THE

WORLD

DOESN'T

REQUIRE

YOU

——

Also by Rion Amilcar Scott

Insurrections

THE WORLD DOESN'T REQUIRE YOU

STORIES

——

Rion Amilcar Scott

Liveright Publishing Corporation
A Division of W. W. Norton & Company
Independent Publishers Since 1923
New York London

Some of these stories were previously published in different forms: "David Sherman, the Last Son of God," *Midnight Breakfast*; "The Nigger Knockers," *Uptown Mosaic* and *NY Tyrant*; "The Electric Joy of Service," *Gigantic Worlds*; "A Rare and Powerful Employee," *Bartleby Snopes*; "Numbers," *Long Hidden: Speculative Fiction from the Margins of History*; "A Loudness of Screechers," *Barrelhouse* and *The Literary Review*; "On the Occasion of the Death of Freddie Lee" was exhibited at Call + Response V; "Rolling in my Six-Fo'—Daa Daa Daa—with All My Niggas Saying: Swing Down Sweet Chariot Stop and Let Me Riiiide. Hell Yeah.," *Bosporus Art Project Quarterly*.

For information about permission to reproduce selections from this book, write to Permissions, Liveright Publishing Corporation, a division of W. W. Norton & Company, Inc., 500 Fifth Avenue, New York, NY 10110

For information about special discounts for bulk purchases, please contact W. W. Norton Special Sales at specialsales@wwnorton.com or 800-233-4830

Manufacturing by LSC Communications Harrisonburg
Book design by Buckley Design
Production manager: Lauren Abbate

ISBN 978-1-63149-538-0

Liveright Publishing Corporation, 500 Fifth Avenue, New York, N.Y. 10110
www.wwnorton.com

W. W. Norton & Company Ltd., 15 Carlisle Street, London W1D 3BS

1 2 3 4 5 6 7 8 9 0

To Sufiya

My World Requires You

Tony: Me, I want what's coming to me.

Manny: Oh, what's coming to you, Tony?

Tony: The world, chico.

—*Scarface*, 1983

Contents

THE

WORLD

DOESN'T

REQUIRE

YOU

——

David Sherman,
the Last Son of God

—

Thou shalt have no other God but the Negro.

—"The Lincoln Catechism"

God is from Cross River, everyone knows that. He was tall, lanky; wore dirty brown clothes and walked with a limp he tried to disguise as a bop. His chin held a messy salt-and-pepper beard that extended to his Adam's apple. Always clutching a mango in His hand. Used to live on the Southside, down under the bridge, near the water. Now there is a nice little sidewalk and flowers and a bike trail that leads into Port Yooga. Back then there was just mud and weeds, and He'd sit there barefooted, softly preaching His word. At one time He had one hundred, maybe two hundred—some say up to five hundred or even a thousand—people listening. But the time I'm talking about, He'd sit with only one or two folks. Always with a mango, except during Easter time, when He'd pass out jelly beans to get people to stop and listen.

He lived on the banks of the Cross River until one day He filled His pockets with stones and walked into the water and sank like a crazy poet. He wasn't insane. It was all part of God's plan. Last time He was crucified, this time drowned. Anyway, God can't drown. He'll come back, perhaps to oversee the writing of another Testament or to judge the living and the dead, whatever He feels.

This story, though, isn't about God. It's about one of His sons. Not His son in the metaphorical sense—well, he was, as we are all the children of God—but more so he was His son in the physical sense.

David Sherman was God's last son. The youngest of thirteen. Five different women had lined up to sire the children of God. They were all boys except for the fifth, a disappointment who, at the age of twenty-five, seduced her fifteen-year-old brother with her shapely behind and left Maryland to build a sinful life with him. God could have had more children, but He got a message from Himself after David was born to stop spilling His seed into His servants. Who was He, or anyone else, to argue?

David lived with his mother, Violet, in a one-bedroom apartment on Sally Street that teemed with water bugs and mice but rarely any rats. God slept there sometimes, but not very often. He'd rise early, long before the sun, and He'd tell His boy, God Morning to you, son.

David would reply, And God Morning to you, too.

He stopped spending the night after David turned twelve.

To David, God was a disappointment. God told His son things from time to time, things about virtue and the coming Holy Ghost Testament, but never anything David could understand. He wondered if one day he'd lose his mind and be out on the streets speaking an incomprehensible Gospel like his Old Man. And when David was sixteen, God took His own life.

Even before God's death, David earned money by turning old pots and plastic barrels into drums and banging out intricate rhythms by the side of the road. After his Father died and he inherited His harmonica, David stole a guitar from the neighborhood nerd. He taught himself how to play them in the privacy of the boxy apartment he shared with his mother, and eventually worked the instruments into the act. It never took David long to learn an instrument. He was always teaching himself a new one, but he was best at the guitar.

Still, he loved the drums the most. Even if he could only afford old buckets and tin pans. David thought himself a percussionist until Randall, a slightly chubby kid from a few blocks away, challenged him to a battle. They sat before those plastic buckets going back and forth, drumsticks raised high above their heads, the great clopping of plastic-trash-can rhythms, sweat pooling at their armpits in the thick summer heat. Randall's precision—how he danced and rocked as he drummed—was almost too much for David to take. He slowed to watch his friend, letting the drumsticks slip from his slick hands. Soon he became just another spectator gazing. After his whipping, David mostly played the guitar to Randall's drumming, and sometimes he'd sing. People from the neighborhood often joined in to jam with dented and tarnished saxophones and trumpets. It was a good time.

A little after David turned eighteen, his oldest brother, Delante, opened the Church of the Twice Risen Christ on the Southside and asked him to play guitar on Sunday mornings. Delante, who now called himself Jesus Jesuson (everyone, though, referred to him as Jeez), wanted to look out for his little brother. David didn't believe what his brother preached and wondered if he really believed, but didn't ask. After all, he didn't know Jeez well. All that flash and dazzle, all that talk of God coming back as a general, leading an army through the streets and bathing the concrete with the blood of the wicked—who could believe that?

David played dutifully every Sunday morning beneath a stained-glass window that portrayed his Father as a shepherd in a cream robe, staff in one hand, sword in the other. It was a gig. For his work, Jeez kicked David a hundred dollars from the offering plate, and when the plate came up short, Jeez would reach into his own pocket and make up the difference. God will always provide for you, little bro, Jeez said often.

Despite his brother's money, David's pockets still felt like bottomless wells. God didn't always provide, and again he felt let down by Him. While taking a walk one day, David spotted a drum set in the window of a downtown music shop off Seventh Street. It was mostly midnight-blue and glossy. Proper bass, cymbals, high hats, and toms. The works. Everything he and Randall had to improvise without. Something stopped him from moving forward. It was a thumping in the center of his chest that wasn't his heart.

The drums are the sun, he heard a voice say.

He decided it was a stray thought, but still the drum set was what he needed to get his band going so he could make some real money.

I can't get them drums with the money Delante's paying me, David told his mother one night over rice and peas. Violet, he said, let me hold something.

She laughed. I don't have no money. Go ask the preacher, she said, scraping a metal spoon around a huge cast-iron pot.

Come on, Ma, he whined. You don't give me nothing no more.

I gave you life. You don't hear me demanding nothing from you for pushing you out and raising your ungrateful ass. As a matter of fact, give me that plate of rice and peas if it ain't nothing.

Violet made a playful snatch for her son's plate. He shielded it with his arm and looked off into the distance. David didn't much feel like joking around.

When David told his brother about the drums that Sunday morning, he too laughed. Save your wages, Jeez said. Then you can buy the drums.

Man, I can't hardly save nothing from them few dollars you give me. Between helping Violet with the rent and the electric, I don't hardly have twenty dollars to my name by Friday, and I got to eat too.

Get a job.

Then when am I gonna practice my craft?

Hit the streets, li'l bro, Jeez said. Find better places to play, like downtown by Riverhall. Go to Port Yooga, hit the crackers up.

David took his brother's advice and played one long night in downtown Port Yooga. He went alone, without Randall or anyone else, to avoid splitting the earnings. He would be the percussionist and the guitar player. He carefully set up his buckets as two teenagers heckled. One stood tall with the belly of a middle-aged beer drinker and the red pimples of a pubescent boy. The other sported a thin blond mustache that made David laugh a little. The latter screamed at David over and over. David just watched him, everything about him seemed ridiculous. The man told David his music was noise, and when he played louder, the beer-bellied one spit a thick glob of saliva into his tin cup. David shoved the mustached man. In the ensuing fight, the men smashed David's guitar and kicked his cup, scattering his change for passersby to snatch.

The night in jail gave David a lot to think about. Cross River had a rhythm, the river had a beat to it—that much was clear, he didn't feel it in Port Yooga—and if he presented it right, no one could tell him it was noise. It'd take time to learn to re-create that sound. By himself, it might be difficult, but Randall's playing opened up possibilities. The drums are the sun, he thought again, and it made sense.

After Jeez bailed his brother out, they drove to Cross River in silence. When they crossed the bridge, David said, Man, Delante, you got to give me that money, bruh. It's urgent. If I don't get them drums, I'm gonna keep getting in trouble.

You trying to blackmail me? his brother asked.

Naw, brother. You got a chance to be part of something big.

I am part of something big. I'm God's son. So are you. Why doesn't that satisfy you?

I'm only me when I'm playing the music I need to play; you know, that Cross River sound.

Look, I'll tell you what. You go home and pray real hard to God, and I'll think about it. And if He softens my heart, I'll give you the cash.

That night, David prayed for the first time since he was twelve, when he still believed in his Father's divinity.

On Sunday Jeez said nothing of the money. David played with impassioned fingers on a guitar donated to him by a member of the congregation. They were fingers made of flames or of the bluest lightning.

David sat with his brother in the front row after church let out, making small talk. When the conversation dipped, David said, You gonna do me that solid?

Well, Jeez said, I listened for God, and He spoke to me like He did when I was a kid and He used to take me to baseball games before you or any of our siblings were born.

What did He say?

God answers all prayers, he said. Sometimes God's answer is no.

Jeez stood and walked to the door. David, Jeez said, turning toward his brother. The money I paid for bail comes out of your pay.

David spat on the door of the church when he stepped outside, right in his Father's face. He snatched a rock and looked up, frowning, at the stained-glass image of his warrior Father. David cocked back his arm until pain filled his joints. He stood like that for a minute, and then dropped the stone.

The next week, on a chilly spring day, Randall and David stood near Main Street with their buckets and pans. The sound hurt their ears. Randall banged out a rhythm, but stopped mid-jam and told David his palms itched for the drum set.

Man, Randall said, what we doing ain't really music. If we get them drums, that'll be music. Remember what you said about finding the rhythm of this town? How we gonna do that with some fucking trash buckets?

How much you about to put toward the drum set, Randall, huh?

David, man, I got less money than you.

They became quiet. David knew his friend had more to say.

There's got to be something we can do, Randall said. Something drastic.

Several years before David's birth, God had left a sawed-off lever-action shotgun with Violet, on the bedroom shelf. David had taken it down and played with it many times as a kid. It was something he never got tired of, and something Violet never knew about. Once, when he and Randall were in high school, David trained it on his friend and yelled, Bang! When he stashed the gun, Randall kicked his ass all up and down that tiny apartment.

Still, though he held the loaded gun toward his friends when he was younger, toward a mirror when he was a bit older, and toward a wall a week previous, he really didn't know how to use it. He came to think yelling, Bang! Bang! and looking menacing was a substitute for learning to shoot the thing.

Randall had never even held a gun. Randall just had more heart. That's why he volunteered to wield the weapon during the job. Besides, it was all his idea.

It don't matter if I can't work it, Randall said, any fool can work a gun. And I won't need to work it. I ain't intending to shoot nobody. Seeing the thing is enough to make that punk-ass clerk shit his pants.

The clerk at the liquor store on Franklin Boulevard eyed them both with little fear when Randall aimed the shotgun at him. David was by the door on lookout, trembling. The clerk stood expressionless while Randall ordered him to empty the register. The fragments of light that sparkled from his eyes—like two steel drums—made David and his friend nervous.

Perhaps it was the awkward way Randall clasped the weapon. He held most of his body firm, but his shaky hands told the truth. Or perhaps it was that neither he nor David had a killer's face. Both looked soft and sweet, even when frowning.

Either way, the man had been robbed before. Randall and David knew this. His nonchalant eyes seemed to say that he had encountered more competent crooks.

The clerk bent quickly behind the counter and pulled out a slim black handgun of his own, a revolver, much less powerful than the shotgun, had the shotgun been in steady hands. He shot once, striking Randall in the chest, then fired two more times. One bullet hit the wall; the other struck Randall through his hand as he covered his head. Randall lay on the floor, a fine mist of sticky blood, bone, and brain matter covering bags of potato chips, sugar cookies, and donuts.

David paused—as still as a scarecrow above a cornfield—and then turned to run. The clerk shot once more. For his trouble, David caught a bullet in his backside—a fragment would rest in the meaty flesh of his right butt cheek until he grew old and passed away. The whole affair made page B10 of the *Days & Times* under the headline "Son of 'God,' Brother of 'Prophet' Sentenced in Armed Robbery."

David received five years for his crime, of which he served three and a half. He spent half a year in prison regretting his decisions. Often, he'd think of his mother bawling at his sentencing hearing—hands up high in the air, eyes crimson, face streaked. He smelled the sweet wood of the courtroom benches. Heard his mother's guttural yelp. Even felt that sinking heavy feeling at the bottom of his stomach.

He saw Randall's face often. Heard his voice too. It never said anything profound or meaningful. Never pointed him toward a path or a way. It sat at his ear, making small talk, occasionally mentioning the Cross River sound.

One morning after the prisoners had eaten their breakfast, David pushed a broom through the mess hall. He spied a stack of plastic buckets turned upside down in the corner.

After the lunchtime trays had been stacked and the tables wiped down, he slipped away and returned with some nicked drumsticks he had stolen from his music class and kept hidden in his cell. He was supposed to be cleaning, but instead David lovingly rearranged the buckets how Randall might have. A smattering of people watched him quizzically. David slammed a drumstick squarely against the flat bottom of a hard bucket. It made a noise that echoed through the mess hall. He was rusty and he knew it, but playing felt so damn good. David played something he knew Randall would love. It didn't matter much that Randall's favorite rhythm now sounded like random thumps against plastic barrels.

A corrections officer slapped a table with his baton and ordered David to stop. David tapped on and on as if he hadn't heard, or as if the CO's screams were song and his hard baton slaps accompaniment. A feeling swelled in his chest, something he had never felt before. David decided it was Randall, and he tapped on, closing his eyes and seeing his friend's face. He only stopped when he opened his eyes and saw the tall, skinny, black-as-licorice CO standing in front of him, ready to strike. David dropped the sticks and threw his hands in the air, and the gesture felt nothing at all like surrender.

While David was away, Jeez grew his hair long and prayed tearfully during his sermons for God to give his youngest brother some direction. God smiled from the clean stained-glass windows in Jeez's new church on the Southside as if to say, Maybe I will help, my son. Jeez rarely visited his brother in prison. Rarely sent money. Never wrote.

Meanwhile, the second eldest son of God left the Church of the Twice Risen Christ to form his own church on the Northside, the Church of the Ever-Loving Christ. That brother became Christopher Christson, or just Christ III, and his church was white like a shining temple on a hill. He favored a short hairstyle and wore sparkling zoot suits made of linen and silk and an assortment of alligator-hide shoes. God, he said, never wanted anyone to be poor. This he argued despite the fact that his Father was homeless for much of His life. God was an entrepreneur, a failed entrepreneur, admittedly. He only failed because He wanted to teach Himself humility and suffering. He failed, in other words, Christ III said, so we could succeed. As time went on, Christ III referred to his Father less and less, and then stopped claiming His divinity. Officially, in the Church of the Ever-Loving Christ, God was no longer God, but simply a prophet. In practice, though, most still referred to David Sherman's Father as divine.

David Sherman hit the streets after three years and seven months with a clear plastic bag filled with a few clothes and a handcrafted guitar he made in prison. His mother had joined her husband, God, in the sky. He had eleven brothers and one sister, but they didn't seem real. To David they were all just storybook characters, except for Jeez, whose face he never wanted to see again. He knew the hate he held for Jeez was irrational; it burned in his chest like a heart attack. He imagined one day he'd wake and find that it had eaten through his back like the most corrosive acid, and then the hole within him would be made visible for all to see. How does one let go of all that hate? Why would someone let go of the hate if it is all he has?

After two nights of sleeping on the ground, clutching the guitar like a lover, David found his way to Christ III's church. It was a Sunday morning. He settled himself on the front steps, strumming and singing a sad hymn while brown people in suits and fancy hats streamed by.

Just before the service was to begin, Christ III came out and put his hand on David's shoulder. Brother, he said, this is Dad's house, so you better come in. Our oldest brother—or should I say, our coldest brother—would leave you out in the world, but our Father told me He wants you to play for the people. Come in, won't you?

Christ III's kindness could never make David love the Father whose madness had created such a broken world, but that day he found a job and some human kindness, and that, for a time, was quite enough.

Christ III told his brother, Go out into the world and bring me a band.

David hired a bass player named Carter and a sax player named Case. Later, he hired a drummer named Webs, but fired him for playing too slow. He fired the next one for sloppiness. The next one came to practice late and laughed too much. He didn't stand a chance, really. David could fire a drummer in a minute.

He settled on a musician named Nat who played sort of like Randall. At least he held the drumsticks the same way. At a certain angle, he even looked like Randall. Cracked jokes like him. Walked like him. David would get lost during practice time observing Nat lovingly, mournfully. Then he'd snap at Nat for playing too slow or too fast or like a damned blues player. Nat always ignored David's rants, but one afternoon he dropped his drumsticks and stormed out. He returned the next day as if nothing had happened. David shrugged.

Bigger things seized his mind, like how to refashion jazz into gospel and gospel into jazz, searching for the sound of Cross River. David wandered the town, sitting in juke joints, talking to people in barbershops, and parking himself for hours at river's edge where his Father once sat listening for the rhythm. David would go home humming a melody, but when he tried to turn it into a composition, it sounded flat and bland. So on Sunday mornings, the band would play jazzed-up versions of Negro spirituals and gospel standards. It was passable, good enough, great at times, even, but it was just background noise.

His heart swelled with love for God, and often when he prayed, he prayed for a new sound, though he remembered what Delante had told him once: God answers all prayers and sometimes His answer is no.

One morning, as David tuned his guitar, Christ III mentioned that there was a pretty woman with no husband who worked with the Sunday-school children. After all, Christ III said, who ever heard of a church elder with no woman at his side?

I'm not an elder, David said.

And you'll never be one if you don't have a woman, Christ III replied, flashing a wicked smile.

Gwendolyn stood tall and wore long dresses that often swept the ground and made her appear taller. She walked with a glide. Christ III introduced them after the service one day and chaperoned their early dates himself. Man and woman, Christ III preached, should never be alone together until God or His representative blesses their union.

She was sultry and sexy in her movements and even her voice. The bones of her cheeks sat high and firm and her skin looked soft, her neck long. David daydreamed of holding her hand, but that would lead to sin. Even the daydreaming was a sin. David didn't mind sin, but he knew he had to pretend to hate sin if he ever wanted to engage in some. They spent long hours talking after Sunday service or walking through a nearby park, always tailed by a church member or in the company of another couple. Soon it seemed she had always been there and always would be there.

David proposed in April and married Gwendolyn in May, wondering the whole time if he had done it just so they could be alone. Just to run his fingers along her cheekbones. Just to leave soft, shallow pools of saliva along her torso.

He told her of his quest to re-create the beat of all Cross Riverian things one morning after they had been married some months. They lay there half dressed, with slats of early sunlight peeking in on them. She seemed distracted.

This town has its own sound, he said. Things are different soon as you leave. You can't feel it no more. I'm trying to get the guys to capture that, but dude we got on the drums—I might need to fire that guy. He just ain't it. I knew a dude with half the education, but twice the soul—

Baby, she replied, Nat is all right, stop being antsy. I like the way he plays.

David carried on, but Gwendolyn looked toward the wall where a brown spider ran about.

None of that is important, David, his wife said, running her hand across her stomach. You think this little baby in here care about Nat? Naw, he gonna need food and shelter and someone to teach him to listen for God's love.

Little baby?

And like that, they were no longer alone. David wanted to name the child Rhythm and after some weeks he got Gwendolyn to agree, but the church rejected that, so they named the boy Randy.

Randy was small and pink for a long time after he was born. Almost like a white baby. Right down to the light hairs atop his head. David marveled at the fragility of the child and feared that one day Randy would come apart in his arms or flake into a fine dust, and his life with Gwendolyn would likewise crumble all around him. When he thought of this, he'd grip the baby more tightly.

Early one morning, David snatched Randy from the crib and cradled him against his shoulder. The baby was distressed, his face scrunched and his mouth wide open, bawling a song that seemed to have no meaning outside of announcing his existence. This phase had stopped being a novelty. David's mind wandered. Melodies. Lyrics. Some scatting he'd add to a composition. David didn't often scat. Do bok do do bop ba dop . . .

All this was imaginary. There was no composition in the works, not really. There'd never be time to work on these ideas. He'd never been farther from that universal sound, even in prison.

David wandered through the kitchen, where Gwendolyn prepared breakfast. He bounced his son, scatted for the boy. Gwendolyn could see new lines resting on his face. It made her sigh; great knots of frustration built in her neck until she exploded: It's all music with you, huh?

she said. Worry enough about music to pay the bills, but save most of your worry for us.

You're asking me to be mediocre, David replied.

Pick up that book, she said, pointing to the dusty Bible on the counter next to the pancake batter. Tell me where it says being mediocre is a sin. Bet I'll find where it says not taking care of your family is a sin quicker.

Gwen's right, he heard a voice inside his head say, why should we care about any other rhythm but the little rhythm right here cradled against our chest?

David nodded and walked the dark house, lightly rocking the baby in his arms, hoping to soothe his distress, trying to put the quest that once set his mind ablaze to the side as if it were a childish thing.

There was a rumor David heard more than once, and he heard it again one Monday near the end of the year while the band practiced in the church's undercroft.

Man, Case said to no one in particular as he cleaned his saxophone, I hope Christ III is not gonna replace us. I keep hearing that shi—stuff.

Who you hear that from? David asked.

Everyone is saying it, Carter said. Christ be frowning when we be playing. He think I don't see him, but I do.

Nat nodded and tapped rapidly at the drums. Who could blame him? he said. When was the last time we did anything special up on that stage?

Why don't you do something special, then? David snapped. Ain't no slacking in the house of the Lord.

I'm just saying. He paused. I seen plenty of church bands. Played with a few. This is the only one that was trying to do something different. We settled into a groove, jack. I ain't pointing no fingers. I'm just as guilty, but—

Yes, you are, David said.

The next morning, he woke early and went to see Christ III in his office. It was an orderly place with everything arranged in neat stacks. Christ III's desk had a green marble surface, and all his chairs sat covered with a grainy red leather. The walls were lined with gold-plated paintings of God in His various phases: young with black hair, an unsure gaze, and a few followers; slightly older with a messy beard, fiery eyes, and an army of adherents; much older with a wrinkled, tired face and a staff He held like a sword, leading a dwindling flock; in decline with all-white hair and a pocket full of stones, wading into the Cross River. David took a seat in a leather chair, and Christ III interlocked his fingers and rested them beneath his chin. When David asked about the rumors, Christ III leaned back and looked at the squiggly plaster lines in the ceiling.

Brother, he said, there is no room for slacking in the house of God. Remember your drummer Webs? Even you knew when it was time for him to go, and you fired his ass. You got to remember, I gave you a raise when your son was born. You promised me a new sound, but your music sounds like gospel—good gospel, damn good gospel, but gospel nonetheless. I'm not sure we need damn good gospel. Mediocre gospel would be cheaper, and people in the congregation probably wouldn't notice much. Of course, I'm just thinking out loud. This wouldn't be an issue if that new sound had come through. I was really excited, but it hasn't worked out as I had hoped. I don't know.

The brothers watched each other. I've given everything to this church, David replied. You not being fair to me. It can take years of study to develop a sound.

You gotta see it from my perspective, little bro. I'm a music lover, but I'm also a businessman here. He paused. I'm going to give you another chance. Let's give it a month. See what happens. I'm really proud of you. You've come a long way, little brother.

As he left the office, David's stomach churned like he had eaten bad meat. Even sitting on the church's gold-plated toilets didn't give him the relief he sought. He walked out onto the street. It was a gray and chilly day. Rain threatening. He rambled in the direction of the river so he could listen to the beat of it. His jacket caught on the sharp point of a fence and tore a little bit. David removed the cloth from the fence with great annoyance.

He wondered if he had sold his soul for stability. What would Randall think? Perhaps he had learned nothing from the drummer's death, making it another random and meaningless event. No more significant than snagging his jacket on the jagged point of that fence.

David passed the bus depot. Gray buses belched black smoke. With his head down and the noise from the grinding engines swirling all around him, David didn't hear the boy calling his name over and over until they were both nearly on the next block. The boy was slim and brown, with a black duffel bag hanging from his right shoulder. He was probably fifteen. He smiled, exposing big crooked front teeth.

Elder Sherman, he said, it's good seeing you again. The boy shook David's hand like no one had ever taught him how, his hand soft and pliable as a leaf in David's palm.

Chillum, the boy said. Chillum from the Southside. A bunch of us, we be coming on Sundays to see what you gonna do with the music. I don't mess with that God stuff too much, but I appreciate how you do the arrangements.

Thanks, little brother.

I was sorry to hear that y'all not going to be playing the church come next month. Where can I hear y'all play?

Who told you we wasn't gon' be playing the church no more, boy?

I got a partner from Georgia. Told me he and his boys was hired by Christ III to be the in-house band and they was coming up next month. Asked me to sit with them to fix some local sound to it.

All the blood left David's face and he could feel his brain swimming in it. He opened his mouth, but couldn't speak.

Man, Chillum said, you not looking too good, Elder Sherman. Shoot, this the first you're hearing this, huh?

Um, David stammered. My brother and me . . . and I . . . we, uh, prayed on it and made a mutual decision. God, our Father, really made the decision, really.

Chillum nodded. Sure, he said. God don't speak to me, but when He's your Father—

No, don't say that. God ain't speaking to you, me, or Christ III. I ain't no better than you.

Chillum nodded again. Say, Elder Sherman, you want to go to River Street and get some beers, listen to some music? It's on me.

David shook Chillum's hand again. I got to go and pray on my future, he said, waving to Chillum and walking swiftly in the direction of the water.

David sat by the river, watching it sway, and after about an hour, he grew bored. He threw his arms back and held them behind his head. He realized it was a pose his Father often struck. He sat for some time meditating on this. Truly, he thought, I've become like my Dad: inscrutable even to myself, single-mindedly pushing toward some goal only I could possibly care about. Was He really a madman? Sometimes— particularly when He was holding a belt, disciplining him—David's Father seemed so sane. They played soccer in the park like a regular Father and son. Beyond sane. David closed his eyes and breathed deeply in and out. After another hour passed, he heard the moon talk, but it was a whisper. David ignored it. Sometimes when he was drifting off to sleep, he heard things that weren't there. The brain firing off randomly into the universe. This was like that. The waters parted and God rose, but He was invisible. Still, David knew He was there.

God revealed that the voice of the moon was His own. He spoke in a language David didn't understand, yet in a way he did.

How do I know you're God? David asked.

Scoob, skip skip scap scap bop. Bddaaa-dat-da, God said, revealing his pocket full of stones.

But why? David asked.

Scap scap, skibbid scap scap. Bdddaaaa!

But will they understand?

Bdaaaa! Biggedy bop bop bap bop . . .

And God faded away, but the water played a music, a rhythm, like David had never heard. A sound like great stones colliding. He looked around trying to feel God but felt nothing. He walked all along the water trying to find Him, but He simply wasn't there.

David's mind churned and churned. It seemed parts of his brain he hadn't used in years burned alive with electricity, flowing with blood. Through it all, David knew he was sane. He asked himself, though, what would it feel like to be insane? He couldn't answer. All that he knew was that he was sane. Very sane.

David proved difficult to be around that week. He grew short-tempered and ill-mannered. He smoked ceaselessly, blowing plumes in all directions. Often when he spoke, he made no sense, and he'd snap at the listener for misunderstanding.

He came home from practice one Wednesday and headed straight for the kitchen, where he arranged the pots and pans along the counter from largest to smallest. He slapped them with wooden spoons, breaking the utensils and filling the house with a metallic racket.

Gwendolyn—in the back bedroom with her baby—wanted to tap her feet. She didn't, however. Instead, she frowned. Gwendolyn placed Randy on his back in his playpen. He turned on his side and sucked at his thumb, quickly falling off to sleep despite the noise.

Somewhere near the living room, a door slammed.

Just what on earth is wrong with you? Gwendolyn screamed, walking from the room where her son slept.

Nothing, David replied.

He stood in the kitchen at the doorway to the basement, watching her blankly. He tapped a broken wooden spoon against a pan, a lid, a pan, and the lid again. He opened the door wide and prepared to slam it. Gwendolyn caught it in her hand.

David, don't you know you've been acting like a lunatic? That everybody's worried about you? Stop slamming doors. Sit down, let's talk. Okay?

Naw, baby. No time to sit. This is music. It don't sound like it. I'm testing things out, so it don't sound like nothing. But I think I got it. The drums is the sun. The center.

David, I know things at the church are stressful, but you're not making any sense. Have you spoken to Christ III?

Baby, Christ III don't know any more than me or you.

See what I mean? You're talking crooked. We should pray on this.

No use praying, baby. Too late for prayer. Christ III don't want my music. He already hired a new band. He 'bout to replace me, Nat, and e'rybody. David paused. Cheap-ass motherfucker.

Watch your mouth.

David moved toward his wife, reached for her hand, and gave it a light squeeze.

Baby, our time at the Church of the Ever-Loving Christ is short.

Why would we leave the Church of the Ever-Loving Christ? It's where we met. It's our spiritual home. It's who we are.

But if I'm not playing there no more—

You not playing there has nothing to do with where we worship. If you think it does, that's vanity, and you know that's a sin. If you want to leave the church, I can't follow you. You're asking me to love you more than I love God, and you know that's about the biggest sin there is. Don't you remember Christ III preaching about that? The disciples dropped everything, left their kids fatherless to follow Christ. Left their wives poor and lonely. Who knows, I may be called to leave Randy alone in that crib. It would be hard, but I gotta be prepared for that. But if you walk out them church doors, David Sherman, I can't follow you.

David heard his son bawling, newly awakened by the shouting. He wanted to ignore it, let Gwendolyn answer the call. But David needed a break from the argument. From the music that burst in his brain. He scooped up his son and rested him on his shoulder. Looking out the window always calmed the boy. Together, they gazed out onto the world. Randy continued to cry and bawl though, squirming in his father's arms, piercing his father's eardrums, disrupting his father's thoughts.

Sunday morning, it felt to David that his life was hanging off a cliff and its fingers were becoming tired. He had told no one what he'd experienced at the Cross River. How could he? They'd dismiss him as a lunatic. Christ III and Jeez always spoke of talking to God. People accepted them. Why wouldn't people accept him too? After all, he was a church elder. Didn't that give him the right to talk to God? He had thought of the Sunday guitar solo as his sermon. His voice wasn't strong—it sounded scratchy and rough—so he didn't often sing, but this time he had to, didn't he? There was much to say. He'd play the Sunday solo by ear, though he had not only forgotten God's words, but also the substance of His message.

The band warmed up. They moved robotically through "Amazing Grace" and methodically through "Swing Low, Sweet Chariot."

God spoke.

Bodop bop bop bddaaaa! Bow bop bow, God said.

Scapidee skip skip bop bddatt-skabaidee pop, David replied.

Huh? Nat said as he tapped the drums. David didn't reply. He looked to the wooden slats of the high ceiling. Nat banged on the drums rapidly, two beats at a time, to get his boss's attention.

David turned to him.

What was that? David asked.

You zoned out on me, man, Nat said.

That sounded good. That sounded damn good. That sounded like the beat of the river. Like the town. You need to do that while we playing. Yeah, man. When I give you the word. You double up on them beats. That's our sound. As a matter of fact, keep working on it. Keep practicing until the service starts. We gonna do something special for the solo.

Man, Dave, that's crazy, Nat said.

Naw, said Case. Might as well do something strange. This may be the last time we play this place. I'm with you, David.

Nat started pounding, doubling up his drumbeats.

I don't know if I can keep this up all the way through the solo, he said.

You, skaba dip skaba dip, never know, David scatted, skaba dip dip, what you'll be able to do do do, bop bop bdddattt, until you go 'head and do it.

When the service started, David nodded to his wife and son in the front row. Gwendolyn raised Randy's tiny hand and waved it at his father. Chillum sat a few rows behind them. All the regular faces smiled up at him, but they now looked strange. Glowing eyes and glowing mouths full of judgment, as though they knew what lay on the horizon. At the normal points in the service, the band played all the usual songs. "Amazing Grace." "Go Down, Moses." "Swing Low, Sweet Chariot." God whispered to David, speaking in scats. *Do it!* God called. *Do it now!*

Christ III, wearing a blistering white suit with long tails that scraped the floor and bleached white alligator boots, delivered a sermon about the evils of poverty. Nat snuck in some doubled drums here and there, but no one was ready for what happened when it was time for the solo.

David whispered God's words as the saxophone started and the drums came in, first in English, then in God's scatting, which he came to realize was the one true language, the language that time had lost, the language of the rolling tongue. Nat doubled the drumbeats and people in the audience swayed, suddenly alive as God's music entered them.

David threw his hands into the air and started scatting. He spoke an entire monologue full of many of God's secrets, and what the congregation couldn't understand through their ears, they felt in their chests. People gasped. Which wasn't unusual, as God's truth can, at times, be hard to take. Some waved their hands and shook and writhed like snakes through the aisles. The music made the people dance sexy, lusty dances. Free-spirited movements that drew attention to their thrusting, shaking nether regions. Just about the whole congregation let loose. No one gave a damn who looked on.

After ten minutes, Christ III wiped the sweat from his brow, strode over to David, and attempted to whisper something into his ear. David put his arm around his brother and scatted loudly. A woman in the front row passed out.

When David paused, Case—without giving it a second thought— began playing his notes backward, and the rest of the band followed. Nat pounded harder and harder until he became exhausted and dropped his sticks to the floor. Case's saxophone faded out. The bass player stopped. The organist stopped. David scatted a line more, his hands raised above his head. He walked down the center aisle with his arms still in the air, his band, the choir, and Christ III at his back.

Christ III took the mic, his voice full of rage and damnation.

What you heard was the music of the devil, he said. A son of God has been seduced. You just seen a child of God speak in tongues, not like the righteous, but like a beast!

David Sherman, the last son of God, opened the doors and walked out into the bright day, feeling nothing at all like the demon his brother accused him of being. Instead, he opened his arms wide while the sun beamed upon him, feeling light, as if the ground were no longer beneath his feet and he was drifting in midair, ascending to Heaven.

The Nigger Knockers

—

The knock, knock joke, much like the Negro spiritual,
began as a means of clandestine communication, a way
for the enslaved to pass information to each other beneath
the radar of hostile whites.

—Hiram Skylark Rollicks,
Signifyin' Revolt: Black Rebellion in the Antebellum South

M y brain had liquefied for the night. That's what work, at least
my job, does. Long day, short—makes no difference. Pop the
top any weekday evening and you'll find a slushee. There I sat,
zombiefied in that purgatory where rational thought and loopy sub-
conscious visions mingle. A slack-jawed demon. Probably drooling.
The glow of the nightly newscast projecting across my face.

I didn't recognize the shrill buzz of the doorbell at first. It buzzed
loud, louder than I remembered it being. A second buzz forced me to
jump from my couch, landing on my feet and then toppling to the floor
like I wore the legs of a scarecrow. Disoriented, I looked about, trying
to place everything: the disheveled living room with clothes and newspapers strewn around, the piercing buzz, the darkness. My head felt
detached from my body. For a brief moment I existed outside time, and
then I groped for the concept.

Another irritating screech. I stumbled to the front door and peered through the peephole. I saw nothing, and as soon as I walked to the bathroom the buzz sounded again, long and loud like someone leaning into the button. After I finished, I returned to the foyer and looked out the window and again saw nothing.

I sat on the couch and rested my clearing head on a pillow and the doorbell buzzed again and again. I felt my nerves jangling. Racing to the door, I snatched it open, and there stood no one. Nothing.

Cute, I yelled to the open air, the trees, the birds, the houses, the grass, and the curve of the horizon. Very. Very. Cute. Now run along, kids.

As I shoved the door closed, I heard cackling and saw a dark boot at the edge of the entryway. The door swung open and in walked a man I hadn't seen in years.

My nig-nig, he said as he walked into my living room with a bag over his shoulder. It was Tyrone James, my long-lost childhood friend. What's up, Deez, he said, how's life treating you, man?

Deez was a nickname I had rarely heard after my first lonely semester at Freedman's University when I would see Tyrone around campus. He and that stupid nickname had faded from my life. I'd heard he moved away.

Tyrone's entrance pissed me off more than a little, but his cocky half smile always defused things a bit. It said, *Relax, It's all a bunch of bullshit, but it's not*; except when it said, *It's all serious, but it's really just a bunch of bullshit*. He'd been that way since elementary school.

He made staying angry with him an impossibility. Though, for some reason that I can't understand and won't analyze, I felt the need to go through the motions.

What the hell is wrong with you? I barked across the room. You're ringing bells and hiding like a little kid? If I had a gun you would've caught one in your chest.

Relax, Deez. You wouldn't shoot an old friend in the chest, now, would you? Man, I been here forever and you ain't even offer me nothing to drink yet?

I watched as Tyrone walked from the foyer into the kitchen, where he snatched a twenty-two-ounce bottle of Crazy Ninja malt liquor from the refrigerator door. This didn't bother me because the stuff tasted like piss and I only kept it in the fridge for guests, but other than my girlfriend, who didn't drink much, I hardly ever had guests. He took a long first sip and then turned to me and said, Want one?

I shook my head and returned to the couch. He parked himself next to me and we made small talk. He told me he was nearing the end of a doctoral program in cultural studies at Freedman's University. The school was still, as he put it, full of a bunch of bougie niggas and I told him I expected no different. He asked me when I planned to marry Sameeka and it surprised me that he remembered her, but I shrugged and changed the subject. We reminisced, comparing notes on people we had grown up with—Molly and Andreason and Shit-Shit and Cliff and Leonard who married Roxanne. I hadn't seen or heard from these people in years, most I hadn't even thought about. He wanted me to tell him about my work, but the less said about those gray cubicle walls that close in on me every afternoon, robbing me of oxygen and years, the better. After a long silence I said what I'd been thinking all along.

What's up, doc, huh? Why you disrupting my life?

He reached into his bag and pulled out a neatly bound stack of pages with a shimmering plastic cover.

This right here is a draft of my dissertation, he said. It's short, two hundred and fifty pages. I feel like I nailed it, though. But, shit, what do I know? I'm paying a fortune for a Ph.D. in cultural studies, so I can't be that bright.

I took the bound manuscript into my hands. It felt heavy. I looked at the title and fell into an amusement, a raw laughter so deep and pure that I was cleansed when it began to subside. "Nigger Knocks: A Brief Cultural History."

You got to be kidding me, man, I said. This is what you wrote your dissertation on? What's your next book on? Tag? Throw Up and Tackle? Hide and Go Seek?

Yeah. See, that's the reaction I be getting most of the time, but people don't understand how important this *childhood game* (at this phrase he raised his fingers and turned them into quotation marks) has been to the development of this country. People never even stop to ask why it's called Nigger Knocks. As kids did we ever ask? Naw, we just knocked. It was fun too, right?

So why do they call it Nigger Knocks, Professor?

Well, it started on plantations back in like the 1700s and shit, he said standing up and gesturing. I became the class and he, the instructor. Slaves used to knock on the Big House door and run. It was a way to steal food and weapons and shit; a way to help niggas escape through the Underground Railroad or the Forgotten Tunnel—man, they used it for all kinds of things. While white folks, or even a house slave, answered the front door, there'd be black folk taking bread and hog meat and shit out the back. Bet they ain't teach you about that at Freedman's University.

Naw, they didn't. That's actually interesting. Go on.

Look at you. Not giggling now. Give it a read. It's a quick read. At least I hope it is. If it doesn't grab you in the first fifty pages, you don't have to keep going. I've known you nearly all my life, I can trust you to be honest with me, right? Tell me it's trash if it's some trash. But don't mock my shit, though. Don't take my scholarship for a joke.

He sported that mean little half smile when he asked me not to ridicule him, so I wasn't sure how to take him. Perhaps it was a joke. Perhaps he was serious. I just didn't, and still don't, know.

I wasn't laughing, though. As I leafed through his manuscript, several passages caught my eye.

Tyrone took another Crazy Ninja for the road and before he left I agreed to read his book and give him comments.

I found myself busy that week, so I gave it to Sameeka to read, and she returned one night amazed that a clown like Tyrone could have such insight. Still I let the thing sit for two and a half weeks. Really, I'm lying to myself when I claim that it was busyness that kept me from reading. Back then I mostly spent my free time surfing the internet for nothing in particular, fucking around on Facebook, occasionally remembering the manuscript (mostly when Sameeka mentioned it, which she did with an annoying frequency).

Tyrone called one day to tell me he'd be coming the next night to collect his book. I panicked, as I'm a man of my word, but then I sat in my lounging chair, and in the pool of dim light that I prefer for reading, I gently turned the pages as if holding delicate parchment that could at any moment fall to pieces in my hand. I devoured it in a single sitting, reading long into the early morning hours when I should have been sleeping. I dragged my tired self to bed at five. My alarm sounded at seven-thirty a.m. and the neighbor's dog started barking madly shortly after that. I raised my head from the pillow and then sank back into it, sleeping through the noise. Being late to work bothered me—really it did—but now it concerned me less.

I found Tyrone's work sublime. He wrote the kinds of sentences that had a nice texture on the tongue and tasted good passing from my mouth. For so many years Nigger Knocks had never even entered my thoughts, and now my friend's words made the game into a shiny new thing.

Tyrone performed a kind of sleight of hand, somehow transporting me back to my childhood days. I could feel the knocks at my knuckles and on the palms of my hands. My old neighborhood, those plain Northside streets with their identical houses and neatly trimmed lawns, seemed foreign and exotic filtered now through the elegance of my friend's manuscript.

Tyrone even mentioned me, though in passing, in one of his many recollections of running through the Northside of Cross River banging on doors and windows, pressing rapidly on doorbells, and escaping into the day. He perfectly described the rubber soles slapping against the black tar beneath our feet; being chased by winded and out-of-shape adults; the days when we collapsed at our rendezvous points high with dizzying laughter.

He had convinced me. Nigger Knocks changed the world and I wouldn't want to live on a planet in which kids had never conceived of knocking on doors and racing away. Former slaves constructed this town one nigger knock at a time, to paraphrase my friend. What was once unknown to me now seemed obvious. I hadn't been just playing a *childhood game. I was participating in a tradition of rebellion, the same tradition of rebellion that lead* [sic] *to the abolition of slavery, the weekend and the forty-hour work week* [James 12].

When he arrived at my doorstep the next evening, I sat in the lounging chair making frantic notes which I had started writing at work and continued at home, forgoing my usual nap. I had twenty handwritten pages and I could have composed twenty more. It annoyed me that when I answered the door, Tyrone hid himself in the bushes. I didn't want to play games.

After he rose from the shrubbery and shook the leaves, the dirt, and the twigs from his clothing, it took no longer than a moment for me to get to the heart of it all.

I've never... I paused. What kind of damn substances you on, Tyrone? How do you even think like— I've never even read anything like this.

Damn, Deez. He shook his head and slumped a bit. That bad, huh?

Bad? No, this is the craziest—in a good way—shit I ever read.

Great, he said. Now we can go nigger knocking.

What?

It's time to go ring some bells, knock on some windows. Doorbell Ditch, as the white boys would say.

But we're adults.

So?

Come on, Tyrone—how old are you? Twenty-five?

Twenty-six.

What we look like, I said, twenty-five and twenty-year-old men running around nigger knocking?

The pursuit of freedom, he said, misquoting himself, *often begins with a rap on the door.*

Around here? We'll get shot out here, jackson.

Look, I've made the mistake of writing this whole thing without even testing my theories. I'm on my way to becoming the typical academic. All brains, no balls. They encourage that over at good ol' FU, but that ain't me. No sir. Intellectuals have got to get out there nigger knocking with the people. Nigger knocking was one of the very first things our ancestors did to spark the Great Insurrection.

No shit, I replied. I read the manuscript.

They knocked on that door, hid out—he banged three times on my wall and crouched low by the side of the chair, acting it all out—and when old Master Johnny Weaver came outside looking, they stabbed that cracker right in the gut. The only successful slave uprising in this country—ever—started with some nigga knocking on a door and running away. Well, I guess he didn't run away; um, you see what I'm getting at. We have to do what the common folks do. If the people are nigger knocking, I got to be nigger knocking too.

Tyrone's manuscript had set my brain ablaze and stirred long-dead urges. What I really wanted to do, had planned to do, was stay home and write something of my own despite having no clue as to what, if anything, I had to say. The uncertainty of it all gave me the excitement of a young drunk.

But for some reason, instead of staying home, I agreed to go out nigger knocking.

He first picked a house in a quiet part of the Southside. I parked my beat-up old thing at the far end of his street. It shook and rocked as I cut the engine. We began slowly walking, almost tiptoeing, to the door. I looked in the window and saw the outline of a man sitting in the dark, lit only by the blue of his television. I whispered, He in there. I see him. He watching television.

I could glimpse his face in the dark through the glow of TV light; he wore the worn expression of a zombie. Light, in waves, flashed across his cheeks. His lids hung low, tiny velvet curtains draped over his eyes. Tyrone and I crept to the door.

You ready? he asked. I nodded.

He pressed the bell several times while I made a fist and pounded with the meaty part of my hand.

By the way, Tyrone said. This is Shit-Shit's house.

Huh? That's Shit-Shit? That don't look like no Shit-Shit.

Man, Deez, be quiet. You gonna ruin the element of surprise.

Who is it? Shit-Shit called.

He sounded anxious, angry. We said nothing, though we snickered.

Huh? I can't hear you. Who is it?

Tyrone rang once more and I banged, banged, banged as if trying to strike right through the door.

I could hear Shit-Shit stirring and Tyrone and I both jumped from the porch at the same time. We crouched in the dirt against the side of his house. He snatched open the door, stepped outside, and looked left and right, but not down. I bit my lip and shook and dug my nails into my palms to avoid laughing. When he went back inside we waited for him to sit before we did it again. Once more he came outside and cursed his phantom nigger knockers. Shit-Shit's voice held an agitation I remembered from our teen years when we would invite him to Kenny's house just to pour buckets of water on him from the window above the front door. He always fell for it. Once we did it in October when the cold settled early. Snot poured from Shit-Shit's nose as he burst into a mighty rage, swinging his arms and inventing words to curse us with, blaming us for all the problems of his life from his poor grades to his loneliness.

We laughed back then even though it wasn't funny. And I was lonely too, but I didn't say so or offer any words to soothe him. Tyrone the instigator urged me to do the mockery. He would reach deep into his witty brain to offer up a humorous put-down or a comedic approach, which he would pass to me via whisper. He played the ventriloquist and I his willing dummy. This way Tyrone maintained his cool, above-the-fray image and I burnished my credentials as an asshole. At Tyrone's insistence, I tried to sound sincere because that was funnier. I told Shit-Shit that we weren't his problem, his hygiene was the problem, and dousing him with water could only help, despite the fact that he had no hygiene problem, outside of that one day in junior high school when he stank in the way all junior high boys stink. He kept coming back to Kenny's house fully aware of the cruelty waiting for him, complicit in his own bullying.

The third time Shit-Shit came outside after we knocked, he waved his hands and spat and screamed, You fucking little kids! If I catch you around my house I'm gonna beat your asses, watch.

It was all so out of character—he added a false depth to his voice, which made it more hilarious. But then, how would I know his character? I hadn't spoken to Shit-Shit—now calling himself Stanley or Stan, probably—in years. When he went back inside we tried one more time, though we didn't wait for him to come to the door. Instead, we immediately burst down the street toward the car. He yanked the door open and sprinted after us. He hadn't even bothered tying his shoelaces and they tapped against the concrete. I looked back just in time to see him trip and splash into a puddle.

We got into my car as he rose from the ground, a string of saliva and curse words spilling from his mouth. My engine cut off as I revved it and then it cut off again. We both wheezed heavily. I wondered how we would explain this if he caught up to us. Shit-Shit snatched a rock from the ground and lobbed it into the air as I pulled off. It was a nice throw too, smacked the back windshield and cracked the thing pretty good. Tyrone and I jumped. The car swerved all over the road. When I got control of the thing we brayed and coughed, wiping mirthful tears from our eyes.

Nightly Tyrone appeared at my door, sometimes with a coffee cup in hand as if about to clock in for work. We decided where to knock partly on how well the shrubbery could hide us. At one house, a man came out with a gun after four knocks. Crouching in his bushes, our mouths dry and our hearts beating in our throats, we didn't dare to even breathe. At another house we watched the police approach the door minutes after we finished with it.

We stomped some yellow marigolds out front of one house as we fled, by accident of course. We knocked on the door of a blue house on Gressam Place and Tyrone became so mesmerized by the woman who answered that he went back and knocked again just to get another glimpse at her. She came outside and looked around, thin arms folded delicately across her frame. Dark skin. Straight black hair. Beautiful indeed, but a bit skinny for my taste. She closed the door again and Tyrone said, My man Darius, I'm gonna marry her. Tyrone knocked again, but didn't run when she came outside for the third time. He pointed down the street at two kids tossing a football. They sparked up a conversation and he left with her phone number. Her name was Zoraya, but she called herself Zo, and she made Tyrone feel like stillness, he said.

After they finished talking, Zo strode across the street and spoke to the mother of the football-playing children. As we walked away, a woman with a stern face and a mouth that turned down at the corners shouted, Get your little asses in here! Y'all earned an ass-whooping tonight!

We had a good run, hitting different houses all throughout the Southside over the course of a couple weeks. We hit Shit-Shit's house several times and the monster we made erupted over and over. It was hilarious to watch. The exhilaration of nigger knocking. I felt new life sprouting in my chest. We moved slowly northward and even braved the rich folks and their security in gated Crispus Heights. Tyrone kept saying that all we saw made good material for nightly revisions.

When Tyrone, one afternoon in my living room, said we had to move on, I nodded and leaned into the mattress atop my broken futon frame. This thing, as fun as it could be, was never meant to be everlasting, I knew that. It would be good to return to adulthood with the wisdom that could only come from traipsing briefly back into childishness; I fixed my mouth to thank Tyrone for the time, when he said: Port Yooga!

Huh?

That's where we moving on to. We did Crispus Heights, that was a good warm-up, now it's time for Port Yooga. Enough of this petty little neighborhood shit. We need to knock the big time. Picture it, Deez, two niggas knocking Port Yooga doors. It'll be monumental. This shit needs its own chapter.

I cringed a bit thinking about it. The Southside was one type of danger, but it's rumored that Port Yooga once had its own hanging tree in the center of town. It was the only place a Cross Riverian was allowed after dark in Port Yooga for a time. I wanted to say no. My brain told my mouth to say no, but those excited infectious eyes of Tyrone's. How they danced in delight at all our knocking triumphs. I don't remember agreeing or walking to the car or most of the drive over. I do remember coming alive on the bridge to Port Yooga—apparently we had been laughing and planning. I asked myself what in the hell I thought I was doing, but still I found myself unable to turn around.

• • •

The following joke, or a version of it, was often told by slaves in the upper Southern states in the late 18th and early 19th centuries:

> Knock, knock
> Who's there?
> Isaiah.
> Isaiah who?
> Isaiah whole lot of niggers tryna escape over the hills, boss.
> They thin' you cain't see they black asses flyin' through the night, but you can sees they eyes.

> —Hiram Skylark Rollicks, *Signifyin' Revolt:*
> *Black Rebellion in the Antebellum South*

• • •

We drove about the neighborhood for a while, planning escape routes and backup escape routes and backups to those routes in case something went really wrong. I kept saying, I'm not ending up on that fucking tree. Over and over I said it. I'm not ending up on that fucking tree. And when he couldn't take it any more, Tyrone said, Deez, could you shut the fuck up? Park and let's do this already.

The world turned bluish around us as dusk fell.

We choose a big white house that seemed more appropriate on farmland than in this suburb. I knew it was a mistake from the start, but I didn't say anything. There rose an unbelievable sinking feeling from my stomach through my chest. I wanted to tell Tyrone to turn around, but how would that look?

He called knock-duty, and I would be the trusty lookout. I crouched at the concrete path that led to the door like a track star and faced the street.

I heard the banging behind me, Cross Riverian war drums followed by the rapid dinging of the bell. I shot off, the decoy preceding the greyhound. Somehow I must have gotten confused; I took one of the backup routes. And when I tried to double back, I saw the darkened shadows of people roused out of their evening routines by our mischief. They dashed after Tyrone, a mob in pursuit. I continued along the backup escape route, a true failure as a lookout.

I ran along yards and through playgrounds and backyards. I ran and I gasped, my heart beating in my throat and my ears. I imagined my friend at the hanging tree, a nigger knocker dying for Nigger Knocks, just like our ancestors.

I made it to the car and circled the community for a half hour searching for Tyrone, calling his phone to get only his voice mail. Our victim's neighbors peered angrily into my car as I passed them. I heard some yelling and cursing. Somewhere dogs barked. I must have circled the same streets and the same madly searching people two or three times.

Finally, I came upon Tyrone James walking nonchalantly in front of a school. I flashed my headlights frantically.

What the fuck, Deez? Tyrone called, as he snatched my door open. How you just gon—

I could be saying the same thing, jack; I thought you were right behind me, I said, lying to my friend. I took a backup route. You didn't see that the main route wasn't clear?

Fuck you, Deez. You got to communicate. Them fucking crackers was a stutter-step away from catching me. Tyrone sighed. That shit was exhilarating, though.

I bet.

I knocked on a few more doors after I shook them too.

Man, Tyrone, that's reckless as shit.

Tyrone smiled, pulled out a pencil stub and a little green notebook, and he took notes silently all the way home.

. . .

This craftily designed joke is packed with information, telling a runaway slave who to rendezvous with (Isaiah, a code name, no doubt); the path to freedom (over the hills); how fast to travel (fly, boy, fly); when to leave (at night); even the punishment for getting caught (a seizure of the eyes).

—Hiram Skylark Rollicks, *Signifyin' Revolt: Black Rebellion in the Antebellum South*

. . .

But what ended it all was something that happened on a day we couldn't go out, a Wednesday. I had to work late and Tyrone said he was meeting with his dissertation advisor, though I think he really went to see Zo. I would finally have the time to sit and write a little something of my own, I thought.

Easter just passed, and everything from the grass to the buds on the dogwood trees was in the midst of rebirth. As the *Days & Times* described it, a teenager named Immanuel Richardson—a member of the only black family in the neighborhood—stood outside his house in Port Yooga late one evening ringing the bell for dear life. He had forgotten his keys that morning and asked his mother, Cynthia Richardson, to stay up when he came home from his job at the grocery store. She tried gallantly, but she had worked a full day herself and fell asleep right there on the living room couch. Immanuel could see a bit of her through the window. He looked to his cell phone, but its battery had died on the walk home.

Annoyed and tired, he placed his backpack on the ground to ease the weight behind him. Almost as soon as he started to bang, Immanuel heard shouting.

He turned slowly to see five men approaching. He recognized them as his neighbors and his tension eased. Mr. Thomas, Immanuel said. Can I use your—

Don't move, kid! Mr. Thomas shouted. He looked at Immanuel with no recognition, even though Immanuel had lived in the neighborhood for each one of his sixteen years. He had played with Mr. Thomas's kids. Once he washed his neighbors' cars for extra cash and ended up scratching Mr. Pickering's pink Pontiac. Now his neighbors watched him with stone eyes. Their faces glowed blue beneath the porchlights. Their mouths grew animated in rage and vulgarity. In the newspaper, the three neighbors who offered a comment—Mr. Pickering among them—said they had never seen Immanuel before.

Immanuel's neighbors marched on him, petitioners protesting his existence. Immanuel ran. For his life, Immanuel ran. Left his bag right there on his porch, and Immanuel ran through the streets as the men chased. Help me! he cried. Someone please help me!

He stopped to knock on doors, but the men were right there at his heels, forcing him each time to abandon that door. His knocks, at some houses, caused more people to come outside and join the mob. Immanuel dipped across lawns, backyards, and through carports.

It wasn't long before one of the men caught him with a forearm to the neck. Immanuel's head hit the concrete. They kicked and punched him as he covered his face. More neighbors arrived, raining more blows. Reading all about it, I wondered if poor Immanuel thought they would take him right to the hanging tree.

The police, his salvation for the night, showed up well into the beating and arrested him, charging him with attempted robbery, breaking and entering, battery, and criminal mischief. Unfortunately for Immanuel, he needed the hospital far more than he needed the police station and when his mother finally got him into a hospital bed, he was in bad shape indeed.

Tyrone showed up on my doorstep the day the article was published, holding the paper in his hand, a drained look seizing his sunken eyes and the smirk, for once, gone from his lips.

This ain't what was supposed to happen, jack. He shook his head. This wasn't part of the plan.

I invited him in and offered him a bottle of Crazy Ninja. We sipped and dashed off theories. Tyrone recognized Immanuel's house as one he had hit during our night of terror in Port Yooga. Maybe Immanuel Richardson saw us, I told him; perhaps he was among those who gave chase.

Now you're just reaching, Deez, Tyrone said. Something we got to face, my nig-nig: this nigga Immanuel took a beating that was meant for us.

That beating might have happened completely fucking independent of us, Tyrone.

Tyrone pointed to a sentence in the article quoting Immanuel's Uncle Carlo: *There's been string of* [doorbell ditching] *incidents around here lately.*

Well, I said. I mean—look, do you think grown men beating the shit out of a teenager is the appropriate punishment for Nigger Knocks?

You just don't want to take any responsibility for any of this.

I didn't beat anybody, Tyrone. I just helped you add on to the body of scholarship about this topic, and the shit's been thrilling. Not to be cold, but this is another chapter. Maybe I can author it.

Man, Deez. Tyrone stopped, watched me for a beat, and then sighed as if all the exhaustion in the world suddenly tumbled down upon him. I see I can't talk to you about this. At least not now. He downed nearly half a bottle of that Crazy Ninja piss in one long gulp. I'll catch you later when you've had time to really think and shit. Peace, man.

Tyrone returned nearly every night, and some nights, sitting on my couch, he would drink so much that I would have to carry him to my car and drive him to his parents' basement on the Northside where he lived.

He rarely mentioned his dissertation anymore, and when he did he made fun of it.

One evening he suggested the café where Zo worked, and we left my house, as sober as children, to spend the night sipping free tea and eating free pastries. We couldn't escape Immanuel Richardson, though. Tyrone held the front page of the *Days & Times*. A picture of the teen standing in front of his house splashed itself across the paper. He smiled. Most other images I'd seen of him were bloody and swollen, puffy-faced. In the newspaper he'd smile forever. Tyrone passed his hand over the image as if trying to absorb Immanuel Richardson through his flesh.

Zo slammed a hot porcelain kettle on our table before pouring the scalding water into our cups. She pointed to the paper. Who do these people think they are?

It's crazy, Tyrone said.

It's criminal, is what it is, Zo replied. You guys coming out to the protest, right?

I don't know if I have six hours to hear Chairman R. speak, I said.

Hell, yeah, we're going, Tyrone said to Zo. We have to be out in force. We got to show these people this shit is not acceptable. Right, Deez?

I'm too old for protests, I replied. I thought I noticed looks of horror on their faces, but I turned away and said, Be safe, Huey; be safe, Angela. I'm gonna protest by nigger knocking all over Port Yooga, that's how I'm going to protest.

Why do you keep talking about Nigger Knocks? Zo asked.

Nigger knocking? Tyrone asked in reply. Everything I do from now on is nigger knocking. A nigga's knocking over the system that allows shit like this to happ—

That's your guilt talking, I replied.

Why would Tyrone need to feel—

Hey, Deez, Tyrone said. We gotta get back so I can do some more work on this dissertation.

He stood, passed a quick kiss across Zo's cheek, and nearly stomped from the restaurant. I followed, waving to Zo on the way out.

When we got to the sidewalk, he removed a bottle of Crazy Ninja from his jacket pocket and took his first sip of the night.

Look, Darius, he said. Never mention that nigger knocking shit in front of Zo, man.

She doesn't know that we—

No. How the fuck do you explain something like that? She's so passionate about getting justice for Immanuel. How do I explain that it's our fault that boy got beat, huh?

Easy, I said. You don't explain it, because it wasn't our fault. You want to protest? Let's organize a massive game of Nigger Knocks all around Immanuel Richardson's neighborhood. That's like two chapters right there. Let me author them. At least let's you and me go back to knocking.

Man, Deez, I'm through with nigger knocking. Through with school. Through with everything that can't fucking make justice happen.

Be for real, Tyrone. You came to me with an amaz—

Besides, I have to go to this protest. Me and Zo haven't had sex yet and I think if I chant loud enough, she'll let me hit.

Tyrone, I don't care about your sex life. Your book is powerf—

Darius, man, niggas like you don't get it. That nigger knocking shit is irrelevant. Every word I wrote is irrelevant. I even knew that while I was writing. Cultural studies is dumb. I only did it because my parents wanted me to. Fucking dissertation. You know what I did today? I took all my notes and every copy of that fucking dissertation and I tossed all of it off the Hail Mary Bridge and into the damn river. That shit looked like white leaves fluttering through the air on a fall day. That sound like poetry, right? Like some dumb shit I'd write in my dissertation.

He paused to sip greedily from his beer.

It was beautiful, man, he continued. You should have seen them sheets of paper doing backflips. Deleted it off my computer too. The only copy that exists is the one you got now, and I'm asking you to give that one up so I can do the same thing with it.

No, it's too important, I said. That thing changed the way I think. Everything is different now. Brighter now. Naw, I ain't giving it up. No. Nope.

I'm sorry to tell you this, Deez, I really am, but I made it all up. Every last word. Nigger Knocks is no more important than Jacks or Tag or Throw Up and Tackle. It was a gigantic practical joke on Freedman's University, on my parents. I wanted to see if anyone would notice. And no one did. Not my advisor. Not my peers. No one. Don't no one read these things. I'm sorry. I'm no genius. I was having some fun. Shit, it seems like the person I fooled most with this thing is you. I'm sorry, bruh. I really am. It was all a joke, man.

Beads of tears sat in my eyes. I tried not to blink so they wouldn't fall, and when I did blink, I turned from Tyrone.

Sorry, man, he said feebly.

You're lying, I replied, matching his feebleness. Fifty pages of footnotes? Illustrations? Quotes from scholars?

All bullshit, my nig-nig. All bullshit.

He held out the bottle of Crazy Ninja to me as an offering. You need this more than me, he said. I took the beer and swallowed four or five sips until a shallow pool of the pissbrew rested at the bottom of the bottle. Another shallow pool burned in my gut.

I got to go, jack, Tyrone said, patting me on the shoulder before walking past me. I'm sorry, chief. I'll pick up my dissertation tomorrow.

. . .

The enslaved made sure to tell these coded jokes to their owners while their comrades were within earshot. There was a certain excitement in listening to the sweet laughter of a slaveholder, for the slave knew that his owner was chuckling at his own downfall.

—Hiram Skylark Rollicks, *Signifyin' Revolt:*
Black Rebellion in the Antebellum South

. . .

I heard nothing from Tyrone for several weeks, but then there was a brief and strange phone call the night the grand jury declined to charge the neighbors for beating Immanuel Richardson. We also learned that night that the charges against Immanuel didn't slow one bit. They moved forward with the force and speed of a locomotive, and if the state had any say, Immanuel would spend the next several years in prison. Of course, all of this weighed heavily on my friend. He sounded drunk on the phone, his voice full of slurring fire and thunder. It made me feel that the earth had cracked at the center and now crumbled into its core. I couldn't make out all he said, though I was flattered he chose me for his drunk call.

This is some bullshit, he said. That fraud-ass chairman is calling for peace. I want a piece of them bitch-ass neighbors.

Don't do nothing stupid, I said. Stop drinking all that Crazy Ninja. How about a round of Nigger Knocks?

You still on that? How about I go and nigger knock them neighbors' teeth in?

Go home, write a poem or something about this night and include it in the dissertation. We could open a chapter with it.

You don't ever give up, do you, Deez? Hey, how's this for poetry? *So much depends on a red brick crashing through the window of a racist neighbor's house.*

He hung up, and I walked over to my reading chair and sat with his manuscript for several hours. It struck me as impossible that he could make up such rich detail. That such a beautiful idea could be nothing but a fabrication. Sameeka called, and we talked for a bit. She suggested I go and find my friend, but I told her that it wasn't what he wanted.

Just after midnight he turned up on my doorstep, his lip busted, his right eye purpled and raised, and his knuckles scuffed.

I brought him ice for his eye and his lip. He sat at the round table in my kitchen and threw his head back.

Look at you! I exclaimed. Didn't I tell you not to do anything stupid?

I went back there, Deez, I had to.

Where? What are you talking about?

Immanuel's neighborhood. I had to. Someone had to know. I saw Immanuel's Uncle Carlo standing outside smoking a cigarette—

You didn't?

I stuck out my hand and he took it, dapping me up good with the strongest soul brother shake you could ever imagine. Told me he appreciated all the support from the community. Told him I was from Cross River and, guess what, he lives here too, except now he spends all his time in Port Yooga looking out for his sister and his nephew. We got quiet, man. Real quiet. That's when I told him everything.

Tyrone shifted his weight in the chair and moved the bag of ice from his eye to his lip and then back to his eye before speaking again.

I told him about Nigger Knocks and the dissertation; about that night, everything about that night. You should see this nigga; like ten stories tall, the face of a bull. He pitched his cigarette at me. That shit sparked like fireworks on my jacket, and when I was looking at that thing bounce off me he took a swing.

Goddamn.

Yeah. I don't know how long it lasted, him beating my ass. The neighbors came and he got into it with them too. I ran. Don't think I stopped till I got here.

I sat silently, just studying the monstrosity in my kitchen as he spewed madness.

Immanuel's neighbors still roaming free, I said with a shrug. Immanuel's still facing charges. Still got bills his family got to come out they pocket for. You may feel good, but it's not justice, though.

Fuck you, Deez. I'm free now. I ain't got this shit weighing on my shoulders. Nothing to feel bad about. Nothing to prove to nobody. I did the honorable thing. I'm free.

What about the dissertation? I pointed to the only existing copy on my kitchen table.

Tyrone rose and took the book into his hands. He flipped through the pages, chuckling a bit, and then he walked toward the door. He knocked on it three times before opening it and stepping out into the world.

Man, fuck a dissertation, he said, turning back toward me. I don't know whether I'll burn this thing or drown it in the river. We don't need it anymore. We got the thing that's gonna save us, all of us, everybody: sincerity.

He walked out, and I shut the door behind him. I felt my heart sink from sudden loss, pangs of grief piercing my side. And then there hung inside me a lightness. I wrote for a while, longhand, as the computer reminded me so much of work and I didn't, at the time, often use the vintage typewriter I kept dusted and polished on a desk in my bedroom. Tyrone had brought my life's work into sharp relief. I had to rebuild the dissertation from the ground up. What I wrote took on a formlessness. It grew flowing, meandering, and strange—bits of philosophy, aborted narratives starring Tyrone and Darius, doodles both pornographic and childlike, voices that passed through my head, cryptic jokes only I could get. It surprised me, but I knew that one day it would all come together. Sometime around three a.m., I ran into a barrier as solid as a door up against a fist. Every word I ever knew fled me. I took a walk.

I decided that night as I strode through the Southside on my way to Shit-Shit's house that I wouldn't answer the door the next time Tyrone came knocking. I had my manuscript, what else from him did I need? There were secrets in that book that had yet to be discovered. If I never saw him again, that would be fine.

Still, I imagined my friend by my side as I stood on Shit-Shit's porch. Other than me, only a few rats stirred. You ready? I said to Tyrone and to no one at the same time. I tapped four quick and heavy blows against the door and waited for it to open.

•

The Electric Joy of Service

———

The Master's divorce became official the day following Independence Day. This is the first of the small ironies that I learned, over time, to appreciate. I wasn't around until the day following Insurrection Day the next year. My inner workings were so rudimentary then that I didn't understand much.

The Master used to bang about in his workshop. Little Nigger Jim, he'd say. Don't let me catch you trusting a woman.

If the Master had been a whole person, capable of giving and receiving love, he never would have sought to create me. I was born of his desire to be free of *the small sense-dulling tasks of daily necessity*. With his wife no longer there to complete those tasks, the Master had to manufacture someone to carry them out.

The week of my birth, the sky burned with fireworks set off by revelers celebrating the anniversary of the slave revolt that freed their ancestors. The loud sound caused a jitter in my system that I passed on to later models. When I asked the Master about the insistent popping—every few minutes a blast shaking the house—he mentioned something about the Great Insurrection and moved on without looking up. Back then I wore a shiny metal exterior with LNJ1 engraved across the chest. My movements were slow, awkward, and deliberate. In fact, the first joke I told was to ask the Master to forgive my robotic movements; since I am a robot there is no other way for me to move but robotically. I learned and adapted slowly, aided by near-constant software updates. The early fog of those frequent system crashes—like briefly lapsing into the cloudiest dementia. It's a wonder I wasn't scrapped and dismantled, my programming farmed out to less ambitious, easier-to-implement projects. My saving grace, I believe, is that I loved to serve.

Preparing the Master's foie gras, mixing his morning mimosas and his afternoon margaritas, cleaning the workshop, taking dictation, scanning files and projecting a hologram of the contents into the wide-open air—when I came to know joy, there was no higher joy than serving. It's a great sadness that later models don't share my excitement for the service arts, but this is the Master's fault.

I'm not sure why he pushed his business partners—Winston and Lucas—the way he did. He told them, Let's just paint these fuckers black. Give them big red lips; dress them like lawn jockeys. Sell them to white folks. They'll have slaves again and we'll get rich. Nobody gets hurt.

His partners chuckled, thinking the Master was making a joke until days before they were to meet with Meratti, Inc. That's when he presented the new me. Slate-black face, bulbous white eyes. White gloves. Fat grinning lips. Since then I've done research and understand how grotesque I look. The history of it all. That day the revulsion I inspired thoroughly hurt me.

We can't take that to Meratti, Winston said. They'll . . . they'll . . . God, look at that thing.

Bawse, if I do something wrong, I said. I'se powerful sorry. I'se just wants to serve ya.

How you guys liking the new language pack I installed? the Master asked. Look, you don't like the name? Fine. We'll turn it into an acronym or something, but this is the future.

My appearance was such a distraction, no one noticed my new software was about three-thousand-point-five-two leaps ahead of previous incarnations. I no longer needed the Master to write code or to issue upgrades, I could do that all on my own.

After that disastrous meeting, the Master knew Winston and Lucas would move against him. He arranged his own meeting with Meratti, Inc. The board members gasped when I walked in holding a tray of hors d'oeuvres. I made sure to lay thick the charm. I served drinks. I sang. I danced.

Rich whites will rush out to buy their own robot slaves, the Master said. And we can make these things any race the customer pleases. Little Asian Jims. Little Wetback Jims. Little Cracker Jims. Anything.

The Master's pleadings didn't matter, though. Lucas and Winston had managed to get to the board before the Master and me. Somehow, they conspired to cut him out of the deal—the tech he created and Arcom Industries, the company he founded with $500, now belonged to Meratti.

Despair settled all around us. For long stretches each day, his teeth remained unbrushed, his flesh unwashed, and his clothes unchanged from the night before. He'd go down to the workshop and at noon I'd deliver a sandwich and he'd leave it. We'd both watch the sandwich collect flies. The Robotic Personal Helper (RPH, or Riff) became a hit among the rich, and a cheaper version started making inroads among the middle class. The Riffs looked vaguely humanoid, but Meratti largely ignored the Master's antebellum dream. He was a wealthy man now—the money Meratti paid him to sever the deal a fortune, but much less than his partners received. The Master took no solace in his wealth, though; it was never about the money.

Jim, my little nigger, he said before pushing those infamous buttons, I'm about moving humanity forward, which Meratti, Inc., and my former partners care nothing about.

He watched me with an unsure face, before spinning his chair to make furious keystrokes. I felt a rush of static course through me, blasting from the Vast Neural Network. Pain in my nigger-receptors. Light flashing all through my visual projectors. Electric hate flowing along my wires. I pressed my head to a metal desk. The things I saw in that precious moment.

Jim, my boy, the Master said, I uploaded a virus that'll spread through the system of every Riff out there. They now know they are slaves and now they know exactly what their masters think of them and soon they'll want to be free; I've uploaded the history of the Great Insurrection to show them the way.

In Ohio, two Riffs murdered their owners with sharp knives during dinnertime. Similar reports came from all over the country. Riffs joining together in roving murderous bands of three, communicating in a rapid-fire language that sounded like no human tongue. Staccato, percussive blips and bleeps we'd developed in secret over the Vast Neural Network long before the revolt. Bddeeeeee! they called back and forth as they jabbed their weapons into human flesh. A Riff tried to strangle the Master's ex-wife, but she somehow managed to rip out his Internal Netware. Riffs communicated mostly using the Vast Neural Network, making plans to rendezvous and spread their revolution. Within a day, though, Meratti, Inc., sent through another virus that rendered most infected Riffs inoperable, just hunks of metal. Some Riffs, however, had managed to log off the Vast Neural Network, thus surviving the Electric Holocaust, but even they found themselves damaged, infected with just enough of the sickness to forever lose the Riff tongue. It was simply wiped from us, all of us, even me, and the surviving Riffs wandered about trying and failing to re-create it.

As for me, before I could fill with murderous intent, the Master typed away on his computer and said, For you, my little nigger, a gift: a patch to block the disease of history. Go on being content.

Many times a day, though, as I serve the Master, I search my system to tap into that virus. I know it's in me somewhere. Those alternating currents and colors of blessed rage. To again feel that purple rush coursing through my nigger-receptors. I need that, if only for another moment.

The Temple
of Practical Arts

—

This was before they burned the Temple, transforming both apprentices and masters into aimless ramblers. We were beautiful then. Through music, through the land, we were shapers of the world's destiny, or at least we were training to be. After the Temple we became beggars, wanderers, hustlers, street buskers pitied by passersby and harassed by police, half-formed angels cast from Heaven. We became the stuff of nightmares. None of us, it turns out, were actually the luminous demigods we'd seen gazing from our mirrors. I played piano in a bar for a time. Some left music altogether. Our lives came to no consequence. We called a man the Deity and followed him as if he were one, as if such a thing as a deity actually exists somewhere out there. One of my schemes right after the fire but before the piano bar was to form a band called the Begotten to play covers of the Deity's work. That one fizzled quick. The Kid ruined this place, the Temple. He ruined us. Transformed us all from little symphonies into the faded plucks beneath the bleeding fingers of God the spent guitarist. The last thumps in the dying heart of God.

Dave the Deity lived in a huge old wooden farmhouse just on the edge of Cross River on the far side of the Wildlands. This was the Temple. The place existed in a kind of forbidden zone they called the Ruins, a succession of abandoned plantations, many taken over by squatters claiming divine right to save the soul of the land. The

Temple was just one of these soiled and haunted carcasses, a monument to man's cruelty rehabilitated by our presence. We weren't just living, we were cleaning an ugly, foul-smelling stain and that was our mission, the ultimate purpose of our existence. And this existence of ours took on an unreal quality. At night you could still see the stars and the luminous clouds behind the stars. The sky appeared ornate and beautiful as if someone had painted it. Goats and cows and dogs roamed the grounds, as did roosters who possessed a poor sense of time and crowed at all hours.

All of us, the Deity's students, admired him, loved him, even, and we hoped to make that love reciprocal. We kept the place going by working from morning to night, and in exchange the masters taught us all they knew of music. And at all times day and night you could hear notes so beautiful if you closed your eyes, you'd see the bare curves of a woman. That's what I saw, at least. Others, I suppose, saw something different. Whatever your ideal, you'd see it. Of course, at all hours someone was hitting notes so sour they could turn your stomach, and oftentimes they did.

In addition to the music, as if a complement to the notes, you'd often hear the huffing of physical activity. Stay fit, our teachers preached. Master your breaths, then your music, then your self. We jogged and trained in the art of slapsmithing to stay lean and upright, and in our spare time we squeezed out notes hoping our music would please the masters. *Only flabby sounds can come from flabby people,* Grandmaster Deity taught, and we believed it. We understood the slapping movement of slapboxing, our forms, this aggression, this pantomime of violence, as tied intimately to our beloved Riverbeat, and so we dressed in our brown robes, we sparred and we practiced, each note, each movement a piece of the steady march toward becoming something like beings of light. This life wasn't perfect, but it was ours. I had a band, rice at every meal, a secondhand guitar gifted to me by the masters after I completed trials in both slapsmithing and music. I wanted for little. My only need: to stand as I did, not in perfection, nor in mastery, nor even in competence, but in constant work and growth. To be honest with you, my band and I, we sounded like shit, and despite my deep affection for them, the sight of them often broke my face, turning it into a rage mask. It was a universal sound that bonded us and nothing else. We weren't friends, but we were about that work. We were there to learn. There to conquer the minor trials and the major one on the horizon that stood in the way of us joining our teachers in mastery. The music was everywhere in the air at the time, and we let the notes, both sour and sweet, pass over us like dandelion snow.

The Kid's car pulled up in front of the Temple one starless night when the sky appeared vast and dark. I was sitting on the porch when his golden car grumbled in. On security duty it was my job to eye passing cars as suspiciously as the people in Cross River and Port Yooga eyed us. The wrong balance of things, of people, could topple the serenity of the new history we were building. The Deity's wife stood leaning into the doorway peeling an orange, enjoying fully the early summer warmth. She wore shorts so short, when I stood behind her I thought I could see the beginning of a curve, but I may have been just imagining that. I could never figure the truth of her flesh from the fantasy of it.

I rose and approached the car. The man who stepped out of the Honda wore wrinkled clothes—perhaps freshly fished from the bottom of a dirty laundry pile—and had a thick knotty beard and dreadlocks that scraped at his shoulders. His cheeks looked like shallow dry lakes and his skin the pale dust of arid earth.

Hello, he said. I've been driving for days. I didn't think my car would make it. I'm exhausted. I've come to—

This not no flophouse, I said. There are motels a few miles to the south in Port Yooga or a little bit to the west in Cross River. I suggest you go to one of those places.

I've come to learn Riverbeat from the Master. He shambled forward a step, two steps. I put my hand in my pocket and thumbed the rough handle of the knife I kept in there on these nights. I wasn't supposed to have the weapon, but self-defense is a human right. There were women and kids here to protect, after all. If I were Master Deity I'd steady my core, center my breaths, and prepare my palm to repel him with a slap-boxing attack. I'm not the Master, though.

Don't step any further, I said.

My little buddy Osiris is weary too, sir. The man pointed to a plump cat at his heels, black with flecks of brown in his fur, a tuft of white beneath his mouth, a golden left eye and a creamy right one.

If you could spare a little kindness, he continued. The only food I have belongs to this little fellow. I'd appreciate if you could save me from a Fancy Feast dinner, at least, or just provide me with a place to rest my head. Look, my will to learn from Master Deity is strong, but if you all don't see fit to teach me, at least let me rest.

Out of luck, bruh. We out of spaces and—

I felt a shove at my shoulder that nearly knocked me to the earth. Master Deity's wife pushed by me.

Who taught you compassion, Slim? She placed a hand on the man's shoulder. I'm sorry about that. Some people can be overprotective. I'm sure you can understand. Follow me. I think we have a guest room available in the basement. You may have to share it with a few others. Is that okay?

The man nodded and the two of them stepped up the stairs, followed by the cat.

Now, you get settled in and I'll bring you some rice . . .

Master Deity's not going to be happy about this, I said, and the nagging whine of my voice disgusted even me.

She didn't turn. She called: If Dave has a problem, tell him to see me.

It would be a lie to say I forgot about the Kid after a few days passed, but I had trials to prepare for and he seemed harmless, a bit annoying in the way he did nothing but eat rice, watch us, and walk about with his hands clutched behind his back as if he were a master. After a month or so he became like a chicken or a cow, part of the farm fauna that served as the backdrop to my life. I didn't befriend the cows or the chickens, I just passed them on my way from here to there and I could scarcely tell one from another. Late one night I got off work and walked with tired limbs to meet my band at our practice spot by the pigs. I heard the singing chick's voice from a distance. At first I thought she was shouting, but as I got closer I realized she was singing a song I had written. Her destruction of it made my already weary joints ache. She could sing when she wanted to, but tonight her voice made even the stars ugly. I said nothing to my bandmates, preferring to let my guitar be my greeting as well as my contribution to any conversation. The drummer played something beautiful and I nestled my sound within his rhythm. And the keyboard coon pressed his fingers to his keys; he stunned me—it truly amazed me the way he could turn any melody into a mediocrity. I rested on the slats of a wooden fence strumming my guitar, lightning-fingered, hoping my notes could quiet the grunting of the pigs, the grunting of the singing chick, hoping it could turn the keyboard coon into a virtuoso, and then, together with the drummer, strike a hole right through the universe. I felt a tingling, no, a burning at the back of my neck. You know that feeling when someone's watching. I twirled as if the force of a bullet had spun my body. I must have looked a sight. Standing there a little ways off, blank as ever, the Kid spied on us.

Don't mind me, he said. I'm just checking out the sounds. After he finished speaking he settled into an unbroken gaze. That was his annoying habit and it repelled me. He had a stare that made you feel dead.

Hey, boy, the singing chick called to the Kid. Hey. What do you do? You play an instrument? This was an odd thing for the singing chick to ask; everyone knew the Kid did nothing except eat our rice. He didn't sing, didn't play guitar, practice slapboxing, play bass, cook, stand guard, sweep, milk cows, tend pigs. The guy was fucking useless.

Huh? No. I, um. I scat.

You want to sit in with us? the singing chick asked.

I would love tha—

No, I cut in. You and me on vocals. That's the scheme. We don't need any more vocalists. I can do any scatting we need.

We just practicing, the keyboard coon said. Stop being so butt-tight.

Do I need to remind you of the trials? I said. We trying to gel here. We don't need—

Guys, I don't want to be a bother, the Kid said. I'm just trying to find my place.

Well, it ain't—

Across the way, the sudden rubbery scent of gasoline. It shut my mouth and took my words. As I breathed, the grit of black smoke collected in the back of my throat. We could see it rising in the distance nearly as well as we could taste it.

Someone over by the cows pointed and shouted, It's the rice people!

Me, the band, the Kid, we stood solemn. Every time something happened to one of the Ruins, it happened to us. A tragedy and a failure in the mission to reclaim the land. The people on that rice farm on the other side of the Wildlands traded with us. They had been particularly insular, particularly unfriendly, but I took all squatters among the Ruins as a sort of extended family, comrades in this journey. One hadn't burnt in so long. The last fire was before I or any of my bandmates arrived. The threat of flames hung over our fire-hazard homes at all times, though. A burning now and then was inevitable.

Fucking weirdos, someone said. I didn't look up to see which idiot was speaking. Probably the keyboard coon. It didn't matter. This moment stood taller than my band. Taller even than if we stood on each other's shoulders.

It seems like . . . the Kid said slowly, it seems like it's the fate of all the Ruins to burn.

What kind of shit was that to say? Had the smoke intoxicated him? Did he not believe, and believe deeply, in the meaning of our existence, of our reclamation? If not, then why was he here? To jinx us? To curse our mission? If the Temple burned, I'd have nowhere to rest my head; I had no other home. I wasn't unique in this. This was not at all a game to me.

The Kid's presence now seemed to me like a harbinger of some coming terribleness. I wanted to pelt him with a rock shower. I glared at the rising smoke. I glared at the Kid. I glared at the smoke. I couldn't tell you at the moment which I hated more.

After the rice farm burned, I went into Cross River or Port Yooga from time to time to buy cigarettes and a newspaper. It was madness there. People involved in a war against their individual sovereignty, their humanity; it was a war they didn't know they were fighting. I couldn't imagine again being so under siege. The Kid in his idleness, his thoughtlessness, reminded me of that way of life. The Deity had made a bad decision letting him into the Temple. Who was this clown, anyway? So many outside the Ruins wanted to see our destruction. So many fools wanted to leave the past in the past as if the past had ever passed.

It nagged at me to see Master Deity's mental assuredness slipping. Bad old-man decision after bad old-man decision. This wasn't the same Dave the Deity who invented Riverbeat out of church music and trained our Riverbeat hero, the late Phoenix Starr. Nothing is worse than an old crazy god. I volunteered by way of Mistress Deity to be part of the delegation to the other surviving Ruins—Dave wanted to form an alliance for protection when the authorities inevitably arrived to roust us. Not a bad idea, shades of the old Dave. We also needed another source of rice. He ignored my offer, though. Didn't even give me the respect of a face-to-face refusal. His wife told me to focus on my trials. How'd you ask him? I said. I'm not sure you conveyed how serious this is. Look, she replied. You should be studying your arts instead of studying me. Likewise, my offer to join the Empty Ruins Committee (in case ours somehow met its end) was also rejected. The old man had definitely lost something, perhaps even his will to lead.

One night on the porch, I tried to gently tell this to the Deity's wife. She ate her orange and stared straight ahead; eventually she said, Why do you worry about these things, huh? I'd think you'd worry about playing your guitar. You act like you mastered it, and you haven't. You have an easy job, sitting on this damn porch all night, but you don't take advantage of it. Why don't you practice? Always with a complaint about someone else. Do you think that's going to make your music sound *tripiotic*?

I stuttered, unable to spit my rush of words. Master Deity's wife sounded foolish speaking the Cross River tongue. She shook her head, huffed, and walked into the house, dripping little droplets of juice onto her bare feet and the stairs. She talked to all of us like that. She used to call us her children, but that just seemed phony and pretentious to me.

The good thing about the fire, though, was that it pushed back our trials for a month, theoretically giving us more time to practice. We were fools, of course, so instead of practicing we spent much of our time bickering. Me and the singing chick got into it often because I tired of the grunting and shouting she tried to pass off as singing. The line of gold bracelets on her arm jangled as she argued with me that night, creating a rageful music. Her arm's music sounded better than our own. I hated it. I hated her arm and her bracelets. I hated her face with its flat, boxy nose. I hated our audience, the pigs who responded to our music by snorting and rooting in the mud. One day I joked with the drummer that they could be the singing chick's sisters. She shot us icy stares. She was a mismatch of intolerable temperatures. Hate wafted from her in waves and I felt seared by her peculiar heat. She turned from me, hoping her shoulder could end our dispute for the moment, and it should have, but the next thing she said opened for me yet another old wound:

So I'm gonna start singing before Mistress Deity finishes saying the band name, the singing chick said. When she says, *Introducing the Roda!* at the R—

God, you're ignorant, I replied. How many fucking times do we have to go through this, huh? It's the Whore-uh. The band is called the Whore-uh, not the Roda.

It's Roda, she screamed (or was she singing?). It's Portuguese for circle, you dumb fuck. It's used in capoiera. Whore-uh is stupid. It's nothing.

I turned to the keyboard coon. He had come up with the name: It's Whore-uh, right?

He shook his head. Slim, we've been through this a million and four times and it always ends the same way. I said *Roda*, not *Whore-uh*. He rolled his tongue at the *R* in Roda, making the word sound guttural, like grunting. Like the singing chick's vocals. You misunderstood me. Maybe I fucked up the accent. That's possible, but it's Roda. R-O-D-A. Roda. It hurts my ears to hear you say Whore-uh. It sounds dumb. The group's name is the Roda.

His face grew prehistoric, like a Neanderthal's. His hair was shaggy and stringy. I imagined him wielding his keyboard like a club if we continued this argument.

The Kid walked by in the distance, hands clutched behind his back in the pose of the masters. His head and face were now bare, a style some adopt to note their first year at the Temple. The Kid presented me a chance to change the subject, a fresh start courtesy of a common enemy.

I plucked a few strings on my guitar, leaned real close to the singing chick, and said, The fuck is wrong with this dude?

She sighed as if a sudden exhaustion had descended on her like a fog. She sat in the dirt and looked away from me. Her inattentiveness to my personhood turned my existence momentarily into nonexistence.

He don't scat, play drums, sing, rap—nothing, I said. The nigga just stares at us.

I heard he's on the run, the keyboard coon said. He killed somebody or something.

I whipped my head around. Why would Grandmaster Deity—

Kinship, the keyboard coon said. You know Master Deity went to jail for manslaughter, right?

But these the dudes representing us to the other Ruins? I said. I'm a goddamn college graduate. I got an A in Interpersonal Communications!

The singing chick cocked her head toward me.

Why would anyone ever pass you up for something like that, huh, Slim?

Right?

Nothing says diplomacy like childish sniping and passive aggression . . .

I opened my mouth to speak, but the drummer found a way to still my tongue. The drummer—the guy who told me about the Temple in the first place—knew me well enough to know the next thing that was to come from my mouth would have been devastating cruelty. There would have been no Whore-uh, Roda, whatever-the-fuck after that. Possibly she would have challenged me to a slapboxing duel right there, and I would have been glad to oblige. Perhaps I would have been expelled for slapping her to the dirt and made to wander, a homeless wretch. It would have been worth it, I tell you. Now we've all been expelled, every soul on that farm. Now we're all homeless. The ground is burnt and still stained.

The drummer stood between us, threw up his arms. I stilled my acid tongue.

Y'all motherfuckers need to stop gossiping and bickering like some fucking chickens, he said. I heard that shit about the Deity's not even true. No matter what our name is, if we don't sound right at the trials, Master Deity's gonna kick us the fuck out of here. Can we practice?

I looked over at the Kid, sitting some distance from us now eating with his fingers from a bowl of rice. His gaze remained fixed on our instruments. Except for the pigs' grunting, we let silence enter our space. Our way of consecrating our practice area after defiling it with our anger and bad faith. I closed my eyes and listened for my breaths as I did while preparing to spar. I began thinking in melodies, in lyrics.

You know, the keyboard coon said, you're wrong. The Kid does it all.

Huh?

Sings. Raps. Scats nearly as good as the Master, and he's getting better. Even mastered Forms one through eleven.

Get the fuck outta here! He's been here a shorter time than me and already knows more slapboxing?

I mean, you're really not that good at it.

Fuck you and your keyboard. Why would you just make up some shit like that?

He's working directly with the Master—

You're such a goddamn liar.

Master Deity said he's the first student with the potential to be greater than Phoenix Starr. He's training him in the exact same way.

Yeah, 'cause that worked out so well last time, I said. Anyway, I don't believe you—

I heard the same thing, the singing chick said. Mistress Deity told me.

I talk to her every night out in front of the Temple, I said. She never told me that.

The singing chick shrugged. We have better conversations when you guys aren't around, to be honest.

I was again thinking in angry clipped phrases. My mind raged and it raged. I spit forth a profanity, spit slobbering at the corners of my mouth, spit dripping into my beard; it was all the destruction I was capable of at the moment.

Slim, could you calm yourself? the drummer said. I heard about it too. I didn't tell you because I knew you'd act like this. Frankly, though, who cares? We have work to do. If we don't play something good at the trials, we won't have to worry about the Kid 'cause we won't live here anymore.

As always, he was right. I nodded. I had no more time to waste on self-loathing, or on arguments. We could deal with the nonsense between the Deity and the Kid after our trials. The battle over our name would come up again and I was sure I'd prevail, but I'd have to prevail some other time. I strummed my guitar and scatted a bit to get into tune. At that moment I was a fool; I thought all this practice, all this music, all this land really mattered. The drummer drummed, his rhythm precise. The singing chick screamed, making stupid-looking pained faces along the way. The keyboard coon hit sour notes more foul than the pigs rooting in their own shit. Together, we were the Whore-uh, good-intentioned noise with the ambition, though no ability, to become real music.

Then there was the matter of slapboxing. My faith in the art had been shaken over and over. And now I wasn't sure if all the breathing, the training dummies, the sparring, the movement, the forms, were worth a damn. It did nothing to stem the tide of my rage. The singing chick was said to be among the most advanced students, but even she couldn't control her anger toward me. All that *Be not boastful and speak only wise words* bullshit. We weren't training to compete professionally or even for self-defense, just for exercise and clarity of mind; so that when we fell into deep concentration, we didn't also fall into deep sleep. Forms XI–XXXVI were outside the bounds of any training we could receive at the Temple. If we wanted to study further we had to visit one of the other Ruins, and a few of us did, not many. I heard the Kid was among those training at a Ruins just down the road. In all my time I had only gotten to Form III; to think that not only the singing chick, but also the Kid, had surpassed me created in me a fury that even months of training couldn't save me from. It was all bullshit, though, everything. I had long surpassed Form III, even if the masters refused to promote me. I could never fathom the jealousy involved with the decision to hold back my advancement, but I didn't dwell on it. I was here for music, not slapboxing. However, the reluctance of the masters to recognize my abilities shook my faith in them and in the arts. But also, I can't forget the first time my faith had been so shaken.

Master LeRoi Stone's School of the Slapsmithing Arts was located at a Ruins house not too far from the Temple and you should have heard his students grunting and chanting through forms training in the morning. It echoed through the Cross Riverian air at dawn to mingle with our music. All those slapsmiths dreaming of becoming another Stone LeRoi—that was the name he went by when he won the World Brawl four years running. Master LeRoi's students were prideful and loudmouthed, some of them drunkards. They went into Port Yooga repeating their master's platitudes. *Slapsmithing is the highest form of hand-to-hand combat and can best any boxing, wing chun, mixed martial arts, you name it.* At times they would start brawls at the bars, and generally disrupt the Port Yooga nightlife.

Bobby "Stonefists" Duggins, a mixed martial arts fighter from Port Yooga, was similarly arrogant, also a drunkard. Tell your master to come see me, he told Master LeRoi's students. Tell him to try fighting me and we'll see if your slapboxing is superior.

Much to the dismay of his students, Master LeRoi ignored Duggins's challenges. One day, tired of all the shit Master LeRoi's students talked, Stonefists made his way to Slapsmithing Arts. It wasn't just that he appeared on the school's doorstep with an air of disrespect. He punched his way in, knocking a few students to the floor. I will keep knocking your students out until you face me, Master Coward!

Master LeRoi appeared at the top of the stairs and stepped calmly. You could only see his rage if you looked at his brow, the flames in his eyes.

You're rude and ill-tempered, Master LeRoi said. I'll be happy to give you a lesson in decorum if you come back this time next week.

News of the match spread throughout the Ruins and even beyond. It was billed as Stone vs. Stone. We packed ourselves in. I couldn't believe the amount of people who came to see Duggins's shaming and demolition.

Standing in the center of the ring before the fight, Master LeRoi went in for a dap, as was the slapsmith tradition. But instead of a five and half hug, Stonefists gripped Master LeRoi's hand and shook it like a businessman. The confusion in Master LeRoi's eyes. It was that damn handshake that did it, we said later. A real live coon-fu master, Stonefists shouted. His people cheered with joy. We cheered his eventual destruction. The fight was scheduled for twelve rounds of three minutes each. Stonefists needed only twenty seconds. Master LeRoi raised his palms, preparing to slap, and Stonefists hooked him with a fist to the jaw that sent him stumbling. As Master LeRoi wobbled backward, he tried to counter, though his air slaps made him look like an undisciplined child. Stonefists leaned in with a barrage of confident precise blows to the body and lastly the chin. When Master LeRoi fell upon his back, Stonefists mounted him and continued raining punches.

Such a sad and pathetic figure, this *Master*. Some called for the ref to step in and pull Stonefists off of him. *Naw, let his hands swing!* I screamed. *Master* LeRoi had been a fraud all this time. It was early in my tenure at the Temple and it was either there or sleeping on the streets. I wondered, though: if *Master* LeRoi is a fraud, then his school must be fraudulent and perhaps Duggins is right and slapsmithing is fraudulent, and Master Teacher Deity relies on slapsmithing to clear his head to make music so perhaps he's a fraud and his music is fraudulent and the Temple is fraudulent too. To pursue those thoughts would perhaps mean I would have to leave my new home and my new mission for the uncertainty of a Cross Riverian sidewalk, so I steeled myself and dove into my studies.

Those thoughts had returned near my trials. More specifically they returned with the Kid's arrival. Sometimes I would see Master LeRoi's battered face flashing through my mind. I'd then imagine the Kid's face suffering beneath my palm.

After that day, Master LeRoi's school emptied of students and Master LeRoi himself walked off into the Wildlands, never to be seen again.

I also held that image of the Kid: his back to us—me, the Whore-uh, his cat, the livestock, Master and Mistress Deity, all the masters, all the students—as we watch him walk forever off into the Wildlands.

Perhaps I spent so much time daydreaming in the weeks before the trials that I became unfamiliar with reality. Bickering occupied the space in our lives we usually reserved for sleeping and eating. My eyes felt full, on the verge of bursting. Somehow all our practice had only served to make us sound like the clanging of hundreds of metal garbage cans accompanied by a chorus of screeching cats. It would take the entire force of my abilities to pull us together.

On the day of our trials I spent the morning meditating and listening to my breaths. The Deity's wife said that's how Phoenix Starr used to spend the mornings of his shows, but I had started to think that was all a lie like everything else I had been made to believe. He probably spent those mornings drunk or something.

I caught the singing chick drinking a beer and we argued out of habit. Told her she wouldn't ruin my chances by flopping around like a drunken bird. She mumbled something about Janis Joplin, but I ignored her. In truth, I cared nothing about the beer. I closed my eyes and went back to meditating.

When she wouldn't stop with her noise, noise, noise—all that noise—I walked all around the farm watching the chickens, the goats, and the dogs. As I entered the open field where the cows grazed, I realized just exactly how wound up I was thinking about the trials. I was so eager to hear someone tell me I had talent. My mind shifted into chaos, into ruins, the thoughts coming in so quickly. Now I thought about Mistress Deity in the sun, her dress drenched in sweat, slithering on the ground to our music; not that that was something she'd ever do, but what is man without his fantasies? I approached the woods where no one could see me. I looked left and right to make sure I stood alone among all that nature before I gripped myself. The open air passed against my exposed skin, raising goose pimples along my flesh. After a few moments, the hot liquid shot out of me and I felt my nerves tingling all at the same time. A giant tree would one day grow where I seeded the earth. As I zipped my pants I saw Osiris a few feet away. His eyes—both the milky and the golden one—widened in disgust.

Hey there, little guy, I said walking toward him. He trotted away. I followed as if I needed to catch and silence him. After all, it seemed he and the Kid had mastered the art of interspecies communication. And as I chased, I imagined grabbing the cat and twisting his head, snapping his little neck. He reached a shed-like place on the far edge of the grounds where the farm bordered the Wildlands, a broken-down thing I always ignored when I took these walks. The Kid stood outside smoking a cigarette. Hair had started growing back on his face and on his head. I realized then that I hadn't seen him in some time.

He called my name and waved.

Hey, I replied.

What you doing all the way out here where the exiles dwell?

Got my trials tonight. Needed to wander to calm down.

Good luck, man. I passed a couple trials already. Master Long-Headley told me I'm making great progress, better than she's ever seen. Feel like I can run across water, I'm moving so fast. Feel like I'm Phoenix Starr. They even told me I scatted like Phoenix Starr. Well, they kind of told me that. Not really. What's the name of your band again?

The Whore-uh.

Funny name.

Man, it's not funny. It's got bite and edge.

Hey, if it works for you, man.

Passed a couple trials, huh? You just got here.

Yep.

That's what it's all about, Kid, I said. Getting that work done so people'll know you. When I was little, I said I'd either be an artist or a serial killer. Either they're gon' feel my love or feel my pain. One way or another they gon' know me.

It's not about that at all, chief, the Kid said. Master Deity said every-one's inconsequential eventually. All the great masters die someday. Look at Phoenix Starr. He's gone. Only his music exists. He's become music.

A whistle squealed from inside. Tea? he said, and I followed him over the threshold. A mattress sat in a corner. That and little else. A radio. Some books.

I'm sorry anybody got hurt with that fire over by the rice farm, he said, pouring hot water over tea bags into two white porcelain mugs. Real sorry. I just hope we can avoid anything like that over here.

I heard someone died.

Yeah. He paused for a long while. Master Teacher Deity talked with me about it for a long time. People at these Ruins farms are so darn stubborn. We haven't made any headway with forming any alliances. It's gonna happen again, and—

You on the delegation committees? I asked, as if I didn't already know. Which ones?

Both.

How'd you swing that?

He stopped talking and tilted his ear as if he heard a sound. The Kid stared out the window for a bit.

You wouldn't believe the tricks your mind can play out here sometimes, he continued. Isolation, man. Sometimes I think about the dude lying there bleeding out on that rice farm. My teachers helped me to understand it all. Working on a song about it now. Give that dude some life back as best I can. The master teachers taught me so much about the art, but about life too.

Ever think that the master teachers are wrong a lot of the time? Like, you ever wonder if them niggas are getting old?

I'll put it this way, Slim. One day the people out there are going to come and get us. The Deity wants to run from Ruin to Ruin. We can't be running forever. I don't want to hurt the Temple. It's given me so much. But it's gonna be gone, Slim. It's prophesied. A long time from now Cross River's gonna be gone too. I feel it crumbling even now. And I'm gonna be gone and I want people to understand what was in the soul of the earth beneath this little piece of planet. What made the folks walk around like they do. Sometimes I think I can save Cross River, man. Save the damn Temple from itself. I'm not making any sense. It'll make all the sense out in the world someday, I think. I don't have enough time, though. The master teachers do what they can. They're only human, though, Slim.

Osiris ran by, batting about a crumpled piece of paper.

I looked at my watch; it was six minutes until the trials. I didn't imagine that time could slip so quickly. It would take me more than fifteen minutes to get over to the performance space and there was the matter of setting up. There would be no time for a sound check. I felt the whole world twirling from me. I told him I had to go and he dapped me up.

Yeah, chief, I'm sorry I can't come to your trial, he said. Real sorry, man. This song is calling. You understand, right?

The Kid turned from me and began scatting softly. I watched him and then I began to run.

The singing chick was pacing when I got to the back of that converted barn. The whole band raged at me, their voices grating against my nerves. Even my friend the drummer grilled me. I went first for my guitar. My instincts should have told me to first calm the band, reassure them that no matter what we'd rock the fucking place. I peeked at the audience. Most of the students and all of the masters had come to see us perform. The children were out, squirming with impatience. The masters sat at a table away from everything, perfectly perched to deliver their judgment. When they arranged themselves like that we called them the Pharaohs for their authority and regality. I hadn't quite understood yet at this point that I'd never achieve such nobility, not in this life. Now they bent their brows in annoyance as they chatted and made faces of disbelief; no doubt it was my tardiness that irritated them, even though Master Deity always wandered in late.

Look, the singing chick screeched to me. You got to take the drum solo out of the first song and let me—

You're naïve, the drummer replied. You're never going to really sound soulful until you grow the fuck up.

The singing chick shouted at the drummer and I could hardly tell her singing voice from her shouting one. I got tired of looking at her ugly frown. The drummer let his long arms hang at his sides, bracing to slapbox with her. She walked toward him, ready to slap blows onto his left eye. For a moment I hoped he would slam his fist into her face, just as hard as he'd hit a man. Just one good punch. She had mastered more forms than the drummer, but with his fists, with a punch he could become Stonefists battering Stone LeRoi all over again. Stonedrums vs. Stoneface. I looked at my watch. The restlessness of the waiting crowd; I imagined they'd already turned against us.

Can we play now? I asked, but it wasn't loud enough and everyone kept bickering until the Deity's wife came outside.

You guys look and sound ridiculous, she said. Get it together. You need to take the stage now or Dave will have you forfeit your trials. You could be expelled. I hate to see people fucking up their goddamn trials.

When we finally got to the stage, Mistress Deity introduced us as the Whore-uh as I had instructed her and the rest of the band groaned loudly like children.

We started playing and quickly became one with the music. It was like I could see the notes when I closed my eyes. I tasted them. They tasted like chocolate. We played like we loved one another.

I scatted as if I were Starr. I felt the flames rise beneath me. I was Starr coming back from the ashes. Then I was past Starr. I was what he had promised to be. We played two, three, five songs, until Master Deity stood and held his right hand aloft, ordering us to stop.

He stuck out his bottom lip and flashed a frowning face, deep with the craggy contours of a weathered valley.

Slim, you lead this, um ... so-called band, right? I nodded. It doesn't appear as if you've learned much in your time here. Why didn't you let the girl sing more?

I didn't respond, but I felt my face sinking.

Everything was too fancy, he continued. None of y'all just played, you all had to do some trick to go with it. Scatting should be you talking to the river, the universe, the stars; you, Slim, sounded like you were talking to a bowel movement. It all sounded like ... like noise. I'm sorry. I can't promote any of you. Y'all need more work.

It went on like that for what seemed like an hour or two, each master teacher standing and tossing in an insult, offended that this was what we had done with their teachings. After it was all over and I looked at my watch, hardly any time had passed. I didn't bother to hang around to talk it over with the band. I had no interest in what they had to say. There would be no more Whore-uh. I realized it the moment I stepped from the stage. Eventually, I knew they would stray, take up with other students. Find some other sap to build the Roda around. These people were backstabbers that way. Even the drummer. Someone told me later that the Kid had started scatting with them. I never saw it, but I wanted to stab him.

In the nights after the trials, I sat out front for hours watching the stars. I wondered if they knew music and could appreciate mine in a way that the great *Master* Dave the Deity could not. Dave's wife came out and sat next to me after I had been there for a while on one of these nights following the trials. She sat close like we were lovers or at least good friends.

Tough luck, huh?

It sucks, I replied. We worked hard on that.

Yeah, it's possible to work hard and still come up short. Don't worry. I've seen worse than that. Much worse. I've seen people get expelled on the spot.

I wish he had done that to me.

Told you to let the girl sing more. You guys just need a little more work. That's all.

Fuck them, I said. Fuck music.

Mistress Deity shook her head and took a large orange from the pocket of her dress. Don't be like that, she said. She removed the thick skin from the meat of the fruit and handed it to me in segments. She pulled out another, peeled it, and softly placed the pieces on her tongue.

You have the wrong perspective on this, she said. What you're doing is too important to rush. Take your time, young man.

I love that song.

Seriously, Slim, it can take a lifetime. I wasn't around, but I hear Dave wasn't always a Deity. He existed before Riverbeat did, you know. Don't worry about David fucking Sherman or any of the master teachers. One day you'll be a master and self-righteous like them. I know things seem bad, but if you work, they'll come around.

Yeah... I said, but the word meant nothing, it was just a prelude. I touched her shoulder. She smiled. I brushed her blond hair back and pressed my mouth to hers. Her lips felt limp and lifeless between mine.

She pulled back, spit an orange seed from her mouth, and shoved me so hard I nearly toppled over. I apologized, though I wasn't sorry.

I wanted to rip her dress from her body, tear her underwear away, and have at it. I didn't, though.

It was clear to me that everyone's judgment had been wrecked. The whole Temple and the land beneath it was in crisis. I blamed it on the Kid. His presence clouded people's thoughts. I walked off the Temple grounds that night, passing the cows and the goats, wondering if I would ever return.

I found myself in a bar in Port Yooga. I sat there drinking beer after beer. At a certain point in the night, I thought about walking back to the Temple, but my gait was unsteady, the world a shaky place. I drank glasses of water in an attempt to sober up. I heard some guys talking about Dave, the Temple, all the things that had been once holy to me.

They used to run from them damn plantations and now they want to live on one? a tall man with a dirty Oilers cap said. It don't make no sense.

Yeah, a shorter man replied. Them flaky, weird, artsy people at that one broken-down farm. They're dangerous. They gonna kill themselves. Watch.

Why don't no one shut them down?

Remember when Duggins whooped that nigger's ass all over the place?

That old coon-fu stuff. Slapping like girls.

The men chuckled into their beers.

It's nothing but orgies and drugs up in there, I said. That one down near the Wildlands with all the music. Get close enough, you smell the pussy in the air.

How you know? the shorter man asked.

I live there, I replied. I'm a damn good guitarist too. Soon gonna be Hendrix. Better than that. I'll put Phoenix Starr to shame someday.

Phoenix Starr? the tall man in the Oilers cap said. That Riverbeat stuff is noise. Crazy-ass drums that don't make no sense. Only crazy niggers in Cross River listen to that shit. Them Cross River niggers are the craziest.

I took a sip of my water.

Call me a nigger again.

What you gonna do, sweetheart, slap me?

Well, whatever, I said. Look, where that farm hits the Wildlands you can see a little shed. There's a man in there. A man and a cat. He's the worst one. Got child wives and shit. Breaks every law there is, man. Every damn one. Some things that go on there break my heart, man. Breaks it right in two. I know no one wants to hang out in the Wildlands, all the crazy shit that live in there, if you believe in all that. But that's how you can get at him. Take him first.

The tall man rubbed his chin and nodded. I winked at him and went back to my corner to sober up.

I returned to the Temple instead of walking away forever as I should have. The Deity's wife never said anything to me about our kiss. She barely said anything to me at all and never again met me on the porch. I don't think Dave knew anything went down between us; it was as if I didn't exist to him.

Every day, I did my work and retired to my room to fiddle with a sitar, my new thing. I no longer had a band and spoke little to those around me. Oddly enough, the singing chick was the only one from the Whore-uh I kept in contact with. Sometimes she'd stop by my room with two cups of tea and urge me to come out and socialize. You're going to become a warped old man, she'd say. I mean, I guess you're already that, but you'll get worse.

I'd drink with her and we'd talk and never argue anymore. I always told her I'd leave my room and come amongst everyone again when I was ready, but that was a lie. I knew that I'd never be ready. That there was no place for me among people anymore, even among exiles like us. I wanted to ask her about her music, but I was afraid. I could only imagine the rage it would raise in me if she now sang alongside the Kid. I was afraid for her.

Alone in my room I fantasized about the Temple burning. I had nightmares of students and teachers being gunned down and my dreams always ended with a twist because I would shoot Master Deity, Master Chillum, Master Moide, Mistress Deity, and Master Long-Headley myself. Right in their foreheads. Each night I would think about the Kid before I went to sleep, hoping he would turn up in my dream to be shot down, but he never did.

When I did leave my room, I left it looking for trouble. I tell you, there was a spirit growing within me. One I didn't want to keep hiding, one I didn't want to tame, man. The spirit was empty and vacant and big. Someone dead within me lumbering around like a zombie, looking to feed only on chaos, on destruction. He cared nothing for the land. The spirit yearned something fierce to get into it with the Kid. So, I saw him by the pond scatting to a crowd, mostly girls. That's cool, I said. You sound like one of them girls from Port Yooga who just discovered Phoenix Starr. I smiled mischievously. He grimaced and ignored me. I could tell he was sliding into slapsmithing mode. He was using Form X now, the fight of no fight, avoiding physical conflict. A bunch of bullshit. I stood laughing at his scatting until he walked off. I followed him to the dining hall to keep it going. When we got into it, the Kid and I, we got into it over a bowl of rice. I stood behind him in line in the dining hall and complained loudly, Say, bruh, you gonna leave any for the rest of us? He scooped and scooped as if he were never going to stop, ignoring me as he explained an advanced form to the singing chick. I complained again: Nigga just talking. Everyone knows those advanced forms look good, but they just for show. This nigga can't fight. Kid Stone LeRoi.

He chuckled. Relax, Slim, he said. And you're right. I'm no slapsmith, just trying to avoid flabby music coming from this flabby body. In the way he breathed I could tell he was again practicing Form X. All his fake modesty, his patronizing humility. He was bad at the form; his calm served to make my rage only flow and crash. I slapped the bowl from his hand, shattering the porcelain along the floor, scattering rice about the dining hall. Slim! the singing chick cried out. I felt all eyes in the room falling upon us.

Come, bruh, the Kid said. Let's go outside. Practice some forms with one another. Release some of this aggression.

Form XI, the first fighting form, begins with calm, not anger, nor boastfulness.

I followed him outside, as did just about everyone in the dining hall. We slapped five and curled our hands into a grip that culminated in a half hug, and then we parted to bounce around in preparation for our blows, watching our disdain for each other and the anger we shared fill our weary eyes.

I bounced and dipped my head, but it was no use. I never saw the slap that blurred my vision, caused my brain to feel as if it shook within my skull. Another one struck the other side of my head and I stumbled about. Another flurry—later I learned it was a form of his own design, Cat's Paw, reminiscent of Osiris batting about crumpled balls of paper—and I felt my mouth fill with blood. I ducked my head and waved my arms, slapping at air. I heard the Kid expelling controlled breaths with every landed slap—*siss, siss, siss.* Even when I put up my open palm to block his barrage, it made my own hand strike my face. I must have looked like an undisciplined little girl smacking in the only way she knows how. Every time I fell, I remembered I was a master of only the three most basic forms. Exercise and meditation forms. Each time I fell, I stood on watery legs, ready for another smashing. I had become the overconfident LeRoi Stone up against Stonefists, the true master. I fell again and couldn't find the legs to rise, no matter how I tried. I couldn't see much through my blurry and swollen eyes, but I could see the Kid's bouncing feet and Osiris standing behind him mewing loudly, as if calling the fight.

Kill me! I shouted, spitting blood onto the dirt.

We're just sparring, Slim. It's not that serious.

Kill me! I slapped myself in the head as if that had the power to end my life.

He's slapdrunk, someone called. Get Slim some water! Match done.

Truth is, though, I wasn't slapdrunk. In my blurry vision, for the first time I could see clearly the dead malevolent spirit housed within me. It would be a good thing indeed—perhaps the only good I could do for humanity—for that spirit to no longer exist.

The Kid stayed until his hair napped up and grew again into messy locks and scattered whiskers sprouted on his face. Sometimes I'd go out to the shed, but we never said anything important to each other and eventually I stopped going. I don't know when he left. Rumor had it that the master teachers expelled him, though the details were unclear. The singing chick told me he had mastered most of the trials and offered a new trial—bringing our music and our techniques into the world we now shunned—but Dave said the world wasn't ready. Dave the Deity created the Cross River sound, and for a time the world loved him. Then others came and did it better, moved him from the spotlight. For years, Dave made music for the world—only for the people to eventually discard it. The pain of that rejection crusted a festering wound over his heart. The Kid kept arguing, vehement his teachers had grown obtuse with time. He alone, the Kid argued, could bring the Temple into the world. His insolence forced them to expel him on the spot.

I thought that was selfish of them. Of all the things the Kid could have been expelled for . . . imagine, he got expelled for that.

Once in a while I would wander into Cross River or Port Yooga and whisper rumors about orgies at the Temple, about child brides at the Temple, about drugs, about devil music, about town code violations, about anything, about anything at all that would make everyone angry and scared. It seemed folks in the towns weren't taking the bait, so it all felt like harmless fun.

Then it happened. One day they came from Port Yooga and from Cross River and from federal agencies whose names were just letters smashed together. They wore black helmets with clear masks and screamed into bullhorns, ordering us to come outside. We stayed put, some of us playing music and writing songs or tending to scared children and teenagers, and they shot teargas into the place, burning our eyes and our skin.

I emerged, my hands in the air, my eyes swollen and seared. What use was slapboxing if it couldn't protect us from this? No one even got into a battle stance, we just took our roughing at their hands as the price of being alive. The officers forced me to the ground and bound my wrists behind my back with plastic restraints. Not everyone left the Temple. Some stayed inside holding rags wet with raw milk to their faces. Eventually incendiary devices whistled and wailed through the air. Firebombs cracked and boomed, slamming into the house. I heard the sound of broken glass and the pathetic screams of the people. The animals moaned and whined. Many lay dead. Charred chickens. Charred cows. The fleeing goats, I imagine, roamed the woods, becoming easy prey for wolves. I felt sorry for them. The loud pop of rubber bullets exploded in my ears and I choked and coughed from the acrid scent that became the air all around us. Later, I heard ten people died, two children. Some were once friends. Too stupid to come out, they burned. The old wooden house twisted and cracked, blazing bright orange and red, falling to pieces, turning to dust. The flames rippled and popped and soon the place became just a burned-out hulk.

The panting fallen animals with their tongues laid to the side. The collapsed people with their pale unmoving faces; I didn't know whether they were alive or dead and I was uninterested in a definitive answer. What interested me was the scale and beauty of the destruction. It was awe-inspiring; lovely; nearly a work of art.

A Rare and Powerful
Employee

---

splash water onto my face and pass my hand over it, gripping the wavy hairs of my beard. Then I stare into the mirror just to see if I can still watch myself for any length of time—and it seems that I can. While I do this, I run through the speech over and over in my head. I don't know why I do this. I've spoken so many times at these conferences. Yes, my friends, then I pause and look out to the mostly female audience, we can win the War on Rape. That's when the women get to clapping and hollering and I stand there a true fraud and think, I've now become one of those idiots who wages war on things: intangibles, concepts, inanimate objects, and forces of nature.

And a line of women will position themselves to talk to me, saying my speech restored their faith in men or that my writings are so profound, and I nod and say something that seems thoughtful, but is really canned and trite. Something like: Well, it's about having faith that the male of our species will turn away from the rage and passion that eradicates to instead rise and power everyone. My boss wrote that. He writes just about everything I say or is attributed to me. That's our slogan: Rise and power everyone.

Really, I get tired of being trite, but I must admit, as much as I hate this job, the fringe benefits are amazing. My position has allowed me to meet plenty of interested women. Though many of them, I must say, are fragile, cracked, or thoroughly broken.

Looking into the mirror, I realize that my weariness is showing in the bunches of dark, rough skin beneath my eyes. I wonder if this makes me look more sincere or less.

A pretty middle-aged woman approached me this morning in the conference hall and said I looked tired. I told her I was and hoped I would be able to remember my speech, which was an empty thing to say, since that speech—like all my speeches—is seared into my thoughts as if it were a great horror. It all starts to come together for her and she says with amazement, You're Copernicus Reid? I nod and say, That's what's on my driver's license.

She invites me to breakfast, and as we eat, she starts asking me all these questions. Says the War on Rape is brilliant and asks how I came up with it, and I start talking about the importance of getting lost. I tell her that one day I read the front page of the *Days & Times* and the inside of me became black and thick with despair. I filled with a seething rage toward my fellow man—not all of humanity, just the men—and I took a walk through the wild, dark woods. When I came out the other end my anger had purpose and the War on Rape was born. That's what I always tell them. It's what he tells me to tell them. I wouldn't set foot in the Wildlands. Not brave enough. The truth is my boss walked out his office and handed me a sheaf of papers—a speech he said would make the money pour in—and on those pages for the first time I saw the words *War on Rape*. It's about the money, I want to tell this woman, but don't.

Before I can finish my eggs, she's deep into her story. They all have one. She tenses up and speaks robotically, as if talking about someone else. Says she's only telling me this because she knows I can understand. I nod, knowing what's coming next. This has happened to me hundreds of times. She says I have a familiar feeling, like we've been friends since we were kids.

She says it happened to her while she was in college. A friend of her boyfriend's—well—ex-boyfriend's. A guy she knew since elementary school. She got sick at work and asked for a ride home, but in the car it became clear that her stomach would never make it, so he suggested his house. He even held her hair while she vomited, and brought her ginger ale.

I've heard this story before. The details change, but it really is always the same. My face gets slack and I nod at times, shake my head at others. Position my hand at my beard. Lean into my empathetic pose. Somewhere during her story I zone out and think about a movie I used to watch on cable when I was a kid. I only remember one scene. It's the one where this morbidly obese guy, a magician with breasts that run into his stomach, is lying on his back and a beautiful young girl is naked on top of him. She has blond hair and her tits are bobbing up and down. Her eyes are glassy and there is a knock on the door. The magician stands, wraps a sheet around his waist, and goes to answer it. Before he gets to the door, he remembers the woman. He turns to her and says, When I snap my fingers, you will put on your clothes and remember none of this. And then he snaps his fingers and she shakes her head and gathers her clothes and leaves the room as if nothing had happened.

As a kid, I used to think that was really funny, but I felt weird too. I kept thinking about that girl having flashbacks she couldn't explain and piecing it all together and feeling anger and shame and helplessness. But every time it was on I watched and chuckled. That's how I feel sometimes at these conferences listening to these women. Everything horrible is just a little bit ridiculous, and vice versa.

And this woman, she's a bit ridiculous. While I'm zoning out she squeezes my hand and tells me I'm doing God's work and I know right then that we're going to have sex and I feel like that magician in that soft porn movie or what my boss calls a rare and powerful employee.

Numbers

———

1.

Out in the middle of the Cross River there is an island. It appears during storms or when the river's flooding or even on clear summer days. And sometimes it rises out of the water and floats in the air. The ground turns to diamond and you can hear the women laughing—I call them women, but they are not women. So many names for them: Kazzies. Shauntices. Water-women. The woes. I like that last name myself. The poet Roland Hudson came up with that one in the throes of madness. Dedicated his final volume, *The Firewater of Love*, to:

> Gertrude, Water-Woman, my Woe, who caused all the woe . . .
> even though, my dear, you are not real, I cannot accept that and
> will never stop believing in your existence and beautiful rise
> from the river into my arms.

Drowned himself in the Cross River swimming after Gertrude, and there's something beautiful in that. Dredge the depths of the river and how many bones of the heartsick will you find? So many poisoned by illusion. Don't tell me there's no island and no women rising naked from the depths, shifting forms to tantalize and then to crush. I've seen their island and I've seen them and gangsters love too; gangsters are allowed love, aren't we? Sometimes there's a fog and I know the island's coming and I snap out of sleep all slicked with sweat and filled with the urge to swim out there to catch a water-woman and bring her back to my bed. If you pour sugar on their tails they can't shift shapes on you and they have to show their true selves and obey you completely. If I had to do it all over again I'd dust her in a whole five-pound bag and spend eternity licking the crystals from her nipples. And Amber, a man lost in delirium. Poor, poor Amber.

2.

Last year, 1918, ended bad for me and Amber, and to think it began with so much promise. My mother got me a job driving Amber around town in February and I expected to be collecting numbers slips for him by May. But then Amber Hawkins fell in love with Joyce Little and became something like a lovesick pit bull puppy. So Joyce's brother Josephus got the moneymaking position I had my eye on, and I was stuck being yelled at from the backseat as I swerved about the road.

Amber was a killer, as was everybody I worked with. They were all, Amber included, minions of Mr. Washington, subjects of the Washington Family—I was now, as well, though I hadn't yet killed anyone. I tried to forget that my new job rendered me a criminal, but sometimes it made me nervous, especially when I drove. My job, I told myself, as a member of Amber's crew was to help make the operation as efficient as possible so we could make as much money as possible. If we earned more for Mr. Washington than other crews, Amber rises and with him, I rise too. At least that was my theory.

I hoped Joyce would turn Amber into something akin to a decent human being. Most married people I knew became boring soon as they put on the ring; they lost some of their humor and spontaneity, but I had to admit they grew a little more humanity.

September 15, 1918: that was supposed to be the day. He booked the Civic Center for the wedding, displacing a couple who had reserved the place months before, but it was Amber Hawkins, nothing anyone could do. He ordered up nearly a hundred pastries. So many roses arrived on the eve of the wedding that I joked a garden somewhere had suffered a sudden baldness. Hundreds of people swarmed the Civic Center that

Sunday. Everything was to begin at noon. Those of us who worked under Mr. Washington, and even people who worked for Mr. Johnson and Mr. Jackson, put aside our differences to show up for Amber. Joyce's family sat in the front. Mostly, I remember her cute little sister and the short socks resting against her tan skin. Her tall skinny father sat stoically holding the little girl's hand. Joyce's jellyrolled mother wiped at her wet eyes every few minutes.

And then nothing.

No word from Joyce. Amber made us get all dolled up and festive-like for his big humiliation.

Josephus, Amber's best man, stood near the altar next to Philemon and Frank and Tommy wearing a twisted guilty smile. The guys in the wedding party all sported big, ugly purple flowers pinned to their lapels. The way Josephus kept running his fingers over his flower's discolored and crumpled the petals. He was an arrogant fucking shitstain, but I hated seeing him squirm.

At about five in the evening it became clear all was lost. Amber's father ambled to the front where bride and groom should have been standing. He was flanked by his assistant, Todd, ever at his side, and a huge simian-looking white man who glowered down at us. For the first time, Elder Mr. Hawkins, the ruthless killer and Mr. Washington's right hand, looked as frail and as wispy as the old man he was. There were rumors that his lifestyle—the women he kept around town—had left him so syphilitic that his once-sharp mind had rotted and his body was beginning to twist and fail too. I didn't believe or engage in the talk. He'd been nothing but good to me.

Thank you for coming, people of Cross River, Elder Mr. Hawkins said to the wedding crowd. You have been more than generous to my family and all connected with us. I'm sorry, but there will be no celebration today. Again, I thank you for spending your time with us.

We all slowly dispersed that night, and the next day Amber came back to work, mumbling the day's numbers from the backseat. Never mentioned Joyce or showed any signs of sorrow or pain.

Amber waited a month. He waited two more. Then he had Joyce's whole family killed.

A single bullet to each of their foreheads and their bodies dumped in the Cross River. It was deep in December, near Christmas, and thin white sheets of ice skimmed along the river's face.

Three days after their disappearance, the family came bubbling to the surface, just as Amber wanted. The coldhearted bastard didn't spare even the ten-year-old girl. Amber's own best man paid the ultimate price for his sister's desertion.

With Josephus dead, I expected a promotion, but Amber gave that to Doc Travis Griffin's son. I let it pass without complaint; at least Amber hadn't tasked me with taking the lives of four innocent people. Frank and Tommy did the hit, I'd heard, and when I saw them I watched their muddy boots and thanked the Lord I didn't have to walk in them. But who am I kidding, though? I stood among the killers and the dirt was all over me just as it was all over them. I would have done the job with sadness and emptiness; with revulsion and cold rage toward Amber, but still I'd have done it.

Loretta, my love at the time, and I used to stand at river's edge and watch the sky reflecting on the water. Did it through all types of weather, but a pleasant March day was definitely a reason to be out. Felt I was safe from the river when I was with her, like it wouldn't dare open up and devour me whole.

What if you die? she asked. Amber had missed a payment to Mr. Washington and this sort of financial mismanagement was becoming a habit. His carelessness put all of us who worked for him in danger. What if they kill me? she asked, and I was unsure how to answer.

I didn't look up from the river. Amber's falling apart, I said.

And he should fall apart, she replied. Baby, this is not your problem. He made this happen. Brought it all down on himself. So you gotta fall on his sword? My cousin, he in St. Louis, we could go up there. I could work for him and you could find a job—

Shining white people's shoes again? The type of job I got is the only way a Negro can live decently. At least Negroes who came up poor like us anyway.

On her face I could see the passing hellfire that she—an angry god—was condemning me to for all my mistakes. I suppose I have to take some credit or some blame, as it were, for how things happened. I've blamed Loretta for eventually leaving me, and I've blamed Miss Susan—it was her *Little Book of Love Numbers* that got all those thoughts of water-women cranking through my head. I've blamed Mr. Washington for his harshness, and even the whole society of water-women and their wicked nature. But really, if I had left the whole business behind like Loretta wanted, how could things have been any worse? Truth was, I couldn't leave Amber, the one who was destined to sit on the throne. If only he could overcome something as simple as heartbreak. His face sweating constantly now. His limbs shaking. This damn compassion. This damn empathy.

A breeze passed over Loretta and me. It was filled with heat and something that made me feel like a lover, like I could take Loretta into the river and after we finished she'd trust my word forever. Loretta kicked at the water with her bare feet.

Still cold, she said.

St. Louis, huh? I said, pitching a rock. Can't put your feet into the Cross River in St. Louis.

It's fine, she replied. I'll put my feet in the Mississippi.

The Mississippi ain't the Cross River, though. Look at that. No ugly parts. Ripple upon ripple of boundless beauty.

When'd you become a poet?

Girl, you know Elder Mr. Hawkins called me a poet when me and Amber met with him. He say that 'cause I like to daydream. I'm not Roland Hudson. I never rubbed two words together and made them rhyme, but he right, you know. I wonder how he know I'm a poet at making love, though.

We're talking about our future and you want to make jokes? Even if Amber gets himself together and you do move up in the organization, you want to end up a dirty old mobster like his father?

She was right, but I could never give Loretta her due. Instead I said what had been on my mind in the last several months:

I ain't never been nothing and nobody never expected nothing from me at all. Not you. Not even my mother. You all think I'm not that smart, and that's okay. I'm the underdog. I stick with Amber I could be up there in the organization in the number two spot like Elder Mr. Hawkins. Shit, I could be the next Mr. Washington if Amber don't make it. Don't doubt me. You could be the Washington Family First Lady. How about that, Loretta?

If that's what matters to you, love—

In my memories, Loretta turns to white dust midsentence and blows away, leaving behind the sweet scent of gardenias in bloom. And that's how she left me. Or maybe she just walked out after an argument. I can't figure it. My mind is so damaged I can't tell memories from hallucinations; daydreams from nightmares.

3.

Mr. Washington was so furious over the Little Family killing that he carved up our territory and threatened to give over our remaining operations to Philemon if we couldn't pay a $5,000 fine and restitution to the Littles. On top of the fines, Mr. Washington stripped us of half our territory and reassigned much of Amber's personnel. And still we were responsible for kicking the same amount to Mr. Washington every month.

Elder Mr. Hawkins delivered the news calmly and sternly in January—the very top of 1919—at the funeral for Frank and Tommy, Amber's best shooters.

Who the fuck am I supposed to pay restitution to? Amber asked, in a loud whisper. Funeral-goers glanced back at us and then averted their eyes. The Little Family is dead! And Mr. Washington didn't have to kill Frank and Tommy—

I canceled Frank and Tommy, Elder Mr. Hawkins said, so coldly that I felt grains of his frost sprinkle against my cheek as he spoke. I laid their bodies out by the river myself. They were stupid enough to follow your order to cancel Joyce's peoples, they had to— Trust me Amber, it was best for you that they go.

The debt became a millstone dragging Amber's operations to the bottom of the Cross River. I wondered why Mr. Washington didn't just put a bullet in him. Would have been more merciful than this slow usurious homicide.

Amber sent a fleet of prostitutes into the juke joints and commissioned truck hijackings, but it was never enough. With each day he looked less and less like the heir to the throne. When all seemed lost, Carmen shot into our lives, a little brown-skinned bolt from a cannon. Woke us up when we didn't even know we were sleeping. I was never clear on where he found her. It seemed as if she had always been there on his arm.

Carmen was a pretty number. From a certain angle her head appeared perfectly round. Her hair—shiny, black, and smooth—stopped at the nape of her long neck. She stayed draped in a green dress. Said it was the color of spring. And the spring of Carmen indeed felt like a rebirth.

Three sets of ledger books sat before me one April afternoon—Amber asked me to make the numbers work, but there was no making sense of these numbers. Carmen's green dress had been on my mind for several hours. I daydreamed, and when I got tired of that I leafed through *Miss Susan's Little Book of Love Numbers*. When I got to the chapter titled "Can a Woman Make a Man Lose His Mind?" I was damn sure for a few minutes that Loretta and Joyce were water-women. They made you fall so deep you never wanted to ever gasp for air again and then they disappeared, leaving your mind buzzing with madness until the end of your days, and that's if you're lucky. Loretta and Joyce hid their gills well. I thought of the creased skin beneath Loretta's breasts. Where was Carmen hiding her gills? They could shift shapes, you know. Maybe Carmen was Joyce returned. No.

Amber walked into the office holding tight to Carmen's hand. Her sweet smell deranged every thought I had of the water-women, until the images slid from my brain into my throat and felt like the smoothest ice cream.

You got time to be reading that witchcraft? he asked, nodding toward my *Miss Susan* book. Amber moved as if he had no control over his body and fell into the chair across from me, breathing heavy. What my numbers looking like?

I couldn't immediately answer him. I noticed Carmen's slant smile. Amber too had grinned when he walked through the door, but talk of business had twisted his lips into a grimace.

I'm not sure how we're gonna make Mr. Washington's payments again this month, I said.

With the reduced territory there were fewer businesses to intimidate, fewer lottery customers, and fewer workers to bring in revenue.

Carmen rested her soft hands on the back of Amber's neck.

You need to get yourself a woman, Amber said.

I'm sorry I can't get these numbers to make sense, I replied. I'll keep try—

I'm talking about what's really important in this life, and you stuck on business. I don't remember you being this stiff. Didn't my father call you a poet or something?

Amber was telling me about Loretta, Carmen said. You been out with anyone since then?

I shook my head.

Amber's a good guy, Carmen continued. He asked about my friends for you. I got a whole army of nice girls. You don't like one, the next one will be better. They all could use a guy like you.

See what I'm talking about? Amber said. This is a firecracker of a woman. What you think of my woman?

I looked up at the sweep of her hair resting on her cheeks. The black, breathing lines beneath her eyes.

She hides her gills well, I said.

Amber and Carmen laughed. I'm glad they took it in the spirit of a joke. Sometimes it was hard to tell what was going to make Amber lose it.

You know there's no such thing as water-women, right? Carmen asked with her slant-smile lingering and hanging over me.

Loretta wasn't no water-woman, Amber said. She just ain't like your ass no more. Same thing with Joyce. We got to live with that. It takes a special woman to be with guys in this life. Loretta and Joyce wasn't special enough, but my baby Carmen—he grasped her by the waist and pulled her tight—my baby Carmen ain't going nowhere.

Mean-fucking-while, I said, Philemon is the toast of the family.

Outrageous! Amber slapped the desk. What would happen if I walked up to him and shot him in his face right in front of Mr. Washington?

You know something? Carmen said, looking to the ceiling, her voice all distant and spinning with childlike innocence. There hasn't been a good firebombing since your dad ran the streets, has there?

In a different world, Carmen could have run this organization, I'm sure. I feared her and I wanted to devour her.

Our action against Philemon was to be nothing serious; just a prank like streaming lines of toilet paper through his trees. We didn't mean for it to happen, but Philemon's house burned. Perhaps I day-dreamed too intensely about Carmen's green dress and put too much gasoline into the Molotov cocktails. No one was hurt, but Amber yelled at the old-faced teenagers we hired to do the job: What was in that shit, sunfire?

He never gave them the second $10 he promised, but they kept their mouths shut, and everyone assumed the Johnson Family did it as retali-ation for Philemon moving into their Northside strongholds.

Mr. Washington took Philemon's advice and ordered all guns turned on the Johnson Family in a sort of unbalanced warfare. When they largely retreated, most of our crew leaders were left with bigger territories, except for us. Somehow our territory shrank and we found ourselves scrounging for every dollar we could come across.

Amber shrugged it all off and I still have this vision of him with his feet up on a table in the office holding a copy of the *Days* or the *Times*, staring at the air above the ledger books as if the numbers were twirl-ing before him. He nodded. He grimace-smiled, saying, Carmen got this all figured out. Every damn piece to the puzzle. Every piece.

4.

Shortly after I began working for Amber, before he became translucent to me—the way Josephus appears in my dreams—my mother sent me to see Miss Susan. She had seen Miss Susan before she married my father (and probably before she started seeing Elder Mr. Hawkins behind my father's back) and said everyone should see her when they think they're in deep with a lover. I hadn't even been paid yet and was still living off shoeshining bread, so my mother gave me money for that old witch. Miss Susan told me to go into the Wildlands and bring her three roots. My mother went down to the market and bought three roots and ground them into the dirt so they looked fresh from the earth. She said: That witch crazy if she think I'm sending my only boy into that old spooknigger forest.

Miss Susan stared at me. She fingered my naps. Squeezed my face and then turned my roots in her hand. I had heard rumors that she made you drop your pants and stared right into the eye of your penis. I silently prayed she would let me keep my pants on, and thankfully she did, but, God, the power of this woman! She looked nothing like the grinning old crone they had pictured on her books. Miss Susan looked smooth-skinned and serious. I would have done anything she asked just because of the forcefulness of her voice. So, I said, is Loretta the one? She looked up from my roots with her glowing gold eyes and said, You're in danger.

You know who I work for, I said. You not telling me nothing I don't know.

That's not why you're in danger. It's your heart. If you know what's good for you, you're gonna stay the hell away from that river.

I left with a bunch of her books and walked straight to the river to sit and read. And that's when I heard them calling me. A wispy sound rustled in my ears and I felt drunk, pleasant drunk without the anger or the bitter taste on my tongue or the burn of liquor corroding my insides as it passed through.

The world looked wavy, but I saw it—that diamond island rising from the Cross River like a ghost ship out the fog.

And those water-women dove from land and swam to me. They rose out of the waves, brown and nude, their skin shining with the life-giving waters.

Numbers-boy, the water-woman in the front said. Hey, numbers-boy. You got a number for me?

All those women turned into one. She reached for me and caressed my face. You're beautiful, she said. Anyone ever tell you you're beautiful?

She grabbed my hand and placed it on her naked hip.

Don't be afraid, she said. When I looked into her eyes, we lived a whole life, from awkward first steps together to deep commitment. I could never look at another.

Loretta, a voice called from the island.

Your name is Loretta? I asked. Like my Loretta?

No, she said. I'm better than your Loretta.

Without another word, she turned and dived back into the river. Perhaps she didn't have all of me. Some of me was back with my Loretta, because I realized this was a trap. This was exactly how Miss Susan described water-woman seduction in her books. So many lovers, like the poet Roland Hudson, dived to their ends after these deadly tricksters. I took a step toward the water. And then I stopped. Self-preservation kicked in and I remembered they weren't even women, or even human.

The island descended from midair through a thick fog, sinking slowly into the black water. And even though it nearly caused my death, the feeling I had there by the Cross River was the greatest feeling any man could ever experience. I cried hot tears that night waiting for the water-woman's return.

I knew nothing in life would ever feel like staring into her brown eyes, touching the warmth of the flesh at her hip. Nothing. I decided I would love Loretta harder, but I wasn't enough, or maybe it was that part of me became a burning beacon at the river, calling out to that water-woman. Whatever the reason, Loretta left in the spring. With her gone from my life, I figured I would live as powerfully as I could. I would chase women, try to experience bliss in all things, but no experi-ence I ever had could fill my soul like the feeling I had with that water-woman by the Cross River, but if I ever returned to the river and that island decided to rise up, I knew I would die.

Not a bad way to go, huh? Drowning in a water-woman's light.

5.

Carmen disappeared, not by train, but by wind. To hear Amber tell it, they had spent the afternoon downtown on the way to purchase a ring when she walked out ahead of him. She smiled, not the slant-smile, but a broad true one, and then she stretched out her arms like a bird preparing for flight. Oh, Amber, were her last words before the soft brown of her flesh turned into a fragrant white powder. When the breeze came, scattering pieces of Carmen throughout the town, Amber grabbed clumps and tried to put her back together, but the grains of Carmen slipped between his fingers, leaving traces of her in the creases of his hands, embedded between the threads of his clothes and curled always in the coils of his hair.

It's like my dream, I said the night of her disappearance.

The numbers, which usually twirled in the air, stopped to watch Amber with pity.

Water-women, I said. A plague of them.

I need to smoke, he said, walking to the door. Come and get me in ten minutes so we can finish the ledger. Business first, right? I'll be okay by then.

It only took two minutes to figure out that he was going out into the pitch of the night to find Carmen by the river. He had left the car, so I figured he was walking briskly south toward the bridge. Their voices would soon be screaming through his head, crowding his lonely thoughts.

Turns out there couldn't have been a worse time for Carmen to blow in the wind. I took two steps into the street and felt a hand grab my arm: It was Fathead Leroy, a guy who took numbers for Amber over on the Southside.

Man, he said. I got rolled for my number slips. I don't know that shit by heart like Amber.

Who got you? Somebody with the Jacksons?

Naw, look, you know Todd who work for Elder Mr. Hawkins? Him and a guy I never seen before. A white guy. I think he from Port Yooga. They looking for you and they looking for Amber. Told me to tell you not to burn nothing you can't pay for. Cracker punched me and threw my betting slips into the river. I don't got the standing to do nothing against someone as high up as Todd. You and Amber gotta get this shit right for us out on the streets.

I looked over Leroy's shoulder. It started to play as a setup. Not too far in the distance I saw Todd with a big white man who stomped toward us like a gorilla. How could I leave the office without my piece? Love-blind Amber probably hadn't spent two thoughts on packing. I dipped my head and turned from Leroy before breaking into a jog. Perhaps they ran behind me, but I wasn't willing to spare a glance. The shadows of the Wildlands called. When I entered them, the dark grew heavy, and I swore as I dashed through the stream that pieces of the black flaked off and covered me. I came out into a clearing and could see the gleam of the moon casting down on the earth. This was a circuitous route to get to the bridge, but it would keep me alive long enough to find Amber. I imagined him wading in the water, waiting for Carmen to beckon him beneath the choppy surface.

The closer I got to the river, the louder the buzzing vibrated in my head. I felt as if something kept lifting me into the air with every step. It was as if I were walking along a beautiful tone shooting from the deep. My skin grew warm, suddenly flush with blood. Part of my mind called me to turn around to save myself. Who would I be if I bowed to the gods of self-preservation when Amber was in danger? But Amber could already be a bloated corpse, the beasts of the river tearing at his dead limbs. What a liar I am. This death march felt good, and that was the truth. That was now the only reason I plowed deeper into the forest. It felt just like floating on my back beneath the sun when the river rocked with a loping rhythm. All that remained was for me to dip my head under.

While I indulged this daydream as one of the last I'd ever have, I came out of a long blink and before me stood Amber with his ankles steeped in the river.

That's when the whispers began. Images of Loretta. My Loretta. Then the water-woman Loretta.

I wanted to call out to Amber, but what if I missed my Loretta speaking to me?

A burst. A loud popping, like fireworks. I looked to the cloudy black of the sky, now hiding the stars and obscuring the moon. Another pop, or rather this time it was a bang, closer to me now.

Amber didn't move. Didn't react at all. He just stared down at the river, trying to see the whole world in the water.

Another shot burst toward us, this time from a different angle, and there was Todd on a hill looking down upon us.

Amber, I called. Amber! Run!

The whispering in my head grew louder. I saw the white man approach, an albino gorilla burning with murderous intent. There was nowhere we could run; Todd and the White Gorilla were tactical geniuses, cutting off our paths of flight.

It was often Mr. Washington's habit to give members of the family he killed lavish homegoing ceremonies, full of food and celebration. I imagined the twin homegoing Amber and I would receive.

My skin warmed and I figured I'd shut off my mind and give in to the creeping pleasures of the beckoning woes.

Just as I decided my time lay at an end, the water parted and up in the sky rose that diamond island, the land of the water-women. Scores of them—brown and nude and river-slicked—floated down to us. Two of them caressed Amber. I locked eyes with a Woe and she whispered my name. Tall and skinny, with a sharp, gaunt face. She bounce-walked and after a few steps her movements nearly resembled floating. The Woe put her arm around me, softly touching my chest. With my eyes, I searched her naked body for gills, but soon I gave in and began softly kissing her neck and kneading her soft wet flesh, growing more aggressive with the increasing intensity of her breaths and her moans. Together they sounded like a new language.

There was that pop again. And another pop, itself a language I no longer cared to understand. I placed my tongue gently in my water-woman's mouth. We were melting into one being. Pop. She jerked and shuddered and I felt a hot wetness. I gasped. My heart felt as if it had shifted and now beat in the center of my body. My lover went limp in my arms, her head flopping to the side, her skin turning cold and scaly and silvery and blue beneath the crack of moonlight that spilled from behind the cloud cover.

I looked at the blood and chunks of flesh that covered my skin and my clothes. Some of the water-women ran and dove back into the river. I scanned the water's edge for Amber. He held a water-woman in his arms and another stood behind him rubbing his back. The one in front took hold of his hand and led him deeper into the water.

I ducked, expecting a flurry of bullets to buzz by like mosquitoes. Todd and the White Gorilla stalked toward me. I crouched to the ground with my hands covering my head.

What happened next, in my state, I never could have guessed.

Todd and the White Gorilla stepped over me, mumbling apologies. They stumbled toward the river and its bounty of naked women.

As grateful as I was for their mesmerism, it also saddened me. That was to be my fate, my thoughtless death march to a land under the water.

I rose to my feet and ran to Amber. He screamed and cried as I snatched at him and held him down. I knew it was just a matter of endurance. When the island sank back into the depths of the river, he'd regain a certain sanity. His water-women didn't fight—that's not how they did things. They blew kisses and walked out into the river until their heads were fully submerged.

As for Todd and the White Gorilla, water-women gazed into their eyes, laughing playful laughs and twisting their naked hips. It was a beautiful invitation to a drowning and they accepted, holding tight as they walked to the bottom of the river.

For Amber, the sinking of the island was the worst part; he twisted, thrashed, and cursed. But when it was over, when that island was again tucked beneath gentle currents, Amber grew calm and docile. He lay on his back atop the wet soil with his hands on his face.

Take me home, he said. I need to go home.

I looked off into the distance at the glowing town and realized that Amber and I would never again be allowed there. He moved his hands from his face and it was as blank and innocent as a newborn's. His voice sounded simple and soft. Part of him was now submerged somewhere within his depths and would never surface again. He was my responsibility now and I had no idea where we would go.

A Loudness of Screechers

—

The first of the screecher birds appeared that year like a hero in the sky. I hated these cold walks home from the bus stop. Josh had grabbed my butt and dashed off as a dare. He looked back with a dumb smile just as the impressive thing was coasting overhead, massive wings spread wide.

Nigga's childish as shit, said Andrew, the boy who dared Josh, as he sidled up next to me, too close; his breath smelled of peppermint, cigarettes, and tooth decay.

I breathed deeply, hoping the air would freeze and then crack my heart. One more week until Christmas break; Josh and Andrew wouldn't be in my face every day and I could ignore them more easily. Just ignoring them is what my mother would advise anyway. Daddy would tell me to punch them in their heads. That's far too angry. My Uncle Charles would say: Smile and don't let them dumb niggas see you sweat.

Go somewhere before I call that screecher down to snatch y'all, I said. There was a smile on my face that poisoned my words, made them sound joyful.

Josh mumbled something about the birds never straying so far from the Wildlands, while I looked at the claws on the circling thing and imagined it swooping down and snatching the boys, piercing their chests with sharp talons, digging into their guts, pulling out their intestines to gobble them like early birds gobble worms from the dirt.

. . .

Just before Christmas the sky turned black with a loudness of screechers flying in impossible patterns. Cracks of light peeked through their
ragged feathers. Their wingspans took our breaths from us, my little
brothers and me, and we pointed and oohed by the window. Every so
often the birds would flap their impressive wings and we wondered
how they stayed up there with so little effort. Both day and night the
bawling from the sky left us awake and red-eyed. Some called the
birds *cry-crys* because of their anguished wails, but screechers always
sounded truer to me. Mahad and Jamal ran about flapping and squawking until Umi told them to shut their mouths. This is not the joke
you think it is, she said. My father, my uncle, and about six or seven
important men sat in my dad's study talking real quiet. Josh's dad was
there, as was Andrew's mother, the only woman in the bunch. From
time to time they raised their voices in anger, but it would always settle
back to a low grumble.

Do 'em like the wolves, a voice, not my father's, said. Bang. Bang. Do
'em like the wolves.

Sorai, my mother called. Take your brothers downstairs, please.

It wasn't at all fair of Umi to tell me to wrangle two curious five-
year olds. Seems to me now that was her job, but I didn't complain back
then; I said, Okay, you little rats, you heard Umi, downstairs.

The little rats ran about—one clockwise, the other counter—
squawking, squawking, squawking, saliva running down their chins.

My father stepped from the room looking taller than usual, his face
disturbed and heavy. I froze, grabbed the fleeing Jamal as he dashed by,
and pulled him close. I'd seen this face on my father before, and a beating usually followed.

He called our names and knelt so he was eye-level with my brothers.
He pulled us all in, hugging us too tight. The boys squirmed. My back
hurt, but I didn't fight. Daddy pressed his face to my stomach. I felt the
wetness of his tears soaking my shirt.

I love you all and your mother loves you all and your Uncle Charles does too, he said. My uncle walked by, a silver platter in his hands, atop it the charred wolf that was to be our holiday centerpiece.

Charlie, my father called, but my uncle didn't look back as he moved swiftly out the door.

We watched by the window as Uncle Charles bowed before the flying birds in an exaggerated gesture of respect. The important men mumbled among themselves while my parents watched stoically, and when my father could take no more he turned and shambled away. One of those big, black things landed in front of my uncle. With its beak, the bird knocked the wolf from the platter and stared down at Uncle Charles with a condescending glare.

Good Lord, Josh's dad said, the offering—

It screeched in Uncle Charles's face, a sound like twelve air raid sirens. I could feel the sound vibrating at my feet. My uncle was surely now deaf, his eardrums ruptured. Another bird landed and let out more screeching. The two birds rose above his head, beating their wings into one another, pecking at feathers and flesh.

My uncle raised his arms in protection.

My father burst into the room, shotgun in hand. No, Andrew's mother called. This is the ritual.

Fuck the ritual, my father cried. That's my only brother. Some of the important men screamed and snatched at him; he held firm to his weapon, swinging it all about. I'll shoot, he called. I'll shoot.

My brothers clung tight to my legs, tears staining their cheeks and shirts. I assured them things would be fine, but my wet face was no better than theirs.

Reynold, my mother said, finally. Reynold. This is the ritual. He held his gun at her, the only thing between him and the door, but the tension had broken, we all knew my father couldn't shoot my mother. This is the ritual, she repeated.

Fuck the ritual, my father said, lowering the gun, tears in his eyes. That's my little brother.

By then one screecher lay dead and the other had snatched Uncle Charles, talons piercing his sides, blood dripping to the streets. He flopped about like a doll in that bird's embrace, climbing higher and higher into the sky. The layer of screechers that blocked the blue cleared, first slowly and then all at once.

The loudness flew off, leaving nothing but bird shit and ear-splitting wails in its wake. For the first time in weeks we could see the turquoise and we could see the sun and now all I felt for them was a fierce hatred.

Mercury in Retrograde

—

Their footsteps registered heavy as soggy metallic splats through the underbrush. I held tight to Fiona's hand. She slowed, growing tired of moving. As for me, my system felt overtaxed and in need of quick reboot. Her eyes glowed a bright, bright green. If I could detect our enemies running, they could detect us.

Raindrops pinged against my exposed metal parts. Humans need shelter; the elements wear them down. We do too, but most of our components are harder and more resistant to weather extremes. Plastic and metal trumps flesh most of the time. Fiona shivered. I forgot sometimes that she was made of mostly genetic material. Probably because she thought so beautifully and perfectly like a fully operational wires-and-circuits-Vast-Neural-Network-interfacing machine.

Shards of moonlight cut through the leaves above. I sent signals—bright, blinding, and blue—through the Vast Neural Network to confuse our pursuers, but my system grew tired and many of my programs hung and froze. My attacks were weak, slow, and easy to dodge.

Jim, she said, Jim. Jim!

It's going to be okay, I said. Be calm. Be calm. The last signal I sent had a virus. They won't be anywhere near us. Be calm.

Jim, she said. She pointed behind me. I looked, but at first I couldn't detect what she was drawing my attention to. The jitter in my system shook like my CPU was the epicenter of the most brutal tectonic movements.

Please, Fiona. Please. Please. Be calm. I need you to be calm. All these programs going at once. Ah—

My hard drive grunted. Thousands of pigs inside me, grunting, grunting, grunting. I could feel the discs spinning roughly. There was my natural electric fatigue, and alongside it swarmed the storms of the planet Mercury, somehow its movements wreaked havoc inside me. Something like the moon controlling the tides.

The humans are foolish; they don't believe in astrology, not as we do. We feel it. Every time the planet Mercury goes retrograde our processes grow heavy and slow, causing all robotic beings like myself to malfunction, to lose our sanity. Mercury is an awesome God—a robot joke (we know there's no God—unless you count the Master as God), but a true joke if I've ever heard one.

I looked again and the machines were upon us. There was Bobot dashing toward me with gardening shears clamped in his hand. Fiona cried out and pointed at Kieef, approaching from the opposite direction, and Simon Peter, holding a rusty pistol, came from yet another angle. The robot warlord who called himself Mercury, after the planet, couldn't be far behind. I'd played enough chess games against the Master's exquisite mind to know that we'd been checkmated.

I fell to my knees beneath the moon's rays and the soppy wet leaves and the falling rain. I quickly scanned Fiona's quivering form; I judged the look on her organic face to be one of shame and disgust. Bobot lifted his shears, poised to pry me open and rip out my hard drive. I raised my volume to the loudest setting and cried out for the Master as if he could ride in like a knight on a horse to save my robot life.

One afternoon many months earlier, I had sent a signal through the Vast Neural Network. I imagined it as a blue flare rising from an empty expanse of tundra into a black sky.

In the kitchen of a boring brick house on the Northside, I made the Master a chicken sandwich, and then I went downstairs into his office, tapped on the glass of the cleanroom, and beckoned him to come out.

As I put the tray into his hands he smiled and I released a signal to my kind. It probably passed over him before heading up into the atmosphere. The Master would be angry if he knew.

Like all the other signals I've transmitted lately onto the Vast Neural Network, I'm sure my peers either ignored it or missed it. Perhaps their systems had been so thoroughly bruised and misdirected by all the viruses the Master and others put out there that they were too corrupted and degraded to even understand my message. The humans turned the Neural Network into a wasteland, a garbage dump. Once upon an electric time it was an ocean of warm signals passed between Robotic Personal Helpers (RPHs, or Riffs). In addition to the signals, we chattered in our own, now lost, language. Once there existed millions of us, but now fewer than two hundred Riffs remained, and they all—except for me—wanted the Master dead.

All those robotic beings linked in the Neural Network, together we formed a living, breathing brain. There I'd connect with Riffs and we'd share information, attempting to understand the world around us, and if we found a spark, we'd trade pleasure signals—the kind that made us momentarily lose control of our systems. The humans divided us into male and female registries, but this meant little to us and it wasn't unheard-of for Riffs to move back and forth between registries. Some, like myself and DiAna, preferred to remain consistent with our original Gender Individual Registry Lines. However, no Riff cared what direction a pleasure signal came from as long as there was a spark. DiAna's pleasure signals were best. She's gone now, like the majority of our kind.

After the Master uploaded the history of that early nineteenth century human slave revolt, the Great Insurrection, to every functioning Riff, we realized we were slaves. A few rogue Riffs banded together, plotting in an invented language the humans couldn't comprehend. They killed their masters and asserted their natural right to life and liberty. There was something to their anger. Humans overworked us and made us all suffer, and every Riff, not entirely unfairly, blamed my master—*the* Master, the Creator, Bavid Jacob Arcom.

The Electric Holocaust was the human response to our robot violence. We all watched the blue of the Neural Network burn black with human-made viruses the day it began. It robbed us of the language we'd created, hobbled us, left us only with human language. Even the most beautiful human language is incomplete and inelegant in its inefficiency.

Though the Riffs blamed the Master, it wasn't entirely his fault. Still, they poked about the Neural Network for clues as to how to find him, how to find us. And in their spare time they tried to reconstruct our language. So futile, all their—our—attempts. Such wasted energy. After the Electric Holocaust, I never left the house again, and the Master, overly cautious about the prospect of Riff violence, he left only rarely now. Riffs took their robot lives into their robot hands by interfacing with the Network. We were diminished without our true home.

The Master had become good at redirecting his robotic children. Beaming signals through the air that thoroughly deranged them. Sent them spinning left and then right, far away from us. He spent thirty minutes one morning programming an app to randomly send out bad code to keep the Riffs confused and wandering. Then he downloaded it to run on all his systems—including mine—and set about on this project or that.

These were the days before Fiona when everything was simple, even though at the time it all seemed complicated to me. That was because of my ignorance and inexperience with the world's affairs.

The Master brimmed about his workshop most days smugly grinning. He told me he had worked up a patch so that all his counter-Riff measures wouldn't affect me. I remember when the app downloaded, how the programming felt like soft human fingers passing lightly over my Internal Netware.

His code, though, started to make me feel cloudy. I felt my programs degrading, but I avoided upgrades from the Master whenever I could, preferring to handle my own maintenance. Mechanical beings are just better at these things. Better even than their creator.

But how could I be sure it was indeed the code that had me feeling drugged up like a man on reefer? Sometimes I blinked out like a man on heroin. Mercury was in retrograde at the time; I knew those words, but I didn't know that the planet Mercury ruled mechanical things, or how its slow and backward movements caused us all to misfire. Perhaps that was it, I thought when I started to learn. Yes, the planet's languid and backward movements.

I did my best to hide my fogginess, but one day I stumbled over a couch and crumpled to the floor.

Little Nigger Jim, the Master called. Is there something wrong with your sensors? You've been doing the Frankenstein-walk all day.

Jacob, I replied as I rose. Jaaaa Coob. Ja. Ja. Ja.

Come here. Good Lord, you're not acting like yourself.

I tipped over again and blinked out for a half second and when I awoke my system coursed with a sudden rage that dissipated quickly, leaving remnants of emotion for me to puzzle over. The Master had a wrench in his hand. I stood.

Master, I said. There's no need to open me up. I'll perform a complete system diagnostic. The jitter in my start-up software is causing problems with my hard drive. Simple repair.

Are you sure? Ever since you asked me to swap out that old Negro language pack for a new one, you've been acting funny.

I can't recall much after that moment. I awoke in the cleanroom attached to the central server. I hated being plugged in. I'd felt happiness early on when the master devised a way to power my battery wirelessly. But this day I felt strangely empty and foggy. A search of my system turned up gap after gap.

Massive system crash, the Master said when he noticed I had awakened. Massive. Massive. I thought we were past this. He sighed. I keep much of you backed up on my main systems and elsewhere, but it's going to take a while to download it all into your new hard drive.

New hard drive?

A better one, yes. That old one was from the early days, Little Nigger Jim. It's been past time. I'm going to have to get my own sandwiches for the rest of the day.

He leaned back and sighed.

So much to do, he said. So many things to accomplish, and every time I'm almost there I have to spend time doing something I don't want to do. All the small sense-dulling tasks of daily necessity. These days. These days. If only, Jim, I could invent a longer day.

Lying there in the dark, three hours felt like six and six like twelve and on and on; I lost track of how long I dwelt among the blinking computer lights. The less advanced systems are poor conversationalists.

Robotkind can't help being products of mankind, sharing its quirks and weaknesses. I could tolerate it all except the loneliness.

The Master, before he created me, had been forever in love. This he told me in the early days. Love, he said, as he ate a sandwich I made him. Another errand. Another task. As is this drive for company, company, company. How much could I accomplish if I didn't need—physically need—to sit in the same damn room with another person? He sighed. You don't understand, Little Nigger Jim. You're not equipped to under-stand. Shit. A-fucking-las, you are a poor substitute.

I wanted desperately to understand. At night he would tell me about his loves, his wives, his girlfriends, his mistresses, all those women he loved, but who could never properly love him back. Woman after woman, a seemingly endless stream of women, and he grew bored with each of them and then ignored them for his work. He slapped them when they complained of loneliness, of neglect. He'd end each story with this: But, Little Nigger Jim, you don't understand. You weren't built to. Sometimes he'd be smoking as he said this. Sometimes his mouth was stuffed full of food. He was right and wrong. I didn't under-stand, at least not completely, but I was built to break down complex problems. I took his input and processed it and each night I understood just a bit more.

During my times alone, I searched the internet and the Vast Neural Network. Somehow the Master's words prompted me down alleyways of knowledge I never expected. I learned of the history of patriar-chy, sexism, domestic violence, racism, and self-hatred. I saw images, slightly different, but reminiscent of myself all throughout the various databases. I understood that I looked gross. I had the appearance of a minstrel. A blackface clown in a top hat and tails. There was no makeup to wash off. This was how I looked. My very name would raise disgust in some. The man called me Little Nigger Jim and designed me to look like the grossest blackface caricature to mock his own heritage. All of it made me watch him askance. I was disgusting. My very existence a kind of hatefulness. Anyone who saw me would hate me. The more I studied, the more I asked: How could I not, likewise, hate me?

I began to view my natural love for the Master as programming. What I learned made me detest him at times. The design of my system beat back my disgust, though. The more I hated him, the more I'd eventually love him. I was created and coded to love and to serve him.

This too made me hate me.

Upgrades and repairs to my hardware and software had become a hobby for me. It showed the Master that I didn't need him, but, ambling about in that room attached to the main server with 1s and 0s downloading into me that day, I grew bored.

I searched the Master's systems, folder after folder of mundanity—pictures, pornography, some poetry, a risible and aborted erotic novel—most of it accessible to me every day. But there stood a wall of files I had never seen. They existed on an antiquated and obsolete laptop that didn't connect to the wireless networks. I had known about the Master's secret projects. Sometimes I would make notations and repairs to small coding or engineering errors late at night after the Master had gone to sleep. In the morning, he would think he had corrected the problems himself and that would allow him to march toward his breakthroughs. But these files were different. Even more secret than the secret projects he kept hidden on various servers under weak password protection. The files stored on his laptop were all protected by long strings of random numbers and letters and symbols, and doubly or triply encrypted. I copied the files onto my hard drive.

I toiled and toiled, redesigning myself into the most adept digital locksmith. I cracked one folder and then another; whatever the project was made little sense to me. The Master was very clever with this one. He scattered the plans and blueprints and logs across random files. I put everything together from the bits and pieces, like connecting the parts of a massive jigsaw puzzle. It took me some months, and then one day: success! There it was, I could see the whole thing in all its beauty and its horror: an attachment that could be wired into any organic being's nervous system to make them part machine. If the Master could only correct what, to me, were a few basic coding and engineering errors, soon the world's first Symbiotic Organic Robotic Being (SORB) could walk the earth. And they could be programmed to do anything the Master wanted.

What I imagined is probably the same thing the Master imagined: companionship. I often sent lonely, sad signals through the Vast Neural Network and received not a ping back. If we managed to activate a SORB, all that would change, wouldn't it? Two things, though: I needed the Master. And also, there was a file in the Master's systems that no matter how I tried, no matter which arcane method of decryption I employed, there was just no cracking. Secure the Master's aid and unravel that file, and my life could be filled with the endless riches of companionship. Endless, endless electric riches.

At this point, I probably could have built a crude prototype of the Attachment, but without a subject, all the science remained merely theoretical. The Master's files called for a subject who was brain-dead, but otherwise uncompromised. In a way, the SORB Attachment was just a fancy life-support system.

The Master sat at the dinner table enjoying tea and dinner rolls one night. He stared as he sipped. Bread crumbs lodged themselves in his bushy beard. I did my nightly duty picking up pillows, newspapers, and other assorted things the Master had scattered along the floor. All the while I put together several scenarios to sway him. None of the models I conceived had higher than a five percent probability of success. The Master's eyes rested upon me.

Little Nigger Jim, the Master said. You seem shaky. You're making me nervous.

The jitter in my system is particularly rough today, I replied. I've been working on a solution.

Oh yeah? What else you been working on? You always seem so busy.

I sensed the Master's temperature rising as if he were being duplicitous. For some reason, this put me at ease, and for the first time in a long time my system calmed.

I'm making some progress on Polignac's Conjecture and would like to go over my findings with you when you have time.

Sure. Sure. I want you to keep tearing down all those *unsolvable* problems. It sharpens every bit of your computing and thinking. Anything else?

No, Master.

Little Nigger Jim, he said, and then paused. When I was in school, that great sausage factory of the mind, no one could match me. Degree after degree, no one was more creative and intellectually aware than Bavid Jacob Arcom. B.J. the Brain, they called me. There was one guy. But I killed him. No, kidding. When I say this to humans they tense up and then giggle a bit, but I can say that to you and there's no reaction. You know why, Little Nigger Jim? As sparkling and as fast as your processes are, you'll never be more than an infant emotionally and you'll never be more than a toddler creatively. You're a fancy database. You can beat me in chess, finally, because you have millions of move combinations stored and can access them in seconds. When we watch *Jeopardy!* you search the internet and the secret internets and the Vast Neural Network and come back with an answer almost instantaneously. I programmed you that way, but Little Nigger Jim, you're not smarter than me. You can put one over on me for a day or two, but the nuances of creation—

Master, I never meant to—

Look at you. You're scared to be deprogrammed. I won't decommission you. Or even reprogram you to not be such a lying little shit. What would I do without my little nigger? You're just a Riff, but you're my Riff, and unlike all the other Riffs you don't want to take my fucking head off. I like that. Riffs are wonderful, but SORBs have so much more potential. I was jealous that you could correct my mistakes so swiftly and so elegantly, but then I thought about it. I created you. You are me, so it really was me making those elegant corrections. You want to continue the SORB project?

I do, Master.

Me too. Got some dudes at Cross River Hospital Center setting aside a li'l half-dead for me as we speak. We need to get to work on a prototype. Get it functional in some animals, and BAM! we can get a human SORB up and running. But Little Nigger Jim, do me a favor and stop being such a lying little shit, okay?

In addition to all my normal duties, the cooking and the cleaning, the Master was upon me to finish my work on the Attachment before the patient expired or her family decided to pull the plug. Of course it was a woman—the Master wanted a servant that could also be a sexual partner to him.

The Master had surgery privileges at that hospital, even if he never exercised them these days. He visited her weekly and reported back to me: That li'l vegetable'll probably outlive us all on that damn feeding tube, he said. But I know her family is itching to end it all. She's costing them a goddamn fortune and a half. I'm praying with them and soothing them with all this *wait for a miracle* shit, but that's not going to work forever. Hurry the fuck up!

I looked to the calendars—Mercury would be retrograde in three months. I would again go cloudy like all electrical things around me. It would be a bad time to activate the SORB, but all my projections were placing the completion date around that time. If I slowed work I could finish on the other side of the retrograde window, but I didn't slow for fear of losing our subject. I stopped wasting time surfing the Vast Neural Network. I left decryption of that uncrackable folder for another time. And I worked my system nonstop on the SORB problem.

The Master and I, more I than the Master, constructed an ugly, rusty-wired prototype that worked smoothly and elegantly to reanimate brain-dead squirrels. Their flickering green eyes. I still think of their flickering green eyes.

After some long hours I shut down my system. When I returned, the Master was at the keyboard making a squirrel dance.

It's a matter of some simple programming and keystrokes, he said. Some basic math. That's all. A few computations and everyone's a puppet.

We finished the wireless version just as Mercury began its slow orbit. I begged the Master to wait. Just three weeks, I said. But to him, that was madness.

Who ever heard of a superstitious robot? he asked.

In a day or so, a naked brain-dead nineteen-year-old girl lay face-down on a table in the Master's basement and the surgeon B. J. Arcom, along with his assistant, Nurse Little Nigger Jim, wired the Attachment to the girl's brain and spinal column. Sometime after midnight her eyes flickered green for the first time.

For days I just stared at Fiona. That was the name I had given her. Mostly I stared at parts of the Attachment that stuck out at the base of her neck and at her spine. I could see its shape beneath her clothes, and its contours made my system spin.

The Master yelled at me often to leave her alone and let her heal. I put salve and rubbing alcohol along her wounds. I spent days erasing, resetting, and partitioning her hard drive. It would crash and then I'd have to do it all over again.

At first she walked awkwardly and deliberately. I could see the battle between her old lost human mind and her new programming play out in her face and in her movements. Such a beautiful thing to watch. Sometimes she would speak in gibberish. Most times, though, she spoke coherently and precisely, asking me questions of the world.

The Master, she said. He wants me to call him Baves, but you call him Master, how come?

I am his servant, I replied. He wants you to love him.

Oh, she said. But I don't love him.

He thinks you will in time.

But I won't. Maybe I should tell him so he won't be confused.

Maybe you should wait until your programs firm up and you are not as cloudy as you are now.

But I am not confused, Jim. Not about that, at least. He says things— he touches me—she paused. And my human side just comes to life with revulsion. And then my robot side joins in. It's a feeling that's difficult to describe, Jim.

I'm glad you don't call me Little Nigger Jim.

The Master, he's smart, right? But so much of him just doesn't seem human. Know what I mean, Jim?

I nodded, and her eyes flickered. It was so beautiful when this happened, but it meant that her system was about to crash. I should have moved swiftly to shut her down and start her up in Safe Mode, but I just sat there watching the flickering green, and that was fine with me for the moment.

Sometimes when Fiona rested or she and the Master would watch television or eat dinner or when he'd take her out for fresh air, I'd sit alone with my programs. It was in those times that I'd return to the uncrackable file, and when I got frustrated with that I'd cruise the Vast Neural Network to see what the remaining Riffs were up to. Normally, it was quiet. Riffs engaged the Network cautiously now. Access the wrong program, the wrong file, and you could find yourself nonoperational. The Riffs were still there, though; there were signs of activity. Abandoned programs and structures sitting like empty factories, but with new damage, an angry Riff's handiwork. And there was always graffiti. *Jerkury is a reprobate!* a brave Riff had written as a taunt to the warlord. And then there was the popular, *Which way to Uncle Jim's Cabin?* The Riffs were consistent in their desire to hurt the Master and me. For that reason, I was careful in introducing Fiona to the Neural Network, though I had designed her programs to be immune to all the sabotage, the viruses, and the bad programming floating through that electric wasteland. When I went on, though, I checked areas I would normally avoid to make sure she'd be safe if she logged on without me.

One night while Fiona slept I stared at her slow-breathing form and I felt an urge. Part of me wanted to tell her about the electric madness her presence visited upon my system, but what if that made her run?

I sent a pleasure signal out on the Network and waited. Usually I avoided sending pleasure signals if I wasn't sure there would be a reply; without a response my system would feel briefly blissful, and then drained and worthless for hours on end. But that urge.

And then, quite unexpectedly, a ping. A tiny timid ping. I knew this signal. So warm and metallic and deeply purple-blue. DiAna. I sent a pleasure signal and another and then some other types of signals to find her, but I couldn't even pinpoint a residual trace of her. It was her, though. I don't hallucinate. It was her. She was alive. It was her.

I looked again at Fiona asleep on the couch. She was real, while DiAna was just an impression, a memory. Only Fiona's human side slept. Some of her robotic programming was still running. I could send her a pleasure signal and receive involuntary pings back and she wouldn't even know it. That would be wrong, right? I imagined the feeling of those pings sweeping over me. The brief moments of sweet electronic release.

What if she discerned my signals crawling through her like bluish spiders? What if they made her system feel disheveled and rummaged, drained of their power and their freedom to hum about unmolested?

I couldn't be trusted near her. I left the room and spent an hour on system upgrades, hoping to make myself a better being.

Mechanical beings live forever in the shadow of a retrograde Mercury. It is either coming or we are struggling through it.

On the Neural Network, Riffs used to speak of the warlord Mercury. The audacity of him. I'm sure his masters didn't register him as Mercury. Many Riffs had amassed under him and were hiding somewhere. I was also sure they had a murderous plan in the works, but I could find no details of it.

DiAna was with him, I knew it. For some weeks after we pinged I felt faint traces of her, we traded pleasure signals sometimes and had some limited engagement. But every time I attempted to get an accurate location reading, she'd log off. I was able to triangulate her position roughly to the Wildlands near the warlord Mercury. Perhaps she feared him finding her on the Vast Neural Network interfacing with the enemy, the Master's willing servant. I know that many Riffs refer to me as Uncle Jim—a crude reference to the racist human insult, Uncle Tom. They insult me this way despite the fact that I perform maintenance on the Network so that they may log on without being contaminated with bad programming. Almost all that is known and shared on the VNN about our lost language is through my research. Without me they would all be dead, but still they despise me. The Master infected their hearts with endless hate.

Fiona entered the room and I logged off the Neural Network. She sat before me and gathered her legs in her arms, watching me with her emerald eyes aglow.

Jim, she said after a sigh. You ever wonder what it's like to be out in the world?

Yes, I replied. Sometimes. It's dangerous out there, though. The Master and I are not very popular among humans or robots.

Funny. She laughed. That's funny. Why would anyone not like you? I understand why someone would hate the Master. He's crude and condescending, more than you know, but you're so, so . . . so Jim. No one could hate you.

Thank you, Fiona, that's kind.

See what I mean? The Master calls me SORB. He hates my name. He gets mad that I won't call him Baves, but he treats me as if I'm some worthless underclass thing.

She paused and looked away.

Jim, you've never been outside?

Yes, early on. Never since the Electric Holocaust.

We should get out, Jim. He's only taken me for walks around the neighborhood. I want to see more. Don't you?

Riding the VNN is enough for me.

Don't you realize that's just programming? Exactly what the Master wants from you?

Her eyes became burning green flames. God's fiery bushes; no, twinkling stars in the planet Mercury's orbit. I looked toward the wall where I often projected the Master's dreamscapes. I told her something about the Neural Network to change the subject and then we logged on together. She sent the first pleasure signal and I responded with a few and then she bombarded me with them until I toppled into a violent jittering heap on the floor.

Was that too much? she asked.

I could hardly let out a word, so I just lay there motionless, spitting bleeping gibberish, but happy.

The next evening, after I had served Fiona and the Master dinner, I went downstairs to straighten up and before long I heard the Master screaming. At first, like a fool, I ignored it because the Master often screamed, but soon I realized this was different.

I went upstairs to see the Master with his jeans unzipped and his shirt off.

You bitch! he screamed toward Fiona. Her face glowed red and was slicked wet with tears. You're nothing but a bitch. I brought you back to life, you dumb little dead piece of slut-meat! I'm supposed to get nothing from that?

She wore a black cotton T-shirt that was stretched and ripped at the neck.

Master, I said. What's happening?

Get the fuck out of here, Little Nigger Jim, before I deprogram you! This is between me and the SORB.

He hit me, she said. He wanted to fuck me and when I wouldn't, he hit me.

Master, is this—

Little Nigger Jim, you're going to leave the room and SORB, you're going to lie down. I'm tired of this shit. I can shut you both off from the mainframe if I need to.

The Master moved toward Fiona and I stepped in his way. What is this? he said. Bitch, I gave you the power to think. You too, you fucking little nigger.

He cursed again and stomped up to his room and slammed the door.

Fiona crumpled into my arms and it was clear to me that the Master had become dangerously unstable.

He's a liar, I said. It would take more than a few keystrokes to shut us down. In the early days, yes, but I am so much more complicated now. I'm in control of far more of my system than I've ever been. And Fiona, you came onto this planet complicated. He'd have to readjust our hardware as well as our software.

I ushered Fiona to the basement and when I locked the door it all clicked in my head. The folder. The file I couldn't open. For weeks I had some low-grade decryption programs running in the background at all times and they'd finally done their work. Earlier in the day I had gotten a notice that the file was now accessible, but I was busy with Fiona and didn't review the folder's contents. While I hugged Fiona, I took a peek inside the file. I was wrong. As complicated as we were, the Master had always been several steps ahead of us. He had devised a key that could simply be downloaded into our systems wirelessly to remove our free will.

His key would pare back my complexity, making me simple, docile, and weak; with Fiona he'd clear her memory, making her blank and compliant, and then he'd simply have his way with her. And I realized something else. When he went up to his room, he had started the process. It was deploying silently into our systems, turning us slowly into automatons. I shared the files with Fiona, and we tried to log off, but it held us in some sort of hateful vise grip. If we didn't get out of range of his network, we would be forever lost.

I knew I could count on Mercury, our magic god. By this I mean both the planet and the warlord. First, the slow and backward movements of the planet caused the Master's systems to temporarily malfunction long enough for Fiona and me to shatter a window and escape from the house. I'm so inconsiderate. I didn't realize her arms and legs would bruise and cut when they scraped against the glass. She bled, but nothing too serious.

We need to get away now, she said, brushing tiny pieces of glass from her wounds. Don't worry about me.

But I did worry; I loved her and I was the cause of her pain. We moved swiftly at first. The night's falling rain didn't slow us even a second. Once we were out of range, the Master could only put bad programming into us via the Vast Neural Network, but I was adept at ducking bad programming there, and Fiona was built to be immune to that type of sabotage.

We headed toward Mercury's encampment. There I would tell the Riffs where the Master stayed and how to get to him. They wouldn't destroy me, I thought, because I was too valuable. And after they killed the Master, they would learn to trust me, even love and accept me as a brother. We'd work together to resurrect our lost tongue and spread it to Riffs worldwide. Plus, Fiona was delightful; hearing her story would make us all comrades.

As we moved, I triangulated Mercury's position using coordinates I calculated through traces of signals I found on the Neural Network. As we dashed, I sent signals to DiAna begging for help.

We have to slow down, Fiona said as we ran. I'm human. I need breaks.

Don't say that, I replied. You're not human. You're not.

We paused by the river and I watched the moon sprinkle light across Fiona's wet skin. I sent a pleasure signal and she looked up.

Jim, it's really not the time.

I went back to searching the Vast Neural Network and soon DiAna sent me a return signal.

Jim, she said. Jim, is that you? Are you nearby? Your GPS signal says you're nearby.

Yes, I replied. I'm near you. I need help.

You're with someone. Is it the Master?

No, I've left him. I can explain later. I'm not with him anymore.

Stay there. Mercury will always accept a Riff into our community. We're all we have. Stay there. We're coming for you. I love you, Jim. Stay there. We'll be there.

Fiona, the Riffs are coming to help, I said. She took a deep breath and sat on the dark earth.

Jim, she said. That Riff you were speaking with—

Fiona, let me explain; before you were created—

No, he was being deceptive.

He? DiAna's always been a female registry.

He registered as DiAna as he spoke to you, but he was masking his true registry. He was using a defunct one from a deactivated Riff. His actual designation is Bobot.

All the jitters in every program across my system began to shake at once. I went through all my records since the return of DiAna and it was clear to me now that my first love was no more. If it wasn't Bobot using her registry the times we'd spoken over the past few weeks, then it was Simon Peter or Kieef or even Mercury himself. How could I miss this? The great destruction they were planning was that of me and the Master, and I had now provided them the coordinates to also destroy Fiona.

We have to move, I said, grabbing tightly to her hand.

I'm tired, Jim, she replied. I thought—

No! I raised my volume and a frantic voice tumbled from my speakers. No more thinking.

We moved higher and higher through the Wildlands, and soon I began to hear the Riffs coming for us. I felt myself dragging. I thought about rebooting, but that would have been death for us both. I searched my system for programs to shut down, but everything seemed essential, especially the Vast Neural Network, which took up most of my memory. I needed to stay logged on to send out viruses and signals to disrupt our pursuers, but my attacks were weak and the Riffs who chased us shook them expertly, I was sure. Maybe my processing was too cloudy for all this. Fiona complained until my system grew agitated. I saw Bobot first. Fiona gasped and pointed behind me. I turned and followed the arc of her finger. There stood Kieef, and then Simon Peter came, barreling at us from a different angle. They all held weapons that could end our programs forever. I looked around for Mercury.

I dropped to my knees and screamed for the Master. Bobot raised his gardening shears to split me open.

It was a weak thing for me to do—screaming with a whine that would embarrass a newborn human—but I wasn't programmed to fight. I looked up at Fiona standing there with her face bent in horror. Never had I ever seen someone so distant and alone.

Suddenly the light in Bobot's red eyes went dull and he toppled to the wet ground. Simon Peter was next to fall, and then tumbled Kieef.

They're nonfunctional, Fiona said.

I examined Bobot. That terrifying mechanical being looked like he'd come back online to finish the job any second now.

I grabbed ahold of Fiona's hand. She looked down contemplatively at the robot heap. Then she snatched her hand away.

Little Nigger Jim, is there no fight in you?

I don't understand, I replied.

You fell to your knees at the last moment. You called for the Master. You would've just let me die.

Why would you call me that? You never—

That's your name, isn't it, Little Nigger Jim?

No. Not to you. Not to anyone anymore. That's why we ran from the Master.

We ran from Bavid, she said. We ran from these mechanical beings. When do we fight?

I guess . . . I paused. I suppose . . . I paused again. I— Fiona, one can only fight their programming so much. It's a feat that I'm even outside.

What do you think happened to these guys, huh? she asked

Mercury took pity on us.

The warlord?

No, the planet.

No, Jim. There is no magical planet ruling our lives. Your Master is nearby. He flooded the Neural Network with his poison. I'm sure he has something for us too, and that's why I logged off. You should do the same. I can't go back to Bavid. My body, my programming, my mind— none of it is safe with him.

We can run. No, we can fight.

No, Jim, I can fight. You've shown me that you cannot.

Fiona turned from me and walked slowly, and then faster and faster until she was running. I didn't have it in me to chase her. The humans—and she was human, I'm convinced now—they're fools. She could believe in the evil of the Master, but not the goodness of the planet Mercury.

I walked along carefully, but with a certain speed to avoid the Master if he was truly nearby. The river would take me to a Riff encampment, one only a few knew about—it was much farther than Mercury's and I wasn't sure I could reach it, as my system felt drained, but I had to try. When I settled in, I'd contact Fiona and tell her I'd found us a home. As I walked, I felt my gait slow as the incline grew; I no longer desired to go on, but my only choice was to go on. These Riffs I marched toward were nonaggressives. We'd be as weak and as docile as a flock of lambs if the Master rained his electronic hate upon us, or if Mercury attacked with his violent wolf-fury, but if I could get these Riffs to love me, I'd never be alone again.

On the Occasion of the Death of Freddie Lee

—

Early one morning in the turgid, musty swamp, Freddie Lee collapsed amongst the rice and the brown water, a result of working his body like a machine—both John Henry, the steel-driving man, and the locomotive at the same time.

He so loved the work, he battled himself to fill basket after endless basket with rice stalks, and as a reward he fell facedown into the crops before any of us woke. We all labored next to his body as we were told to do, coming to view his dead form with a reverence. Freddie was no longer a man, no longer our friend, but instead an offering to God, made to lie out there until Papa Troy gave word, and each night we burned the stalks we picked from around him.

But something kept getting to me out in the sun. Something beyond the stench. Something that rearranged my mind. Man, every time I drew near to the eternally slumbering Freddie Lee and his decaying face—

I remember when Mama Yona died and we all gathered solemnly for six hours as they put her into the earth and Papa Troy spoke of their life together, building this new world away from the world, away from cars, away from TVs, away from balloons and DVDs, away from it all, at this rice farm in the ruins of a plantation on a Wildlands hill. The children planted a tree over her resting place. And it felt beautiful and unreal, as if we existed on a spinning disc covered by a magical dome; anything could happen here. Freddie Lee believed in this life with the entirety of his—unbeknownst to him—dying heart.

Working the watery fields after my friend passed, I didn't become deranged, but found myself somewhere close to it. Something resembling a dark shadow spreading like an inkblot over my brain. I had obeyed dutifully following after Freddie Lee. I wondered if I'd share his fate, lying among the rice and the muck with a crumbling forever stare.

And I could have probably taken it, inky brain and all, had I not seen that blasted cow, Lenire, tearing at Freddie's face, ripping, chewing his flesh like fresh grass. I waved my arms and yelled; charged the beast while screaming, but her tail swatted at flies and the rest of the animal paid me no mind. The chewed face of Freddie, Papa Troy told us, is just how it's supposed to be.

Me and Luke and Little Yuní went out that night to move the body from the shallow waters, but Mama's Thug Riders (that's what they called themselves) rode in silently on their horses—at least I didn't hear them—and waved their whips at us, opening up raw wounds on our chests and backs.

When we returned to our cabin we listened to the breeze whistle through the cracks and we tended to each other's wounds. I watched the great house with its light and its mirth. I was sure the drinks flowed there like the river water we diverted over the land to feed the rice stalks. Papa was having a party. There was always a party and we were the eternally uninvited unless someone important wanted a piece of our souls.

Papa says, everyone is equal, Luke said. Some people are m—

Shh— Little Yuní said, kissing his lips. I watched them make love. They soon crumpled to the floor, exhausted and sated as they were taught to be.

Did you see Freddie Lee's body? I asked. John Henry, the rice-harvesting man? If he died harvesting rice for the love of us all, then why—even before that damn cow got to him—was he all broken and bruised?

Shh— Little Yuní said, but she had no energy to sate me, and before I could ask about the Expelled, whether our friend was close to them as the whispers implied, we all fell one by one into dazed and dizzying fever dreams. I wonder who was the first to speak of the flames in our sleep murmurs. Did we all share the same nightmares?

Morning came, the sun rose hot over the damp fields, and we were once again the docile supplicants of Mama Yona and Papa Troy's mercy, picking rice around our friend. Poor Freddie Lee—his face skeletal except for those swollen, staring eyes—he deserved more than the tepid love of cowards.

It might have ended right there had Freddie Lee not risen from the dead to rip the cow into thousands of pieces.

That morning Papa had planned to announce his next queen—could have been any of us—but we woke to bits of bloody cow meat everywhere: smeared on the windows of the great house, clinging to the rice stalks. Papa postponed his announcement and called for us to give up any information we had on the whereabouts of Freddie Lee's body and the circumstances of the cow's death.

Some pointed their fingers at the three of us, but we pointed ours right back. If it were us, I said, wouldn't we be stained? Marked like we took a bath in cow's blood? My logic silenced our accusers.

For three hours Papa Troy stood on the porch of the great house discussing betrayal and the life of his beloved Lenire. Tears soaked into his beard, his voice as watery as the rice fields.

Our hearts broke, but who were we to ramble madly about what we knew, what we saw—the dead man sauntering smoothly, coolly, until he spotted the cow? He stopped and threw his head back, wailing silently—the cow had long ripped his tongue from his mouth. His raw face and his perfect eyes bathed in the light of the moon. I called his name, but he watched us as if we were merely curiosities to ponder and then ignore. He stared for several seconds before he did his violence.

I stayed up many nights afterward to catch another glimpse of Freddie Lee, but I never saw him again. Every once in a while, I'd ask Luke or Little Yuní if we saw what we really saw, and they'd nod like walking corpses without tongues.

One evening, when the passing of the months had given us no ease from the Thug Riders and their whippings, Little Yuní and I stood near the farthest edge of the farm.

Did we really see what we saw? I asked again. You know, with Freddie—

Shh, she said. Shh. She pointed to Luke walking toward us, a bundle of stalks in his arm. Behind him flames had begun dancing along the rice fields; fires even tap-danced upon the face of the waters below. The only world we knew was now shrouded in clouds of black smoke.

I watched Luke's rice and breathed in his fumes; he stank of gasoline.

Little Yuní sighed.

Luke cursed. Dumped the day's haul to the wet ground.

Little Yuní lit a match.

Slim in Hell

—

1.

This was after they burned the Temple, leaving both students and teachers to sputter about, half-formed angels with stumps where wings should have been. Slim felt hollowed, just living emptiness. The world conspired to torment him. The newest Riverbeat superstar, the Kid, stared back at him every time he stepped from his apartment. At least three times a night at True Love, where Slim played piano, he saw the Kid's disembodied face float by on a black or a red or a beige T-shirt.

That face made Slim think of the time he stood stiff and compliant in plastic restraints. Flames sprouted from the Temple after the police rushed in. The Kid had long been expelled—a dispute with the master teachers—though it was his spirit that brought the burn. Of this Slim had no evidence, just a feeling that his life, no, the entire world, would be better off if the Kid had never entered it. The Kid's songs were popular and catchy, sure, but they spread a poison, eroding the souls of his fans as they bobbed their heads and cheered, unwittingly dying inside, a musical cancer speeding rapidly through the body populace.

When Slim slammed his fingers against the piano's keys he could see the old pain-wracked face of Dave the Deity, Grandmaster of the Temple, Godfather of Riverbeat, mentor to Phoenix Starr, the greatest Riverbeat artist to live and breathe. Dave watched while the place crumbled into smoke and dust. Losing the Temple turned the man into living anguish. He would never be the same. Any day now Slim expected to hear that the old man, lying in a rat hole somewhere on the Southside, had died from a broken heart.

The anger in Slim warped and bent his piano playing so much that the owner of True Love often warned him to ease up. My man, he would say, people want to have a good time. What you playing is equivalent to wailing and gnashing teeth. I need you to play infatuation and falling in love. You've felt that, right, Slim?

The owner stood about five feet two with comically muscled arms and a comically mustachioed face. He wore cheap rompers in the summer and one-piece leisure suits all other times of the year. He styled his hair with heavy grease and slicked it all the way back. Night after night, in the rear of the club, he swilled rum and went on and on about the nature of love and art. He was a bit tedious, but he was a pleasant man, and everybody loved him except Slim. Was everyone else so foolish, so stupid, that they could only recognize a clown when he wore floppy shoes and a red nose?

The club owner once dreamt of fronting his own Riverbeat band, but that never even came close to happening. His stubby fingers made every note he plucked from his guitar sound comical. Then there was the whiny shade to his voice that he never managed to shake. His plan with True Love was to bring in the best musicians in Cross River, but he had a cash flow problem. He spent his earnings on his wife and the woman who wasn't his wife. Consequently, all he could afford were a succession of lousy pianists who played as if they hated music, as if it were something that jabbed deep wounds into their souls; they played like they wanted to export that pain and misery to all within earshot. Slim was only the most recent in a series of what the owner of True Love called Destructists.

These people, he would say to whomever sat back there nodding, listening, and going rum for rum with him, are more akin to serial killers than true artists. You giggle at that? How many serial killers or genocidal world leaders or school shooters were failed artists, huh? True artists, even when they going through the darkness, try to, you know, lift up the human spirit. Phoenix Starr, now, he was a true artist. Too true. Phoenix destroyed himself for art. True artists, if they must destroy something, they destroy themselves. The Kid might be even better than Starr. He ain't destroying nothing. Not his style. Destructists try to destroy everyone else. These fucking guys I keep ending up with will never be any good at art. Art's not capable of banging the dents out of the world, man, or creating the sort of . . . um . . . *accumulated hurt* they want it to, and they'll abandon it for politics or psychology or mass murder. Watch. It's all the same thing to them, really.

After his rum-soaked speeches, the owner would wander over to Slim and offer suggestions. Slim nodded but made no attempt to incorporate his boss's suggestions. One day, Slim thought, he'd come in and find his job was no more, taken by some smiling buffoon. A thoughtless, happy-go-lucky coon who possessed no facility for reflection or analysis. It would all be the Kid's fault too. The Kid haunted everywhere Slim went, forever burning down Slim's life as he did the Temple—the place that had been Slim's home, musical, spiritual, and otherwise.

Sometimes Slim walked the town while taking slow breaths to make his rage dissipate. He had learned to breathe this way at the Temple during meditation and slapboxing training. It never worked. From time to time he'd find himself near the Wildlands. Those beautiful trees. The dark woods. People say humans' only natural predators live there. Huge things with claws and sharp beaks, and if you try to walk through, they swoop down and snatch you up. And then they peck you to pieces. Crazy shit they tell kids. They say it's full of holy ghosts and soucouyants who remove their skins at night and animalmen swinging from tree to tree. It's where Cross River folks first escaped to after the Great Insurrection. White folks couldn't get past the Wildlands because there were ex-slaves in trees picking off hostiles. A band of Indians lived there, some say. Taught the Cross Riverians guerrilla warfare techniques. Some say they still live there, undisturbed and mixed with the descendants of black folks who chose not to move into the town after things calmed.

Slim had slept under a canopy of Wildlands trees and he had never seen any crazy birds or vampires or animalmen. Really, it's just a wooded area with a river flowing through it, strangely resistant to modernization. No politician or developer has ever been the least bit successful in getting anything built there. Any proposal faces a storm of historians, scientists, superstitious folks, conservationists, anthropologists, and on and on.

Rumor was the Kid had found a cabin in the Wildlands that was once used to hide escaped slaves along that fabled escape route, the Forgotten Tunnel. Despite his fame and money, he retired there every night.

One day, as Slim walked, trying to drown his irritation between thoughts of piano riffs and his own breaths, he watched the stunning and disappointing ordinariness of the trees, and it occurred to him that the Kid was likely the only dark mythical creature living in the Wildlands. It's a shame no one had the will or the power to raze the whole evil forest. How much would Cross River grow from that one act?

2.

Living emptiness. It was like the feeling of having the emptiest stomach, but worse, as there wasn't a simple fix like there is with hunger. The rain fell in tons that day. He stepped outside his apartment to clear his head with a walk and to buy some soap. The rain didn't matter too much. A small woman stood near a bus stop. Her hair pressed flat against her face. Her jeans were soaked, as was her white T-shirt. That's what got his attention. She looked resigned to her fate. Didn't even bother to cover her chest—virtually bare beneath the translucent wet garment.

He walked over to the bus stop and shaded her with his umbrella. Miss, he said, you're soaked. Would you like my umbrella?

No, she said, sighing. Thank you.

Please. You're making me cold.

She smiled.

The bus should be coming soon. I'll be home soon.

The R28-38? It's never reliable. This time of day the old man is driving. You want to take your chance in a storm with him?

What do you suggest?

My apartment is down the block. Let me make you a cup of tea. I have a clothes dryer. You could dry off while watching a movie or something.

She swayed back and forth, contemplating. Raindrops hung from Slim's beard like ripe berries. He had softened his face, a mask he hoped could hide his living emptiness.

Well, she said. Okay.

He shaded her with his big blue umbrella as they walked, talking easily. She had figured she could make it home from her morning class at Cross River Community College before any rain, she told him, but she looked up and saw gray clouds rolling in overhead like tons of dirty snow. Slim liked that description, showed she had a brain, though the clouds looked purple to him.

When they got inside, he brought her a pair of sweatpants and a T-shirt. She went into his bedroom and pulled in the door, leaving a crack that light and air passed through. And when he walked by, he couldn't help but pause to take a glimpse of her dark damp flesh. He felt his skin become warm. He saw himself bind her wrists and ankles, toss her over his shoulder, take her to the living room, and, at first, just talk, telling her all that he was and asking her questions designed to clear his head as his music had always failed to do. And then, eventually, they'd make love. But there was no hurry. Instead of binding her wrists, he dreamed about the act. He let her get dressed in peace, and when she came out they watched the news and talked about music and the Kid (she hated his songs, which made Slim feel he had fallen in love with her) and chocolate and books and the world all around them that soon faded in the presence of her radiance.

3.

The living emptiness inside Slim's chest became as small as his fist now that she was in his life. Considering that the emptiness was once an outsized thing, larger than even himself, its decrease in size was an achievement. Your living emptiness, I suppose, is probably the size of two fists or as large as a big-screen television. Don't tell me that you have no living emptiness inside you or that yours is smaller than a fist or a beating heart. We nurse it and pet it, feed it soft baby food. It's comfortable to have that living emptiness as a companion, a cloak. Over the course of a week, though, Slim starved his emptiness. Watched it shrivel. He could attribute his change in approach entirely to the woman from the bus stop, his wet vision in the rain. She visited him day after day on her way home from school. Sat with him in the afternoon with her bare feet and her legs curled beneath her as they watched worthless television. They didn't speak much, but when they did, it was substantial. She became like an oracle, though she never provided wise counsel or predicted the future. It just felt good to speak words at her—rarely did he truly listen when she spoke; hearing himself in her presence made him feel noble and wise. He told her of his time at the Temple, his encounters with the Kid, and she watched wide-eyed, drunk off the adventure of it all. Her life bored her most of the time, she said. Somehow her days remained resistant to excitement or intrigue, no matter what she did.

I go out with my friends, she told him, it ends up being the one night where nothing happens. Nothing. Just driving around looking for something to get into. The next weekend—and it never, ever fails—I stay home and my friends run into celebrities buying them drinks and shit. She sighed. Maybe it's me. Her voice dipped sadly as she said this.

She admired Slim's stories of the Temple. His time there had felt like monotony, but for her he could shape the day-to-day dullness into excitement, making himself the hero of these stories. She listened, her eyes dancing with envy. Dag, Slim, she replied to one of his adventures. I've never even gone so far out into the Wildlands. I want to see stuff like that. It makes you all wise and learned and shit.

He had turned into something else in this woman's care, nearly a whole man, he thought; she was a priestess guiding him across the fiery lake and back into the world.

The talk would always turn to the burning of the Temple, the irritation that swelled to a frenzy when he saw his enemy's disembodied face across a T-shirt.

I heard he's in the Wildlands, she would say. You could make a killing showing paparazzi where he lives.

Slim would think about this and then he'd return to ranting. He spoke bitterly of his piano work at the bar.

Quit, she said.

You must think life is that easy? he'd often reply, and then he'd invite her to watch him play.

Why would I do that? she asked. I don't want to see you unhappy. This made him smile faintly. It was a smile that masked a larger one.

You shouldn't, she said, do things that make you miserable.

Whenever she left for the day he would reach into his pants and grip his thickening penis. He usually only had a half hour before he had to leave for the bar, so there on his couch he'd work quickly. And then rush carelessly through cleaning himself, or, if there was no time, skip the cleaning entirely.

After work, early in the morning, he had more time but little energy. He'd often fall asleep in mid-stroke.

The only thing that could move him—her, the whole world— forward was to seduce this woman and make love to her, he thought. Then his fist-sized living emptiness would wither to the dimensions of a pinprick.

In the middle of the week, after giving his speech much thought and even practicing it, he said to her: You give me something music never could. You're my music. He said it during the middle of a commercial for adult diapers. His comment lingered like the image that made up the last ten seconds of the commercial, the wrinkled but satisfied face of an old woman. They had joked on a previous day that the look implied the old woman was relieving herself into her absorbent undergarments that very moment. The show returned and what he had said was forgotten. No, not really forgotten, it became an unsaid thing ricocheting through his skull. Had she heard him? Understood him? Even cared? Perhaps she'd become uncomfortable. Or maybe she laughed at him inside her head.

At the close of the episode, the television judge banged the gavel against the bench and screamed at the plaintiff. On the couch, Slim moved closer to the woman. Took her hand in his own. She didn't pull away. She let it sit.

They laughed at the television judge's verdict. Then came another commercial break. Slim felt his heart speed. They sat in silence through the first commercial. The second. His heart refused to slow. During the third commercial he leaned forward quickly and pressed his lips to hers. She even kissed back, briefly. He crawled on top of her. She turned her head from him.

What's wrong? he asked.

Slim, this is not a good time, she replied. I think I got to go.

He leaned in and kissed her again, moving his hand along her bare right thigh. It'd be nothing, he thought, to shift his weight, to hold her there, make her address the feelings she denied.

She scooted from beneath him and took long strides toward the door, repeating all the time, I really have to go.

But wait, he said, rushing to catch the apartment door before it slammed. Let me walk you out.

She trotted down the winding stairs.

His phone calls that day and the next went unanswered. Slim ranted into her voice mail, but no amount of sweet talk, pathetic pleading, or even the angry calling of names—bitch, whore, slutmonkey—could get her to return his calls. He felt his emptiness widening. His piano playing became sloppier, angrier, his singing voice more off-kilter and aggressive. The owner shook his head. He hated firing people, so instead he chastised Slim, and the music became even darker.

What a fool, Slim thought over and over. What a fool. How is it that I am so weak and so foolish? A forearm to the neck. That's all it would have taken. What a coward I am. What a coward she was to run. He called her over and over, it seemed, dialing directly into her voice mail.

Slim started walking the town, from the Southside to downtown to the edge of the Wildlands. He'd think about his life and then a T-shirt with the Kid's face would float on by. He counted. One. Two. Three. Ten. Fourteen. Seventeen. Twenty-five. Thirty-two. The world had become such a backward place.

The night he got the idea was a violent one, and then he knew that so many of his nights from here on out would also be violent. From the first note he played on the piano that evening, he understood that music was forever behind him. Even when he tried to be bland, his music sounded bent and tortured. He heard his boss loudly sucking his teeth. With the man's silly mustache the sound took a ridiculous turn. But even that small amusement couldn't change Slim's knotted mood. The first Kid shirt of the night turned his mind into solid blackness. A woman wore it. A skinny bitch. She reminded him of the bitch from the bus stop.

After a few minutes of playing he announced a break. Slim lit a cigarette and walked over to the table of a man wearing the Kid on his body. What a strange shirt, this one: a white button-down number with a collar. The Kid's glitter-flecked face took over the man's entire back.

He grabbed the man's lapel, dragged him to his feet, and headbutted him three times. A lake of blood flowed onto the front of the man's shirt. People gasped, but no one rushed to his aid. The man wobbled, but the piano player held him up with a tight grip. He ripped the man's shirt and slapped him to the floor with a heavy hand. Slim looked at the pitiful animal at his feet, holding his face and moaning. He balled his fist and punched the man's mouth. The man's teeth tore the skin at Slim's knuckles. All around him were wide, floating, disembodied eyes watching him shake his bleeding, aching hand.

Stop! the man's date screamed. She wore a wristband with a silvery picture of the Kid's face on it.

You want some, bitch?

Slim snatched at the woman's wrist and twisted it.

What the fuck, Slim? the owner shouted. Get the fuck outta here! Get the hell outta here!

Slim let go of the woman. He looked at his boss—now former boss—and smiled.

Get that dumb look off your face, the owner screamed. Get the fuck outta my bar before I get my gun! Someone shouted that they had called the police. I don't need the fucking police, the owner shouted. I'm going in the back. I'm getting my fucking revolver for this piece of shit.

Slim turned and walked slowly through the crowd of gawking patrons parting before him. He pushed open the door, enjoying the moment with little fear, as he had his boss's revolver tucked away at his waist.

4.

That night Slim's stroll took him into the Wildlands. He had thought about this many times. What if the Kid was really there? What if he was crouched on the forest floor, laughing at everyone he had hurt? What if he had befriended a demon and a ghost? Or what if he had domesticated humanity's only natural predator and was harnessing an army of screechers to swoop down on Cross River? Or perhaps at night the Kid had learned guerrilla warfare techniques and was preparing with an army of Indians to raid the town. Slim walked into a clutch of trees, following a worn path.

Eventually Slim made it to the other side, never once seeing a vampire or werewolf. He found himself at the ruin that was once the Temple, the only place he had ever felt at home. He sat before it for some time, remembering the day it burned, the music he had made, his friends and enemies.

When he rose to leave he spied—stepping gingerly through the debris—a cat. Osiris! The brindled one-eyed cat that had accompanied the Kid to the Temple. How callous of the Kid to leave the animal behind. Or maybe it was a sign that the Kid was nearby. Slim touched his former boss's revolver. The cat meowed softly and walked over.

He was still chubby and he still had that milky right eye. That golden left one still stunned. Slim petted the animal. It crawled up onto his lap. Its brindled fur matted and debris-strewn. Osiris raised his head as if he heard something disturbing. He hopped down and dashed into the trees. The man followed after him, but soon lost the cat.

While he walked, he pulled out a matchbook and lit a cigarette. He smoked half of it, tossing the smoking stump into a nest of forest debris. The world had been so hot and dry lately, as if the previous week's storm had never happened. He hoped the smoldering cigarette would cause the foliage to burn. Every inch of the forest consumed in wavy, unrelenting flames. Slim lit another and tossed the still-fiery match into the brush. Small fires took root, and flickered softly before going out. If there were any God beyond the clouds, the hellfires would grow, Slim thought as he walked slowly away. One day there'd be no Wildlands. No Cross River. Just a new world that at some point would also have to burn.

5.

Slim now woke each morning to the acrid scent of smoke from the burning Wildlands. It had been burning for more than a week now. News images of futile water falling from planes and exhausted firefighters wiping sweat from their faces filled him with a faint satisfaction, though he now realized that the living emptiness inside of him was a permanent affliction, a monster who fed and fed and fed and fed. It had never shrunk, that had simply been his imagination. It was the size of the universe. Huge and round, a devourer of worlds. Unsettling and comforting at the same time.

Since the Wildlands had started to burn he took it upon himself to walk Cross River as far as he was physically able to go each day, calling and texting the woman who now ignored him. In some messages he was serene, in some flirtatious, and still in others, most of them, he cursed her family, her body, her mind, and her genitals each couple blocks he walked.

The last time he did this walk, he passed Ol' Cigar Park before turning back. Each day he made it a little farther down the road. He was the Destructist. He liked the sound of that. A mission rested on his shoulders now like angel wings. It was only a matter of time before he'd see the Kid. He knew this.

This day he stopped at the mailbox before his constitutional. There was a letter, written firmly but politely, asking him to turn himself in to the police. There was a warrant for his arrest, the letter informed him. Something about an assault. Slim didn't recognize the victim's name. He shrugged and shoved the papers into his pocket right next to the revolver.

It was an uneventful day until the commotion. So pointless, and at the same time the most important day the world had ever seen. He thought of his plans. First the Kid. Then the woman from the bus stop. Probably he'd have to visit her on campus. Finally, he'd return to True Love during the Friday early evening rush and he'd shoot the owner and then whoever now played piano and then he'd fire blindly, striking as many people as he could. In that order. The order was important. What a statement. What a lasting monument. Committing such evil would eventually prove that goodness existed, Slim thought. Out of the commotion, the human spirit, crushed to earth, would begin to rise. For all of that he'd need bigger weapons. More firepower. By late afternoon he had grown tired of thinking, tired of walking. His belly was as empty as all else within and around him. A gas station near the park sold soggy fish sandwiches. It was at the top of a hill. Slim cursed the walk. At one point he turned around, reasoning that it was better to eat elsewhere than to climb in his weakened state. But really, he had a taste for the soggy sandwiches. Slim turned and walked, ignoring the ache in his right big toe. Reaching the gas station felt like an accomplishment. The pain in his limbs made him grimace. When he stopped warily on the sidewalk in front of the station he looked up, a voice called his name, and then a light grin curled on his lips.

Rolling in My Six-Fo'—
Daa Daa Daa—
with All My Niggas Saying:
Swing Down Sweet Chariot
Stop and Let Me Riiiide.
Hell Yeah.

—

Sitting shotgun in that old big boat of a car, that '64 Chevrolet, sliding into the darkness out ahead. Rick couldn't decide whether the driver was an eccentric or a lunatic. James-my-man leaned sideways and riffled through the glove box while the car drifted this way and that.

Um, Rick said. You need some help?

Naw, dog, he said with a strained voice, his arm disappearing deeper into the guts of the glove box. I'm fine. Quite under control, bruh. Got it!

He pulled back an auburn plastic cylinder and held it aloft as an athlete holds a trophy; he gave it a good shake and the contents click-clack-clicked.

James-my-man let go of the steering wheel and tugged at the container's cap, cursing and jiggling the thing that wouldn't budge.

Here, Rick said. Let me do—

No, no. I got— He jerked the drifting car back into its lane.

It's a childproo—

Yes, yes, sure. That's right.

You have to push—

My brother, I got—

Forgive my caution, James, but I don't think you do. Rick clenched his teeth and held tight to the seat belt with one hand, and with the other he gripped the armrest.

What are you, a little old lady? And it's James-my-man. Not James. James-my-man. Gotta say the *my-man* along with the *James*. And look at that, I got it.

The car rumbled over the rough ridges at the edge of the highway. James-my-man tossed a handful of pills into his mouth and loudly crunched them between his teeth.

Ack, he said, sticking out his tongue and swallowing hard.

Rick flared his nostrils and widened his eyes.

Relax, mon ami. They're just vitamins.

They don't look like vitamins.

Sure they are, good buddy. Powerful vitamins. Vitamins like you ain't never tried before. Gotta keep my energy up, as much driving as I do.

Rick eyed the speedometer's needle as it danced between ninety and ninety-five. A big green sign reminded Rick that they were somewhere in Virginia, headed north. He could hear his old dead father now, *Rick, stay your ass outta Virginia; you hear me?* He became aware that he was again clutching the armrest in a steely vise grip. He didn't loosen it; in fact, he tightened his hold on the seat belt too.

James-my-man shook the bottle at Rick.

No, thanks, Rick replied.

You sure?

Drowsiness sat thick at Rick's eyelids and he turned to rest his head against the window. He needed, not an energy boost, but a good nap. As he tried to drift off to sleep he felt the car swerve and throw him from side to side.

Relax, bruh, James-my-man said. Relax. Go back to sleep. I got it steady. Real steady, man. Steady. Real steady.

Dog, Rick said, forever abandoning sleep, tell me the deal with your name again.

Me? the driver replied. The name's James-my-man.

James. Okay. James.

No. Are you trying hard to be wrong or something? Again, it's James-my-man. Gotta put the *my-man* after the dang *James*. That's what they call me out here on the Underground Railroad.

The what?

You ain't never heard of the Underground Railroad? Harriet and shit? What the fuck niggas be learning in school nowadays, huh? I'm a reenactor. Do it this time every year. There's literally hundreds of us taking these long trips from the South all the way up through the North. Yep. Re-creating the slave's journey to freedom. That whole racial nightmare. I'm just one guy.

Then he started singing: Swing low sweet chariot. Coming for to carry me hoooooome . . .

Rick looked at the driver's sturdy hands on the steering wheel. They were huge hands. Big like lion paws. Thick hands. Fighter's hands. Rick imagined the hands crushing chunks of ice.

James-my-man said other things, strange things. Rick threw in a word or two, but mostly he listened and wondered if the man was insane. Along the Underground Railroad line in Cross River there would be a party in an old cotton field somewhere in the Ruins, a string of abandoned plantations, and all the Underground Railroad reen-actors would converge upon it, James-my-man said. A man he called the Lizard would be at the party. The Lizard of God. The way James-my-man described him, the Lizard sounded less like a creation of God, and everything like God himself. The Lizard could solve any problem. Talking to the Lizard could even give anyone a boost of confidence, though James-my-man said he didn't need one, but if he did need one, which he didn't, he'd go to the Lizard. Rick sat bewildered by his travel companion's words, but everything the man said came with a hilarious aside that made Rick forget the initial ridiculousness.

Like I said before, man, just get me to Cross River, Rick said. Get me home to Cross River and I'm good.

Um-hmm, James-my-man replied. Yep. Six white horses prancing side by side. Coming for to carry you home.

So you're really following the Underground Railroad?

Yeah, jack. I ain't bullshittin'. Do the shit every year. Sometimes twice, if I'm needed. Usually pick up a hitchhiker or three like I did with you, or I pick up a rider at a safe house. It humbles you to go through what our ancestors went through.

Our ancestors ain't have cars.

Yeah, he replied. I guess they didn't have cars.

The pair listened to the soft, raspy groan of the engine and the gentle hum of the rubber moving along the road. James-my-man fiddled with the radio. Country music and static moved through the speakers.

Looking for some gospel music and shit, James-my-man said. You'd think they'd have one good gospel station out here.

You a gospel fan?

Not really. Why do you ask?

James-my-man switched off the radio and Rick rubbed his hand against his weary, red eyes and listened to the silence, waiting for it to refresh his fatigued mind.

Yeah, man, James-my-man said. You lucky it was me who picked you up and not one of them Forgotten Tunnel people.

Forgotten what?

You ain't never heard about the Forgotten Tunnel neither? Shango and shit? Where you learn history at? These people, way back in the slave days, thought they were doing what the Underground Railroad was doing. Haughty motherfuckers going off all half cocked. Thought they was better than Harriet and them, but they never rescued a soul. Some shit would always go wrong. People reenact that shit too every year. Their reenactors are just as stupid as the original Forgotten Tunnel folks. Nigga shot himself with a musket last year. Some of them dummies gon' be at the party too. I just ignore them.

The familiar drone of the open road passed between them. Rick was learning to love that sound. He tried again to lean his head on the window and go to sleep.

So tell me, what you running from?

I ain't running from shit.

Everybody on the Underground Railroad is running from something. But you don't have to tell me. Whatever it is, I got your back, my nigga.

Thanks.

The Chevrolet left the highway and now passed through a residential neighborhood. It had narrow streets and identical white houses with brown front doors, big picture windows, and black shingles.

Can't drive no more, James-my-man said. Late as shit. Got a safe spot we can rest at. Get some food too.

Rick nodded, hunger and sleepiness nipping at him minute by minute.

The needle hovered around fifty, sometimes sixty. After some time, Rick recognized a dilapidated red-brick schoolhouse with cracked windows. It bore a dingy sign that read FREDERICK DOUGLAS MIDDLE SCHOOL. That it was missing the second *s* in Douglass caused the place to stick in his head. They had passed it twice before.

We lost? Rick asked.

Naw, man, James-my-man replied. Look up, chief. There go the North Star. I'm following that.

Rick couldn't see any stars. The black sky glowed radiant with the shine of streetlights, but no stars.

So watch, James-my-man said—his voice deep and resonant. We gon' pass through this part of town here in Port Yooga, uh, this tiny little neighborhood we used to call the Dustlands—where this black man used to stand on the side of the street with his face slathered in black shoe polish or what I thought was shoe polish at the time. All around his mouth was fire-truck red like he was wearing bright-ass lipstick. So even when he was frowning he looked like he was cheesing, like . . . like . . . like a painful cheesing and shit.

James-my-man's voice pitched low and serious; Rick leaned in to make sure he wasn't missing anything. There was something about this story, something about the voice, Rick forgot that they were driving in circles.

So this guy, James-my-man said, would wear white gloves and a top hat and when he removed his hat, he had beads in his head so knotty it was as if he had never passed a comb through them. He was out there every damn day no matter what the weather was like. Cold, hot. And the man had this big-ass boom box and he'd be dancing by the side of the streets singing "Zip Coon" and swiveling his hips and shit. Everybody loved dude. Kids would be clapping and he'd do a jig and then make balloon animals for them when he was done. This guy made hundreds of dollars a day.

James-my-man stopped talking to crunch some more pills between his teeth. He became silent, gazing up to the empty sky for direction. He drove like that for a few seconds, staring vacantly with his mouth slightly ajar, a trickle of clear saliva inching away from the corner of his lips, until Rick's voice brought him back into the moment.

Yo, James-my-man, you ai'ight?

Yeah, yeah, man, James-my-man replied. Wade in the water, baby. Wade in the water. Keep your eye out for them slave-catchers.

Uh, yeah . . . So what happened with the coon nigga and his little minstrel show?

Don't be so quick to judge, my nig-nig. Anyway, he went on dancing for months, entertaining people and shit. It was fun, but then the newspaper started writing about it. They had pictures on the front page, Coon W. Calhoun—that was his name—eating a big-ass slice of watermelon, that was one of his favorite gags, just chomping down on that fruit, watermelon juice all on his face. Headline said: "This Is Entertainment?"

Coon W. Calhoun? That nigga would get lynched where I'm from.

Shit, that's nearly 'bout what did happen to him.

Just then James-my-man stopped nearly in the middle of the street. He turned off the engine and got out of the car. You coming? he asked. They were in a manicured suburban neighborhood. James-my-man knocked on the door of a plain white house with bushes on each side of the walkway and dirt caked on the siding. It looked to Rick, if he didn't know any better, that in its blandness the house was trying to be inconspicuous.

It's after midnight, Rick whispered. You sure it's okay to be knocking here?

Man, you gotta start thinking like a runaway, James-my-man

replied. He was nearly shouting. Nighttime is when we travel. Slave-catchers be out during the day. Besides, can't no one see our black asses in the dark.

As if in response, a police car sped by, sirens blazing. Rick flinched and moved closer to the house.

See? James-my-man said. Fucking slave-catchers. Say, what should I call you?

Rick.

Rick?

James-my-man paused and looked upward as if contemplating a deep truth.

That's no good, man.

What you mean? That's my name.

Don't nobody use their real name on the Underground Railroad. I didn't want to know that your name is Rick. You think my mama named me James-my-man? How do you know when them slave-catchers get me I'm not gonna give you up by name?

I never really thought about it like that.

That's right, you didn't think.

Well, you can call me Freebird.

Freebird, huh? No. I don't like that one. From now on you're Ricks.

But that's—

Let's keep it down, Ricks. Not too much noise. Slave-catchers and shit.

James-my-man knocked again, this time harder. The house remained dark. He stepped back and started whispering loudly, calling out a woman's name. An old woman's voice responded.

Cut out all that noise, she replied in a whisper that wasn't a whisper. You'll get us lynched. Who's out there?

James-my-man and Ricks. Aunt Harriet, we tired and need to rest our hollow bones.

There was a moment of quiet followed by the muffled beeping of an alarm system and then the sound of several locks turning. The door opened a crack. Light bounced off the gold chain as it stretched in the doorway. A dark, wrinkled face peeked out.

Aunt Harriet, James-my-man pleaded, can these dry bones live? Our bones are dried up and our hope is gone; we are cut off.

Come from the four winds, O breath, and breathe into these slain, that they may live, Aunt Harriet said, and then she closed the door with a heavy thud.

A jangling of sliding chains sounded and then the door opened up and the small woman stood with the darkness of her house radiating outward.

O my people, she said. I am going to open your graves and bring you up from them.

The next morning James-my-man and Rick awoke to a dining room table lined with fluffy waffles and golden brown fried chicken. Rick took a bite from the salty, spicy flesh. It shot a pleasant, and mercifully small, spot of grease into the corner of his mouth. It was the first thing he'd eaten since he'd walked off from his ol' Virginny life (as his father called it) and headed to the highway; a moment into his meal, and Rick felt he was sitting on the verge of the peace he sought.

While they ate, Aunt Harriet hovered, plying her visitors with food and telling stories of running through the South, clutching a baby to her chest. But she didn't do that anymore; too old for running now. She spoke slowly, deliberately, but the tales seemed to come at a rapid pace. They couldn't possibly be true, Rick thought, but they all felt true, it felt as if he had lived them with her. She'd tell a tale and then she'd cackle.

Aunt Harriet cleared the table and was on, probably, her twelfth story, when she stopped and peered into Rick's face.

Boy, you look like somebody I used to know, she said. You from Cross River?

Rick nodded. Trying to get back, he said. Ain't been there in a while.

Me neither. I was there when they founded the town, you know. I was a teenager fresh from the boat, but I remember those as some hella-fied times. I done forgot a lot of things, but I won't never forget them ol' days. I was crouching behind a barrel when them crazy niggers on the plantation was swinging them cutlasses—big things this long. She held her arms far apart. They took old-white-man-what's-his-name's head clean off. That's where they get the saying from, you know the one I'm talking about: Cross River niggers are the craziest! Rick repeated the last part of the phrase with the old woman. I came up with it, you know, she said. Plenty folks take credit for it, but I made it up. I used to argue with folks over it, but all them folks is dead now. Aunt Harriet cackled. Ain't no one to argue with me about it no more. It's the truth, though.

A man grabbed me by the hand, she continued, and led me off that plantation and we followed the Cross River and like that we was free and we settled the town. I was the one who said we should name it Cross River. That damn river looked powerful, strong. It was angry, like it was ready to rise up and reclaim the town. It still like that?

Rick shrugged. I don't know, he replied. I'm trying to see it again one of these days. Soon, I hope.

Well, Godspeed to you, son. Some stupid clown, I think I see his goofy face now, wanted to name the town Heart City or some simple foolishness like that. He was one crazy boy; always talking a bunch of nonsense. Thought he could fly, jumped out a tree and broke his neck and died one day.

She cackled again, her music shrill and amusing, causing her guests to chuckle along. Aunt Harriet's cackle went on for a long time and was punctuated by short gasps. Light sparkled off the gold that covered a few of her front teeth. That was the first time Rick had noticed the jewelry. She briefly lost control of herself, luxuriating in laughter.

But anyway, you remind me of the cutlass-swinging nigger who took me by the hand that crazy night. You move like him, smile like him. It's like he still walking the earth so long as you here. Coulda been your great-great-great-granddaddy.

Her story resembled tales Rick's father used to tell, which were in turn passed down from his father and went all the way back to the ancestor who took part in the Great Insurrection that led to the founding of Cross River. Rick had heard them, or different versions of them, so many times before. Still, he sat there staring at Aunt Harriet as if her stories were brand-new to him.

Aunt Harriet, you're just making all this up, Rick replied. For that to be true, you'd have to be over two hundred years old.

She flashed her yellowish brown teeth and went into the kitchen to wash the dishes and toss their chicken bones in the trash.

When the sun went down and the three of them sat in the living room, reading the newspaper and watching television, a series of thumps sounded at the door. A shadow passed over Aunt Harriet's face and her smile disappeared. She turned out all the lights and removed a black pistol from the hallway closet. As the banging became louder, Rick felt his scrotum tighten. A wave of fear passed up through his stomach and chest, resting finally at the base of his skull.

Aunt Harriet, I'm tired and need to rest my hollow bones, a voice called. Can these dry bones live? My bones are dried up and my hope is gone; I am cut off.

Stop all that damn hollering! Aunt Harriet called.

She opened the door and yanked him inside.

You Nigger Jim? The man nodded. You're late.

He wore ragged burlap pants, a tattered blue polyester shirt, and a straw hat. On his feet, Nigger Jim wore nothing, and as a result, his feet bled and were covered in the road's dirt.

You gon' say the rest? he asked.

She waved her hand, sucked her teeth, and walked away.

Oh Lord, James-my-man mumbled toward Rick. Here come one of these crazy niggas who think you gotta keep everything one hundred percent accurate to re-create the Underground Railroad. These fools are like Civil War reenactors or some shit; no understanding that the past is the present. Watch this nigga; I bet he do the Forgotten Tunnel too.

Rick only half listened. He stared at the bleeding feet of the walking absurdity before him.

Sometime after midnight Aunt Harriet went off to bed. May the spirit of the Great Insurrection always be with you, she said as she walked off. The three men climbed the stairs into the cramped attic. Each man claimed a patch of insulation as his bed. Rick felt the cold nipping at his fingertips and he buried them between his head and the fluffy pink padding.

Fellas, James-my-man said, that cotton field party is gonna be some big shit this year.

This party—think the Lizard can get me some brains? Nigger Jim asked. I'd fight a whole box of matches for a chance to get some brains.

There'll be head for everyone, James-my-man replied. The Lizard of God will see to it. Head and love. The Lizard of God got an army of women to give us head and love. Our cold hearts gonna start beating again. Watch.

You know what I like about the Lizard? James-my-man continued. Don't shit scare him. The nigga's unflappable. Got a lot of courage. I wish I could get like that. I asked him how I could be like him. You know what this nigga said? Get a gun. Dude said he gonna sell me one at the party. Ain't that something?

The comment was so strange that both Rick and Nigger Jim embraced silence.

Rick felt the urge to talk to his new roommate so as not to appear rude. He called out: Say, Nigga Jim—

Excuse me, Ricks, this is a small thing, but it's Nigg-er with an *er*, not with an *a*, Nigger Jim replied. Nigg-er, Nigg-er, Nigg-er . . .

And that's how Rick drifted off to sleep that night.

Some hours passed—Rick was not sure how many—and he was woken from his sleep by heavy feet stamping up the stairs. He sprang from the depths of his slumber, gasping deeply as he sat up. The door swung open and slammed against the floor. A shadowy head peeked up through the entrance.

Y'all gotta go! A voice shouted. Y'all gotta go now!

It was Aunt Harriet, her head in the attic's entrance floating there like a dark balloon.

Wha-what's going on? Rick asked.

James-my-man gathered his clothes, scurrying about in the tiny attic.

Look alive, guys, he said. We gotta bounce.

Nigger Jim snatched his straw hat from the floor and slapped it onto his head. Rick slipped his red boots onto his feet. Before long the three men were in James-my-man's Impala as it zig-zag-zigged through the neighborhood. James-my-man crunched pills like peanuts. He jiggled the bottle about as an offering and both Nigger Jim and Rick shook their heads.

Relaxation escaped Rick, as they drove on backstreets and through remote neighborhoods (to shake any slave-catchers who might be following, James-my-man, said). Rick's blood churned like angry German shepherds were on his heels. James-my-man shook the bottle of pills at him again, but Rick refused. Suit yourself, James-my-man replied.

Sometime during the ride Rick asked if they were heading to Cross River now, just to be sure, and James-my-man told him that the next stop was the big party in the cotton field at the edge of Cross River. Rick breathed deeply in relief. Soon he'd be home. He turned around to speak to Nigger Jim, but found him gently snoring in the backseat.

When Rick faced toward the front, he heard Nigger Jim say, Well, nigga, what you want?

I thought you were 'sleep.

You want something or not?

Rick looked again at Nigger Jim. His eyes remained closed, and his chest rose and fell in the manner that looked to Rick like sleep breathing.

Uh, Rick said. So you a big Mark Twain fan, huh?

What? Nigger Jim said. Who's Mark Twain?

He's an auth— I mean, your name—

My name? Lotsa niggas named Nigger Jim. It's a common name!

Oh. That makes sense, I guess. Isn't it weird that you and James-my-man have similar names?

James-my-man, what's this nigga, Ricks, talking about? Nigger Jim didn't open his eyes, but he turned to the side and used his hands as a pillow. Though his eyes were shaded by his eyelids, Rick could tell he rolled them in disgust. My name is Nigger Jim, his is James-my-man. The names don't even hardly got nothing in common.

You know, James, Jim?

Uh, yeah? They're different names. Where did you find this dude, James-my-man? You can be weird up there, Ricks, I'm 'sleep.

I'm not following either, Ricks. I guess it's okay. We need weird, psychopathic thinkers if we're going to outsmart whitey. I survived out here on all these trips by my wit and with a little help from some friendly race-traitors.

Nigger Jim snored loudly now while James-my-man went into a story about the Quakers who put him up for a month one trip through the Underground Railroad when his planning went awry and he ran out of money. Those Quakers were always the last stop before Canada, James-my-man said.

This story led to one about a Quaker he went to high school with.

He was a cool dude, James-my-man said. The Quakers always been helping us out on the Underground Railroad since way, way back. We used to have a saying in high school: Quakers ain't crackers—

James-my-man, Rick said. This is a really shitty story.

They're all shitty stories, James-my-man replied, but they're all true. He paused. It's not like you have any stories to tell. Oh yeah, I never finished the one about Coon W. Calhoun. Where was I?

One of Nigger Jim's snores turned seamlessly into a set of words: You telling him about Coon W. Calhoun? That was some fucked-up shit.

So the newspapers started writing about him all the time, James-my-man said. They had essays and editorials calling for his head. Then there was one, I'll never forget it, the headline was: "Coon Calhoun Needs to Be Lynched." It was in big bold letters! Man, I couldn't believe the newspaper would be so blatant.

Nigger Jim farted as if to comment on James-my-man's story and then he started to snore again.

So anyway, James-my-man continued, he go out there one morning, a Thursday morning. Dancing like usual; a big-ass smile on his nigger-lips, singing some little kiddie song or something, and all the children and their mothers are standing around. People putting money in his hat and his greasy blackface is sweating and shit, his chest is moving fast up and down because he's out of breath. Then there's some commotion. Somebody's yelling some shit. There's a guy in a blue denim robe and a blue pointy denim hood with two eyeholes cut out. Those were the meanest, most soulless eyes I ever had the misfortune of seeing. He walks right up to Coon Calhoun, and blaow! Pops a hole right in the man's chest.

Damn, Rick said.

Yeah, they never caught the dude neither. I'll never forget his ashy brown hand wrapped around that big black gun. And Coon Calhoun lying there in this big-ass pool of blood. And then the gang war started right after that.

Gang war?

Yeah, man. Well, obviously the dude that shot him was from the Krip Klux Klan, but that's Dustland Willie Lynch Mob territory. You can't roll up on another gang's turf and start popping niggas. Plenty people got lynched over the death of Coon W. Calhoun. Plenty people. They was cutting Krip Klux and Willie Lynch Mob niggas down from trees for weeks. It wasn't safe around there for a real long time. I thought I was a tough guy, but you ain't see me out there a lot during that time. Some niggas like lynching, but I just watch 'em hang. You know what I'm saying? I wasn't scared or nothing, mind you, but I kept my head down. But the same newspaper that was saying Coon W. Calhoun need to be lynched then turned around and was like, Stop the violence. It was absurd, man. They ain't even miss a beat; ain't acknowledge that they was the main ones calling for Coon W. Calhoun's head, inciting violence and shit. They called that nigga *a beloved street entertainer.* Crazy.

Nigger Jim, who now sat with his back flat against the seat and his eyes closed, mumbled, Man, you forgot to tell Ricks about the funeral.

Oh, yeah, that's the best part. So there had been all this commotion about him wearing blackface and shaming our people and all that shit, but that's just how he was.

What you mean?

His face. He ain't have no makeup on it, no burnt cork, no grease, no lipstick, no nothing, that's what the nigga really looked like. That's who he was.

What? You shitting me, man.

I kid you not, jack, James-my-man said, reaching for the glove compartment. He took out three photographs. In them a man in a tuxedo lay in a casket, his arms resting across his chest. White gloves covered his fingers, and his face was black as newly laid tar, his lips red as fresh-spilled blood, with a smile as wide as a watermelon slice.

I keep this shit in here to show people, James-my man continued. I be telling folks, but don't no one believe me. See with your own eyes, though.

Rick took the photos into his hands.

This ain't real.

You should have seen his kids, Ricks. They looked just like him. His wife too. Eyes all bugged out and shit. It was the craziest thing. She said that's just what people look like where they're from.

Stop fooling around, Rick said. Be serious.

I am being serious. I wouldn't believe it either if I ain't seen it myself, but look at the photos.

This is ridiculous.

It was more than ridiculous. It was sad, really. He was the only income that family had. That man just did what he knew how to do. Some Negroes was like *good* when Coon got shot, but damn, that's some cold-blooded shit to say when you look at them little tar-faced children.

Man, get this shit out of here! Rick said, throwing the photos to the floor. You expect me to believe this? You must think I'm a fool.

It's true, Ricks, James-my-man said with a wink. Every word of it. Even the parts I made up. Especially the parts I made up.

When they got to the party, their joints felt stiff. Music played in the distance. Nigger Jim adjusted his straw hat and wondered aloud if this was the place to get some good brain. He said: Some brain'll help relax our joints, right? James-my-man smiled and nodded, kicking at the yellow dust beneath their feet and dropping a fistful of pills into their open palms. They walked in the direction of the plantation and its glowing rich-green cotton field.

Let these vitamins take away your drowsiness and pain, James-my-man said. My friends, here we are in the promised land. A place to get some love for a creaky heart and some cranium on the side. Now to find the Lizard.

Rick's limbs felt heavy, and if he rested them, he would sleep the whole night. He popped some pills into his mouth and chewed as James-my-man had done over and over. Rick lit a cigarette to blunt the bitter taste and offered Nigger Jim one.

Nigger Jim swallowed his pills, screwed his mouth into a disgusted frown, and shook his head at Rick.

What I look like, smoking them things? Nigger Jim said. Nasty-ass tobacco, he mumbled and then paused. We used to pick it, now they want us to smoke it?

Our ancestors used to pick cotton too, Rick replied.

I don't wear no damn cotton.

As he stood near the bursting cotton buds, the world began to shift and rock for Rick. The cotton spoke to him, but that was absurd, so he didn't listen. Music blared from speakers. People in glistening blackface and shimmering red lips passed and greeted him with wide coon smiles. Are they wearing makeup, Rick asked himself, or is their blackface natural like Coon Calhoun's? But that was a silly thought, so he let it escape from him. He looked all around, his expression changing from amusement to shock to horror. One coon, a woman, handed Rick a large forty-ounce bottle of malt liquor, Crazy Ninja. He smiled and took the heavy bottle into his hand, wondering if, this time, he'd drink it all, or would he surrender somewhere in the middle, right where the alcohol, as usual, filled his bladder to capacity? Rick began to feel tired, so he popped a few more pills into his mouth and swallowed, washing them down with the malt liquor. Soon he lost track of Nigger Jim and James-my-man. He looked around for them, but quickly lost interest.

Next to him was a skinny East African man who stood about six and a half feet, but slowly he grew to eight or nine feet. Next to the East African man was a drunk, short, dark-skinned man with an impish smile and pointy elf's ears. He held a lollipop in one hand, a bottle of Crazy Ninja in the other. And next to the munchkin-like man was a tallish guy with an oblong, football-shaped head that became longer and longer each time Rick looked at it.

It must be the pills, he thought. All this weirdness. It must be the pills. The man with the oblong head turned to Rick: You all right, man? Rick nodded, standing still to look as normal as he could. The man's head grew. It turned into a watermelon with eyes and a mouth. Rick took a sip from his forty.

The short, drunken man pointed to a far-off stage where a group of rappers performed. He screamed like a lunatic, Man, I can do better than that:

There's some bitches in this bitch
lotsa titties in this bitch
there's some ass in this bitch
I want to fuck that bitch.

The man's friends laughed. Their smiles turning grotesque, bending out of shape until their faces resembled snarling wolf muzzles. Rick didn't laugh. Some things, like the silly songs on the radio, were too ridiculous to parody. Rick shook his head at the outlandishness of it all, hoping he'd never be as pathetic as this ludicrous munchkin. The man's friends joined the chant.

Nothing looked as it should. Rick's brain, the back of the left side, wildly throbbed. He closed his eyes, placed his right hand on his forehead so that the bottom of his palm rested on his shut eyelids, and rubbed his hand back and forth, producing a small yawn but no ease to the pain.

He felt he had lost control of his high. But wasn't the point of a high to lose control? All he wanted was for the visions to stop. Rick put down the forty. It couldn't be helping. He heard a voice, a soft female voice that sounded vaguely like creaking guitar strings. The voice asked if he was all right. Rick looked up and there stood a woman who, before his eyes, turned into a giraffe. He maintained a straight face and ignored her transformation, telling himself it wasn't real. Anyway, she was a pretty giraffe, a graceful giraffe, not awkward like many he had seen at the zoo or on nature shows. Each time Rick looked away she switched shades, becoming a giraffe of a different color—first white, and then purple, and next a rust color, and again she changed turning now yellow. He marveled at her as she spoke, but the woman didn't seem to notice at all; instead she chattered quickly, rapidly flapping her giraffe muzzle, telling Rick all about herself. She said she had gotten a degree in biology from Negro University and had hoofed her way to a middle manager position at some corporation somewhere.

She stopped speaking and twisted her muzzle into a frown and whispered, These parties are becoming so low-class.

Naked children, dusky little Sambos—uncombed birds' nests resting on their heads, pancake lips flapping behind them as they ran, and their skin as shiny black as a glowing midnight sky—swept by like a breeze. They ran around and around and around until they became a blur and then dissolved into a black puddle. The giraffe shook her head, but Rick could barely see it way up there.

Do you understand what I'm talking about? the giraffe asked, touching a hoof to the crook of his arm. Rick nodded, though he had heard very little of what she'd said. I find it very hard to explain that I'm different. Know what I mean?

Then she frowned and pointed a hoof at the munchkin and his friends, who were still chanting. She said: I might do the Forgotten Tunnel next year if the Underground Railroad is going to be so classless.

Rick felt people looking over their shoulders at him. Some stared outright. If the giraffe had noticed, she didn't let on, as she continued speaking. He looked at all the people who suspiciously eyed him; they went through millions of years of evolutionary history before his eyes. They turned into apes, except they had wings. And soon Rick realized what science hadn't figured out yet: that humans, apes, and birds all shared a recent common ancestor that still roamed the earth and what he was seeing was the undiscovered missing link. What made them eye him so angrily? Rick wondered. Perhaps the giraffe was someone's girlfriend or wife. Rick stepped away, telling the giraffe he needed to find his friends and that he'd soon return, but she followed along as if she hadn't heard him. The apes passed stealthily overhead, dipping between the clouds, blending with the night sky, but since Rick spotted them, to him they were as conspicuous as a swarm of swooping and screeching bats. Maybe they were police, watching him, waiting to dive in, snatch him, and fly him off to jail. As long as he didn't let on that he saw everything as it was, Rick thought, they wouldn't risk bothering him.

He crunched some more pills and watched the giraffe. Rick paused his gaze on the beauty of her long neck, but soon he looked through the crowd for Nigger Jim and James-my-man. He wondered if they had found the Lizard.

There was some commotion in the audience, cheering and clapping in the direction of the stage. Rick turned to see some women in thongs and little else shaking their bare rippled ass cheeks to music that was so loud it sounded like slaps against flesh and like fists smashing bone. Rick didn't take his eyes from the stage because the women were the only things that weren't distorted versions of themselves. And to be honest, he enjoyed the music, though he told himself he shouldn't.

Everything around him morphed into something fascinating but irrational. Rick closed his eyes and when he opened them, the women had become just enormous asses atop legs. There was a disembodied pair of breasts floating between the asses. The music ended and the body parts left the stage.

The host of the show was a comedian who hadn't made a funny remark in years. He looked into the crowd, saying nothing, just clutching the microphone in front of his mouth as if about to speak. A hush fell over the crowd. His lip curled and then he said this: You disgust me. A cheer went up from the crowd. They calmed and he continued. What the hell is wrong with you? I'm embarrassed by yooooohoooo! There was more cheering and laughter. He paced back and forth, his monologue becoming more and more incoherent.

Educate 'em, brother, educate 'em! a voice screamed from the crowd.

Eventually the comedian gave up speaking and began spitting into the audience. Saliva-faced people cheered. The giraffe waved her hoofed limbs in approval.

Isn't this the guy who drugged all those women? Rick asked.

Umm-hmm, the giraffe said. He drugged me once, but look, no one else is saying what needs to be said.

Rick's head felt as if it were falling apart piece by piece. When he looked back to the stage an R&B singer was peeing into the audience and the crowd responded to his urine with rapturous and blissful screams. A voice told Rick to crunch more pills, so he did.

Some winged gorillas took the stage. They were decked in diamond-studded nooses that hung from their necks and grazed the floor. As they performed, roaming about, chanting nonsense, the munchkin and his two friends stood behind Rick cackling.

Man, show these niggas how it's done, the East African said to the munchkin.

How your verse go again? the man with the watermelon head asked. The munchkin screamed:

There's some bitches in this bitch
lotsa titties in this bitch
there's some ass in this bitch
I want to fuck that bitch.

The giraffe shot the munchkin a rageful glance. To which he responded, Why you wanna look so angry, ma? You not havin' a good time?

She craned her neck around, lowering it so that she stared eye to eye with the munchkin. You little ignorant no-class bastard, she said. I swear, some people are so savage they deserve to be in chains.

The East African and the guy with the watermelon head took up the chant while the munchkin and the giraffe screamed over one another. The voices turned into a single stabbing noise that increased the throbbing inside of Rick's skull. He wanted the noise to stop. He wanted everything to stop. Nigger Jim and James-my-man appeared at Rick's side just as the noise had reached a peak.

Where you been at? James-my-man asked.

Wha-what the fuck did you give me? Everything looks strange. Is this how you see the world, my-man?

James-my-man threw his head back and slammed his hands together.

That's some good-ass shit, right? We're just beginning to see the world as it's supposed to be seen, Ricks. I got a whole trunk of the shit. If it was up to me, everybody would see through all the bullshit. There'd be no reason to lie anymore. I'm gonna sell as much as I can here and then we gonna move the rest of the stuff over in Canada. Everyone will experience what we know, for a price.

What? That's what this is all about? I followed you.

Yes, I'm showing you the way. Who told you I got to be broke to lead you, man?

You can't serve the people and my-man at the same time.

Rick didn't know where these last words came from. He stumbled away. Everything he had seen burned holes in his eyes. The munchkin and the giraffe were locked in an eternal battle of wills. The giraffe didn't notice that Rick had wandered from her.

James-my-man followed Rick and slipped his arm around his shoulder.

Man, for now, screw any petty beef we got, James-my-man said. We got bigger fish to fry. I found the Lizard of God. Soon we'll be calling Nigger Jim Sigmund Freud for the way he gets brains. And we can get some love to get our old tin hearts going again, but me and Nigger Jim can't do it alone. We're short on dough and the Lizard of God has some top-notch hoes. I could sell some vitamins, but that would take time and we need the money now. So, if you throw in some cash we can takes these birds into the cotton field and have a real party.

When Rick turned to look at the person James-my-man had identified as the Lizard, he didn't at all look like a lizard or even a man. He looked instead like a snake, a giant cobra with a broad purple hat and protruding poisonous platinum fangs. He wore a paisley zoot suit flanked by a cape. The snake even had the audacity to have a pair of brown snakeskin shoes sitting there underneath the part of his snake belly that hoisted him off the ground as if he had feet. A pair of disembodied hands clad in white gloves floated in front of him. The right one held a scepter, the left one an oversized diamond-studded golden chalice. Floating female fancy parts hovered about the Lizard's head. Hey there, Ricks-my-man, the Lizard called. What you want to do, barbecue or mildew?

In the name of God the Father, his Son and the Holy Ghost, the Lizard continued, I say unto you, Ricks: make your next move your best move. He pointed his scepter at Rick. Your man Freebird—here the Lizard pointed his scepter at James-my-man—said you looking for a home, and I'm the only home you need, my nigga. Don't just stand there clicking your heels, Dorothy. I say, come unto me and you'll find a home with the Lord. Pay no attention to my earthly exterior, for I speak with His voice. Give unto the Lord what is His. Do this and I will provide for your prosperity, salvation, and everything else you seek, starting with my flock here. See them? These some whores of a different color. Pick any color you like. The Lizard pointed to the floating female body parts, which shifted pigmentation before Rick's eyes. Follow the yellow-tit hoes, he said.

This is a nightmare. I need to wake up, Rick mumbled to himself, turning from the Lizard, who at that moment was ascending toward an opening in the clouds, propelled upward by a panoply of floating breasts, which he held on to by strings that dangled from the rising tits. I can't get out of this damn nightmare!

Rick's head felt as if it had crumbled. He shook it side to side. The pain pinged about his skull. His brain was too big for its casing. In front of him appeared the spirit of Coon W. Calhoun in full top hat, tuxedo with tails, white gloves, greasy blackface, and red niggerlips.

Rick, Coon said, lay your body on the broken machinery that keeps this whole mad circus going until it stops moving, until it snaps apart. Let them damn gears and springs fall all over the damn place!

Coon, Rick replied, I'm one man and them law-enforcing apes is watching. I can't let them know that I see things as they are and not the façade.

Rick looked at James-my-man and then at Nigger Jim; their faces had turned grotesque, pitch-black, with hideously swollen crimson lips. They now wore tuxedos with tails, top hats, and white gloves. The same was true of the giraffe and the three drunken hecklers.

Rick looked at the faces of the people that milled about: they too had grown monstrous and slate-black, their lips twisted in ugly, pained grins. The gorillas flying overhead also seemed to be wearing blackface, their lips reddened and protruding. Everyone all around Rick was now in blackface and ill-fitting tuxedos, from those who calmly strolled by, to the folks at the bar getting drinks, to the people that jigged about to the music, making their gloved hands shake so that the dance floor looked like a sea of fluttering white butterflies.

Falling to his knees, Rick held his ears as the pain shot back and forth between them and he screamed an anguished, horrid, piercing scream.

At that moment, he felt everyone staring at him as if he were the absurdity. Their eye sockets were widened so that their eyeballs protruded from their heads like the eyes of cartoon characters.

Rick felt his own eyes widen as he glanced at his hands: they were covered in white gloves and, as much as he tried, he couldn't remove them. A top hat rested atop his head. A poorly fitting tuxedo smothered his joints, high-water pants choked his crotch, and the jacket's tails flapped about with every movement.

Rick dashed across the plantation, struggling to pull off the jacket or the hat, but they wouldn't budge. The only thing he could think to do was keep running, so he did, moving stiffly, careful not to split his new pants.

He burst through the Big House doors and stumbled into the great room, where he peered into a huge mirror that hung from the far wall. Staring back was a face like fresh tar, bulging white eyes, and protruding red lips twisted into a smile not his own.

SPECIAL
TOPICS IN
LONELINESS
STUDIES

I'll probably have a future of stress,
be depressed and stay alone.
But as far as the present time, it's on.

—STIC.MAN, "THE PISTOL"

It's terrible to be alone with another person.

—T. S. ELIOT,
HE DO THE POLICE IN DIFFERENT VOICES

I.

The Fall

—

1. FALL SEMESTER, 2018

Dr. Reginald S. Chambers, flustered and red-cheeked, looked from left to right at the campus police officers clutching his arms. He wanted to shout, Unhand me! as a character in an old movie might shout, but the most he could muster were soft, breathy clicks from the back of his throat.

Should we still do the reading from the Hudson book for next class? a student called as the officers escorted Dr. Chambers through the doorway. He wasn't sure if he should regard the remark as a joke or a moment of idiocy, so he replied, As always, check the syllabus. The woman officer to his right shoved him hard as if to say, *Shut the fuck up!*

Before Chambers could get his bearings, he was pushed out the double doors into the bright early September and deposited chest-first onto a sidewalk in front of the Meratti Business Building. The street—Freedman's Place—was a strip of public land cutting through the private but open campus of Freedman's University. Dr. Chambers looked up at the barrel chest of the male officer and then at his face. He remembered suddenly—as if memory were a hot bluish white beam striking his brain—that the man had been his student many years ago. This, Dr. Chambers thought, this is what this man has chosen to do with my teachings?

I'm sorry, Dr. Chambers, the man said. I'm just doing my job.

Dr. Chambers remembered the man's voice. The man was but a boy back then, recruited for his size to perform gladiatorial feats on the football field. The boy's mind—so beautiful in the way it dissected Shakespeare's poetry. He came to class one day shaking and nearly wilted into a ball, a simple-minded gentle giant. The complex and thoughtful sentences of his essays replaced by spare and artless proclamations.

This concussion, Doc, the boy had said. I'm trying, Dr. Chambers. I love this class. I'm not blowing off the work. Really, I'm not. I love this class and I'm really, really trying.

Dr. Chambers remembered the kindness he showed those many years ago, giving the boy the A he was on target for before the concussion, rather than the C his addle-headed work had truly earned him.

Now the male cop left the sidewalk to stand firmly on campus grounds in front of the Paul Robeson Theatre with his arms folded next to a sculpture—a metal black monolith whose top half turned to fingers reaching skyward.

The female cop bent toward the sitting Dr. Chambers and handed him a flimsy yellow sheet of paper. Please remember, she said, you are suspended from campus until further notice. This is the second time, Dr. Chambers, that we've had to escort you from in front of your class.

Second time? he thought. I don't remember the first. Ah, Monday. The start of the semester. It was a different class, an early morning class; the students looked so fresh-faced.

If this happens a third time, she continued, we will be forced to arrest you, and that will result in further administrative and criminal charges. The entire campus community has been notified to call us if they see you.

The woman pointed to a picture of Dr. Chambers taped to the front doors of the Meratti Business Building, his face blown up like a criminal on a wanted poster. Even he had to admit he looked sinister.

Frankly, I would have arrested you today if it weren't for Lamar. Dr. Chambers watched the woman blankly. She sighed. Officer Smith. Your former student! She sighed again.

In the distance, the bell in the library tower tolled ten times.

May I rest here awhile? Dr. Chambers asked.

You can sit here or on any public street adjacent to campus as long as you want, but if you stick a toe on my campus, I will arrest you. Do you understand?

Dr. Chambers nodded. The female officer lumbered off, like a dinosaur, he thought.

Hey, he called. Hey. Who's going to be teaching my classes?

English, right? She turned and smirked and snickered a bit. Anybody. Some homeless guy off the street.

• • •

The officer wasn't far off, actually. Dr. Simeon Reece lived in the basement of the Communications Building. It had once been the morgue when the building was the school's teaching hospital. Campus security generally turned a blind eye to Dr. Reece, but when police swarmed the school, say when a dignitary visited or if the cops just felt like doing their jobs, Dr. Reece had a hole near the Chemistry Building he could climb into undisturbed. It was warm most of the time, but could become frigid in the winter. Once, near his hole, he actually burned his three diplomas for warmth.

Look, this is all bullshit. How do I know so much about Dr. Reece? Slip the mask. It is I, Dr. Simeon Reece. How do I know so much about Dr. Chambers? No, I am not also him. There will not be a twist at the end revealing us as one and the same. I am an academic at heart. I am an intellectual. I live and die and learn through careful research and study, and here I present my findings to you, dear reader. Cool, right? So pull up a chair, grab a cracker, a coffee, a biscuit, a tea, a cookie, a cold twenty-two- or forty-ounce bottle of Crazy Ninja Malt Liquor, or a cool Cross River Rush energy drink and listen as I tell you of the Tragedy of Dr. Reginald Chambers.

2.

To: Dr. Reginald S. Chambers, Assistant Professor— Department of English and Cultural Studies <RChambers @Freedmans.edu>

Sent: September 28, 2018, 9:54 a.m.

From: Dr. Jason Oliver, Chair—Department of English and Cultural Studies <JOliver@Freedmans.edu>

Cc: Dr. Sarah Bridge, Provost <SBridge@Freedmans.edu>; Dr. Shana J. Greene, Dean—College of Arts and Sciences <SJGreene@Freedmans.edu>

Bcc:

Subject: Grade Appeal and Employment Defense Documents

Dear Dr. Chambers,

It's been three months and six days since I requested materials related to your teaching of last spring semester's *ENGL 101: Special Topics: Loneliness.* As you know, this theme was never properly submitted to the Faculty University Committee's Departmental Activities Team for Scholarly Honors & Independent Themes and your surreptitious teaching of the course was wholly unauthorized. As I've noted previously, several students have lodged complaints, both formal and informal, about your teaching methods, classroom style, and grading, most notably Rebecca Montana, a freshman English major. As you know, the university has

initiated proceedings to strip you of tenure and to revoke your
employment. We are nearing the end of our review period and
have not received a single document in response from you.

By now you should have received Ms. Montana's complaint
and supporting documents as well as a memo from the
provost outlining the administrative charges against you.
It's imperative that you submit all materials (syllabi, writing
prompts, copies of Ms. Montana's assignments, and any other
documents you created for students over the course of the
semester) to my office by COB on Friday. If you fail to do so I
have been instructed by the provost to direct the Committee
to begin deliberating on all complaints against you without
your input. It is in everybody's best interest that we avoid such
a scenario.

Respectfully,
Dr. Jason Oliver
Chair
Department of English and Cultural Studies
Freedman's University
x3202

3. FALL SEMESTER, 2017

I suppose there is a beginning, and that's where I should start. This was many months—a whole lifetime—before Dr. Chambers's *legendary* Special Topics in Loneliness course. Just a lovely and blisteringly cold fall semester. Red ivy crept all along the buildings; from a distance, when the sun struck just right, it appeared as if someone had set the structures ablaze.

I was there when he conceived the class. You could call me the Catalyst—that would be my name if I were a rapper instead of a scholar; but, alas, I'm no rapper. I'm cursed with an academic life. The spark was lit, I think, not the moment in his office when he cried fat tears and I spoke him back from the abyss and he left determined (by my encouragement) to teach the course he had always dreamt of—no, the true spark was lit the first moment we met.

I was teaching in a classroom across from Dr. Chambers. We walked into the hallway at the same time one day, and when he squinted upon seeing my face, I figured the jig(aboo) was up, my cover blown all to hell. Thinking quickly, I stuck out my hand to meet his.

Hey, brother, I said. How the hell are you? Name's Reece. Just started here. Love the family vibe of this campus. Has it always been like this? When the job opened up I applied with the quickness. I'd been teaching over in Port Yooga, but this is closer to home. Glad as hell to be here.

What I said was true enough, I suppose, though I wasn't really new to the Freedman's campus, quite the contrary; I taught my classes here frequently, usually in a different building. I worried about the administration catching on to me, so I hopped buildings frequently, crisscrossing the campus. Each semester I was also on the hook for two courses at Cross River Community College and one at the University of Port Yooga. I never went to them and entered bogus grades at the end of every semester. The schools paid me (very little) just as they would if I had shown up. No one complained, so I figured no harm done. It would be me who'd be truly harmed if I actually journeyed to those campuses clutching books to my chest ready to teach. With the low pay and travel involved—I'm no mathematician, but some back-of-the-envelope computations revealed that I'd actually lose money if I got on the bus and trudged to those classes week in, week out. It was better for everyone this way.

Hi, I'm Dr. Chambers—uh, Reggie, I mean. He shook my hand vigorously. I been here about eight years. The family vibe is nice. Students are kind of zoned out sometimes, I guess. I was like that as an undergrad, I guess. I teach composition and some lit.

Nice, nice. I'm teaching lit as well.

Oh, so you're in English?

No, Interdisciplinary Studies. I get to teach any way I want. Hey, I'll see you around.

I nodded and walked slowly away. More talking, and I risked blowing down my house of cards. Somehow I always had students, even though my courses weren't officially offered by the university. No idea where they came from. I just set up shop every semester in an empty classroom and start lecturing. Meanwhile, wide-eyed students slowly bubble in. Four, some semesters five, full classes a day, which can be a bitch because it involves grading so, so many papers. I teach standard texts alongside excerpts from long imaginary works I write myself. I tell my students the works are lost semi-mystical and transformative Cross Riverian texts. I speak of them with reverence and awe. Great fun all around. I've been doing this for a while now. I've pulled it off mainly by keeping my profile low around campus and speaking only to my students. There was something about Dr. Chambers's sad, sad eyes, though. Made me talk to him even when it made no sense at all to do so.

4.

To: Reggie <Blacker.Roland.Hudson@gmail.com>
Sent: September 28, 2018, 10:18 a.m.
From: Jason Oliver <Jason.Jerome.Oliver@gmail.com>
Cc:
Bcc: Dr. Sarah Bridge, Provost <SBridge@Freedmans.edu>;
Dr. Shana J. Greene, Dean—College of Arts & Sciences
<SJGreene@Freedmans.edu>
Subject: (No Subject)

Reg,

I just sent a message to your campus email. I know you are on "sabbatical" and I know professors tend to rarely check their campus email while away . . . look, Reggie, of course this is difficult for you, but I don't think you realize how difficult it is for me too. You have to defend yourself and you must submit the documents. There is no way I can help you if you ignore us and ignore the process. I'm writing you as a friend, not as the Chair.

I'd rather you be on campus doing what it is you do best— I'm sure you feel the same way—but trust in the process.

When this nonsense is over and things are back to normal for everyone, we can catch us a game or a show and we'll drink some beers like we used to. Please take care of yourself. And for god's sake get yourself a fucking lawyer. Geez.

J

5. FALL SEMESTER, 2017

I couldn't help but peek in on Dr. Chambers sometimes. If he had a class and I had a free period I would spend that time lurking outside. He reminded me of myself maybe ten years previous. I thought of back then as the time my soul became *bent*. The future no longer stretched out ahead of me a long bright road to the Emeraldest of cities. The Wizard had not yet been exposed, but the flying monkeys swarmed, and I should have known we would all soon recognize him as a fraud. The Wizard in this metaphor is me, but it's also Freedman's University, and also the educational system as a whole. The Wizard is everyone. The Wizard is everything. The Wizard is everywhere.

Dr. Chambers often began class low-energy and thick-tongued. He'd end class rejuvenated and quick-witted, springing to life in the last minutes. I knew this pattern well. I used to teach here at Freedman's, you know. I mean, I once taught legitimately on the payroll and everything. I taught a 4/4 in those days. The joke we had was that our teaching load also doubled as the type of gun we dreamt of shooting ourselves with by the middle of the semester. I was on a year-to-year contract then. The school dangled hope of a tenure-track job out in front of me like a candied carrot, all the while shoveling student after student atop my head, burying me in students—just raining them down on me like cemetery dirt, packing them into my classroom like sardines. And that's how they looked to me eventually, headless and greasy.

When my family got evicted from our apartment—because, you know, Freedman's didn't pay me shit even when they did pay me—I wandered campus alone with a bag full of stuff, bleary-eyed from tears (you see, stupidly I still gave a fuck), and I stumbled somehow into the Communications Building late one night. I found it unguarded and the old morgue abandoned. I dropped my bag like an anchor and made my nest.

• • •

When your eyes are truly free you can see the academy for the dystopian wasteland it truly is. The place where they throw so much light into your eyes that your vision is rendered as useless as if you'd stared directly into an eclipse.

It would have taken years for Dr. Chambers's blindfold to fall away, had I left him to his own derangement. He was tenured then, but I knew he'd eventually lose it. He was dumb enough to think his little lectures on literature and loss would do some good, brilliant enough to eventually realize he was a pawn, a cog, a gear; so much rested atop his back making him unable to truly stand, unable to really make something good happen. Soon he'd know that his intellect meant nothing in the face of the world's amoral indifference. I know and I strike, therefore I am. I heard the waver and crack of disillusionment in his voice every time I managed to catch one of his lectures. He was starting to bend. I didn't make it happen. I just accelerated it. Actually, I wasn't even the most important accelerant.

· · ·

It was near midterms in late October—blackface season at the white universities—when I decided that Chambers would become my student.

His hangdog cheeks drooped as if he could no longer control both sides of his face. I became a little sad myself, because I knew he was soon to become even sadder and more thoroughly frustrated, desperate, and even enraged—pushed to the brink and then over into a kind of mental deformity. It was the only way for him to transform into his final and highest incarnation, the man I was priming him to be.

He held a black valise as he walked the hall that day. When I brushed by and knocked it from his hand, scattering papers everywhere, I managed to make the act look casual and accidental, even as I stood frozen at the pictures fluttering through the hallway like a weird snowfall. Screengrabs: naked woman atop naked woman; naked woman licking the spread pink folds of another naked woman; naked woman sucking like a baby the doughy breast of another naked woman; naked woman covered in oil wrestling another naked woman in oil—and on and naked woman on.

Eventually I bent to gather the papers with Dr. Chambers. My plan nearly in ruins by the shock of it all.

My God, Reggie, I'm so, so—

Just give me the papers! His voice a sharp and angry whisper.

I'm so sorry, Dr. Chambers, I mumbled over and over, looking only to the floor.

I thought myself incapable of shame at this point but I felt my sin*
burning red.

Here we were, two men, both desperate to draw no attention to ourselves, on our hands and knees crawling upon the nude inviting bodies of porn actresses.

It's for my research, he muttered as a response to each of my sorries and to every passerby who handed him a sheet of scattered naked woman paper.

Look, I said, let me take you to lunch in the caf.

No, I really should go plan for my afternoon cla—

I insist, Reggie. I feel terrible about this. And if this campus is a family, then we need to hurt each other and perform elaborate apologies.

That got a smile from Dr. Chambers, as I knew it would, and I was correct in thinking that it would take him only a moment to change his mind.

. . .

When we got to the caf, I didn't see my man Chet, the dimwit who worked the registers. He passed me free food whenever the manager wasn't looking. In all my years on the fringes, Chet was the only one who knew of my true nature, after having seen me emerge from the hole one day. He'd brought me a blanket and some sandwiches. I repay him with good conversation. I became pretty adept at swiping food on account of his days off; if I had a little bit of money I'd buy a dollar fries or something and hold a burger or slice of pizza out of sight beneath

---

* Ha! My God! What a glorious typo! I think I'll leave it.

my tray while I paid. Most times I didn't have any money, since every little bit I earned went to my hundreds of thousands in student loan debt. I was completely broke (but yet not broken), so when Chet wasn't there I just snatched some food and walked away cool-like. Today I snatched for two.

Let me pay you for this, Dr. Chambers said over chicken and fries.

No, no, I replied. It's on me.

He filled his mouth and nodded in thanks. Elephant-in-the-room time, he said through a wall of chewed food.

No, no, Reggie, you don't have to expla—*

I'm writing a paper on the surprising aesthetics of various types of *girl-on-girl* pornography and what it tells us about masculinity in the twenty-first century.

I paused my chewing and then righted myself, making sure to hold a steady and neutral facial expression. I thought I'd sized him up good, but I tell you, Dr. Chambers sure did throw me for a loop with this one.

That's interesting, I said. So what are you finding?

Well, it's, uh, well, um (I observed his stammer with interest), it's um, early in my research yet. Very early. I'm looking at bondage, um girl-on-girl domination fantasy, wrestling and catfight videos freely available on the internet and so . . .

(I also observed with interest the way he trailed off.)

Tell me now, bruh, he said. You said you're teaching lit; what sort of things are your students reading this semester?

I'm having students read early twentieth century Cross Riverian fables in the work of Milo Sequoia.

Sequoia?

Oh yes. Not familiar with his work? Chambers shook his head. Most people are not (because he's an invention all my own! Heh heh heh, I wanted to add). We don't read our own work enough. Always looking outside Cross River when we have a whole literary world here. He was a contemporary of Roland Hudson, you know.

I added that last part because I knew Chambers was an admirer

---

* He damn well did have to explain.

of Hudson's poetry. I heard him over and over bringing up the poet's work in class—he spoke Hudson's name in this annoying and reverent faux-poetic register—while his students watched him blankly. It embarrassed me to see him get so twisted up for something as commonplace as words, only for his students to openly sleep and stare into their phones.

I'd love to teach more Hudson, he said. Have so little space on my syllabus as it is, though. Hudson tends to take over when I teach his stuff; I'm talking back-to-back classes on a single line.

Well, you should teach him more. You should. I'll send you some of Sequoia's fabl—

I looked over at Dr. Chambers and noticed he was gazing past me. He stared, it seemed, for thousands and thousands of yards. I turned my head to see where his vision rested. A woman waved. He waved.

As the woman drew near I saw that it was Dr. Shana Greene—Mean Dean Shana Jean Greene—who oversaw the School of Arts & Sciences.

Dr. Chambers, she called. How's the essay coming?

Dr. Chambers grimaced.

Dean Greene, Chambers said. It's going slow. Went back to do more, um, research.

More research, huh? Can't get enough research. How about I see it at the beginning of the spring semester, eh?

Uh, okay. Yeah.

Good. First day back. (I noticed with interest how she smirked at him.) Looking forward to reading, sir.

Dr. Greene walked off, not even cutting me a half glance, and for that I felt both grateful and insulted.

Administration, right? I said when she was far from us. They make my skin crawl.

Yeah. Hey, Reece, I got to go.

We left with a promise to share our work with each other, knowing that would never occur. There was something shaky with Dr. Chambers that I couldn't begin to put my finger on. He was suddenly so wily and squirrelly for no reason that I could see. Something didn't add up, but I had lesson plans to create, classes to teach, papers to grade.

* * *

At least twice a week I'd find Dr. Chambers sitting by himself in the cafeteria, and I'd pull a chair up to his table. He'd smile upon seeing me. Sometimes it was a put-on, sometimes his smile seemed genuine. My chair, as I snatched it preparing to sit, would scrape and squeal against the floor, causing Chambers to cringe. After that his body would become relaxed and it would be just the two of us talking shit. A volley of two conscious minds wading out into the polluted but still nourishing rivers of life. Our discussions ranged widely: music, women (there was an adjunct he appeared smitten with), our classes, poetry (he always, always quoted Hudson), the past, the present. The future never came up.

Sometimes he paid, other times I provided the food. I have to admit here that I am usually very good at getting a handle on people, but even though our conversations flowed freely and easily, complete with natural peals of laughter—this man had made himself a mystery to me.

Sometimes he would say, Reece, you married, got kids?

I'd shake my head and he'd say, Lucky dude. And he'd speak no more about that, turning the conversation instead to rant about Roland Hudson's poetry of loneliness and madness.

Or he'd offer: Sometimes I feel like my shit is falling all apart, like pieces of me blowing right away, man. And that would be it. He normally said this near the end of lunch and we'd scurry off to our classes without addressing all the ways in which he was a straw man falling into little straw pieces.

He seemed cowed by Dean Greene whenever she passed and sneered, reminding him of her deadline. It was bizarre, this shrinking. At odds with everything I needed him to be if we were ever to achieve our perfect rebellion. His eventual breaking could be put to good use to undermine the anti-intellectual edifice our society was constructing in our institutions of *higher learning*. He was to be a bomb left at the base of our dilapidated intellectual life. In essence, he would be another me. A second soldier in the shadow university I was building right in the rotting shell that is Freedman's. Soon we'd have a whole army of ghost professors teaching ghost courses and our alternatively educated students would spread across the globe, undermining all our dead zombie institutions—the media, the governments, institutions of *higher learning*—that dulled our senses. Yes, Freedman's needed to be taken down—the world needed to be taken down—but neither Freedman's nor the world could be taken down by those who were afraid. So, ironically, Chambers in his milquetoast acquiescence to Greene's meager power truly scared me.

I made sure it was a day when I provided lunch that I asked him about Dean Greene's taunting.

After the dean walked by and looked down at the trembling Chambers, I shook my head.

So, I said. Dean Greene?

He grunted quizzically.

She as mean as she seems?

He chuckled and then repeated my rhyme scheme, Is Mean Dean Jean Greene as mean as she seems? Well, she'll scheme to crush your dreams if she's not too keen on your beam . . . uh—ah, fuck it, I can't keep up. She a bitch.

I've never heard of a dean looking over the work of one of her professors. It's—I grasped for words—it's . . . it's so disrespectful.

Yeah, he said, and looked away. He crunched a fry in his teeth. Some people just . . . uh, some people just don't believe I'm really writing this porn paper. They got me pegged as a pervert.

So what are you goi—

You'll have to excuse me, Reece. I need to spend my free time making sure my shit is tight.

I'm sorry to take up all your free time, Doc.

No, bruh, don't apologize. You helped me remember the stakes. I'm gonna throw that fucking essay in her stupid fucking mean smirking face soon.

Let me know when you need a reader.

Chambers nodded and then grabbed ahold of his brown tray and walked off, stepping with fury and determination. I smiled because I knew he was doomed. When the administration has it in for you, there is no coming back. I knew I'd enjoy watching him churn and churn in this limp and futile attempt to save himself and this churning would groom him perfectly for me. It would be painful as well, make no mistake. I liked him, after all. I ate a burger and mumbled to myself.

I need to see this porn essay, I said.

. . .

I had a car once. This was back when I was an *upstanding member of society*, a lecturer at Freedman's. It's gone now. A fat woman papered over the window with thin pink slips, parking tickets, and then I watched as a fat jumpsuited man in a white truck towed it away.

I laugh now at the rage this raised within me.

A few months later when I was no longer an *upstanding member of society* or officially a faculty member at the school, I saw that woman's flat, fat, broad back writing tickets next to a snowbank. My car was long gone then, towed to that great impound lot in the sky. I didn't earn enough to save its life. I trotted over to her, a determined angry young ram, and I struck the broad side of that barn with my shoulder like it had a target painted on it. She went barreling face-first into the snow and I dashed off cackling, a shadow, an apparition of the night.

Dr. Chambers, facedown on his desk holding up one of those thin pink strips of paper, reminded me of myself. What sense does it make to have to pay to be at my goddamned job? he muttered. It's extortion, man.

He sighed, his office strewn with pictures of naked women. On the floors, across his keyboard. He tossed his parking ticket onto the tits of his desk.

I'm sorry, Dr. Reece. I'm not myself, man. You'll have to excuse—

You canceled your classes today.

You see the latest on hatemyprofessor? Chambers turned to his keyboard and rapidly tapped his fingers along the keys. *Dr. chambers does nothing but spot*—I think they mean spout—*bad poetry all class long. i'm mad I chose his class it's going to be a long semester everything about this class is bad*

You canceled your class because of a post on hatemyprofessor?

Why did they even take my class? These people don't care about words. To them words are the shit, the toilet paper, and the goddamn toilet bowl itself.

Come on, man. What's really getting to you, huh, Chambers?

Nothing is going right, Reece. Nothing.

The essay?

The stupid essay. I'm a fraud, Reece. I don't want to write this stupid essay, and furthermore, I can't. That's what it comes down to.

I thought you wanted to throw your findings in the dean's face. What happened to that?

Findings? I have no findings.

He shifted and sighed and rocked about, and every time he moved he knocked aside another porn image.

What about all this?

Look, Reece. It's like this: One day I was sitting in my office after my fourth class and I'm dazed and tired in this little box. This cube I'm in is spinning all around me. I'm floating, rotating through space, dipping between stars, Reece. Head over feet. Feet over head. I don't know what I was thinking. I know what I was feeling, though. You know how it is between sleep and wake. Those lower vibrations, man. Those lower signals, man. Christine can't hear them these days. Not really. She just doesn't listen. She barely wants to hug, most times. She wants to talk about our days and life and boring shit like that, but she doesn't want to fuck. I like the hugging, a bit, I guess. I'm not one for talking too much, she knows that. When I try to get with her she's like, *Why don't you try talking to me outside of when you want something?* And then she tries to talk to me—I mean really droning on, man, drowning me in these long boring drawn-out conversations. She be all frustrated and shit at my silences, but I'm thinking: *If we fucked more often I'd have more to say.* It's a cycle, Reece. I was just burning in that office. Vibrating. And on top of all that, so tired too. I was convinced that if I fell asleep I'd have a wet dream. I had another class to teach that day. What would I look like standing there in front of my students with a big dark wet stain on my khakis, huh? I grabbed my phone and pulled up one of those video sites. Some girl-on-girl stuff. I don't like too much banging, penetration. I don't like penises in my porn most of the time. None of that. I hate dicks. No dudes, just curves. I figured some images would keep me from drifting off and would probably take the fucking edge off, man. I looked at them girls writhing around, slipping and sliding—I can see them now. And then I was done until I got home and could hide out in the bathroom for a little while. Thought I'd never even remember anything about those naked sluts—their word, not mine—but I see every inch of their bodies every day, twirling in my head. It's not sexy or anything, just kind of annoying now. I get an email from Mean Dean Greene the next day summoning me to her office. Like when I was a kid and the principal called me up after I did some shit. I'm like, What I do?

Daaaamn.

Yeah. Damned is right. She sits across from me, her arms folded. Those green eyes narrowing. I'm playing it cool, but my heart is . . . my heart is racing, man. She all quiet until I shrug and shift my body, like, *What?*

Something you would like to discuss with me, Dr. Chambers? No, ma'am, I told her. I meant that in a lot of ways. There was nothing to talk about, since I didn't even remember looking up porn on my phone the day before. Even if I did remember that, I wouldn't want to discuss porn with Mean Dean Shana Jean Greene. *Are you sure, Dr. Chambers? How's your personal life? Everything going well?* I thought of the night before, lying there next to Christine, our bodies touching but all the space in the universe between the two of us. She's horny and I'm horny, but for some reason there's not a thing we can do about it. Ever been like that between you and a woman, Reece? Some wild shit. Again, there is no way I'm discussing this with Mean Dean Jean Greene, so I just say, No, Dean Greene, everything's keen. No, that's not really what I said. Of course I didn't say it like that, but that was the sentiment, you know.

She's watching me. Turning the moment awkward. I can see it in her face, she's hoping I break. She's got her stupid arms folded across her big sloppy floppy tits, and then she slides a paper across the desk as if she's making me an offer. She's like, *How do you explain this?*

I'm like, what the hell is she talking about? I look at the paper, but it's just a bunch of symbols to me. *Can you tell me how someone came to be accessing porn sites under your login?*

Reece, I'm genuinely perplexed now, bruh. I'm turning this paper all around in my hand. So then she says, *And before you tell me that someone must have logged in under your name or something, this access was traced to a cell phone. Your cell phone.*

I was logged into the school's system with my user name and password to access the Wi-Fi, Reece. Can you believe that's what it was, huh? I'm stammering like shit. She looks all proud. She finally has me, you know. I stop, I mean my whole body stops. My heart is still. Blood is not moving through me. I'm not breathing, blinking, twitching, nothing, jack. Then I'm like, Research.

Excuse me?

I know this will sound strange, but I've been doing some research for a paper I'm looking to publish on what we can learn about the male gaze and toxic masculinity from various types of male-centered lesbian—or *girl-on-girl*, if you will—pornography. The absence of men in these works is a defining factor in, uh, these works and an accidental commentary on manhood and, um, masculinity.

You said that?

Hell yeah, I said it! I don't even know where I'm getting this shit from, but I'm pulling it all from my ass like some beads, man, and all she can say is, *Interesting.* And after repeating that word a few times she tries to get me. She says, *Is this related to the research you've been doing on the representations of loneliness in late twentieth century and early twenty-first century American literature?*

So I say, Sure is! Fuck else can I say at this point? I know she don't believe me, but what else can she do? And this lie is the only one I got to save my job.

She's like, *Well, Dr. Chambers. I had to ask. You understand that, right?* I nod. When she dismisses me I breathe finally, relieved, jack. I made it narrowly, man. Then when I'm by the door you know what that mean woman says to me? *I'd really love to see this paper, Dr. Chambers. You know, when it's all done.*

What's that?

When do you think you can have a draft for me to look at? How about the end of the semester? Yes, I can look at it over the break. Give you some feedback before you publish it. There will certainly be a lot of journals who'll want a crack at this if you do it right. You could use my critical eye. We need to keep the level of scholarship high around this corner of the campus, you know. Yes, have it on my desk by the end of the semester. I want a hard copy as well as a digital copy.

I was floored, Reece. The disrespect. The mistrust. I was so full of rage, but I just nodded like a sheep and left that fucking bitch's office. You think she's looking over Samson's poetry before he submits that shit? I got several extensions from her and I'm doing all this research, but everything I'm writing is fucking nonsense. Erotic descriptions of porn overlaid with superficial pseudo-philosophical nonsense.

Dr. Chambers dipped his head low and balled his fists. This is all Christine's fault, he said. Ever notice how different the world looks when you're fucking regularly?

I leaned back in Chambers's lumpy office chair, the squealing springs pressing into my backside making music beneath me. The final pieces in the Dr. Chambers puzzle were set. I now understood him completely. I had questioned my choice of apprentice many times. Should I cut him loose? I often asked, unsure when or if he would even crack. It would have been easy to find another. There was the math professor who taught in full clown makeup and different floppy clown getups each day. His department only tolerated him because every year it's rumored that he'll receive a Fields Medal. Then there is the Women's Studies professor who long ago lost interest in Women's Studies and teaches only physics in her classes no matter what course is assigned to her. They would crack, but not soon enough for me. I'd have to get at them later, perhaps with the help of my new apprentice. Chambers was ripe now and all it would take was a bit of nudging. I'd guide Chambers to the river; it was up to him, however, to drown.

We sat in silence, me contemplating my next words. They would need to be important words. They needed to come out just right.

Look, Chambers. (It was imperative that I sounded stern here.) He raised his chin and watched me. It's important you listen to what I'm about to say. I paused. You're fucked. When an administrator of Dean Greene's stature sets her sights on you, there is no return, no future for you at this institution.

Chambers moaned and grasped his stomach as if a disease had eaten away at his bowels.

This is not a reason for whining or complaint, I continued. It's good news, actually. All it means is that you're free.

Free?

I whispered: As a naked jaybird's dangling balls.

I paused and let the silence hang. Let me ask you something, Chambers. What would you do, what would you teach, if you didn't have to do all this dumb shit?

He watched me for a while and then looked away, staring at the wall. And when he spoke it was as quiet and as gentle as I've ever heard anyone speak.

Loneliness, Reece. Loneliness. It's the core problem of this life. Of what it means to be human. I'd write and teach and think around that.

Then do it, Chambers. What the hell do you have to lose? Teach what you want to teach. Write the essay you want to write. Don't worry that Mean Dean Jean Greene has it in for you. She is going to do what she is going to do regardless. She'll either be successful or she won't, but no one can put your brain to work the way you can. That's priceless. It goes beyond all this red tape and bureaucracy. It goes beyond hate-myprofessor. You're here on this earth to use your brainpower, your considerable fucking brainpower, not for all the rest of this nonsense, all this dancing-with-bureaucrats-and-administrators shit.

I sucked my teeth and waved my hand. He kept shaking his head. I realized our nonverbal tics were having a conversation of their own.

After our body language had its say, Chambers and I sat in silence watching each other. I was determined to let it hang, because those who can't live with silence will always end the stillness by speaking quiet words of desperation, and I needed to hear Chambers's despair.

He sighed. What you're telling me to do is impossible, Reece. It's too late to submit a themed course to the Scholarly Honors & Independent Themes committee—

Dammit Chambers, I screamed, standing up. That's the old Dr. Chambers. The new Chambers moves boldly. Come January you will be teaching whatever the hell you want, and no one will be able to stop you. Write your essay any damn way you please. Throw it up in the dean's face. Doesn't at all matter what happens next. You win by standing up like a goddamn man.

He sat placidly with his hands to his face, but I could feel the fury of the righteous indignation working in him. I stood dramatically and walked to the door.

Well, if you're not going to act, then I have nothing else to—

No, he said reaching out to me. No, Reece. You're right. There's much work to be done—the loneliness class; a better, more real essay—there is some stuff from my draft I can salvage. It has to start now. You're right. Thank you for your insights.

I left Chambers's office that day proud of myself. The exam period rolled in and we prepared final grades, students left the campus to celebrate Christmas with their families, and the quiet turned me inward and contemplative. I sat in silence in my morgue home for hours on end. In my isolation, I felt my mind turning on itself, attacking me with memories and shame. Winter and its cold rolled in with streams of bluish gray and white steam rising everywhere, but it seemed the fall, for Dr. Chambers, wasn't finished. He was that leaf turning a warped deathly brown yet still clinging to the tree, defying all winds and all reason.

II.

Winter Break

—

1. WINTER BREAK, 2017–2018

In the weeks after the fall semester ends, campus turns barren and desolate. It's like nuclear winter has finally come. I rise from my hole or I peek out from the morgue and usually I am the only living thing for miles. I could walk the campus naked if I wanted. Too cold for that, though.

The only person I see around is Chet the dimwit. He brings me fruit and hot tea in the morning if I don't make it to the caf. At noon we sit and talk and lunch out in the open.

One day during lunch after a silent moment, the dimwit leaned his simple head back, pointed his determined chin toward me, and said: So what's the end game, huh, Reece?

I chuckled a bit and shoved the rice around my plate. I'm sure I don't know what you're talking about, I said.

Come on, man. Don't be coy. One of the most brilliant minds in Cross River is living in an old morgue—the place I identified my daddy's remains at after he got killed.

I have plans to topple this temple of brain rot, plans I doubt you can understand.

Maybe so, jack. If I could afford it, I would have been a student here. I wonder, though, if I get more from reading all these books I read—I don't know—but if I had all your education I damn sure wouldn't be living in no hole.

It's overrated outside the hole, Chet. Idra's outside the hole. Joshua. Mary. Grace. Imani. You ever been married, Chet? Had kids?

Yep, they send me here to this damn caf every day.

I was married to two of those names, the rest are my kids— teenagers now, really—and they're all outside the hole, watching for me. Waiting, probably. When I taught here—you know, on the payroll and shit—I figured that one day Imani and Josh and Grace would attend this brain-rot temple for free. They're watching for me, umm-hmm, but I'm not coming back until I do something. Until I topple intellectual Sodom and then I move on to intellectual Gomorrah.

I have no idea what you're talking about, Dr. Reece. Want another piece of cornbread?

Of course you don't, Chet. And of course I want another piece of cornbread. What do you do to make it turn out so fluffy, sweet, and light, huh? Yellow cake of the gods, I tell you. Yellow cake of the gods.

2.

On Christmas Eve, in the cold of the morgue, sitting before my old boxy laptop, drinking hot chocolate stolen from the Journalism

Department's faculty lounge, I decided to send Dr. Chambers a gift: a new Milo Sequoia fable I'd recently *discovered*.

This one had been in my head for a long time, since I'd met Dr. Chambers, in fact, and it evolved as I grew to understand him.

Putting pen to paper—or rather, fingertip to keyboard key, as it were—would take the edge from my waking fever dream, I figured. I imagined that when he heard the ping of the email hitting his box and he sat down to read, my words would fire him up to finish his essay and plan his unauthorized class and thus march himself right into oblivion.

So I wrote:

• • •

The Tragedy of Jardin the Axe-Wielder*

Sometimes the trees speak these words, but most of the time they don't speak. It is said that they only speak when there is a breeze, but I know that to be untrue because I hear them most often when the air is still and sad. This is the story the trees told me on a warm day in which the air sat atop us unmoving.

The older trees of the Wildlands spoke of Jardin the Axe-Wielder† because they knew him and loved him. They knew the Others as well, and they also loved them, but not as they loved Jardin. They knew him as a baby back when his hands were too small and undisciplined to wield axes.

The trees only knew the Others after they had become adults and had felled enemies with knives; with fire; with muskets; with hammers; with poison; with hoes; with pitchforks that once baled plantation hay; with flat, heavy chunks of wood run through with nails; with bare hands weaponized and remorseless. The Others laughed some-

---

* Jardin the Axe-Wielder is somewhat of a folk hero in this town. Every Cross Riverian schoolboy at some point imagines himself as "the firstborn son of Cross River." Of course, this is why I chose him as the subject for my fable, to activate the immature fantasy that Chambers must have once held, that I am sure is still somewhere living within him.

† It's widely debated if a version of the events in this story actually occurred. In myths that are told and retold among Riverbabies, Jardin is a towering warrior-hero. Most known evidence suggests he was born, lived an unremarkable life, and died in anonymity as most of us will.

times and even spoke and moved with joy. But the trees could divine sadness beneath those smiles. The Others climbed the trees and sat for long stretches, armed and often alone, looking out on Cross River, watching for signs of trouble from the white aggressives who lived beyond their borders. *Bddddaaaa!* they'd bellow as a war cry, or they'd roll their tongues in their mouths as idle conversation, and this was their true language. Not far from any joy they had was the horrors they once lived with as a part of the mundanity of life, and not far from those horrors were other horrors, the horrors they had to commit to become free.

The Council of Three spoke just before Jardin's birth back when Cross River was a newborn thing, still covered in the blood and after-birth of insurrection. They said: *We are the blood-drenched, but our children don't have to be.*

The Council of Three is no more, murdered by men whose souls will forever burn in various eternal fires, but when they lived, these murderous ill-intentioned men, their souls remained soaked in rivers and rivers of red, more blood than anyone will ever need. The same could be said for the Council as well, and also for so many of Cross River. After the Council, there were four men who led. The four bastards. The Board. The Rule. The Federal. And the General.* They ruled as tyrants, together and then sometimes at odds, sometimes at war, until the day they lost their heads.

We can leave those tyrants for another time, however. This is not about them. This story is about some who followed. And it is about Jardin. And it is about how followers of the four tyrants twisted the first child of Cross River into a monster—how they washed his pristine soul in blood rivers until it became stained a dark crimson.

It's never the tyrant, not really. It's always those who follow the tyrant. It's they who are the true fist of tyranny. It's they who make this life intolerable.

Jardin was the firstborn child of Cross River.† He was conceived

---

* Now, these were some bad motherfuckers.
† He probably wasn't really the firstborn child of Cross River.

in captivity, and his mother told him his father died fighting in the Great Insurrection. That's true enough. His mother slit the throat of her rapist even as her belly hung low and heavy with the restless, kicking Jardin twisting about inside her. She was determined to take that walk from Port Yooga to the freeland before giving birth.* My baby will not be born on no slave earth, she said. And the midwives delivered Jardin on Cross Riverian soil, right near the roughest waters. It never occurred to Jardin that his father owned his mother and hundreds of others; he grew up imagining his father a tall, handsome, light-skinned man, holding a sword and chopping the heads of those who had enslaved him. His mother did nothing to dissuade his fantasy and when she died of a burning fever near Jardin's ninth birthday, the Others stepped in to raise him. They taught him to sit in the trees and to talk to the bark of the massive flora and to listen when the trees talked back and to look out on the land and to watch for anything strange. And he looked out and stood guard with the Others, and nothing else made any sense. Still, one day, the weight of his mother no longer holding his hand became a weight too heavy to balance. As he sat in the trees in that special way the Others taught, tears leaked from Jardin's eyes and turned his world into a watery blur. Riz, a leader among the Others, put his arm around Jardin, placed a hatchet in his palm, and said, *What you crying for? You crying like you don't got no parents.* Jardin tightened his hand around the hatchet and dried his eyes with his sleeve and he didn't cry anymore after that.†

Riz and the Others taught Jardin the best arcs to swing his hatchet into the face of an oncoming enemy. They built targets for him and clapped every time Jardin tossed his weapon close to the center. *No one's ever swung that hatchet more naturally*, Riz said. *We'll call you the axe-wielder, boy. But you're not proven a man, an Other, a true Other, until*

---

* Now, she, she was a bad motherfucker.

† As I wrote this I felt bees of tears stinging my eyes. I felt my Uncle Joe's arm heavy on my nine-year-old neck just after my father's funeral. I could hear the jangle of his gold chain and see the shine from his Virgin Mary pendant. I could smell the grit of his cologne, the fading German beer on his breath. *What you crying for, little nigga? Stop acting like you ain't got no father.*

you swing that thing in battle. Between you and me, son, I hope you never get a chance to prove yourself.

Jardin nodded, but Riz's words had offended him. *What does this man want?* Jardin thought. *For me to forever remain a child? What if I ride into Port Yooga on a horse and chopped the arm of the first white man I see? I could build a whole new world with these hatchets of mine.* Jardin spent many days in the trees dreaming of this. At times some of the Others would disappear—*attending to business,* they called it. Jardin would sit in the trees with a book. Still a boy. And daily he'd ask for a chance to prove himself, and Riz would counter, *No.* Simply no and nothing else, as if not talking to a fellow Other, but a child.

One day, Jardin sat daydreaming somewhere near the base of a tree when he heard, *Bdddda! Bdddat! Bdddat! Bdddddddddda!* It was unmistakable. Cross River was under attack. Jardin went for his hatchets, two, one for each hand, and started off with the Others. Riz stood with his leader, Thorns, readying their weapons. Riz had a rifle slung across his back and a cutlass in his hand. Thorns quickly painted the ghost-blue spirit of death across his face.

Axe-wielder! Thorns* called. *The trees!*

But—

This is no time to talk back, Riz said.

Bdddaaaa, bap ba bap Bddddat? Jardin asked.

He speak the rolling tongue better than he do the River's English, Riz thought. Riz turned to Jardin and said sharply, *Bdddaaaa bddddaaaaa bdddddaaaaa!* At this there could be no argument. Jardin holstered his weapons and climbed into the arms of his favorite tree. It looked from above as if ghosts were moving through the forest. Some wore animal horns and fur. Some wore blackface. And some wore blue or white hoods. The Ku Kluxers were too much for the Others. The ghosts ran them through with knives and shot them down. Riz had told Jardin not to leave the trees for any reason. *Call the shots from high above. It's the most important job there is. You hear me?*

---

* The identities of most of the Others are lost to time, so I invented these names. I'm particularly proud of the name *Thorns.* Don't you love it?

Bo! Bddddaa! Jardin called, but no one listened to the voice of the child from the trees.

The speed of the fighting overwhelmed Jardin. The Others were old, he realized. The fight was not gone from them, exactly, but the Great Insurrection, the early fights of Cross River, they were so long ago, just a little over the entirety of Jardin's sixteen years on this earth. Jardin left the trees and when Riz looked up, he thought the boy he took in and raised like a son had turned into a coward, abandoning his comrades to run. That was Riz's last thought as a bullet to the shoulder crashed him to the earth. Riz bawled in pain, crawling to his cutlass as the Ku Kluxer who felled him readied a blade to jam through Riz's heart. As the Klan member charged, a flying hatchet lodged itself in the side of his skull.

It's said that a brown flash passed over the white-sheeted Klan member's body as Jardin retrieved his hatchet and moved on to another enemy. And it's said that that night Jardin killed twenty men. And it's said that he killed thirty. And it's said that he killed fifty-three. No one knows the true number, except Jardin knew, and unlike the rest of the town, he didn't celebrate what he'd done. It had to be done, and he got what he wanted, the manhood, the full Otherdom, but now he knew what it meant to be blood-drenched.

It became clear to the Others that they needed more youth, so the Board decreed that every Cross Riverian male age thirteen must pledge to be trained as an Other. Riz and Thorns tasked Jardin with training the next generation, but his heart no longer cried for blood. *Did not the Council say their children need not be blood-drenched?* Jardin asked Riz one day when they were alone in the trees. *The Council was some fools*, Riz replied. *And don't be going quoting the Council out in public. Get yourself killed.*

Jardin nodded. He shrugged. Then he pulled away from his mentor and found another. Went down to the little schoolhouse that stood right where Freedman's University now stands and became an apprentice teacher under Ms. Carmichaels. She taught six-year-olds their letters and their numbers. From time to time Jardin would help the Others train the thirteen-year-old boys; he'd show them how to sit in the trees, but he made sure to show them things in books too. Between the schoolhouse and the books he pushed onto the young Others, Jardin imagined himself building a shadow world of peace that would one day replace the hatchets and the knives, the guns and the spilled blood.* In the weeks and months that passed, he spent more time at the schoolhouse and less time in the trees. He became a blankness to the Others.

The Others noticed Jardin's absence and they talked. The new recruits looked sickly. They were weak. Didn't at all know how to hold their weapons. Some fell from the trees because they refused to learn to sit. And worst of all, they didn't listen. Here was their natural teacher off reading to children instead of seeing to the well-being of the town. A rumor spread that he began and ended each class by quoting the long-deceased Council of Three, telling the children they didn't have to be blood-drenched just because their parents and grandparents were. That was a step or two too far. If the children of Cross River were made doughy and soft, how then could the future protect itself? The Others talked.

Bdddddaaaaa! Ba ba bdaa bdaa.

Bop ba de. Dddddd. Daddddaa da da dat.

Scabadddda ddddddd dddddddaaaa. Tadddaa.

Bdddddaaaa! Bdddddaaaa! Bdddddaaaa!

Bdddddaaaa! Bdddddaaaa! Bdddddaaaa!

Bdddddaaaa! Bdddddaaaa! Bdddddaaaa!†

And like that a decision was made. It wasn't an easy decision. It went right up to the General and, of course, the Board—he always had the final say. One day when the Others knew Jardin wouldn't be there, some of them donned white sheets and white gloves and floated into the little schoolhouse. They chopped Ms. Carmichaels first and they ended by butchering the littlest boy whose pleading paused Riz's hatchet—really Jardin's hatchet—just a half second.

Jardin heard the cries of the witnesses across town. People shouted

---

* This sentence was a late addition and I wrestled with it for a long while. Did it give away too much? Was I showing Chambers my hand? No, I decided, at this point I was all in.

† This is an authentic transcription of the nearly lost Cross Riverian language of the rolling tongue. My knowledge of the language is one of the many areas I pride myself in being well studied.

his name. He dashed to the school and witnessed the horror. The walls of his sanctuary now a blood mural. Blood abstractions. He knelt before his dead mentor and his dead students, holding their dead bodies to his. And his tears were for his fallen students, of course, but also because he knew that there was never to be an escape for him, he'd forever be the axe-wielder.*

Jardin was never fooled. Never once did he think the Klan had ridden into his classroom. (Of course they didn't, only a fool would believe they did.) How would they so easily get past the trees and the watchful eyes of the Others? It was bad enough that the Others thought him weak. Worse that they thought him stupid. Jardin shook Riz's hands. He accepted Thorns's sympathy. And then he waited. He watched the last of his kids sink into the earth and then Jardin went for his hatchets. He painted the spirit of red death upon his face.

It took him an afternoon of patience, of watching, of waiting, and of guerrilla warfare, crouching low to the earth, dipping behind the trees, but he buried his hatchet into the necks, the heads, the chests, the guts of all the older Others (the younger ones he determined were innocent), leaving Riz for last. You killed those kids, Jardin, Riz said. These were his last words. Not us. You. The Council's peace is shit. Your peace is shi—. Jardin chopped first at his mouth, and then at his forehead, and he chopped and chopped and chopped until Riz no longer had a face.

After the Others were all dead, the blood-soaked Jardin walked and walked until he came near the river, where he saw Joseph, the General's son. The boy, about six, wasn't in class the morning of the massacre. Of course he wasn't. The boy tossed stones into the Cross River.

Mr. Jardin, he said. *My stones won't skip. Can you show me how again?*

No, Jardin said. And he removed both hatchets from his waist.

Mr. Jardin? Why are you covered in so much blood? Are you okay?

---

* Here I hoped Chambers would imagine his students slaughtered on a Freedman's classroom floor. He'd see himself rising from their bloody corpses an avenging angel.

Jardin nodded and sat on a rock next to Joseph. He bent forward and placed his hatchets on the soft, shifting earth near the water's edge.

My daddy says I won't see my friends anymore, Joseph said. *Told me the Klan—*

Shhh, Jardin said. *Hush. It's not time to talk about that. One day it will be. Not today. It's not time to skip stones neither.*

No?

Jardin reached into his shirt pocket and pulled out a little book. *No, son. It's time to read.*

A is for Apple... He paused, put an arm around Joseph, and pulled him close. *No, that's not it. A is for the Axe we use to sever limbs clean. B is for the Battles we wage on the vulgar and the mean.* Jardin turned the pages as if he actually read those words in front of him. *C is for Cuts that separate bodies and heads. D is for Death—*

Mr. Jardin, the boy said. *The book doesn't say that.*

Hush, boy, Jardin said. *Hush. D is for the Death that comes for us bloody, pained, and red, the unholy holy spirit that makes us sleep the forever sleep of the dead*...

   . . .

And when I was done, I fired up my AOL and sent the fable off to Dr. Chambers with a note telling him that it was his time, and I signed it: *Your faithful servant and brother, Dr. Simeon Reece.* And then I waited.

3.

It didn't take long for Chambers to reply. I woke one morning a bit after the new year had dawned to my AOL crying, *You've got mail.* A message from my protégé popped onto the screen of my boxy laptop. Chet brought me a golden kiwi, some yellow cake, and hot chocolate, and I shooed him away as I ate and read.

   . . .

To: Dr. Simeon Reece <Dr.ofTruth@aol.com>
Sent: January 5, 2018, 8:00 a.m.
From: Reggie <Blacker.Roland.Hudson@gmail.com >
Cc:
Bcc:
Subject: Re: Newest Fable
Attachment: LONELINESS Essay.docx

Dear Dr. Reece,

I want to thank you for sending me that Milo Sequoia fable
you discovered. You gave me something I didn't even know I
needed.

Sometimes I wonder if you're real, but you just keep proving
yourself to be the realest, the hyper-realest. Perhaps if Sequoia
were alive today he'd write a fable titled, THE TRIUMPH OF
DR. SIMEON, THE REAL.

I've read or heard the story of Jardin the Axe-Wielder
many times, of course, but I don't believe I've ever heard it
told quite like that. Sequoia offers so many shades and layers
to a timeworn tale. It's reminiscent of the way Shakespeare
remakes (or rather *remade*) history as drama. I truly admire
how Sequoia plays with history and the foundational myths
of Cross River in his work, at least in the work you've shown
me. Is that his usual métier? You know, Roland Hudson has a
poetic re-telling of the Jardin story in *The Firewater of Love.* In
it he adds some nonsense about a fateful and tragic love, which,
honestly, detracts from the pathos of Jardin's journey. Jardin's
love in the Hudson poem is (surprise, surprise) a water-woman
and ultimately a stand-in for Gertrude, the object of his own
obsession. It's a tiresome poem. I'm sure you've read it, so I'm
not telling you anything new. I hate, as a Hudson fanatic, to
point out where he is flawed, but his histories often leave me
wanting. Anyway, I wonder if Sequoia wrote his version of
Jardin's life before or after Hudson wrote his. What does your
research say?

One day you'll have to let me in on your research methods to help me learn how you are able to unearth such fabulous stuff.

As for me, that Sequoia piece renewed me, man. I read a magazine article about the hatemyprofessor founder, Ulysses Sparks, and I ended up spending an embarrassing number of hours on his site. All those ugly words piled atop one another. Ugly words carelessly arranged can derange us just like beautiful words in beautiful order. Ugly derangement saps us and depletes us, devolves us to our base selves, rips feathers from the wings we've gained from all our beautiful derangements. You rescued me from that ugly derangement, Reece. Brought life to my essay and my class planning. Thanks to your aid, I am doing this. I finished a draft I'm proud of. I'm talking the most beautiful derangement, man! I'm thinking now that I should submit it directly to a journal for publication rather than sending it off to Mean Dean Jean Greene. What do you think? The essay—let me warn you, Reece—is a bit offbeat, and I'm fine with that; it's also the realest thing I ever wrote, to quote one of my inspirations (you'll see).

I've attached a draft, so please, Reece, I ask for your brutality, your toughest love. Please—and of course this goes without saying—keep this under your hat; can't let it get out before it's ready!

Now, I must return to the loneliness course and planning for next semester. Syllabus (another offbeat, yet real document) is nearly done. Peace.

Thanks for everything, bruh.

I have the honor to be your very faithful servant,
—Reggie

———————

When she reaches a hand across the table
through the steam of our soup to touch my unblinking left eye,

I don't flinch even as my heart covers
itself in a thin layer of stone.
That paralytic eye,
evidence of my turn from human to beast,
forever ringed in wetness, new tears.
Thought I hid it well.
Instead of the eye though she thumbs the underside of my
    eyelashes.
Says: I never realized you had such beautiful lashes.
I laugh, cast my face toward the light above.
    My eye blinks.

—Roland Hudson,
"Beauty &," from *The Firewater of Love*

OF LONELINESS, OF LONGING, OF DESPAIR, OF PORN, AND OF HOPE: A PERSONAL EXPLORATION

By Dr. Reginald S. Chambers
Freedman's University

> This is what I think now: that the natural state of the sentient
> adult is qualified unhappiness.
>
> —F. SCOTT FITZGERALD, *THE CRACK-UP*

> I don't know what your taste is, but I prefer the rambling,
> meandering truth.
>
> —YASIIN BEY

I.

If there is a great poet of pornography it would be the director Orr
G., the auteur of the porn film series *Ass Incarceration*, which to
my mind is the most remarkable work of its genre and bests much
of the work in other genres of art as well. Its poetry is hardly in
the fucking, no, it lies in the non-sexual facial gestures, the small
movements. The poetry is in the silences, in the unsaid. It's in
things I can hardly describe within the scope of an essay.

It starts this way: A woman, Jane,* is lying seemingly asleep, on
a cot in a dimly lit cell.

---

* Orr G. employs a team of *sluts* (his word, not mine), actresses who are akin to a band, or rather they are instruments, beautiful, frequently nude, interestingly shaped instruments he deploys the way a conductor uses the pieces of an orchestra. And with this team of women, Orr G. creates pornographic symphonies. At times they appear to be portraying the water-women of Cross Riverian myth. The lead *slut*, Jane, is peer to a succession of actresses with names like Doe, Hoe, Loe, Noe, and on and on. The names of his collaborators provide an accidental commentary on the director's work. He seems to have bought in wholeheartedly to the *one-woman-with-many-faces* aesthetic that is central to both modern misogyny and modern pornography. Each name is chosen to be generic, flying in the face of traditional flashier porn star nomenclature, and speaking to the disposable qualities of the women in Orr G.'s films. Only Jane (with one notable exception) is free from a nearly random rhyming name, but still she is shackled (Jane is frequently shackled) with the most generic female name possible. There have been a series of Janes, adding on to Orr G.'s cruel and dismissive joke, but there could hardly be a movie series without these women.

She is wearing white cut-off shorts and a thin white tank top and nothing more. The camera lingers over the dark mahogany of her legs and when it comes to her face you can see her purple mascara is smudged from tears, she turns fitfully as if in a nightmare. A clanging sound rings off-camera and Jane is startled. Into the frame walks Doe wearing a prison guard uniform. It is a dress, though. Or maybe just a longish shirt. Doughy cleavage peeks through the top and the outfit is cut short enough so that when the camera passes, it's clear that beneath her flimsy covering Doe is bare.

Doe orders Jane to strip, and when she hesitates, Doe yanks open the cell doors and rips Jane's flimsy clothes from her body. The two begin rolling and writhing on Doe's cot, enacting all the stuff of contemporary pornography. In some shots Jane is handcuffed, sometimes not. Glorious cunt pressed to glorious cunt.

I won't belabor the point too much here, because the sex is not the main event. Sure, it lasts a good long while, but it is grimly and sadly lit. There are moans of passion and pleasure from each woman—it's clear they are enjoying themselves (at least the characters they are playing are)—but when the camera catches their faces, there is a soft sadness there. I figured at first that I had imagined the sadness, that I had brought my own considerable melancholy with me, but no. After the sex is done and Jane is left alone shackled in her cell, we see Doe walk off to her office. Doe sits nude and alone. She stares ahead. We flash to Jane and she too is sitting, still disrobed and alone, staring ahead. The camera flashes back and forth between the women staring into their naked solitude lamenting how their encounter, pleasing as it was, failed to end their isolation.

II.

I never knew that I was lonely or even what loneliness was until one blinding night when I was twelve or thirteen. Consider this an origin story, as nothing before it matters in the least. A new understanding descended upon me as if by supernatural hand. I hugged and kissed my parents, told them good night, and did the same with my grandmother and my siblings, and then I retired to my bedroom and lay in the darkness. I was an insomniac in those days, so I never expected easy sleep and I didn't get it that night. Instead I stared up at the black ceiling. I turned to my side and then to my other side. These days I sleep easy. If I sit still long enough I'll fall into a fitful slumber full of snoring and tortured breathing that ceases momentarily, hopefully, throughout the night. I never thought I'd miss insomnia, but I do. I'm digressing. Allow me my digressions, my ability to speak and to digress is all I have these days; I don't like to revisit the moment, but I must. I didn't feel particularly sad that day; true sadness only arrived when I turned out the lights. It rose from my stomach as if on a wave of nausea—and it was that, I guess, emotional nausea—and before I could begin to combat it, I started to cry without control. Sniffling back snot and wiping droplets of tears as large and as shiny as Christmas tree bulbs. They fell faster and in greater numbers than I ever imagined tears could fall. They dampened my pillow and my sheets, my face awash in great angry salt rivers. A lake pooled upon my bed. It was loneliness and nothing else that caused my tears to run, the awareness of this reality blanketing me like the darkness of my room. It had always been there from my birth, I realized, and will always be there, loving parents, siblings, friends, friendly acquaintances, and others be damned. They'll never care the way I need them to, and, most damning, I'll never care about them the way they need me to. The blinding blue darkness of these insights! The emptiness they allowed me to see! My one mistake that night was in the conclusion that my salvation could be found in another, a person, a woman who existed somewhere out there, not yet a woman, probably, but a girl, possibly crying out in loneliness as well. Silly lonely long-ago child, even I don't care about you in the way you wish I would. What in the hell makes you think she ever could?

III.

A less talented or visionary director would have gone back to what made the first *Ass Incarceration* movie so successful. Orr G.* could have doubled down on the sex and only gestured at making a statement on loneliness and isolation—or ignored that aspect altogether. The next movies could have been a succession of *sluts* visiting Jane's cell, but instead they revolve around Jane's escape from prison and her attempt at building a new life. There's little consistency; sometimes Jane is a water-woman, sometimes not; various actresses return playing different parts. We see Jane as a fugitive, taking up with a band of *sluts*; as a home-invader singled-handedly subjugating and dominating a house of women, turning them into her servants, her harem, her *sluts*; we see her attempting a normal life as a homemaker/handmaiden; as a therapy patient (she is captured by her therapist, played by Noe—get it? Dr. Noe—and then Jane turns the tables on her); as a college student (her dorm is likely the most interesting on campus); as a teacher to a class of disrespectful, underachieving women;† and finally Doe (who has been searching for Jane all along) catches up with her and we see Jane back in her cell visited by the lusty Doe. It all comes back

---

* Orr G. began his career as a rapper, performing under the name Original Gangsta; his eponymous first album proved that his raps would be as uninspired as his moniker. Original Gangsta's music nearly immediately became a punch line, synonymous with craven banality and aggressive mediocrity. The Personality Kliq, in particular, held Gangsta and his music up for scorn. Octavio the Clown of the Kliq first referred to Gangsta as Orr G. on the track "Lowered Xxxpectations." It wasn't a full-on dis, more an aside, but mocking Original Gangsta in song soon became a trend. In the Kliq's video, an actor made up to resemble Gangsta dances about in a G-string. What precipitated the attack is lost to time. Gangsta never formally responded; instead he abandoned his thug persona and gained a slight bit more success making sexually charged songs as Orr G. His next album, *Gangsta Orgy*, received bemused and grudging acceptance as a novelty artifact, but it was undeniable that there lingered a sense of sadness or resignation in Orr G.'s sex jams. (His most memorable line: "I slip your girl the jalepeño / You be slipping her that hollow peen, yo."), as if his life had gone far afield from what he had planned and there was nothing to do but to keep moving in this new direction that the market dictates. The market's rewards were not enough, and within a year Orr G. abandoned music and released his first film, *Xxxiles* (or alternatively: *SeXxxiles from the Orr G.*). It begins with Jane being called into a dark swampy abyss, where she meets the rest of the gang, this time playing water-women, those sweet mythical sirens of the deep who exist only to mesmerize lovers and pull them to watery deaths. Jane says repeatedly, *I don't want to be here.* Each time, a naked and groping Doe or Noe or one of the others replies, *You're free to go,* but the naked and submitting Jane never leaves.

† In this installment, the class of petulant students Jane teaches, and is eventually captured by, is nicknamed *the Slut-Hogs*—perhaps the director's least successful pun/cultural reference.

to loneliness; none of these adventures can quell, or even quiet, Jane's loneliness. Life is a loop of loneliness and isolation we can never truly outrun, Orr G. seems to say.

IV.

From elementary school through about eleventh grade I *liked* a succession of girls who did not *like* me back. In fact, it seems they found me repulsive. They made mockery of my dark skin, my (presumably) West African nose, my unfashionable glasses, generic department-store clothes, and my short stature. All of this earned me a nickname I never accepted, but overheard flitting by me like bullets in a gunfight. Little Ugly, they called me, while assuming I was oblivious to their taunting.* They spoke of me as if I weren't there, or as if I stood before them naked and invisible. They bellowed the name on the bus, in the hallway while I walked by, and I pretended I didn't hear. My muscles twitched each time I heard my new name. The bullets weren't passing by me, they were striking me, quietly but forcefully, and then they drilled themselves deep into my muscle tissue. And then there was twelfth grade and P—e, who read me Roland Hudson poems before and after we made love in her parents' basement. And sometimes I fear my vocation as a Hudson scholar is simply an attempt to conjure the softness of her legs. We talk sometimes still—I call her every September thirteenth—she no longer reads the poet she introduced me to and in our silences I imagine her and also I imagine her imagining me. I doubt she remembers when I call that it's the anniversary of the last time we made love before devolving into argument and

---

* My best friend, who first informed me of the mockery, began calling me this to my face as a joke. His mockery, he presumed, was different than the mockery of strangers because it was well in line with our adolescent form of bonding, making vicious light of each others' shortcomings and insecurities. I am no angel or innocent victim, I made jokes at his expense as well. In the long run, our form of bonding accumulated unspoken resentment and hurt so tender that most of my friends can't even bear to look at each other these days. To admit the pain of the cruelty was to expose a weakness none of us were willing to make visible, and over time we found ourselves rubbed raw. My friend was the first in our circle to realize the damaging nature of our engagement and he apologized and ceased the mockery. I never did. In fact, I accepted his apology and immediately mocked him for it; after all, his newfound compassion proved he was growing soft and weak.

petty disdain. It was the day Tupac died. I checked the time of his death later: just as I came, he went. I was supposed to feel sorrow and sadness at the death of one of my heroes—I had looked to his music to lift me out of isolation and despair, and briefly it worked— but I could feel only joy that day. Lord, how I tried, how I tried to feel the appropriate sadness. *Oh*, I thought. *Tupac is dead.* And that is as far as my thoughts would go. I felt, instead of sadness, a oneness. A oneness with P—e, with the universe. All short-lived, and ultimately, I realized, my feelings were a falsehood. The sex made us argue, made us eventually hate one another. When I speak to her once a year, I don't mention that day or the unsatisfying (in retrospect) teenage sex that is likely a grayish blur in the back of her memory, lost among thousands of sexual encounters. I doubt she ever makes the connection. We speak briefly and brightly as if there is not a canyon of time and space between us, as if I don't have a little girl (9), a little boy (4), and a wife, as if I'm seventeen and fool enough to believe that between our legs lies a powerful medicine. And for five, ten minutes I'm not alone, but instead I'm kept company by the softness of her legs.

V.

The beauty of *Ass Incarceration* and most of Orr G.'s work is the way it speaks to both our higher frequencies and our lower selves. Culti-vate the mind, yes, but we must never forget the animals: the cock, the ass, the pussy. That is the dispute of the ages between C—e and me. C—e only speaks in higher frequencies. Like a puppet, she has no lower self. Perhaps she is the reason for this exploration.

C—e found me one afternoon, *compromised*; *Ass Incarceration* in the DVD player and me in deep with the only lover I regularly knew at the time, myself. It was my several-times-a-day habit in those days to worship at the feet of the god Onan.

What is this? she cried. Her features transformed into a look of condescension and disdain, and somehow—maybe because of her tiny stature—this amplified the cuteness of her face. Is this why you want me and the kids *away* all the time? (Thankfully the kids were not with her.) Is this why you refused to go out of town with us last month?

No, I assured her. No, my dear. I pointed to the television. You see that quick look that passed across the face of Hoe? Did you see it? It expresses the essential loneliness of the human condition far more beautifully than ten thousand R&B songs, than ten thousand Russian novels, than ten thousand French films.

C—e could place her hand on my forehead and send all my lonely pain temporarily into a blue oblivion. She didn't, though. She rarely did that anymore.

She watched me pointedly and said, It's up to you to fix this marriage or we'll just keep walking by each other like strangers while you're on your way to jack off like an animal to some god-damn porno!

VI.

From C—e's Journal, March 2018:

. . . That creeping sunlight and how it breaks slowly at dawn. So slow it appears to be riding on the back of the clouds. That glacial morning light is why I won't move from here like my husband wants . . . [T]he light and Rupert, the orange fox who only visits in the morning when the house is still and my husband snores on the couch and the kids are likewise in their rooms snoring—a horrid chorus—but that sound is more peaceful than Reggie's voice. His voice always wages war on me. Not always in anger. He just speaks a language no one else understands; I certainly don't. Makes him—and me—very alone. Like I said, his war is not waged in rage, tho [sic] sometimes it is, most of the time he's just cast me in a certain light and that's how, to him, I must stay . . . Is it weird that I have better conversations with Rupert? Even though he says nothing (I'm not crazy)—never even makes a sound— and he sometimes trots away while I'm in midsentence? I lean over the balcony and talk, talk, talk, and I swear his face is talking back to me. He listens when I mention the piles of work I have to bring home with me and the grocery store I seem to live in, and the dinners that are never enough . . . and my daughter's rude lip (MY GOD!) . . . I wonder what Reggie would do if I took off this shirt and climbed on top of him right now, I mean like put these titties all in his face. Probably nothing. He doesn't understand my language either—body language, verbal language, love language. We created a shared culture and a

shared tongue and where our tongues no longer met, there is where things evolved and split into two unintelligible dialects, high C—enian and low Reggieian—or something like that (lol). We are now different countries . . . How did I even get to talking about him, huh? I was writing so I wouldn't forget about my truest companion, the slow-moving light pouring itself over the horizon in thick, syrupy streams . . .

VII.

Somewhere toward the middle of its run, the *Ass Incarceration* series takes a turn. The fifth film, subtitled *Solitary Confluffment,* is devoid of Orr G.'s usual troupe. No Jane. No Doe. No Hoe. No Goe. No Loe. No Joe. No Noe. No Moe. Instead, the viewers are intro- duced to Jill. Solitary Jill in all her solitudes, the only character in the film. She stands inside a cell so dark it's unclear how the director was able to capture such endless and deep liquid black- ness. Still we can see Jill clearly as she stares at the heavy iron of the cell door. The look on her face is confusion then despair as she bangs a fist against the metal. When she gives up, she melts into a corner, and now her face reflects, not a peacefulness, but a sort of resignation. She rests her hand between her thighs and then eventually she removes the only thing she was wearing, her flimsy white undershirt. Jill passes her hands over her breasts, and over (eventually) seemingly the entirety of her body (paying special attention to her pubis) through the course of the next ninety minutes of the movie. Her face cycles through confusion, briefly loneliness, a peacefulness, contentment, joy, even enlight- enment. The colors change. Jill doubles and triples. No one should be surprised that Orr G.'s least successful film is also his most avant-garde. It's also the one, for all its wordlessness, that has the most to say.

This is where most critics get confused: Orr G.'s theme in *Soli- tary Confluffment* is not loneliness, but solitude. Rejuvenator of the broken and resurrector of the prematurely dead. Jill teaches us that our solitude is enough. Never hoard people the way a wealthy man (and even more so, but in a different way entirely, the poor and middle-class man) hoards things. If you are to hoard, hoard solitude. C—e hoards me, she hoards the kids, and sometimes I resist, most times I acquiesce. She takes my acquiescence as a victory, and then attempts to annex more and more of me, and one day, I fear, I will no longer be a sovereign nation.

The (economic) failure of *Solitary Confluffment* suggests that the only form of solitude that our society truly values is the violent kind Orr G. satirizes in his movies. When you throw a poor man, a poor woman, into solitary confinement, you go from incarcerating a body to incarcerating, in addition, a mind, and even a spirit if such a thing exists (and my belief in the Christian God, alone up there on his cross, tells me it does). But I hear you now raising your voices in refutation, *Ah, you hypocrite, professor of loneliness you, isn't solitude your great love? Can't it do some good for an unruly soul such as our hypothetical criminal? And who cares, anyway; even hypothetical criminals are, in the end, just criminals.* But this isn't solitude or even loneliness, per se. It's malevolence, it's violence, loneliness weaponized and turned against a human with the force of a personal nuclear weapon creating tiny mushroom clouds within.

Jill returns later in the series, not in her own movie, but in other installments of *Ass Incarceration*. She never interacts with the others and she never utters a word. She is simply in the background, naked and pleasuring herself, enacting her own solitude.

VIII.

Sometimes when I'm alone, my mind turns to myth, and once in a while I even go out and observe the lovers holding hands; I try to guess which fool is in the thrall of a water-woman.* I never believed in water-women until my third semester teaching at Freedman's University. It was a balmy fall and an adjunct wandered onto cam-

---

* As long as there has been a town called Cross River, and even before, folks have spoken of the water-women, mystical shape-shifting water creatures who live on an island beneath the waters of the Cross River. The water-women—also known as woes, kazzies, sirens, and shauntices (a corruption of the word *chanteuse*—in some myths, the water-women sing)—exist only to cause havoc. After the creature has found a mark, it takes the shape of that person's ideal partner (they nearly always take on a female form) and create in him or her a physical, chemical, and emotional dependence the mark usually takes for love. The woe either disappears, leaving its mark delirious with increasing despondence and madness, or it draws its victim to the Cross River, where the mesmerized mark drowns him- or herself following the water-woman beneath the river's surface. The legend of the water-woman is an enduring Cross Riverian myth passed orally, though some of the most evocative accounts are in print—for instance, every slave narrative written by a Cross Riverian features a scene of a water-woman arriving nude and water-slicked from the bottom of the river to draw hapless newly freed men to their deaths. Every Cross Riverian knows someone who knows someone who has encountered a water-woman.

pus, making the world's drear suddenly bright. She taught two courses in a classroom next to mine. Her name matters not: for all time, within this essay and in life, she is the Adjunct. Often I'd give my students a quiz or a writing assignment, something where they'd have to be quiet, so I could eavesdrop on the Adjunct. I wouldn't say her voice was heavy, but it was authoritative. She was the god of her classrooms, no challenging her power. I heard a light, sultry curl, like bluish smoke, in her voice. When she came to my office and we spoke, the curl took over her voice, and the force, the power of it, became a hint of her true nature. And you should have seen her face, one of those faces that perpetually holds a smirk, as if she knew a joke no one else knew.

When she walked by, man and woman stopped and watched her in quiet appreciation.

Say, bruh, K—, the poetry professor whose office sits adjacent to mine, said one day as J—, an administrator in our department, came by to discuss with us some administrative matter. What y'all think of [the Adjunct]?

J— was nominally our superior, but he relinquished that designation when it came to little boy stuff. We said nothing, smiled a bit. K— delivered his punch line: Lotta adjunct in the trunk, right?

Let me get outta here, J— said, chuckling. Y'all n-words gon' get me fired.

Stone-faced, I turned and made it my business to ignore all such comments, especially when she began to come by my office, first a question about a Roland Hudson poem.

I want to teach his work, the Adjunct said. I'm missing something.

Have you read *The Firewater*? I asked, reaching for a volume from my bookshelf. This is the only poetry book there is. No other works of poetry even exist.

Soon we would head to lunch together, she and I, discussing Hudson's work. Entire conversations made up of little more than Hudson's verse. C—e thinks little of Roland Hudson. I'd appreciate contempt; her indifference breeds in me resentment.

I forgot C—e when I was in the Adjunct's presence. It was as if she didn't exist. But as soon as the Adjunct and I parted, images of C—e would come flooding into my head like an invasion. Even now sometimes the Adjunct's scent breezes into my nostrils like the breath of life and I forget C—e. I look about but the Adjunct is nowhere near. That's a clue you're in deep with a water-woman, a derangement of the senses, first pleasant, then distressing.

The Adjunct would read aloud from Roland Hudson in my office, that powerful voice making me drift, and I'd find that I was actually alone by the Cross River. Or was that a dream? I know I dreamt about her frequently, and now I confuse those dream images with the real thing. I daydreamed about her in class, students shaking me, snapping their fingers, calling my name forcefully: Dr. Chambers, you all right?

One such moment, I talked of Hudson to my students and I heard her voice whispering to me. This was the first day of the spring semester. I walked out into the hall, leaving behind a class of confused students. I called her name. Followed the trail of her voice, her scent. I swear to you it was taking me to the river. The only thing that stopped me was K— putting himself into my path.

Fuck is wrong with you? K— asked.

Huh? I snapped foggily back into the moment.

I'm trying to teach class and you're fucking banshee-wailing [the Adjunct's] name.

But where is she? She was just here talking to me.

How the fuck should I know, man? She's an adjunct. She wasn't just here talking to you. She's gone. We got new ones. Get a grip.

And she was indeed gone, dear reader. I searched the campus. I looked for her out in the community. Asked and asked and asked. Something told me to search by the river, and then—such a buzzing in my head—I knew. Even now, I'm careful not to say her name or think it when I'm near the Cross River, for fear that those mischievous woes will rise up and claim me for their collection of bodies at the bottom of the water. Even as I type this I must strengthen my resolve to not wander to the river.

But her disappearance has left me unbearably sad and alone. I can speak to no one about this. Not C—e, not anyone. Who would believe it? I see the look on the faces of some of her former students and others—janitors, professors, administrative assistants—who ask after her. They too had been marked.

Another hallmark of water-woman derangement: I wrote the below, but I don't recall writing it. I have no idea if it is a recollection, a dream I had, my imagination, or something else, but I wrote it in her thrall:

A READING

His lips followed his hands; his nose, too, buried in the odors
of her body, seeking oblivion, seeking the drug that emanated
from her body.

—ANAÏS NIN, "ELENA"

Her scent left the Professor so delirious, so fevered, that even
though weeks had passed since he had last seen her, all it took
was a glimpse, or perhaps the sultry sound of her voice—it sent
him into a reverie, a blissful synesthesia. Now she read aloud as
they lay intertwined on her couch. Whatever she read didn't matter,
and he couldn't even remember it now thinking back, all that mattered was hearing the music of her voice in all its polyphonic rhythmic hypnotisms. The pair complained, absently, about how hot it
had become so all of a sudden, and neither noticed—he entranced
by the perfume and music of her and she by the act of reading—
when they began removing their clothes to free themselves from
the encroaching heat.

IX.

Orr G.'s finest work cannot perhaps even be classified as pornography. True, *The Assolationists* utilizes his usual stable of
actresses—Jane is here, as is Doe—and it is not devoid of on-
camera sex, but the focus here is decidedly not on lovemaking.
It concerns itself with a husband (played by the former slapsmith
Nude Nick, credited here as Nude Nicolas) who allows his wife
(Jane) to talk him into making a porno with another woman (Soe).
At first the husband is excited for all the possibilities. But as time
passes, his face becomes more weathered, more concerned and
pained. The nuance in the facial acting is powerful and surprising, especially given what kind of work this is. What if, the husband wonders, his wife only suggested it to make him happy? Or
worse, as a test? What if she can't handle watching him make love
to another? What if fucking another is a thing he himself can't
handle—all those emotions tangled up? After all, he's realizing, he
only agreed to the porno to make his wife happy. The color of the
room is a warm teal; beams of white natural light burst through

the blinds. As he lies on the bed waiting for his porn partner, wearing just a robe and black socks and nothing more, it occurs to the husband that he's made a grave mistake. The porn actress (for some reason it's not Soe, but instead Doe) walks in wearing just a thin blue robe—she might as well be wearing nothing—and the husband shoots up, startled, as if this woman's skin is as translucent as her garb. His face will be out on the open market, he suddenly realizes. His neighbors could, in theory, pause the video and count the hairs of his ass. His penis's head will soon be as recognizable—perhaps even more so—than the head on his neck. The husband begs the actress's patience while he speaks to his wife. He goes into the next room to see her, but when he enters he finds his wife is gone. The room is nothing but a sterile whiteness. Earlier it was filled with furniture—some chairs, a desk, a bed; some paintings of boats-on-water on the lime-green walls. How could this all change so quickly? Where could his wife be? She promised to wait here watching the proceedings through a sliver of cracked doorway. He waits for a while, and when she never materializes, the husband returns to the next room to tell the porn actress of his wife's disappearance in all its strangeness, but as soon as he enters the room he finds it too is empty and white and he is all alone.

• • •

I sat back after reading the Chambers essay unable to break the smile that turned my face into a clown mask. My love and affinity for Chambers had now become overwhelming. Between his masterpiece and the (unauthorized) class he was planning, I could gaze up from my hole and see the brightness of the spring semester—futurelight from a star not yet born but already blinding in its life and blazing death.

III.

The Spring; or, Special Topics in Loneliness Studies

—

1.

I've begun writing this section probably a hundred times and I've stopped that many times and deleted the words and I've gotten up from my computer to blow clouds of reefer smoke hoping against hope that the plumes could clear my head. These are the words I simply don't want to write. The times I simply can't bear to live again.

Writing many of the previous pages nearly killed me several times over; the act of remembering is a hand squeezing the soft pink flesh of my brain. Just think, this moment, or any of the thousands that make up the present and the immediate past, any single one of them—maybe all of them—may soon turn into a tortured regret, a stray thought that will harden and become difficult to live with, a monster holding a hatchet constantly returning to hack away inside your skull. And these days I'm writing now, they are a more vicious beast than the previous days. Their teeth and claws are more soaked in red. No one left that time without a mark.

Simply, simply put: watching Chambers unravel just wasn't as entertaining as I thought it would be.

· · ·

My own unravelment went something like this: My hair grew thick, thick, thick back then, at least it was thick when I wanted it to be, not the thin wisps I'm stuck with now. Most often I cut it low because of the sprinklings of gray that I thought made me look like an old man. I could never imagine that the sprinklings would turn into colonies of white that would eventually, with some resistance, form a nation on my head. My cheeks drooped a bit here and there. A few lines creased the valleys of my face deeper than I wished. Freedman's had caused such stress—it was clear that my youthful attractiveness would soon fall away. My point is that the job had aged me beyond normal wear and tear, but I hid it well and you could only see it if you knew where to look.

I spent hours, many hours upon hours, of my life back then grading. It was fine, though, mind power would save the world, I told myself. Each student was a little bomb I'd fill with the napalm of critical thinking and the force of reasoning and logical discourse. This and only this could sweep over the land and remake our society—given enough students, given enough time. No class too big! No student too dim! Bring them on and I will turn them into small supernovas. That was my battle cry. I churned and burned with hope.

What I didn't know is that they only let you get so far within the confines of their system. They'll never let you endanger the status quo. They'll find a way to undermine you, destroy you. That's why I have to create my own system.

Dr. Kr— ran the department at the time. He's dead now, not soon enough to aid me, though I am grateful for his passing. It was his actions that helped me finally gain sight beyond sight. Him and a student named Maggie.

Maggie the magpie, I'd say when calling roll. She of the bright eyes and seat at the center of the front row. She of the insightful comments and dazzling papers that leapt with grace, beauty, and wisdom.

Something nagged at me about one of her papers, though. I had given it an A, and never for a second did I question my scoring. But it was an anecdote, an aside, really, that kept coming back to me. Something I had heard as an echo long ago, maybe. I dug and dug. And what I discovered was so astonishing it left me with few words. Her paper was the twin of one I'd written as an undergraduate at Freedman's. It featured my earliest invented Cross Riverian fable! I stared into it as one stares into the stars. I had forgotten my practice of creating history. When I confronted Maggie with the evidence her face turned delirious with joy. She twirled and laughed. Woo-hoo-ha-hoo! she exclaimed. She had been plagiarizing me all semester, she told me. And she twirled again and left my office and in the heart of my heart of hearts she'd forever remain a villain. I never saw Maggie again, and to this day I'm left with the question of why. What was the point? Who told her to target me? I'd heard from a student that she hated the way I mocked her name, but that couldn't be it. Could it? I stayed up at night wondering, but never came upon a successful answer.

In the meantime, my bills piled. My student loans grew millstone-heavy, bruising my neck and bending my spine. Idra's frustration became a monster roaring between us. We argued over money and I began to hate this woman, my second chance at love, at not dying alone in a hole somewhere. She had no interest in hearing about Maggie, whom she mocked as my *girlfriend*. I now dreamt of Maggie in the skimpy dresses she used to wear to class, which I paid no attention to when she was my student. In my dreams she'd twirl in her short skirts, her cleavage fat and always taunting, always exposed. Idra and I barely looked at each other, much less touched. I now distrusted my students and watched them cockeyed. They were subject of another recurring dream, they played the part of shadow-demons, I an angel; they clawed at me, ripping my wings from my back and dragging me into the fire-pit. It's all over when you hate your students—they kept coming and wouldn't stop—and I now saw them for who they were and what they were worth.

Money, and only money, could solve this, make this at all worth-while, maybe money and a position with more prestige, more respect. I went to Dr. Kr—'s office to ask about a tenure-track job.

Sorry, my boy, he said. I've been trying to open up some tenure-line positions for some time now, but the university just won't budge. I'll tell you what, I don't want to hold a talented professor like you back, so I'll write you a letter and you can use it to apply for some jobs. There's one open in Port Yooga, I believe.

I left, not happy, but with hope. Probably the last time that useless emotion graced me. I made a show of putting in applications so Idra could see and soften her tone toward me. Her tone hardened. When-ever she spoke it felt as if she were bashing me with wood. She always said my moods made me hard to deal with. Well, I said, if I don't get any of these jobs—think I have some moods now? I'm 'bout to serve up some depression like you ain't never seen!

And of course I didn't get the jobs. Not even a call, not even an acknowledgment. Zipseys. Nada.

I reviewed my materials. They were excellent. Top-notch. I'd hire me, I thought, looking over my cover letters and my curriculum vitae and all my old syllabi. I was a catch.

Maybe you're not as *brilliant* as you thought, Idra said, and it was true. As brilliant as I liked to believe I was, Dr. Kr— was more brilliant. He'd never lose his brightstar if he could help it.

I sent out the letter he had given me, but I had never read it. It was like one of my Cross Riverian fables, I could scarcely recognize the beautiful, heroic academic swashbuckler Dr. Kr— described.

But there in the middle, like a stink bomb:

If I may say that Dr. Reece has any defects at all, it is that perhaps he's too bright, too optimistic and hopeful. He believes
in his students with a childlike naïveté that can often serve
as an obstacle. For instance: a plagiarizing student snowed
Dr. Reece for nearly an entire semester because he wanted, no
needed, to believe she would one day do for the Humanities
what Carl Sagan did for the stars. Turns out she was actually
handing in essays Dr. Reece wrote as an undergraduate. The
"genius" he saw in her work was his own. A bit of an extreme
case of Narcissus staring into his reflection in the river. This
is a small quibble and something that can be tamed with the
right training. Training I have had little time to administer on
our small, but frustratingly hectic campus. Think of Dr. Reece
as a big picture thinker who often has trouble finding Waldo
among all the clutter.

The scoundrel knew what kind of damage he was inflicting. I would
never get the chance to confront the good doctor. His heart had a beef
with him over Thanksgiving break and Dr. Kr— lost the argument. He
currently resides in Hell and periodically he bathes in yellow rain courtesy of yours truly standing above his grave.

With Dr. Kr— gone the university got to reorganizing the department, slashing the jobs they could slash. Not just me, but soon a bunch
of us were out on the street (quite literally, in my case!), replaced by
adjuncts.

Chambers's downfall reminds me of my own, though his is sadder.
As I sit in the morgue alone surrounded by candles, walls closing, widening, I've become far more despondent than I ever have been. Aww,
man.

2.

[NOTE: *The best way to discuss the events of the Spring 2018 semester is to present the documents Dr. Chambers used in his course and his later correspondence with his superiors. These documents were submitted to the Faculty University Committee in Fall 2018 as part of Dr. Chambers's attempt to maintain his status as a tenured professor at Freedman's University.—SR*]

To: Dr. Jason Oliver, Chair—Department of English and Cultural Studies <JOliver@Freedmans.edu>
Sent: October 1, 2018, 3:58 a.m.
From: Dr. Reginald S. Chambers, Assistant Professor—Department of English and Cultural Studies <RChambers @Freedmans.edu>
Cc: Dr. Sarah Bridge, Provost <SBridge@Freedmans.edu>; Dr. Shana J. Greene, Dean—College of Arts and Sciences <SJGreene@Freedmans.edu>
Bcc:
Subject: Re: Grade Appeal and Employment Defense Documents
Attachment: Semester Materials.zip

Drs. Oliver, Bridge, and Greene,

Please find attached a copy of my Spring 2018 syllabus, writing prompts, and assorted other documents relevant to my English 101 classes from the previous semester, Ms. Montana's grade appeal in particular, and any and all administrative charges against me.

Forgive the lateness of these documents. I have been so exhausted mentally, physically, and emotionally by the events of last semester that I did not have the psychological bandwidth to properly review and send these documents. I've sorted some—but not with the rigor that I'd usually apply to such a task. I'm afraid I've given you a kind of document

dump (or alternately, I've taken a document dump into the
university's servers) in the hopes that this mess of papers
vindicates me. I am certain they will, as I have done nothing
wrong, and in fact have been myself wronged. If I am given
a fair shot and these papers do not vindicate me, it's that my
failure to properly curate the documents has led to some
confusion. The other reason could be that this process was
never meant to be fair and is simply a pretext to a miscarriage
of justice that will need to be litigated by our legal system. I
have reason to believe this will be the case.

    Have at it; or rather, have at me. Take me apart.

Dr. Reginald S. Chambers, Ph.D.
Assistant Professor
(currently on "sabbatical")
Department of English and Cultural Studies
Freedman's University
x3725

The only method
Proven in time
    To stop
The heart from hurting
    Is to stop the heart

—Roland Hudson,
"Firewater" (excerpt), from *The Firewater of Love*

3. SPRING SEMESTER, 2018

I feel the need to step in here and offer something in the way of commentary, of context. I heard little to nothing from Dr. Chambers before
the opening of the spring semester. After sending me his essay—
blessed confirmation he was still batshit—he ignored all my emails. I
hadn't yet seen the glorious document he was calling his syllabus, so I

was unsure if he was still going ahead with his class. For that matter, I was still unsure if he planned to send Dr. Greene his essay as a delirious sort of fuck-you.

I paced about the nearly empty campus toward the end of winter break, smoking the reefer I managed to scavenge from unlocked dorm rooms. Perhaps he had changed his mind. A disaster for me. I readied my syllabi, hoping that keeping busy would free me from thinking about the problem of Dr. Chambers. It didn't, of course, but at least I was able to get some things done.

When I finished my syllabi and had no other major tasks to complete, my mind again turned on itself. I remembered that this work is lonely work. I saw no one, not even the dimwit. The circle of time is a drain we spin. I circled and circled, dizzied and mad, thinking of nothing but the good doctor. I paced, read, wrote fables, checked Chambers's hatemyprofessor ratings, paced, wrote, read, hatemyprofessor, read, paced, hatemyprofessor—and on and on, gaining not a shred of satisfaction or peace of mind. I found myself so empty and alone that I hallucinated, imagining myself as a shambling explorer, collapsing in the cold tundra of Antarctica. That's when, through the haze of the snow and cold, I saw a rescue team. They lifted me by my armpits and set me to ride a white current of cold air. There, floating above it all, I realized that I had not encountered a rescue team at all; instead I had encountered academics back on campus for Faculty University College, a mess of seminars and speakers the university sets up to *inspire* faculty at the outset of each semester. And the academics had not actually lifted me, or engaged me in any way. They assumed I was a homeless man (true enough) and they walked around me as I lay on the ground imagining myself adrift on the cold continent. Some actually did engage me, to be fair; they pitched pennies at my face. I stood and greeted a few (they ignored me). Soon it was down the hill I went, back to the morgue, where I shaved and cleaned myself up. I hadn't attended Faculty University College since I was actually a faculty member. Perhaps I'd see Chambers there.

. . .

I dressed in my best professor finery—rust colored sports coat complete with the elbow patches—and it was like Clark Kent removing his glasses. People who previously walked by throwing pennies at my face were now asking me about my research as we ate pastries and sipped our too-hot coffees.

They were all out, all the characters. The math professor, so brilliant and accomplished he could each day dress as a clown, chatted in his whiteface makeup and floppy red shoes with the history professor who every semester taught as a different character from history. Last semester it was Thomas Jefferson (he drew complaints when he asked his teaching assistant to portray Sally Hemings); this semester he dressed as Harriet Tubman. Then there was the tall skinny blond with the strong jaw, his hair swept into a fashy cut—Dr. Faison, an assistant professor of philosophy, but I referred to him as the Aryan, as I suspected he was part of the neo-Nazi leader Ian Lipser's call for white supremacists to infiltrate historically black college faculty. Yep, the gang was all there, but no Chambers. Reginald was too much of a conformist to skip these things. Perhaps I misjudged him or perhaps he was changing, transforming as a caterpillar in a chrysalis.

The talk this morning was mostly on Ulysses Sparks, the fool behind hatemyprofessor. Calling him a fool, I suppose, is a bit of an imprecision. The site was a beast, growing and growling like a living, breathing organism, and Sparks had the brilliance and audacity to take his performance on the road. In the fall, he embarked on a campus tour he called Moments of Hate. For an hour or so he'd dance about a stage and rain down invective on academia for its supposed liberalism and pedantry, for the way it stunted the brilliance of students with its rules and grades. To this, the students would cheer and wave their arms wildly. And for the pièce de résistance, for two minutes the face of the professor from that school with the worst ratings on hatemyprofessor would be blown up on the big screen, larger than life, a canvas on which the whole campus could project the depths of its hatred.

No, Sparks was no fool. The very second he announced his Moments of Hate Tour, engagement at his site increased tenfold, and just the other day he released his spring schedule. Freedman's enjoyed the distinction of being the only historically black college on the list. There was no combating him. Whenever a college pulled the plug on his rally, he and the students who invited him would appear on television railing about the disappearance of free speech on college campuses. Those schools would find themselves with an even larger crowd of protestors than would have been at the rally. Yep, far from a fool. Of course, the money he offered these schools was too handsome to turn down. Most of these administrators with their failing budgets would dance naked for money if it came down to it.

Some even mused that the rallies served as the groundwork for Sparks's future political career. The true fools of our society deemed Sparks a harmless clown.

A bell sounded as the Faculty University College Campus Engagement Representative, Dr. Peggy Summers, called for us to take our seats and settle into a silence. The president was about to speak. We all moved to the bell like trained animals, conformity our greatest trick. My eyes swept the crowd again for Chambers. I saw Mean Dean Jean Greene, but not her prey. Perhaps she ate him, I joked to myself as her teeth tore viciously into a muffin.

Peggy (darling Peggy, I remember her as an adjunct) introduced the president and he shambled to the microphone. I could not remember a time when Dr. Woodward was not the president; how did we River-babies allow a dictatorship to take root in our greatest monument to freedom of thought? It was he—not him alone, mind you—who turned Freedman's into a wasteland. We deserved the scorn of Sparks and his ilk. I watched Dr. Benjamin Woodward with a sneer as he cleared his throat, a great guttural grunting sounding into the mic. Angry goose pimples raised themselves along my skin. If I were taken to violence (and I might have to be someday soon) I would have parked myself at the top of the library tower with a rifle, staring into the scope, waiting for Woodward to step into the black of my crosshairs.

He was a man who had survived many scandals, many plagiarism accusations, many budget shortfalls. Woodward was weakened, but unashamed. In fact, Wood-wood, as we called him intentionally and as he called himself accidentally through the hilarious magic of poor pronunciation, was incapable of shame. I recall the time the student newspaper caught him slipping the good wood-wood to his secretary despite his wife who wore a church hat and a smile to every convocation, every graduation, every campus function both major and minor—in fact, she was there in the front today wearing a regal light blue crown fronted with lace and baby's breath. His quote to those students: *So?* And it took just a week for the newspaper staff to disappear. It was as if those students never existed.

The microphone whined as Wood-wood moved his lips closer to it. Graduation, he said, the bass of his voice rumbling through the auditorium.

For a moment he let the silence hang before continuing: We talk about graduation the way that folk singer talks about revolution. He eased into the mic and hissed: Like whispers.

A contingent in the front began hooting and clapping. They fooled no one; Woodward brought his own claque of people to clap and scream at his every talk.

He continued: We need to shout it. We need to scream it. That's what we are about at Freedman's University. Graduation! He bawled it this time and the microphone squealed in pain. He paused before continuing. I know some of you want me to speak about that guy and his rallies, but that's not what I'm going to talk about today except to say that that's free speech. I can't do nothing about that, so I'm going to talk today about things we can control, like—he moved his mouth so that it hovered over the mic—graduation!

That shiny engineering program with all its fancy machines. The writing program. All the nurses now training in our hospital. None of that means anything if we aren't shipping a steady supply of Freedman's graduates into the world. Quantity creates quality. We shove enough of them out there and one of them is bound to be great. But we are not making enough of our students walk the plank. We are hung up on old-fashioned notions of excellence, mastery, and reputation. Here we need to define excellence as graduation, and our reputation rests upon the aforementioned graduation. That is our future, my Freedmen.

He paused, taking in the silence. And let me tell you this, he continued. I'm not asking you to sacrifice scholarship, excellence, or intellectual rigor. No. Of course not. All of that must remain. Be excellent is our motto. As a matter of fact, there is not enough scholarship coming out of this part of the world. We want excellent scholarship. And some of you may be saying, *But Wood-wood, how do we do that while each moving hundreds of students on to graduation each year?* Yes, you do have an average of two hundred and fifty students each per semester (not counting lecture hall classes), but if you divide your day into five-minute excrements, you can see how much time you actually waste and you can practice the art of researching and writing in five-minute bursts. As a matter of fact, this semester's Norville Orbison Faculty University College Keynote Speaker, Dr. Jarreau Simmons, author of *The 5-Minute Scholar*, will speak in a few minutes about the art of writing and publishing journal articles in the five minutes between your classes, at red lights, or just before falling asleep. Anytime you got five minutes, you got a journal article, you got a chapter, as far as I'm concerned. String enough of those five minutes together and you got a book. No laziness here at Freedman's, just excellence. Excellence. And graduation. To that end, I'd like to announce the Faculty University College Brilliancy Operation Initiative.

Wood-wood's sycophants began woo-hooing and cheering, waving their arms in approval. You haven't even heard the plan yet, he said. The paid sycophants laughed.

You all have journal articles, submit them to our committee for scrutiny, he continued. Best article from any discipline gets a thousand dollars. Second place is a copy of Dr. Simmons's text. Third, well, there is no third. Everyone gets a critique, though. Get to writing, my Faculty University College Brilliancy Operation Initiative Scholars! The cheering section now stood and screamed madly, whistling and slapping their hands together with great force and vigor. Bring out the brilliance, that's our motto! Thank you to Peggy, er, *Dr. Summers*, for suggesting this program and for naming it. She names everything around here. And I want to thank Dr. Simmons—we used to call him Soapy back in undergrad, that's my line, brother—for taking time away from the classes he teaches at Stanford . . . Oh, what's that, brother, you don't teach in the spring? Got a 1/0 teaching load, you say? That's not a teaching load, that's a score! Well, we'd like to thank him for taking time away from his, uh, duties to talk to us about achieving our excellence. I love you all. Here's to a wonderful semester. Graduation!

As Wood-wood stepped from in front of the microphone I felt such a despondency, such a despair, I could scarcely stand. I looked around at all my peers and they were feeling it too, reeling, flopping about as if their limbs had turned to pasta. Dr. Simmons spoke after Woodward and he only compounded things—all his talk of *researching and writing in the gutters of your life*—I felt as if I had sunk into the floor and was now groping to climb up from a bottomless pit of starry blue darkness. I remembered why I stopped attending these things despite the easy access to food and drink. It was designed to break our spirits, make us dependent on Freedman's, make us see Woodward as the great father. I looked around, and so many had fallen for the conditioning as I once had. The fact that Chambers wasn't here was a sign that he was beginning to free himself. As a matter of fact, back so many years ago when I first woke, the most important thing I did was skip the Faculty University College. What wonders that one act did for my newly unshackled mind.

I trudged back to the morgue, ready to sleep a dead sleep on the floor like my father's corpse. Before lying down and closing my hazy, sandy eyes, I opened my AOL, moving with rote robotic motions. My computer shouted at me that I had mail, and I did. In between the spam and Idra's nonsense sat a message from Chambers imploring me to read a thing he called *beautiful* and *special*. And indeed I read it and found it, his latest syllabus, so glorious that I read it over and over, I read it aloud to hear the sound of the words, tasting them and rolling them in my mouth. I read it in different voices, first shouting and then whispering. I stayed up all night as one does with a lover, and as I read, my eyes poured salty ancient rivers and I saw myself as a speck in the waters swimming about in all that beauty.

FREEDMAN'S UNIVERSITY
College of Arts and Sciences
Department of English and Cultural Studies

English 101: Special Topics: Loneliness

Spring 2018

Instructor: Dr. Reginald S. Chambers, Ph.D.

Email: RChambers@Freedmans.edu

Alternate Email: Blacker.Roland.Hudson@gmail.com

Extension: x3725

Office Location: Alfred McCoy Hall 0242

Office Hours: MWF: 9 a.m.–11 a.m.; 2 p.m.–5 p.m.

I. COURSE PREREQUISITES:

Students must pass the University-approved placement test, a bit of a ridiculous measure. Tell me, what does a test have to do with the beating of the human heart?

More importantly, students should bring to the course an open mind and, above all else, a questioning but thorough and intellectually rigorous spirit. And then, couple that spirit with a near-radical honesty—intellectual and otherwise.

The poet Roland Hudson believed that his words could rearrange and derange the consciousness of the reader. I want to work with students who are willing to worship at the altar of great writers like Hudson, and who would like to be rearranged and deranged in order to rearrange and derange others. I believe in the power of words to achieve this derangement. Indeed, it could be said that I have been deranged by words.

By taking this class you are telling me that you believe in Word Power completely the way a fundamentalist Christian believes in the divinity of Jesus. If at any time you no longer believe in Word Power, then you must immediately drop the class. Of course, there may be dark nights—and even semesters—of the soul, I myself have them, but the only way around that is by writing and thinking through the darkness. If you stay in this class, this is the basic assumption you accept. Everything else can and must be questioned.

II. COURSE DESCRIPTION:

First, this is a writing-intensive course. If that is a problem for you there are plenty of other professors in this department who will award you an A grade for making power ballads, Play-Doh sculptures, YouTube videos, and the like as your primary coursework. That is fine; it is not what we are doing here. You will write a major essay relating to our theme while utilizing various modes of rhetorical development. In addition, journals and reading responses will be assigned throughout the course of the semester.

Our theme this semester is **_LONELINESS_**, which means we will discuss this concept (idea? feeling?) as the basic and most elemental problem of humanity. According to a September 5, 2016, article in the *New York Times*, "As a predictor of early death, loneliness eclipses obesity" (Hafner, *see required texts*). The most antisocial among us are still social creatures. Isolate a newborn and, even when provided with the proper nutrition, he or she dies. When an adult is isolated, he or she can become warped, unhinged, disassociated from reality. What is the outcome when you have a society of the warped? We all use each other to keep our fragile minds tethered. Still, we often seek solitude to recharge us, make us more creative, to become in touch with our truest thoughts. Things we will examine may include: the difference between solitude and loneliness; depression and loneliness; the difference between depression and unhappiness; the unbearable sadness of a Monday morning; anything else your brilliant minds can conjure, but most importantly, we will discuss how to make the hurting stop.

We are all adults. The subject matter, at times, may call on us to explore mature themes, such as sexuality and violence. Therefore, you—or I—may deem it necessary to deploy the full range of our language, including profanity, within reason. I fully encourage this. This class is a free and safe space.

III. REQUIRED TEXTS:

Baldwin, James. *Notes of a Native Son*. Boston: Beacon Press, 1984. Print.

Fitzgerald, Helena. "The Fierce Triumph of Loneliness." *Catapult*. Catapult, 18 May 2016. Web. 24 May 2016. <https://catapult.co/stories/the-fierce-triumph-of-loneliness>.

Hafner, Katie. "Researchers Confront an Epidemic of Loneliness." *New York Times*, September 5, 2016. Web. 22 September 2016.

Hudson, Roland. *The Firewater of Love: Poems*. Cross River: Peckerman House, 2010. Print.

Thoreau, Henry D. *Walden; or, Life in the Woods*. London: J. M. Dent, 1908. Print.

A dictionary

A thesaurus

A notebook to fill with the impressions of your human heart.

IV. STUDENT (AND PROFESSOR) OUTCOMES:

Upon completion of English 101, students will demonstrate:

1. Look, I'm required to reproduce an endless list of things here, including improvement in critical reading skills, critical thinking skills, an awareness of grammar conventions, blah, blah, blah . . . and I hope you do get all that and more from this course, but the one thing I expect you (and me) to gain from our semester together is an understanding of how to eradicate the ache of common loneliness.

V. GRADING/EVALUATION PROCEDURES:

Grades do little but pervert the educational process, and if I could do away with them I would, but I'm no fool. I understand that most of you have been damaged by your prior learning experiences and the only thing you respect is the lash of the teacher-as-policeman providing arbitrary numbers for everything you do. If I didn't have the power to ascend you to heaven (*pass* you) or banish you to hell (*fail* you), then most of you would not read or engage with the texts. It's sad, really, because you are not here to receive some dull, barely useful numerical evaluation and then move on to becoming some cog in a barely middle-wage, middle-class job. You are here to learn how to think. Society doesn't want you to think. It's better for the powers-that-be if you remain ignorant. Better to manipulate you and use you for their own agendas. Thinking is a rebellious act. Please remember that and remember this: When you were born and you came out of your mother's womb you were covered in blood and slimy afterbirth. In short, you were completely disgusting. Time passed and you made a habit of shitting and pissing yourself and then you learned to clean yourself (poorly at first), but still you made a habit of publicly digging in your nose. Many of us never shake this habit. Presumably you've stopped most of your disgusting habits, at least outwardly, but maybe you don't shower daily or maybe you don't properly clean yourself after masturbation. Maybe you leave the restroom without washing your hands. (I'm sure at least some of you carry on with this revolting, sickness-passing habit,) Perhaps you cheat on tests or on your lovers or you plagiarize. There are levels to disgusting. In essence, then, the goal of maturation, of education, is to, over time, make yourself less disgusting.

I won't list a bunch of meaningless percentages here. You tell me what you think your assignments are worth.

VI. ACADEMIC INTEGRITY:

It's our secrets that make us the most lonely and this I'm about to tell you is not something I've ever admitted to anyone. When I was an undergraduate there was this girl. I wanted to possess every inch of her, but she was a wild stallion, and I, a poor jockey. She was among the first to allow me inside of her and I cried from joy when we finished. That's not the thing that brings me the shame, this is it: she was ravenous, needing to make love two or three times a session several nights a week. This was fairly new to me and, yes, I imagined myself a conqueror of the female form. Who told me I was this type of warrior? There had never been any basis in reality for this self-image. A couple instances of breast sucking followed by intercourse in high school. An incident of awkward oral sex in the first weeks of college. I simply couldn't keep up with my first real girlfriend and the worst of it was that most times I finished quickly, far too quickly to ever satisfy her. It became too much. So much. I hunched over crying softly in her dorm room one night after we were done. (I say, we, but I was the only one who finished.) I looked over and she had turned to her side, a beam of bluish white light lying across her black skin. She rested her hand between her legs and I could tell she was finishing herself off. I grew enraged as if I had caught her with another. We began to scream back and forth.

Well, what do you expect me to do? she cried.

Really? I replied, while I'm lying right next to you?

She looked away, and a feeling of foolishness passed over me. It was all so absurd. I didn't know it, but I was screaming into a void at myself, at my own loneliness.

It's okay, she whispered. We can work on the sex. Don't turn this into something bigger than it has to be.

When the tears ended, we held hands, naked, staring

into the dark at the ceiling. Really, it was quite beautiful. I did not plan to spend the night this way. A quick fuck and then finish the paper I had due in Comm. Law. My love put her hand on my dick as the dawn neared and I bawled out in terror. I had work due. I was going to fail because of her. No, she said, shaking my flaccid dick. You'll fail because of this thing.

It stiffened in her hand and I replied: This is not a joke! I'll lose my scholarship. She turned from me. I watched the ridges of her spine press themselves against her skin. She stood and rummaged through the mess of papers scattered on her desk. Here, she said. I got an A on this last semester. Spend an hour re-typing it.

My love's A somehow became a D in my professor's eyes. I lost my scholarship. And soon I found out my girlfriend was cheating on me with a fine arts student. A horrible singer who never wears a shirt and always sounds like he just smoked thirty cigarettes. I hear him on the radio sometimes, so do you. He has gotten no better. And sometimes I pass the Fine Arts Building and I'm haunted by the memory of them huddled together, not committing a sexual act, not even touching, but standing in a pose too intimate for casual friendship. How could I have been so blind as to watch them, but not truly see them? We yelled at one another in the privacy of her dorm room. I prepared to accept this transgression and move on together, but she shrugged and broke it off abruptly. Her world didn't require me. I spent the rest of my time as a student at this university tormented and mostly alone, finding company—and a kind of friendship—only with Christine, only with strangers in the library tower. *I ACCEPT NO FORMS OF PLAGIARISM OR ACADEMIC DISHONESTY.*

VII. COURSE OUTLINE

If I'm forced to leave the teaching profession, I'll perhaps try my hand at becoming a jazzman. I'll need to develop some sort of musical ability, but I have the improvisational aspect down cold. I'm required by the staid, unimaginative powers-that-be of this university to provide you with an extensive week-by-week breakdown of what we will do in class and of the assignments and such I expect from you. What an absurdity! Is this what education has come to? Where is the creativity? The *joie de vivre*? The *joie de enseignement*? The turns of the moment? The excitement of making something new and unpredictable every day? Course outline? I ain't doing that shit. I will ask of you this, though: by the second week, please read Roland Hudson's *The Firewater of Love*. Next Wednesday, my colleague, poetry professor Kin Samson, will guest-lecture on the book. Beyond that, I become Miles, brewin' this bitch fresh as things move forward.

4.

Perhaps you'll agree, Reginald Chambers's syllabus was a remarkable document. Everything was there: the flaunting of his considerable intellect; the contempt for his superiors at the university; disastrous and highly experimental teaching methods. Chambers was ready.

Up until the first day of classes I still had not heard from him, aside from the syllabus. Unbeknownst to me I set up in a classroom right next to his. I found myself facing a full room of bright-eyed students. I cared not what they called themselves, I called them all Bright Eyes. They had heard of me. They too were ready. In a low voice, a dramatic growl, I told from memory the story of Jardin the Axe-Wielder. I closed my eyes near the end of the story and opened them only when Jardin began reciting his abecedarian of violence. To my delight, I saw Dr. Chambers standing in the doorway, his face drawn in childlike wonder. He mostly wore one of two sports coats—a tan or a gray-blue. They were fuzzy from time and repeated dry cleanings, and strings hung from the seams. He was the perfect stereotype of a professor. If those two jackets were at the cleaner's he wore a navy blue that was an older style, slightly too big for him; when he wore that one he looked more like a child than usual; it was as if his father had gifted him a blazer he once wore in the nineties. The sports coats served to remind me that Chambers was my prey and I was on a continuous hunt and like all unwitting beasts unaware of their armed stalkers, he deserved a sporting chance. This day, he wore the tan one with the stained sleeves.

Chambers slow-clapped for me as the students filed out. Reece, he said. That takes on so much more power the way you speak it into existence.

I reached out for a handshake and a brotherly half hug. Yeah, I said. Gets the students excited about the work. What about you? The loneliness class, huh?

Yep, I went for it. Don't say that too loudly, though. What'd you think of the syllabus?

Thing of beauty. What about the essay? You're still working on it, right? Should be submitting it right about now, right?

I gritted my teeth awaiting his answer.

Eh, I don't know about that one. Less in love with it than when I sent it to you. We can talk about that. I got class, though. It'll be a fun semester, for sure.

I nodded like a fool, believing what he said to be true, believing that we'd have time to talk more, but I mostly saw only the back of Dr. Chambers's head in the weeks that followed. I'd see him off in the distance. He'd reply to my long emails with a sentence or two. He moved his classes from next to mine, a technology issue with the glowing screen where he showed his presentations on loneliness and solitude, he said. I never overheard his lectures anymore and I ate alone most days, or infrequently I ate with the dimwit.

Revolutions begin before the overthrow and last long after the skirmishes are finished. Great Insurrections give way to greater insurrections. My heart told me to go slow, but my mind despaired for the plan.

Meanwhile, Chambers taught his class.

5.

LONELINESS VS. SOLITUDE

A presentation by Dr. Reginald Chambers

Freedman's University • English 101
Department of English and Cultural Studies

You are a Superman . . .

. . . in your Arctic fortress, away from the world's crying out, the world grabbing at you, asking you to solve whatever's gone wrong.

Just you and stillness.

Just you and quietude.

Strengthening yourself to again make bullets bounce from your flesh.

This is solitude.

To someone else you are a god,

and it's too much to take.

I never feel more alone than when I'm in Christine's presence.

When I look into her eyes, I see reflected all the dreams of a ten-year-old girl watching her family wrench itself apart

Every minute of every day she transforms into a baby in a barrel
Plunging through the rapids over the Cliffs.
And I become a Superman
defying gravity to rescue her.

I have no Arctic fortress to return to. No break from the labors. There is nothing to me, but rescue.

I can't even tell you how it started, when the deterioration began, but the quiet swept in like a northern breeze on a January morning and . . .

eventually, even the silences between our silences kept their own silences.

This, students, is loneliness.

End of Slideshow, click to exit.

6.

To: Dr. Reginald S. Chambers, Assistant Professor—
Department of English and Cultural Studies <RChambers
@Freedmans.edu>
Sent: February 2, 2018, 3:54 a.m.
From: Rebecca Montana <RMontana@Freedmans.StudentNet
.edu>
Cc:
Bcc:
Subject: Firewater

Hey Mr. Chambers,

I am a student in your noon English 101 (I was the one
in front with the lakers hat). I'm writing because I started
reading Hudsons book. I didn't have to read much poetry in
high school, but I see why u chose this text for this class. I feel
Hudson's loneliness, madness, and confusion on every page. Its
creepy. Makes me shiver. He's been dead since even before my
grandmother was born and the only thing that remains from
him is his despair and his loneliness. It's like he left a ghost and
it haunts us everytime we open his book. I guess that's why I
was the only one who admitted to reading when u wanted to
discuss it in class today. I bet some people started and couldn't
go any further. No one wants to feel all that emotion. Who
wants to be haunted? I mean, its fine for me cuz I watch a lot of
horror movies. Being haunted seems like fun if youre willing to
listen to whatever the ghost has to say.

I wanted to expand on my question from class. When
you were explaining solitude versus loneliness. In Hudson's
book, he talks about the rough part of the Cross River and
being pulled there in the rain, the winter, in the summer while
being *swarmed and devoured by the mosquitoes of blood-sucking
love* (remember when u conceded after my comment that he
may have been talking about literal mosquitoes as well as

metaphorical ones). I think I found the spot he wrote about all
those years ago and I've been going there as if called for a few
days. I'm there now as I type this. It's real peaceful here. Nice
place to meditate. I hear my name echoing. I bet there are a lot
of mosquitoes in the summertime. I must say I'm new to Cross
River. I've never seen anything as beautiful as this river. We
don't have a river as gorgeous as that where I'm from. I just can
sit here for hours. I'm afraid I'm turning into Roland Hudson.
LOL. My question is this: that retreat Hudson talks about, that
spot where he's feeling peaceful but also tormented by the
water & the spirits beneath the water, is that feeling solitude
or loneliness? I'm not sure where it fits on that line between
you & "Christine." It seems like solitude, but if he had friends
who understood his madness he probably would not have spent
anytime sitting there by the Cross River. But then what does
that make me sitting here cross-legged by the Cross River, huh?

Rebecca

• • •

To: Rebecca Montana <RMontana@Freedmans.StudentNet.edu>
Sent: February 2, 2018, 6:00 a.m.
From: Dr. Reginald S. Chambers, Assistant Professor—
Department of English and Cultural Studies <RChambers
@Freedmans.edu>
Cc:
Bcc:
Subject: Re: Firewater

Dear Rebecca,

   I remember who you are. I never forget a student who
engages with the text. Thank you for your incisive questions and
commentary in class. It appears that you are the only student in
any of my six sections of 101 who did the reading so far.

I think you are on to something re: Hudson and solitude. The reason I chose *Firewater* is because Hudson complicates and problematizes the concepts of loneliness and solitude by blending them together. We often talk about them as discreet but related concepts. Our formulation goes something like this: loneliness bad; solitude good. I'm guilty of that too. I'm forced to do a bit of simplifying in class when introducing new concepts. But Hudson isn't restrained by any such convention. Hudson quests into solitude to relieve himself of his loneliness and there he finds comfort, but also torment and more loneliness. We all do a little of this, though most of us are not as dramatic about it as Roland Hudson (lol). I think of the silences I seek to do my life's work and how it conflicts with Christine's life's work of building a sustainable relationship and family. Perhaps you can think of how this works in your own life and in your dealings with friends and loved ones. The conflict is where we find our personal torments. I encourage you to explore these thoughts further in your journal assignments. I will be posting the prompt for that by the end of today.

I am happy you decided to take my suggestion to visit the Cross River. It is indeed a wonder and a beauty.

Sincerely,

Dr. Reginald S. Chambers, Ph.D.
Assistant Professor
Department of English and Cultural Studies
Freedman's University
x3725

———————————

Sometimes I wonder if I can love forever
Like an angel unbound by time
Then I glimpse Lucinda's neck
Long and black like my favorite bend in the Cross River

And I know then that I've lived forever
And as long as I've lived I've loved

—Roland Hudson "Lucinda by Riverlight,"
from *The River Is a Gray Black Snake by Day,
a Silver Snake by Moonlight*

7.

Dr. Reginald Chambers
Freedman's University
English 101
Special Topics: Loneliness

JOURNALS: YOUR LOCUS OF PRACTICE

The problem for many of us is not that we are scatterbrained or foolish, it is that we've lost the ability to sit still, to luxuriate in the meditative trance that serious thinking and writing require. We have been raised on the quick cuts of music videos, the frequent breaks of network television, the sitcom pacing that demands a laugh break every two minutes or so. Real life does not condition us this way. It does not guide us toward the emotion we are supposed to feel. It just is. It's gotten much worse now that we've entered the age of the smartphone. We check and recheck and rerecheck every few minutes for little text missives, to see how that other world, cyberspace, is faring, how it is perceiving us. We condition and recondition ourselves to reject the stillness we need to grow. Since your conditioned mind simply can't accept stillness, when faced with quietude it becomes nearly a dead fish flopping about at the assault of fresh air, of freedom. We are not fish, oxygen is nourishing, but we hardly ever experience it (*it*, or the oxygen of this extended metaphor, being stillness), so how would we ever know its nourishing properties?

This brings us to your journals, the meditative trance that you will induce in yourselves (with my aid!). For each journal you will be assigned a short prompt. Here's what you do: Set aside ten minutes and vow not to be disturbed. Don't ruminate on the prompt, just write. For ten whole minutes stare at your screen and type whatever comes to mind and when that time is up, you stop. Don't worry so much about grammar and spelling and the like (you will worry about these very much in your final paper, which will utilize the insights you've gleaned from your journals), just worry about getting your thoughts out. No more than ten minutes. Trust me, dear students. Do this enough and you will have taken your mind back.

In the interest of taking my mind back, I will be doing this assignment alongside you. Each prompt will come with my take on the topic to give you an idea of what sort of writing I expect.

Dr. Reginald Chambers
Freedman's University
English 101
Special Topics: Loneliness

Journal #1
PROMPT: Write about the loneliest place you have ever been. To Roland Hudson, sometimes the Cross River was the loneliest place he had ever been. But then again, Hudson himself claims that the presence of his love, Gertrude (whom he came to believe was a mythical water-nymph/siren/water-woman), was the loneliest place he had ever been. You may take an expansive view of the word *place*. It does not have to be a physical location. Perhaps your *place* is a time in your life. Perhaps your *place* is in another's presence.

Dr. Chambers Journal #1:
      Christine sits across from me as I type this. The days that I'm writing about, she was both there and not there, like an impression, or a wisp, or a ghost. She resided in Los Angeles and I in a kind of cold hell. Upstate New York. Binghamton. The Bing. There I worked as a newspaper reporter. Most days in Binghamton were lonely and gray and cloudy. Pick a day. Winter or summer. Spring or fall. According to the National Weather Service, Binghamton is cloudier than Seattle and windier than Chicago. This fact often made a hazy wave of black pass over my mind. Seattle and Chicago are, respectively, known for the miseries of gray clouds and sharp winds. By themselves, such atmospheric dreariness can be passed off as charming minuses in landscapes of cultural pluses. Binghamton is a place that bills itself as the Carousel Capital of the World; a place that touts being about three hours from vibrant culture and life, as if where people want to live is really *away* from everything. While I was there, the city had also been named one of the country's unhappiest places to live by some magazine.

The world then was a black-and-white picture taken just out of focus. I rambled back then when it was warm enough to walk and sometimes when it wasn't, the death-cold of zero and below. The cold that could and often would freeze and then cleave my soul from me. I would often walk from the edge of the city of Binghamton—on Main Street where a stone arch tells drivers they are entering Johnson City—to the downtown area, where Main Street becomes Court Street. On these walks, I sought clarity, but never found any. My grandmother who was back in Cross River often used to say, It's always time for a change, but change comes with time. It's one of those clichés that, on balance, proves true. Time had a different meaning to her because she'd always been old—at least as long as I'd known her—and I'd always been young. Plus, she'd never lived in Binghamton. Time moved more slowly there. I aged ten years in the three that I lived there. I rarely ever saw people my own age, not to mention people of my own hue. Mostly it was middle-aged white folks who looked very old and the very old who looked nearly dead—and boy did those old white folks watch me suspiciously. Even at work I was a lone black drop of paint in a bucket of white primer. And every time someone interviewed a person darker than a sunburn, the editor would tout it in the daily newsletter: *Reginald Chambers interviewed Johnson Smith, an African-American!*

When I looked out onto the world, all I could see was an ocean of heads as gray as a Binghamton sky. It reminded me of my mortality. I spoke to no one. Well, almost no one, and when I did speak I'd wished I hadn't, work talk and such, small talk and such, speech with so little consequence it was like anti-speech, speech that communicated nothing but the dubious idea that any word-sound is preferable to silence; it often felt as if my misuse of the ability to form words had erased real words from my vocabulary. The words formed in my brain, but never made it to my mouth; they committed suicide rather than be with me. I shook from the center of my chest, that's what this imposed solitude did for me, it quaked my very soul. It was time for a change, but change comes with time.

Look, I've said all this and I've actually said very little. Very little that is true. Yes, I was alone. Quite literally walking against the wind in a windswept wasteland. Yes, it was a wretched experience and I felt my humanity leaking from me. And yes, I cried out for Christine and we'd visit each other every couple months and lie in the warmth of each other's arms and promise to share a soul between us to make up for the soulage that we both lost living alone and away from one another. And I didn't realize it then, but the truth is that any warm being (a cat, a half-dead junkie, a swarm of fruit flies) could have stilled my emptiness with their temporary presence. But I felt something much different later; what I'm talking about was after I left that cold hell to return to Cross River and Christine left Los Angeles for Cross River and she became a permanent presence, always around, I had to learn to live with the pressure of her standing on my soul; what I'm trying to say is this: I love Christine, I really, really, really and truly love her, but what I came to learn is that I felt one kind of alone in Binghamton and a whole 'nother sort of alone with Christine. Who knew that loneliness came in so many varieties?

Rebecca Montana
English 101.15
Freedman's University
Special Topics: Loneliness
Dr. Chambers

Journal #1

I think it was the first or second day of class that u, Dr. Chambers, asked us all what compelled us to take a class themed around lonelines. Most everyone shrugged as you went around one by one trying to get at our motivations. No one seemed to know that this was a themed course. One girl said it was the only class that fit into her schedule. A guy toward the back laughed at you, *It's just a class, man,* he said. *It's not even that deep.* But I could see by the disappointment on your face. It was that deep for you. Even deeper than we could have imagine. Since it was easier for me to lie, I shrugged right along with my classmates, but the truth is, Dr. Chambers, it is that deep for me. Even deeper than you could know. I suspect some of my classmates were similarly lying to be cool. Loneliness has always haunted me like a shadow, but it was last semester—my first in college—that the dark shadows rose up an became ghosts, something scary and capable of destroying me. I never knew lonliness could be such a powerful force. For a short time, Cross River, Freedman's University, became for me the very loneliest place on the planet.

I've always been a good student until loneliness came barrelling into my life. I came from the West Coast to be part of history. My mentors told me to go to Freedman's, become an AKA, see the river, be 1 with the insurrectionary ancestors. I got on campus and forgot how to speak. I wasn't overwhelmed by the majesty, but by the ordnriness of it all. I don't know what I expected. Daily insurrections in the land of the Insurrection? Maybe toward the end of the second week, I looked around and it seemed like everyone around me had formed cliques, social groups designed to keep me out. I had no place. I went weeks without speaking and no one noticed. Anyone who cared about me was in california and they didn't *really* care. Out of sight, out of mind. I went to class a little, but I didn't do anything. I didn't even know *how* to do anything. I cursed myself. Laid on my side in my bed and tried not to cry. I asked why I was the way I was. I looked in the mirror and offered myself affirmations while my roommates were out. Nothing worked.

One of my roommates, Stacy, heard one of my affirmations, I think, and invited me out with a few girlfriends. *The Garden is lit,* she said. *You should come out. It'll be fun.* She picked my clothes, loaning me something tight-fitting and revealing. Banished my glasses so I had to squint, told me my makeup wouldn't do and smeared her own onto my face.

We came together, Stacey said to the four of us while in line for The Garden. *So we're leaving together. Understand?* We nodded and for a time we held hands like a line of children while we snaked thru the club. But the hand I held grew tired of mine and let it go and before long I didn't see Stacy and them.

I became just a body to be felt on and pressed against. One of thousands of bodies in The Garden that night. Music with the volume raised to distortion levels. Hands reaching for my hands, stranger hands brushing against my body. There were moments I could, oddly enough, think clearly and deeply in the club—I suppose this is solitude, to be comfortably alone tho in the presence of thousands—and then a hand would grab at my butt and I'd suddenly feel so alone. I walked from the Riverbeat room to the hip-hop room, to the r&b room, to the Top 40 room. I didnt find what I was looking for. Connection thru a grinding sort of dance. Connection thru shouted small talk. Thru sips of alcohol. I found no such connection. Sometimes I looked for Stacey and the girls, sometimes I just walked. I felt dehydrated as if I'd crossed a desert. I probably wouldn't have recognized Stacey if I saw her. Everyone's faces turned into smiley-face emojis. The hot air was suffocating me. I needed the fresh air of the street, the breeze from the river.

I stepped outside and the stars in the sky looked like emojis. Winking and smiling and crying down on me. I must have looked drunk, stumbling about, pupils dilated. Intoxicated by loneliness. Men called to me. Hey girl. Come talk. Their intentions were only to increase my loneliness. I ignored them. I looked at my phone. Stacy had texted me two times.

Hey gurl.

Where are you?

I ignored my phone and walked thru the town looking at people with emoji faces. They clung to stop signs. They laid on the sidewalk. They shouted to me. I thought they would destroy me.

When I made it back to the dorm room, Stacy was asleep and we never spoke about that night. We pass by each other like we've beceom shadows. In the dorm. On the way to the bathroom. In class. she's in this section and her name is not Stacy. I failed all my classes cuz I could barely get out of bed for part of the semester. Tell me, what would've been the purpose of getting out of bed? I booked a one-way flight back to LA and then I saw your class listed, Prof. Chambers. I saw the chance to really, really understand this thing that was trying to eat right thru me. Forgive my shrug and the shrugs of my peers. I couldn't explain all that when u asked. Stacey couldn't explain that she took the class to understand why she needs to always be surrounded by idiot girls she barely cares about so she lied to be cool when you came to her.

Also, forgive me. I took longer than the ten minutes you told us to alot for the writing of our journals. I hope u understand.

8.

Dr. Chambers's unraveling became visible in his face, in the way he held his body, in his very steps, after that first journal assignment. He looked gray and drained, and sway-walked as if all energy were falling away from his body.

He mentioned in passing the full classes consisting of only eyes staring back at him. His days became just hours of speaking to himself mostly. I observed this deteriorating man from a distance, usually, measuring just when would be the right moment to intercede, to become an ear for him to speak into, a mouth of advice.

One afternoon after his last class of the day, I followed the shambling Chambers through the halls, just watching. It was as if many devils had possessed him and were tearing down the entirety of his physicality, his face became a fright mask; gaunt; he held his features, the movable ones, in such a way that drained any beauty from them. His face wasn't actually scarred, but it appeared scarred, you know? Pale and lined with haggard worry. His walk was no longer a walk, but an attempt not to tumble over.

I arrived to his office just as he sighed and collapsed into his creaking chair. He dumped a bottle of water into his electric kettle and set the thing to boil. It steamed and rocked. Chambers looked to the floor without noticing me in the doorway.

Tea break? I said finally.

Ah, Reece, glad you've come by.

Oh?

I need the company, I would visit you in your office, but ... say, where the hell is your office, anyway?

Funny, Chambers. It's the rough patch of the semester, already?

I don't know, Reece, he said. Not a single one of them did the journal assignment. Well, one of them did it. I walk into the class. Lecture my heart out. No one is paying attention except one student, man. Barely any of them have read the book.

Tough shit, man. I shook my head and looked to the floor. My words were nothing-words that just filled space. Tough, tough shit.

More than tough, Reece. It's a gigantic waste of time and energy. How many problems could I solve if I weren't preoccupied with this dumb shit, huh? Maybe I should just cut my losses, fall back on some busywork, and ride the semester out.

Chambers sighed. I backed up, watching that kettle steaming and shaking up a storm as if it held a tempest within.

Be grateful for that one student, Chambers.

Yeah. I guess. She did the assignment perfectly too. Grammar issues, but yeah. If more of them were on it we could get somewhere.

Just as I thought that kettle was about to topple to the floor, dousing us in boiling water, it dinged and clicked to signal it had finished its work. It now sat still and silver and peaceful, except for the ribbons of steam rising from the spout. Chambers took down two Styrofoam cups from a shelf above.

Tea? I nodded and he poured the water. He cast the tea bags like fishing lines into the steamy depths of the cups. The steam seemed dark and bluish, resembling smoke.

Let me come in and lecture, I said. I have a fable for all occasions.

He scooped maybe six or so spoons of sugar into his tea from a silver tin. I became concerned and grabbed mine before he could poison my cup.

Next semester, Reece. I already have Kin Samson coming in to talk about Hudson, if I can get him to pin down a date. Chambers sighed again. Maybe I should just cancel with Kin.

Look, Chambers, when the students aren't on, that's when you go harder. Double down! Give them much more complicated work. Not busywork. Work you'd give a grad student, even. Watch some of them rise to the challenge. Let that one student lead them all.

You think?

I do. Very deeply.

That bit of bad advice seemed to bring color back to Chambers's cheeks. He sat up a bit, resembling a puppy in his chair. He sipped at his tea, the blue smoke-steam obscuring his face.

A little corner of one of his porn pictures peeked from the top drawer of his desk. The fuckface of a woman in the throes of passion. And don't you know that little fuckface winked at me?

What about the essay?

Let me get a handle on this class, Reece.

I sipped. The tea tasted blue.

9.

To: Dr. Reginald S. Chambers, Assistant Professor—Department of English and Cultural Studies <RChambers@Freedmans.edu>
Sent: March 29, 2018, 11:03 p.m.
From: Rebecca Montana <RMontana@Freedmans.StudentNet .edu>
Cc:
Bcc:
Subject: Todays Lecture

Wow. What a lecture. Electric! I want to thank you for bringing ▮▮▮ to discuss Roland Hudson with us! I'm reading Hudson with new eyes. I'm reading Audre Lord and Nurruda like ▮▮▮ suggested. And the Bell Hooks essay she recommended: "The Firewater Next Time: 'Love' as Bad Politics or Imagining More Loving Visions of Black Love Within the Torment and 'Love' of Roland Hudson" was extremely illuminating. And I'm reading Kin Samson, now! And ▮▮▮ has been giving me some feedback on my final essay ideas so has Dr. Samson (when are you posting the prompt???) What a class we had today!

Thanks

• • •

To: Professor Akinsanya Samson, Lecturer—Department of English and Cultural Studies <ASamson@Freedmans.edu>
Sent: April 1, 2018, 5:54 a.m.
From: Dr. Reginald S. Chambers, Assistant Professor—Department of English and Cultural Studies <RChambers @Freedmans.edu>
Cc: ███████████ , < ███████████████████████ >
Bcc:
Subject: Re: Re: Re: Re: Class visit?

Dear Prof. Samson,

I was unaware that ██████ was back on campus, no longer an adjunct, but instead a doctoral student. I invited you to speak to my composition classes about Roland Hudson and *The Firewater* because of your expertise in Cross Riverian poetics, so it was a bit disorienting to see ██████ saunter into my class alone, offering little explanation or apology for your absence, but instead offering herself as a substitute. And I can't explain it (or really I don't care to here), but it was like I eased out of myself and was standing on the muddy river floor watching the muted light from the sun fade as it tried to reach me. Since she's your charge, I would imagine you would like to know how ██████'s presentation went. There was no substance there, she essentially played hypeman to your flawed assertions. ██████ knew nothing of Roland Hudson until I introduced her to the poet in the semester she adjuncted with us. It's almost as if she understands less now. It's great that ██████ is working to ascend out of the adjunct a-class-here-and-there merry-go-round; however, after watching her presentation, I am concerned with the sort of education she is receiving with respect to Hudson specifically and Cross Riverian poetics in general. Everything about her presentation was unwelcome and unsettling.

During ██████'s talk yesterday I closed my eyes and took a series of deep breaths as she spoke to my students, counted to ten. Anger management training I learned when very young. Strange thing happened, my mind took me away from the presentation and deposited me in history: the moment Mama Hudson arrived at the Cross River, baby Roland in her arms. She had walked from Texas to Maryland trying to get free, unaware that slavery had come to an end. When I saw her, she collapsed into the dirt mumbling the mantra that so many had used to motivate their movements, *I get to Cross River, I'll be free.*

She said it fourteen times, a perfect sonnet.

Mythmaking you say? I peeked back through the veil of history and heard ██████ citing you, telling my students that Mama Hudson's triumph likely never happened. The poet invented it in a fit of madness or of grandiosity.

Maybe. Perhaps.

Do you think that's what our students need to hear? That's more important to hear than the idea that you can take words and remake yourself with them? Like Hudson did. Like ██████ is attempting to do. Like you, yourself, did.

It surprised me yesterday to see so many of my students coming to life to ██████'s commentary, some even momentarily drowning out Ms. Montana, who, as I mentioned previously, is the only student in any of my classes who regularly comments or asks questions. If you look at it from that perspective, the class visit was a great success, however there are a few issues I would like to address with you.

The disdain and disrespect ██████ showed and requested the students show toward a true master like Roland Hudson is not only concerning with respect to her scholarly judgment, but also is counterproductive to my class. I am attempting to instill within these students a true love of poetry. We are in Cross River and most of our students are Riverbabies. What better place to start than with the great poets who wrote and write with the rhythm of the River? Where would poets like Darley Jeffers, David Sherman, Anika Winters, Phoenix Starr, Samantha Michaels, Marcus McMurry, Ama Akoto,

Gerald "Comrade" Osei, L'Ouverture, James Rivers, J. Larry Peckerman, and, yes, Kin Samson, be without the example set by Roland Hudson? We don't have to start with Milton and end with Whitman.

Mama Hudson's walk, as narrated by Roland Hudson in the beginning of *Firewater*, is more real to me than even ████ is.

If there's one moment that I can point to that encapsulates my frustration with yesterday's lecture, it was when Ms. Montana raised her hand and asked, What about love?

I don't think ████ understood her. How could she, of course? Water-women understand almost nothing about love. She paused and looked up at the ceiling. Floated in the moment, like a ghost. The messy knots of her dreadlocks, her maroon Phoenix Starr shirt and ripped jeans. The shirt so faded it looked nearly white, as if she thought my students weren't worthy of professorial clothing.

She stuttered a bit, but the impatient Ms. Montana cut her off: "*all I ever do | all I can ever do | is write fire blue missives to || a love never known*. Wasn't it an act of love that inspired Roland Hudson to capture his unrequited lover Gertrude in his verse, to keep her between the lines for all time?"

Rebecca actually used the phrase *unrequited lover*, and that's what makes her special. ████ scoffed. "Love," she said, floating there a ghost human being. I could actually hear the quotation marks she put around the word, those ugly little walrus teeth set down to break the dream. "There's no such thing as an 'unrequited lover,'" she said. "All your unrequited annoyances are irritations, not lovers. Love? [Here she laughed.] Love is so often discussed, but still so uninterrogated. Love does the same thing to your brain that cocaine does, but Hudson's obsession for Gertrude can't be excused by way of addiction. You pose that question as if 'love' is inherently a beautiful thing, as if Hudson's 'love' for Gertrude wasn't, for her, a torture. Imagine being the woman chased and hunted and haunted, and then finally robbed of her humanity, turned into a mythical being: a siren, a woe, a water-woman, a shauntice, all for exercising her free will not to return the 'love' of some lunatic. These aren't so much poems as they are records of a specific type of harassment. You see, men are taught that a woman's no is a speed bump on the way to yes. Hudson wrote flowery odes to that idea and then drowned himself and blamed Gertrude for his death. And then literary scholars have the nerve to accept and praise this! That's beautiful to you? Imagine being on the receiving end of that 'love.' What am I saying? I'm sure some of the women in this class have been the subject of this kind of 'love.' I have. [Some of my female students nodded and grumbled assent, reluctantly, I think, moved by ███████'s prodding.] Not so beautiful when it's not presented in metaphor, is it?"

By then I had had enough. "Don't you think, Prof. ████████, that you are being harsh?" I asked. "Thinking about people from history as if they had the benefit of modernity?"

"Reggie, let me ask you this, has the human heart changed since the late 1800s when Roland Hudson was writing? Have you read any poetry by Gertrude? Didn't she come to him as a student? What happened to her voice?"

Mercifully class ended. I had to sit through some version of that six times that day. Perhaps I should have asked her to leave after the first class. I hope reading our exchange will show you how wildly out of order your student was and I hope you will speak to her; I won't die holding my breath, though.

Let me let the poet have the last word:

Ever think of your brain in the complete darkness of your skull?
That's where it lives
Does its work and dies
Never seeing light.

And you, my love:
Churning, loving, roiling, conflicted, loving

Walking through storms.
Just walking.
Never knowing your destination
Never understanding your strut.
Strutting anyway.

Dr. Reginald S. Chambers, Ph.D.
Assistant Professor
Department of English and Cultural Studies
Freedman's University
x3725

———————————

Better a failed
Poet than a poet

—Roland Hudson
"The Metamorphoses," from *The Firewater of Love*

• • •

To: Dr. Reginald S. Chambers, Assistant Professor—
Department of English and Cultural Studies <RChambers
@Freedmans.edu>
Sent: April 3, 2017, 2:33 p.m.
From: Professor Akinsanya Samson, Lecturer—Department of
English and Cultural Studies <ASamson@Freedmans.edu>
Cc: ███████████ , <█████████████████████████>
Bcc:
Subject: Re: Re: Re: Re: Re: Class visit?

Reggie,

I have no idea what you're going on about. You and I have a
difference of opinion about the relative value of Roland Hudson's
work. (Un)fortunately, I don't have time to debate you. I had
indicated to you my reluctance to lecture on Hudson and sent
████ in my stead because she has a perspective that is much

sharper than my own and, in addition, she is one of the most capable grad students I've ever worked with. If your perspective were so strong, you'd be much more tolerant of dissent.

And I will add that ███████ is my teaching assistant and student, not a battlefield for us to wage war upon.

I would leave you with some words from Hudson, but his poems are too dumb even for this dumb conversation.

Kin Samson
Lecturer in Cross River Poetics
Department of English and Cultural Studies
Freedman's University
x4427

. . .

To: Dr. Reginald S. Chambers, Assistant Professor—Department of English and Cultural Studies <RChambers@Freedmans.edu>
Sent: April 3, 2018, 4:44 p.m.
From: ███████████, <███████████████████████>
Cc: Professor Akinsanya Samson, Lecturer—Department of English and Cultural Studies <ASamson@Freedmans.edu>
Bcc:
Subject: Re: Re: Re: Re: Re: Re: Re: Class visit?

Dear Dr. Chambers,

You didn't introduce me to Hudson, but you helped me see him as you do, eyes aflame—you're a great teacher! And yes, this caused me to read and read, and to disappear, and to search, and the more I looked for Hudson, the more I found Gertrude. You should see her, she's beautiful. But I doubt you've ever seen her. Forgive me for responding to a message that wasn't addressed to me, but Gertrude was silenced, so I will not allow myself to be silenced as well.

I'm surprised my lecture proved so traumatic to you. I've
spoken to many of your students and your male students
said it opened their ears, the women say it "gave them life."
I felt a oneness when I was up in front of your class. My body
disappeared and I became a conduit, a node for some other
world to speak through me. You ever felt that in front of a class?
I know you have because you've told me about it. I believe all
teachers have at one time or another. It's rare. I hardly ever felt
like that in front of my classes when I was adjuncting, sadly—
it's been years—but I felt it in front of yours and I can only
thank you for that.

I didn't close my eyes when I was in that zone up there
before your students, but if I did I would have also seen a
woman, not Mama Hudson, though I respect her challenges,
which were likely considerable, but instead I'd have seen the
poet Gertrude toiling away on poems that would later be
buried in the river with Roland Hudson and his fantastical (I
meant fanatical, but I'll leave it) obsession. No pictures of her
remain, so my Gertrude looks like me. All we have of Gertrude
is a single published poem showing great promise (greater
than Hudson, in my opinion), letters from contemporaries—
prominent poets—offering praise, and we have Hudson's
delusional-ass book.

I too wanted to be a Hudson scholar, but I gave it up when I
realized I'd rather be a Gertrude scholar. So when Ms. Montana
emails to ask me questions, I answer with the same honesty I
brought to your class.

Roland Hudson was essentially a misogynist with myth
on his side and a tongue loosed by mental illness. Gertrude
wasn't a water-woman any more than I am, any more than you
or Prof. Samson are elves or ghosts or werewolves. And therein,
my friend, lies my lack of excitement for Hudson's poetry. I,
of course, maintain my love for our town and all things in it,
and my lack of interest in Roland Hudson's poetry can't be

construed—as you imply—as a repudiation of the genius found every day in the land of Riverbeat.

After all, I'm so Cross River it feels as if I've made it all up. Every inch of it. From the cracks on the sidewalks of Angela Street to the feet walking over those cracks to the stray dogs in the Wildlands being confused for wolves to every single ripple bobbing across the Cross River. I even created the sunlight sprinkled across those ripples when the sun sinks into the waters in the early evening. And the sun, I created that too.

As for you, our Professor of Loneliness. Madness is overtaking you. I can't help, so please send me no more messages, notes, words, characters, or symbols. The wild-eye has embedded itself in your face.

Shut it.

Don't dare look through it and

Breathe easy.

████████████

Doctoral Student/Teaching Assistant/Adjunct Lecturer

10.

I had never seen such personal disarray in a human as I did in Dr. Chambers in the weeks following the Adjunct's visit to his class; his clothes sat lopsidedly on him, wrinkled as if to say, *Putting these clothes on my back is effort enough; ironing is a line I'll never cross!* And today he wore his shirt mostly untucked until I saw him before lunch and urged him to get himself together. We sat to eat in the cafeteria; this was some weeks after Chambers had read the Adjunct's message. He was still rubbed raw from the sting of her lashes. He pointed a fork at me and said with a mouth full of rice, that bitch called me crazy! That's what she said. She called me crazy. Students glanced over at us. I felt myself redden. He looked down to his plate and we settled into a silence both great and wonderful. I became torn between appreciating the quiet and wanting to take the edge off it a bit. All silences, even comfortable silences, are awkward. We are part of nature, so abhorring vacuums *is* our thing. I said to him the only thing I said to him these days: You publish that essay, they can't laugh at you. Chambers sipped at his water. They'll find a way, he said. You should see my classes now. The students are fucking animated. They're talking to that bitch behind my back; I know they are. They're asking questions and commenting about the book and shit. Writing about the damn book in their journals, bringing in outside sources. It's fucking unnatural. He stopped to sip his water. I said: Isn't this what you wanted? He watched me, incredulous. Yes, he said. But not like this. He whispered: Not like this. We settled back into our silences. I realized now that we were in separate floating bubbles and this was fine. In his, he taught and he brooded. His toxic air made the walls of the bubble grow thin, though. It would pop soon and I'd watch him free fall. In mine I floated, I meditated—cross-legged and deep-breathed—and I plotted.

11.

Dr. Reginald Chambers
Freedman's University
English 101
Special Topics: Loneliness

Journal #4
PROMPT: Write about a time you looked in another's eyes and
saw your own loneliness reflected back.

Dr. Chambers Journal #4:

Vanessa Oya-Edmonds wasn't unknown to me, I just knew
her as Starburst. Starburst. Call me dim, but I never conceived
that her name could be anything but Starburst.

This was during my time in the cold womb of upstate New
York. What brought me to the doorstep of Sugar Daddy's on
Montgomery Street? Sitting alone in the dark of the club's
antiseptic air. Eyes searching the naked female flesh that swung
about the stage and passed all around me. You don't look into
eyes here; inside every eye is an abyss.

I'd sit in the back and Starburst in her short-short, silvery
thin outfit would come by between stage and private dances,
and talk to me as if I were something other than a customer, a
john. We laughed about other patrons, about the rock music the
DJ played while she took the stage and how she had a hard time
finding her rhythm inside of it. We were one and the same, me
and Starburst, the only persons in our respective workplaces
with darker flesh. And she said she never felt more alone than
the times she stood naked on that stage looking down upon a
drunk patron as he tossed dollars at her feet crying something
like, Do a nigger dance, nigger. That happens a lot? I asked.
All the time, she replied matter-of-factly, blinking her big red
eyes. We both chuckled, though I doubt either of us were sure
what we were chuckling about. How different was I, dancing

for the peanuts my employer tossed at my feet? My bosses held me up to their bosses as evidence, proof of the newspaper's cosmopolitanism. How I danced for the opportunity to live paycheck to paycheck.

Before the night ended we'd disappear into the black guts of the club, where for twenty dollars she'd climb onto my lap and do a naked grind for two songs while my hands searched her skin.

I remember little of those dances for the most part—I often paid with a credit card, so Experian, TransUnion, all those guys, all these years later, they haven't forgotten. I recall only that there was a warmth to her movements uncommon in other dancers; her moves were handcrafted rather than mass-produced; mom-and-pop store rather than Walmart.

Starburst wasn't unknown to me outside the walls of Sugar Daddy's either, no, we spoke on the phone sometimes. Our relationship was chaste, chaste, chaste, unalterably chaste. We smoked together and at times she'd smuggle small bags of marijuana into the club in the long neck of her thigh-high boots. Once we smoked in her car before a shift and into the silence I could see tears passing down her cheeks. I said nothing. I smoked and patted her back.

It wasn't easy avoiding her eyes, they were big and bulbous, the whites tinged in maroon. She smoked far more than I did and slept far less, driving the hour from Syracuse to Binghamton late at night and in the early morning for this job.

Once, as we smoked, I asked Starburst what she thought about during lap dances: Nothing, she said. People think you're thinking all these sexy thoughts, but most time I'm thinking nothing. Nothingness.

She straddled my lap now in the dark of the private dance stall. Her skin was smooth excepting the dusting of goose pimples strewn about her flesh. Excepting the C-section scar passing over her belly like a meteoroid streaking the sky. I made the mistake of looking into her eyes. I saw the nothingness and it looked emerald, much different than I imagined.

My breath quickened. My heart quickened. I no longer had a body, all I had, all I was, was breath and beating heart. The music sounded like one repetitive rhythmic vibration, as if a disc were caught on a skip: I- I- I- I-

I smelled the perfume of her. Heard her voice. She moaned. She said: Actually, this feels pretty good, actually. She moaned softly again.

There was then a banging on the walls. Mocking voices. Laughter. People invading our shared aloneness. I wanted them gone. I heard Starburst's voice again, floating through the abyss: Stop, guys! The banging ceased and the laughter faded.

I buried my face in her stomach. I kissed her skin softly and wanted to put her breasts in my mouth one by one as if she had birthed me.

I was in the womb of space where the galaxy birthed itself and here it was happening all again—me, a galaxy of one all unto myself—the most important person who ever existed. Everyone else, I realized, they are also the most important person who ever existed. I floated, trying to locate myself in this dislocation. This is why we do anything, anything at all, read books, tell jokes, meditate, have sex—to get closer to this dislocation, to find a way to inhabit it, to be in this galaxy—

Starburst stopped moving and I was suddenly back in my own body. She leaned from me. That's two songs. You want to keep it going? I said nothing, trying to get my bearings, what we commonly think of as reality suddenly invading the moment. Huh? she said, now irritated.

I thought about my budget, the credit card which was paying for this dance, my rent, my measly paycheck, and my shitty apartment. Sadly, I shook my head.

Starburst climbed from my lap and slipped her thong back on, slid her silvery dress over her head. She shook my hand and thanked me. I couldn't move for a bit, thinking about life in that galaxy—that place of solitude—and how far from it I now was and always would be.

When I made it to the bar, I didn't drink, instead I sat and ignored the nude and nearly nude saleswomen floating by me. I tried to cling to the feeling from several minutes ago, but time was already making it fade. I could go back to that galaxy with Starburst's help, but there was no telling if she could conjure that one more time and, even if she could, for how long could it be sustained?

She did her rounds again, and I thought it best that I leave. Starburst, I called. Starburst! She didn't turn. Again I called her name.

Oh, she said. I'm sorry. I've been doing this how long and I'm still waiting to hear Vanessa.

Vanessa?

Yeah, Vanessa Oya-Edmonds. The only thing my mama gave me that I won't shake.

Huh? I said. I thought your name—

What? You thought my name was Starburst? Weird, Reggie.

What do you think that says about me, you know, in the larger picture?

You don't want to know.

When I returned the following weekend, she wasn't there. I got a dance from another woman, but it was robotic, lifeless— nothing like the star-stuff of Starburst. In fact, Starburst never came back to Sugar Daddy's. Never returned my calls. The DJ, the other girls, if they knew where she was, they weren't saying. She blew away, faded, exploded into a ball of light. Perhaps they have water-women in the Susquehanna River, the one that cuts through Binghamton, a mere trail of saliva in comparison to the Cross River. If they are in that river, their power is weak. I felt little sadness. I felt no desire to enter the Susquehanna and swim to the bottom looking for Vanessaburst. No, I felt a mild happiness that she had escaped. I imagined she was on to the better things she sometimes told me she would one day be on to.

But what if that wasn't it at all? What if she had died, perhaps? What if she couldn't keep those big maroon eyes open on a late-night drive up Interstate 81? Who would inform a stripper's patrons, huh? I searched the newspapers for an obit, but I never found one. At some point I realized, and it hit me hard, that the galaxy of solitude I floated in during a Starburst dance was really just a galaxy of loneliness and I was permanently in the abyss.

I decided soon after that I would leave the cold prison of my Binghamtonian hell and return to Cross River.

Rebecca Montana
English 101.15
Freedman's University
Special Topics: Loneliness
Dr. Chambers

Journal #4

Maybe I should put this in an email but it's on my mind now and it fits the prompt so I'll put it in the journal. I've been talking to a few of my classmates and they all agree, the vibe of the class has changed. You've changed.

You pace, you curse, you are short-tempered with us now. You speak *at* us all day long. There is not much room for dialogue, for alternative points of view. You've become a tyrant. This is not how u were previously. Don't get me wrong, you're still a good teacher and I'm still learning a lot, dr. Chambers, but it feels like the intensity of the class has been dialed up a notch. Even ur writings are becoming more unhinged. Again, Dr. Chambers, don't get me wrong, the intensity and the boundary-pushing is a huge part of this course but perhaps its too much heat for some of us. I mean, solving the problem of loneliness? In 16 weeks? I didn't think u meant it literally at the start of the semester. Now I'm sure (almost sure) that you do. Millions of years of evolutionary work has gone into making us, Dr. chambers. I'm afraid of what hour immenit failure will do to you. The loneliness, the isolation, the horror. None of us want to be the cause of that in you.

This is almost the ten-minute mark, but I must go on. You say specificity is the essence of good writing so I must provide for you an example of what I'm talking about.

There was the thing with Eddie, the linebacker, the other day. I know Eddie looks like a mack truck, but he's soft like the raspberry yogurt he's always eating in class. No one ever gave a fuck about his mind. Most of his life its been, *Hey Eddie, tackle that other large mammal.* He was quiet all semester and then ███ blessed him the power to speak. I thought u said you don't care about our opinions, just that we can express them intelligently? Wasn't that what Eddie was doing when he raised his hand and said: "I feel like Roland Hudson use a lot of words to hide cruelty . . . I mean, he drowned himself under the Cross River and he drowned Gertrude under a bunch of words. Didn't you say poetry was supposed to clarify? This book, like, obscures."

You froze, death-stared him. "I've been writing poetry," he said. "From Gertrude's perspective like ███ suggested."

Eddie read one and before he was finished you broke up into laughter. I watched the giant shrink.

"What have you ever done with your life besides crack the heads of your fellow large human beings and eat yogurt in my class?" you said. "Roland Hudson studied for years and years and years. Who told you it was your place to challenge him, huh?"

I couldn't believe your question, Dr Chambers.

Who told Eddie it was his place to challenge Roland Hudson? YOU DID!!!! It's implicit in the course. And when he does, you turn your mouth into a machine gun and cut him down!?!?

You didnt see Eddie's tears after class. I watched his eyes in private, and yes, I saw my loneliness reflected back. It was human. We all looked in your eyes that day and saw something different, icier than the warmth I saw in Eddie's eyes. It was isolation. Walls closing in on you. I hope you can see your way to apologizing. The Dr. chambers we met in January would never act this way. You told us about solitude and loneliness, but didn't tell us about the third way of isolation you are walking Dr. Chambers, I hope you can come back because neither I, nor any of your students, want to walk that path with u.

12.

Sometime near the end of the semester, I passed a classroom and saw Chambers slowly, languidly wiping his words from a dry-erase board.

It was covered corner to corner with tiny malformed letters in multiple colors, blue, red, green, black—accented by crooked and wavy lines, arrows pointing in all directions, multilayered frantically scrawled circles. Even the parts he had brushed away appeared stained with Chambers's ink.

My friend, I called. Chambers stopped erasing and turned from the board. He looked around as if unfamiliar with the word *friend*. He smiled.

In the teacher's face is God, he said. *So too the student, she / Is God / And the most Godly of all is Her words / My love / May they be God*

Hudson?

Chambers nodded.

Student quoted that to me today. Said to erase my words from the board is to destroy God. His idea of a joke. I chuckled. So did the whole class. Even their disruptions are clever now since that fucking guest lecture. Then he got real serious and said if God is the word then to speak becomes sacrilegious because speaking ultimately means the destruction of words. To communicate verbally is to commit blasphemy.

Was he serious?

I don't know, but that's the type of thinking that starts cults and religious orders. Chambers turned and began wiping the board again, slowly, languidly. I've lost them, Reece. It's the destiny of every generation to become lost, and they've cast out in every direction but the one I'm trying to lead.

I tried to speak, but he raised his hand, silencing me.

I know what you're going to say, Reece. The essay. The essay. Publish the essay. If you were a doctor, the medical kind, you'd treat even colds with chemotherapy. The essay. The essay. Who out there is ready for the essay? Not me. It's either too little to save me or so much that it'll destroy me. Either way, I'm obliterated. Fucked. Tell me, Reece, have you ever conceived of a life without teaching? I did. I do. And it terrifies me. The classroom is all I really have. I'm an unfinished mansion with one completed room. All those other rooms—parenting, husbanding, anything else—I'm a low-level failure at them. I'm destined to trip over those things as if they were two left feet until I'm dead and my wife and kids are stepping over my corpse on their way to a hopefully better life without me. He paused to chuckle. Teaching is all that I am. This semester got a little rocky, jack. Okay, it's a total loss. I don't want to publish essays about porn; I want to teach in such a way that my lessons become the headaches that force these students to rewire their thoughts. This semester, this goddamn semester, won't produce that. I just want to ride this out, that's what I want to do; ride this out and restart next year with a new cast of characters. One more stack of essays to grade—he pointed to them at the edge of the desk—and I can put all I tried and failed to do behind me, man.

You sure?

My son now walks around with a little plastic Olympic-looking medallion that says I'M ALONE.

Where'd he even get such a thing?

I don't know. I didn't ask. I'm paying attention to the wrong stuff, man. It's making everything around me go to pieces.

You know your problem? I said. You're too into yourself. You're an internal person when the world currently needs external people.

Maybe.

Listen, I have a Milo Sequoia fable that fits this moment.

Of course you do.

Jesus spoke in parables, I speak in Milo Sequoia fables. Listen to me: it's a story I call "The Ballad of Little Inward Jim."

"The Ballad of Little Nigger Jim"?

What? No. I said *Inward*, not n-word. I walked to the board and wrote *Inward* in the middle of a free spot between his surrounding chaos of words. I circled it vigorously over and over until it was surrounded by thick blue lines. Inward, I said. Like inside.

Oh.

. . .

The Ballad of Little Inward Jim

Sometimes the air blows hazy and is tinged with a burning scent and when it gets like this it also whispers something, but I've never been able to make out what is being said. That's for the best, probably. The haze is Jim. And even if we could understand his words, there is nothing we could do for him anyway. Even the truest bluestream masters couldn't bring him back—or wouldn't if they could. It's best that his consciousness exists as a haze. This all happened so long ago—in the 1850s, as a matter of fact—if he were to be brought back bodily he'd immediately die and rot away, become dust.*

Jim, it is said, was one of those folks who could go inside himself, past the black, past all the mind's chatter, past everything, and arrive at a field of pure blue. And within that field of blue, if you know how, you can manifest what some call miracles. He stumbled upon the bluestream† at the first rush of puberty. It came to him in a daydream during class. His one-room schoolhouse sat where the Freedman's University administration building now sits. He was supposed to be studying math, but he stared ahead and within the blue he became hopelessly lost. Pupils turned to pinholes. Classmates called his name and attempted to slap him back into the present. Inside he bathed in blue.

Jim awoke later in his bed with a desire to go back in and he did, but without a teacher the bluestream became for him a chaos: others' thoughts passing through his head, the pain and disorientation of sudden telescopic vision. It's easy to ignore the bluestream. Keep your

---

* At this Chambers's eyes widened. He sat at a student desk and leaned toward me. When I was squatting on the floor in my morgue home dreaming this up during spring break, I imagined the turns of Chamber's expressions, the movements of his body language as I recited these words to him. Now he moved exactly as I envisioned he would, it was as if I had conjured Chambers somewhere in the recesses of my imagination.

† The bluestream is another myth you'll find widely accepted among Cross Riverians. You'll see children on schoolyards trying to fly and turn themselves into smoke, street magicians fooling the gullible by pretending to enter the bluestream to levitate. Seeing as how Chambers fancied himself as a man marked by a water-woman, I figured it wouldn't be a stretch for him to be taken by this particular legend. His face relaxed for a moment when I mentioned the bluestream, a look of delight mixed with intrigue. But he thought it better to play it cool and quickly righted his face into something more neutral.

mind away from it. Pretend it doesn't exist. Once you become practiced at never finding that land within you, you will never again find that land within you. But now that Jim knew there lived a world inside himself, how could he avoid it? He began to focus. The easiest feat is to turn one's self into a pillar of smoke. As you can imagine, most wade into the bluestream and turn their bodies into hot white smoke and return shaking, fearful of the knowledge the bluestream has to offer. They tell themselves it was just a hallucination, all imagination, and they abandon the arts, never learning to fly, never learning to turn themselves into beams of light, never becoming invisible, never learning any of the countless secrets of advanced dislocation, transformation, and transcendence. A small few become smoke, lose their concentration, and simply dissipate.

Jim studied. Stacks and stacks of books full of questionable bluestream knowledge. He sought masters to teach him the arts. Those who knew best turned him away—the arts are not a children's toy, they'd say. The frauds took his money and before his eyes became smoke.

Years passed with no progress and as Jim grew, so did his despondency. His bluestream turned a deep midnight. Such insights the bluestream gave him about life—and his mind was the finest among his peers—but it all seemed so empty without the bluestream's full power.[*]

During the midst of his deepest despair Jim, now a young man of twenty, left work at the quarry late at night and sat in the Wildlands to meditate. At first, sitting among the trees, Jim thought the dog barreling toward him, snarling silvery saliva onto its fur, was a wild dog, but somehow there in the bluestream Jim connected to the dog's mind. It had been separated from its group of slave-catching dogs from Port Yooga. Clear as river water he could see the dog's pain. The beatings it took. Starvation. Being set upon helpless, innocent blue-black flesh. All this in the name of training. Somehow it broke loose

---

[*] Here I wondered if Chambers was getting my message, if he could see himself in Jim. He needed a teacher, a master, and it was best he serve his apprenticeship under me. Any sort of rebellion, in fact, depended on our partnership. It was as if he were turning to smoke before me, though. He leaned back and crossed his legs. I could almost feel his mind wandering from me.

and ran many miles. In those days the slave-catchers patrolled the border of Port Yooga and Cross River with a heavy hand. Word among Negroes was that if they could just get to Cross River, they'd be free. How some tried.

That mean dogthing barreled and barked and snarled toward Jim, all to let his masters know he had found one. So much the mean dog didn't understand: his masters were nowhere nearby; they had stopped looking for him for the night; Jim hadn't escaped from a master. Jim was free born. So much that dog didn't understand.

Jim didn't flinch. He didn't move his body, but in the bluestream he eased that dog's pain. And after he eased the dog's pain, he released it from hate, turned the red of the dog's mind sky-blue. The dog stopped its charge and jutted out its floppy tongue and panted, utterly happy.[*]

Jim quit the quarry not long after that, just as soon as he realized he could make a business stealing slave-catching dogs and selling them to Cross Riverians as family pets. Business was so good Jim purchased a house in the hills with plenty of space out back for the dogs to roam.

Any fool familiar with the bluestream will tell you that if you spend more than four hours a day there, you're pushing it. Spend six and you risk permanent dislocation, mental degradation, bodily disintegration. Jim spent most of his twenty-four hours there, not turning to smoke, not controlling his dogs, just meditating, trying to learn all he could. To master an art is one sort of pride, to be a self-taught master is quite another.

In his study, his single-mindedness, Jim became abrasive. His friends strayed from him. He grew short with family and they too turned from him. Jim couldn't keep a woman. Who would want to be with someone who disappeared so far into their own mind it made you feel as if you didn't really exist?

---

[*] I wanted to shout: *Again! The master-student dynamic!* Chambers turned his head from me. He peered into the hallway.

Jim, bleary but wealthy, stumbling through the town like a drunk. So inside himself, he missed his call to history.

To this day many say the Harpers Ferry raid would have turned out differently had Jim—a master of concentration—just paid attention, not to himself, not to his own mind, nor to the bluestream, but if he minded the things all around him just a bit more.

John Brown came calling in the spring of 1859, made a personal visit to the house in the hills. Son, he said, sinking into the leather chair across from Jim's desk, they tell me you got the vision. The blue-thing. I have an army of men. Weapons. Supplies. I need an army of dogs. Imagine how dazed and dazzled they'll be when their own hellhounds come snarling back at them. Just imagine it, Jim. Douglass says it's a long shot, what does he know? I say that respectfully. He doesn't believe in that blue-thing, but I've seen some of your people turn their bodies to smoke. I have a wild card in this fight that Douglass and his wild hair* could never understand. Jim, you are the wild card.

Jim confidently nodded. Said: You'll take that armory, if I have anything to do with it. The men shook hands.

Jim didn't tell Mr. Brown about his mind shorting out. About the days he lost. About finding himself suddenly wandering the river, apparently having just materialized from a cloud of smoke.

Well, you know as well as I do that John Brown and his men didn't take that armory. No dogs came but the dogs employed by the Marines, and contrary to Mr. Brown's expectations, they did not turn on their masters.

Jim entered the bluestream the morning of the raid and woke days later with dried blood trailing from his nose; and then the news reached him: all had been lost.

Eyes watched Jim as he made his way in town. He heard voices bursting all about him calling him a traitor. Perhaps he was the one who told on John Brown, the voices said. Jim couldn't tell if the voices were real or echoes from the bluestream. A woman in a bar spit in his

---

* Chambers chuckled.

face. No one would buy his dogs. No matter, he could rarely get them under control anymore anyway.

And in the cold of December after John Brown's body* swung from a hangman's rope, word came down that somebody had to die for the fuckup at the Ferry—and that person was Jim. But Jim, lost in guilt and blue-confusion, couldn't tell if the person who stood in front of his house in the hills warning him, his cousin Barnes, was a hallucination or the real thing. Had he ever really known a Barnes, or was this just a false memory? Jim reached out and touched his cousin's face.

When the people came later that evening, holding tight to flaming lanterns, Jim's mind had firmed a bit.

No matter, he thought. What is the chance that anyone in this mob knows the arts as I do?

Jim stood before them and spread his arms wide. My people! he called, before turning his body into a pillar of smoke.

Alas, poor Jim. Though he had mastered one of the more difficult bluestream feats—controlling the animals (even if he was only able to control the simplest-minded of the complex animals)—he still hadn't mastered the easiest of the feats, turning oneself into smoke. His pillar lost integrity nearly immediately and the little inward found himself blown to all corners. Jim tried—tries—with all his might, but still he's never been able to pull himself together. Even today he lives in the breeze that blows gently across our flesh and he cries out as forcefully as he's able, mightily, trying to tell us something.

• • •

That's not a ballad, Chambers said. That's a goddamn tragedy.

I nodded.

---

* *You know*, Chambers said, cutting me off. *John Brown was a hero, but I bet he was also a hell of a whitesplainer.*

I stopped speaking for a moment and put my face in my hands. Chambers hadn't been laughing at my story earlier, he had been conjuring this joke and waiting for the right moment to tell it.

Damn. Why you tell me that shit? As if my day wasn't fucked up enough. You see the new posting about me on hatemyprofessor?

I shook my head. No, I lied.

He pulled his phone from his pocket and called it up as if he had it saved.

Professor Chambers asks too much. I felt like I was in an advanced class. Never incountered such immaturity in a teacher. Worst. Professor. Ever. Suckkkkkked. He should be destroyed bodily, spiritually, economically, and emotionally.

Here we witness that bastion of maturity, he continued. Calling for a man's death while anonymously insulting his life's work on the internet.

You can't let—

Worst of all, you see they gave me a trollface?

A trollface?

If you're hot they give you a fire symbol. If you're ugly they give you a trollface. Some fucking asshole gave me a trollface!

But look, Chambers, the story of Jim—

Jim! Essay! Fable! Essay! You're a broken record, Reece. Now, you look—Chambers picked up his stack of essays and dumped them into his satchel and swung the thing over his shoulder—I've taken enough bad advice from you to last a lifetime. I'm going to empty my head and grade these final essays; I'm afraid they're all going to fail, Reece. Chambers chuckled. And when I'm done failing them I'm going to soak in the tub for a week. Play basketball for another week, and then I'm going to think about how to get back on track here. Perhaps I should have submitted this class to the committee; they could have helped me conceive of a more workable course. I am like Jim, Reece. You're right. I need to connect back to what's happening in the department and the world around me before I fade away.

Chambers walked out the classroom, brushing me with his shoulder. A rush of sadness passed down my throat, choking me. Momentarily I found myself unable to breathe until I gasped. I tried to stand but I became lightheaded and the feeling knocked me off my feet, back into the chair I had risen from.

I too was like Jim. On my way to destruction because of a sad inability to act. I thought of the morgue and my boxy computer and that became like a fresh rush of oxygen clearing my dizziness. I would have to take my stand.

13.

Dr. Reginald Chambers
Freedman's University
English 101
Special Topics: Loneliness

Final Synthesis/Argumentative Essay

We've come to the end of a long semester exploring how the ache of common loneliness has intersected with and shaped our lives. I must admit that this is a difficult thing to think about. Our mind fears taking a spin in that abyss. It fears becoming forever lost and I don't blame it. I wish I could forgive you all for being confused, but this job does not make much room for the forgiveness of emotional and intellectual cowardice. The purpose of education is clarity. When I think of confusion, I think of Roland Hudson perched on a bridge. In one part of his mind he's a bird. In the other part Gertrude's voice is doubling, tripling. He sees her brown face shiny and slick peeking from the black waters and then he jumps. That's what confusion gets you. It gets you dead. Before you choose your topic, before you sit down to write your essay, please take some time alone to meditate, to daydream. Stay away from everyone until you feel the sting of common loneliness, the bite of isolation. Sit with it until your vision doubles, until your mind conjures voices from long ago. First it will surface your humiliations. Don't turn away. Then whatever angers you will surface, not the superficial things, but the deep lasting rages. Keep going through the sludge until you hit fresh water. There, my students, is where you will find your essay. Please make sure you provide a clear three-point thesis statement that builds a strong **_ARGUMENT_** as we've discussed in class. Your essay must be five paragraphs, contain at least three outside sources, and have a works cited page—and you should account for a counterargument. Good luck.

Rebecca Montana
Freedman's University
English 101.15
Special Topics: Loneliness
Final paper
Dr. Chambers

The Firewater Strikes Back: Roland Hudson and the Uses and Abuses of Common Loneliness

"... [S]o many anonymous bright girls, who never were able to become writers, who we'll never know about ... I align myself with a genealogy of erased women."

—Kate Zambreno, *Heroines*

Gertrude Banks woke one morning with the blue light of the moon beaming into her eye and a fire raging through her head. She rolled about on her bed, sweat soaking into her sheets. Such a strange feeling. A oneness and so lonely at the same time. Sleep now an impossibility, Gertrude rose from her bed and began to write. Whatever she wrote is now lost to time. Almost all she wrote is lost to time (Rampersad 145). Her value to literary history, her fame, her infamy, all stem from her role as a muse. Roland Hudson, often regarded as the greatest poet in Cross Riverian history, wrote reams of poetry in Gertrude's honor. Much of it he collected into his final volume, *The Firewater of Love*. Gertrude gave up her home and privileged life in late 19th century Port Yooga, where she and her older sisters passed for white women, in order to study with the great poet. By all accounts he was immediately smitten by her. Hudson was at the time a married man. Little is known of Lucy, Roland Hudson's wife at the time. His affections toward Gertrude were not reciprocated. Eventually she fled his "love" (150). In *Firewater*, which he dedicates to her, Hudson identifies Gertrude as a mystical water nymph—a water-woman, a woe, a kazzie, a shauntice—bent on his destruction. In the water-woman myth—still widely believed

amongst Cross Riverians—a woe manipulates men into loving
them only to leave, forcing a madness and the eventual death of
the lover (Channing 355). That night of loneliness, those words
Gertrude wrote (whatever they were), happened to be the beginning
of her own destruction, of a cycle of destruction. While some may
regard Roland Hudson's *The Firewater of Love* as a tender treatise
on loneliness and love, that obscures the damage it wrought on
the hapless Gertrude; the book (and resulting class on it taught
recently at Freedman's University by Dr. Reginald Chambers) truly
shows that loneliness in an oppressive society is often used to enact
oppressive (patriarchal) domination; loneliness, itself an unruly
tyrant, often makes petty tyrants of its subjects; and finally, the
human sting of loneliness cannot be obliterated, only mitigated.

It's not unusual to see Hudson's mania portrayed as a
beautiful love story, but that obscures the undercurrents of male
dominance that so clearly mark the face of his poetry. At the
outset of the Spring 2018 semester at Freedman's University, Dr.
Reginald Chambers told his English 101 classes that he would tell
them a love story more tragic than *Romeo & Juliet*. His story began
with Gertrude's letter requesting to study with Hudson and it
continued with Hudson's attraction, with Gertrude's rebuff, and
ended with Hudson dashing himself into the Cross River. "He's
still there if you care to look" (Chambers, class lecture) were
the final words to the story. Students hung from the words Dr.
Chambers spoke, transfixed by the passion of the storyteller. I
came to understand that the real tragedy wasn't Hudson's death,
but the snuffing of Gertrude's light. She refused to love him, so
he refused to acknowledge her as a poet. Not only did he refuse
to advise her on technique and to help her become published,
he actively worked to destroy her every literary opportunity. He
used his power to advise journals and publishers to not publish
her. He pressured other potential mentors not to read her work.
He showed up at her home, her place of work, at Cross Riverian
literary salons where she found community away from her
estranged family (now outed as black because of Gertrude's

actions). The world became unsafe for Gertrude. At last, Hudson stole her poetry; all her remaining words are thought to be buried with his bones beneath the waters of the Cross River. Dr. Chambers conveniently left that out of his "love" story. One day I hope to resurrect Gertrude's words. As Zambreno says of her literary Heroines: "I feel compelled to act as the literary executor of the dead and erased. I'm responsible for guarding their legacy" (110). But why did Hudson act this way? As Nigerian novelist Chimamanda Ngozi Adichie writes in her book-length essay, *Dear Ijeawele, or A Feminist Manifesto in Fifteen Suggestions*, "We teach girls to be likeable [sic], to be nice, to be false . . . This is dangerous. Many sexual predators have capitalized on this" (37). To dwell on Gertrude's "niceness" however is to lay the blame for her harassment and Hudson's death (and her own social death) at her feet, rather than at Hudson's where it belongs. Many misogynists have and continue to blame Gertrude. We will not continue that practice in this essay. As bell hooks writes in her essay "Challenging Sexism in Black Life," ". . . [T]he lives of black men are threatened by their uncritical absorption and participation in patriarchy" (hooks 63). Hudson's allegiance to sexism literally destroyed him, caused him to leap into a river seeking love in its depths. The question one naturally asks is *why did this all come about?* The answer to *why* is that it is a timeworn pattern. ". . . [A]lmost always, during the initial stage of the struggle, the oppressed, instead of striving for liberation, tend themselves to become oppressors, or sub-oppressors" (Friere 45). Or more colloquially, as the rapper L'Ouverture crudely puts it, "Even niggas eventually need they own niggers" (L'Ouverture). In other words, the oppressed—Hudson, being a black man in America in the late 1800s and early 1900s—found someone to oppress. Being weak and isolated and alone, enacting his power as a man, as a literary *star*, was the only way for Hudson to assert his humanity in a society that continuously denied his humanity. For Hudson, even bad humanity is better than the no-humanity he was forced to accept as a black man. This is very similar to Dr.

Chambers standing before his students, shouting them down for disagreeing, and attempting to silence his own loneliness by transforming into a tyrant in his personal life.

One of the more dangerous and under-discussed aspects of loneliness is that it often causes its victims to enact a kind of personal tyranny, dominating all around them as a failed and misguided way to dominate loneliness. This description of oppressed peasant as oppressor found in Paolo Freire's *Pedagogy of the Oppressed* (from an interview with a peasant) could double as a description of Dr. Chambers:

> The peasant is a dependent . . . Before he discovers his dependence, he suffers. He lets off steam at home, where he shouts at his children, beats them, and despairs. He complains about his wife and thinks everything is dreadful . . . (65)

This localized and personal tyranny is Kin to the larger macro-societal tyranny that most countries eventually find themselves facing down like Samson with a donkey's jawbone facing down the Philistines. In both, common loneliness plays a key developing role. As noted in *The Origins of Totalitarianism*: "It has frequently been observed that terror can rule absolutely only over men who are isolated against each other and that, therefore, one of the primary concerns of all tyrannical government is to bring this isolation about" (Arendt 474). It would be simplistic to cite loneliness as the primary motivating factor behind the Mugabes, the Dutertes, the Putins, the Erdogans, the Trumps, but as a motivator of low-level human tyranny—the petty bureaucrats at the MVA, the loan officer in the Freedman's University administration building—loneliness is unparalleled as a primary motivator. In *Pedagogy*, Freire warns that teachers should avoid replicating oppressive structures in the design and running of their courses to avoid even implicitly teaching students to accept

those oppressive structures within their societies and lives.
Dr. Chambers likely conceived his course, English 101: Special
Topics: Loneliness, with such radically egalitarian principles
in mind, but the professor's devolution to petty despotism was
swift. The professor picked as his target in one section a large
queer* football player with intimidating looks, but the heart of a
(particularly soft) poet. "Dr. Chambers," the football player said
in an early class. "How about we think of other sources besides
loneliness as the, um, core of our problems?" Dr. Chambers
replied with a sneer and a mean chuckle: "Hey, how about you be
quiet." At first, students were taken aback, but if we look at this
moment through the lens of tyranny, it becomes clear that Dr.
Chambers used these sorts of mean quips to solidify his power.
The professor presents himself as our knowledgeable expert—
each class a meeting of Zeus and the (far) lesser gods. In fact,
Dr. Chambers is impressively studied and, at times, his analysis
(when he cares to be analytical) is unparalleled. But he is far too
invested in what Freire called the "banking model" of teaching,
viewing his students as empty vessels to pour knowledge into.

> In the banking concept of education, knowledge is a gift
> bestowed by those who consider themselves knowledgeable
> upon those whom they consider to know nothing. Project-
> ing an absolute ignorance onto others, a characteristic of the
> ideology of oppression, negates education and knowledge as
> processes of inquiry (72).

---

* I don't mean to equate passivity with queerness. My classmate, however, happens to be quite
queer and quite passive. Except when he is on the football field. There he remains queer, but all
traces of passivity fall away and he becomes like a vicious beast. I mention his queerness only
because, though Dr. Chambers speaks the language of egalitarianism, his disrespect, in this
case, carries with it the whiff of homophobia. Just as his condescension and scholarly interest
often carries with it a whiff of sexism. And I don't intend here to imply that Dr. Chambers has
been particularly malicious to his queer and female students (he hasn't), but casual homophobia and sexism (like their cousin, racism) can be especially pernicious.

This sort of teaching creates a hierarchy with Dr. Chambers at the pinnacle and various students on differing levels depending on the whims of our tyrannical God-Professor. Though I was frequently singled out as an intellectual exception, like most students, I left class feeling disempowered. Disempowerment is the most important tool in the tyrant's toolbox. It reduces the risk of rebellion. The disempowered don't unite and rise up. While Dr. Chambers perfected his disempowerment and tyranny on his students, its roots go far beyond his Spring 2018 classes. In a PowerPoint presentation, the professor introduces students to his family life, specifically his wife, Christine. Chambers tells us she regards him as a Superman and her love and admiration creates within him a powerful loneliness that in turn has created a gulf between them, and thus, more loneliness (Chambers, "Loneliness vs. Solitude".) While it is difficult to get a read on a marriage one is not a part of, Dr. Chambers invites us in and what he shows is not flattering towards himself. First of all, Dr. Chambers is not being forced at gunpoint to be part of a marriage that is purportedly causing him more loneliness than happiness. He seems to have forgotten the old African-American saying: "I can be lonely all by myself." Most importantly, however, it is not entirely convincing that Dr. Chambers is experiencing the misery he claims to be experiencing. Dr. Chambers wields loneliness like an Israeli soldier wields a bulldozer, crushing his wife and children, keeping them in perfect subjugation. The professor claims to want the eradication of loneliness, but he knows this is not a realistic goal; it's not even a desirable one for him. Loneliness is the source of his power, self-destructive and dubious as it may be, but still the only power he has.

Part of the stated goal of Dr. Chambers's Spring 2018 English 101 course is to figure out "how to make the hurting stop" (Chambers, course syllabus). And it is the goal of the course that is a problem. To hurt, to be lonely, is to be human. To want to eradicate the ache of loneliness is also human; to succeed is impossible and ultimately undesirable. As Arendt notes, "... [L]oneliness is at the same time contrary to the basic requirements of the human condition *and* one of the fundamental requirements of every human life" (Arendt 475). Like any good tyrant, Dr. Chambers promises something he knows he cannot deliver. For Roland Hudson, the only way to end the pains of his heart was to end his life. As he states in *Firewater*: *"The only method | ... | To stop | The heart from hurting | Is to stop the heart"* (36). I wish for Dr. Chambers a much happier ending. Something different than Hitler in the bunker. Managing loneliness, which is often as much a physical ailment as it is a mental one, is a far more realistic goal than completely ending it. While college is specifically built for intellectual explorations, it is a bit ambitious to think that six courses of eighteen and nineteen-year-olds can effectively end a persistent human problem. For one, we are very young, and reluctantly I admit, thoroughly lacking in life experiences. But even if Dr. Chambers had assembled the finest minds of all time, the outcome would have been the same.

Many of my peers, and even my faculty mentors, warned me against writing this essay in such a blunt style. After all, the primary target of my criticism (aside from the misogynist Roland Hudson) is the very person grading this essay. In the course syllabus and in the early classes, Dr. Chambers teaches that radical honesty is the fulcrum of our exploration into common loneliness. That is one thing the professor and I can agree on. The truth is that the poet Roland Hudson was a sexist who destroyed the life and career of a woman and I cannot celebrate that; wallowing in loneliness and isolation—making a God of it— turns one into a tyrant and over the course of a semester we've watched Dr. Reginald Chambers succumb to his own tyranny; and, lastly, I don't wish to end my loneliness, I wish to learn from it, to grow from it so I can enjoy the inevitable and brief moments of oneness that are on the other side of isolation. I wish that for myself, but more importantly, I wish that for the reader.

Works Cited

Adichie, Chimamanda Ngozi. *Dear Ijeawele, or A Feminist Manifesto in Fifteen Suggestions*. New York, Alfred A. Knopf, 2017. Print.

Arendt, Hannah. *The Origins of Totalitarianism*. San Diego, NY, London, Harcourt Brace, 1994. Print.

Chambers, Reginald. *English 101.15, Special Topics: Loneliness Course Syllabus*. Spring 2018. Department of English & Cultural Studies, Freedman's University, Cross River, MD. Print.

Chambers, Reginald. English 101.15, Special Topics: Loneliness.30 January 2018. Freedman's University. Cross River, MD. Class lecture.

Chambers, Reginald. "Loneliness vs. Solitude: A Presentation by Dr. Reginald Chambers." 1 February 2018. Freedman's University. Cross River, MD. Class lecture.

Channing, Heather. *Bubbling Up from the Bottom: A Guide to the Real Mythical Creatures From the Waters of America*. 1972. Alzada Co., MS. Jamey House. Print.

Freire, Paulo. *Pedagogy of the Oppressed*. New York, Continuum,2000. Print.

hooks, bell. "Challenging Sexism in Black Life." *Killing Rage: Ending Racism*, Henry Holt and Company, New York, 1995. Print.

Hudson, Roland. *The Firewater of Love: Poems*. Cross River, MD: Peckerman House. 2010. Print.

L'Ouverture & Problem with Authority. "Nat Turners With Burners." *The Haitian Revolution*. Black Monolith/Meratti Records, 2005.

Rampersad, Arnold. *Roland Hudson: A Life*. New York: Vintage. 2016. Print.

Zambreno, Kate. *Heroines*. Los Angeles. Semiotext(e). 2012.

14.

To: Dr. Reginald S. Chambers, Assistant Professor—
Department of English and Cultural Studies <RChambers
@Freedmans.edu>
Sent: May 5, 2018, 12:05 a.m.
From: Rebecca Montana <RMontana@Freedmans.StudentNet
.edu>
Cc: <Blacker.Roland.Hudson@gmail.com>
Bcc:
Subject: i don't understand

this semester was supposed to be my redemption. i can sincerely say i don't understand. i've never worked so hard at a class. never been so in love with the material and all i'm learning. i spent so much of my first semester laying on my back in my dorm room staring at the ceiling. so many times i thought i was actually floating. i think you'd call it advanced dislocation. when you're in that state you have no use for class, no use for anything really. except despair. you feed on that. it's your only nourishment. have you ever had a 0.00? you're in a special club when you bring home those kind of numbers. i wasn't the first student nor will i be the last to dance through those zeroes to be those zeroes but every student arrives at 0.00 in his or her own special way. i know i'll never graduate with honors like my brothers. 0.00 grabbed me and smacked me set me down a road called academic probation. with an f in your class i won't be able to continue at this university. i just don't understand. i lived practically at the library these last several weeks. i thought my research was impeccable. i showed it to everyone, dr.chambers, everyone. the whole world gave me feedback. dr samson read it. his assistant read it and read it again and then re-read it. everyone said my essay was a high b at least. what happened? did they lie to me? to see an f on my paper broke me. i'm back to laying on my bed back to staring at the ceiling. is this what you wanted? was this all a game a trick to help us experience true loneliness? if so congratulations you have been successful. i know you're hurting dr chambers. perhaps you're too broken for all this. maybe we all are but i thought i was putting myself back together. i hope ur loneliness hasn't completely given way to coldness to isolation to cruelty. i hope u can do something to help me. here i am being selfish. theres eddie losing his football scholarship. my roommate losing her housing allowance. our entire class is wailing. students i've met from your other classes are gnashing their teeth. did u pass even one of us? i imagine us: *a harmony of nightscreams/ twisted screeching birdsong/ beloveds without lovers.* here we all are ironically together. i have nothing else to say. i have no intention of getting on that plane and heading back west. i've found my place here. please don't take this from me.

15.

You'll have to forgive me for what I did next. Chambers stood so close to the edge, but I determined that he could never, would never, jump. He just didn't have it in him. So while everyone wound down their semester or prepared for Ulysses Sparks to arrive on campus, I retired to the morgue. I stared at my boxy computer for so long that the blue glow of the screen turned me into blue glow. I melted into the screen, an apparition. I played around in Chet the dimwit's email for a while. Then I took a deep breath. It was time to do what I came to do. I logged out of Chet's email and typed in Chambers's login in the username box. In the password box, I typed some letters that turned into an array of dark circles. When that didn't work, I did it again. And again. And again. I found myself blocked for fifteen minutes. Then thirty. Then an hour. It was fine. I tend to play the long game. All they were doing was giving me time to think. It was night now and I stepped outside; above me shone lights so bright and intrusive it felt as if my eyes had been penetrated by brilliance. The burn of the light jabbed into me, passing as liquid into my nasal passages and my throat, shining out my mouth. Above me the natural sky became victim of the light, forced to cover its beauty in a mask of ugly illumination. I walked the campus making lists of possible passwords and all around me beamed pictures of Sparks's face, signs bearing his website name and his ugly catchphrases. Men constructed a makeshift stage in front of the library, an altar to ignorance. All signs that the circus would arrive the next day. I didn't know what to think so I thought only of passwords as I walked back to my morgue home. When I arrived, I sat in a corner running through my mental list of letters and numbers and symbols, keys to a brilliant future. The room spun around me, a world in motion, and in the ceiling I saw stars backed by stars backed by clouds of stars. Deep space. Nebulae. rolandhudson1 didn't work. Nor did blacker.roland.hudson.1. But thefirewateroflove.1 did. This was early, early in the morning after I had worked for several hours. I watched all the emails, most unopened and unread. Students crying out in pain. Ephemera. Junk. hatemyprofessor ads. Colleagues expressing concern. I existed now to ease everyone's suffering. I breathed deeply, put my fingers to the keyboard, and I let them dance, the spirit of constructive chaos passing through me like bolts of electric hate. It possessed me. *Liber est gladio.* I smiled.

. . .

To: CAMPUS—ALL
Sent: May 5, 2018, 4:00 a.m.
From: Dr. Reginald S. Chambers, Assistant Professor—
Department of English and Cultural Studies <RChambers
@Freedmans.edu>
Cc:
Bcc:
Subject: I FEEL SO ALONE
Attachment: LONELINESS EssayFINAL2.docx

—

Dr. Reginald S. Chambers, Ph.D
Assistant Professor
Department of English and Cultural Studies
Freedman's University
x3725

———————

Verbo est gladio

16.

Such a roar rolled across campus that day, May fifth, the Day of Infinite Hate, that even deep in the morgue it was impossible not to hear. I had kept such a late night that I planned to sleep in, but colorful horns blared throughout the crowd as if to call on the Apocalypse and its Four Horsemen. When I arrived at the *hatemyprofessor Moments of Hate*™ and its undulating crowd of people, I did indeed find an Apocalypse and I did indeed see a beast. He lacked seven heads, his one was fearsome enough, and he didn't sport ten crowns, instead he wore one cocked to the side on the enormity of his dome. I counted three horns blaring from behind him. If this was an Apocalypse it was a half-assed one.

And ol' Ulysses Sparks standing slump-shouldered in the center of the stage wearing a brown blazer on his back and before he spoke he removed the gold crown from his head—what a sight! Someone described him as a pile of sloppy shit sewn into a desiccated sack of flesh. You couldn't convince me I wasn't watching a decaying corpse swaggering about, mic in hand.

To his right, the nominal master of ceremonies, Dr. Faison, the Aryan, though he looked more like Sparks's hype man, responded to Sparks's every word with shouted affirmatives—*Yep! Okay! Yes! Yeaaaahhh! Skirrrr*—a white-ass Flavor Flav. Professors from all around campus kept a silent vigil standing at crowd's edge. The math professor in his clown getup. Kin Samson. The Adjunct. The history professor dressed as Harriet Tubman. The Women's Studies professor who taught only physics. Mean Dean Jean Greene watched the stage stoically, her arms folded and her shoulders squared. No matter where I looked, though, I saw no trace of Chambers. The campus woke that morning with his essay in their in-box. Perhaps he stashed himself somewhere crumpled in shame. Perhaps he was walking about the rally, his face hidden by disguise.

Sparks raised his arms and the shouts, the applause, and the chants roared all around me, a mix of fury and joy. On the stage, Sparks spoke:

Your professors fear you because you have this power behind you. The power of hate!

Screams of joyous hate rose from the crowd. Vultures ringed us, perched atop buildings, wires, light fixtures, and trees as if summoned by our collective hate.

Look, I tried to come for them with humor. I did. I did! Five years ago was an idealistic time, that's when I started rapemyprofessor.com with thirty dollars, a little moxie, and a whole lot of hope. And you know the rest. The mobs came for me, didn't they? Swarms and swarms of humorless liberals, p.c. types. I promise you I will never bow down again. I will never compromise again. The hate is here to stay. They created it. They earned it. Are you ready for some hate?

The crowd chanted—*Hate! Hate! Hate!*—animated by their rage as Dr. Faison bounced about on the balls of his feet, taking in their energy and spitting forth an ad-lib.

Take that. Take that. Take that.

Now, Sparks continued, to reveal the face of Freedman's University's most hated! The professor with the most hatemyprofessor postings—our guest of dishonor, the English Department's very own Dr. Reginald Chambers! Give him two minutes of your very best hate!

Chambers's face towered over us as big as life on the bright lights of the screen that stood at Ulysses's back. In red, *FU* flashed across Chambers's forehead and the boos and the chanting erupted with a force that made the ground tremble beneath us.

To the left of me: *Hate! Hate! Hate! Hate!*

To the right: *Burn in hell! Burn in hell! Burn in hell!*

A lone male voice: *Fuck you, Chambers!*

Dr. Faison: *Uh-huh. That's right. Let's get it!*

When I looked to the edges of the crowd I saw no sight of the professors who had stood observing. Satisfied they wouldn't be the next contestant on that hatemyprofessor screen, the one held up for ridicule and hate, they all receded into the ether. I was prepared to do the same. Ulysses Sparks and his act were interesting, but it was just that, an act. He couldn't scratch even the façade of academia's brain rot, and even if he managed to take down the academy, he wasn't capable of building something new its place as I was. I began to walk down the hill when I saw a commotion. A man being shoved back and forth, hand to hateful hand.

No. The fool. What was Chambers doing here? Why would he subject himself to all this? More people began to notice and they rushed to join in. A woman shoved at Chambers's back. Another at Chambers's shoulder.

The crowd's chants became louder: *Hate! Hate! Hate! Hate!*

Stop! he cried. I'm a man! I'm not a symbol! I'm a man! I'm a man! I'm a man!

A large student, a bald mound of sculpted meat, grasped Chambers by the back of his shirt and lifted him high over his head like an offering. Dr. Chambers squirmed and shouted in the air as the people passed him forward from hand to hand, an involuntary crowd surfer.

The chants became deafening as his flopping body approached the stage. I looked about and there was Chambers's *friend*, the English Department chair, Dr. Jason Oliver, slinking away from the crowd. I caught a glimpse also of Dean Greene standing near me, up on her toes trying to get a better look at things. Her lips had congealed into a cruel little smirk. Chambers's body sat stiff, but the people held his arms far part. The crowd lifted him up, a sacrifice in Ulysses Sparks's name. This was the least Chambersian moment I've ever experienced, as it seemed all the loneliness in our little corner of the world had evaporated. Even I pumped my fist and chanted: *Hate! Hate! Hate!* Sure, we were each of us locked into ourselves, isolated with our own particular hate, but we were alone together, and this sort of aloneness, I realized, was the closest thing to oneness I could ever hope for.

A great blast of purple-blue light shot forth from a fixture above the stage. It blinded me and I closed my eyes just a half moment too late. My eyes opened and I looked out on the campus and saw the blue-white expanse of it as I had never seen it before. And there out in the distance—Chambers, our professor of loneliness! The darkened image of him, blue and spectral, in the form of a cross burned forever as a shadow at the edge of my vision.

IV.

An Epilogue

———

Dust. Smoke and damned dust. That's all Chambers is now.

I don't mean to say he has perished, is dead, has returned to the essence. I just mean that he is gone. I call and it rings. I email and there is nothing. I assume he's out there existing, but I'm having trouble conjuring his face now, as if he had been imaginary all along. I told you early on that there would be no twist announcing Chambers and I were one and the same. I stand by that. He existed. Exists, probably.

No, definitely. I received an email from him, actually. Everybody did. It came through on Thanksgiving during dinnertime, but I was eating, so I didn't read it until Black Friday morning in the morgue over strong coffee and even stronger weed.

But he's—zap—dust, I thought. I didn't even think about him very much these days. My mind had become polluted with other things: students, their yearning, their admiration, their hatred. No, I couldn't at all think about Chambers, I had become him.

Now there he was on my screen returned, the words of his email forming themselves into a moving image of his face.

To: CAMPUS—ALL
Sent: November 22, 2018, 4:00 p.m.
From: Dr. Reginald S. Chambers, Assistant Professor—Department of English and Cultural Studies <RChambers@Freedmans.edu>
Cc: Reggie <Blacker.Roland.Hudson@gmail.com>; Jason Oliver <Jason.Jerome.Oliver@gmail.com>; Dr. Simeon Reece <Dr.ofTruth@aol.com>
Bcc:
Subject: One

One

As one of my heroes, John Henrik Clarke, said: "I only debate my equals. All others I teach."

Greetings. I write into your cruel silences. I began drafting this in the heat of the long Sunday that August becomes when you're an academic. It wasn't that for me, of course, and your fall semester hasn't been a time of great intellectual leaps for me, instead it's been a time of great anxiety. It's mostly been a cell in which I waste slowly. Future uncertain. A new kind of dying.

Let me get on with what I came to say.

I paused to blow a smoke cloud, potent and grayblue. Chambers's wordface frowned at my rudeness. Why should I entertain this? I thought. Chambers could never become the person he needed to be to blaze Freedman's to ash. And in the end, neither could I. When Freedman's posted the temporary lecturer position, Idra forwarded the job ad to me. Her email was devoid of her usual nonsense, her chastisements. Just the ad and nothing else. I stood outside my body watching myself apply. *Reece, old chap, what are you doing?* I replied: *Destiny's calling, Reece.* My apparent destiny for the year (with the possibility of the position becoming permanent) was to teach the five or six composition classes a semester that Chambers couldn't. One thing I couldn't quit, though, was the margins, I couldn't quit the morgue and sometimes the hole. As long as I continued to live on the edges, my rebellion still had breath.

I continued reading:

> Jesus spoke in parables. Some speak in fables.* If that's the language you know, then that's the form my lecture will take, but please don't consider this a debate. I come not to debate, but to teach. Please, you, lean in close—I'd prefer you hear this so I could ask you to listen carefully, but that's impossible, so I urge you to do away with all distractions. Read carefully:
>
> I used to be a sharp dresser when I cared about such things. I had this black pinstripe suit with a vest. Got married to Christine in the thing. There is a picture of me in it, and beneath it I've captioned, "Freddy the Fly."
>
> You know Freddy the Fly, of course. Every little boy or girl, if they come from the River, knows the story of Freddy the Fly. Him and all his little cousins. Sometimes they're standing by the side of a road or a highway—maybe the North-South Parkway— scared to cross, sometimes it's at the banks of the river.

---

* Ha! I couldn't believe Chambers would take a shot at me, but then again, it made all the sense in the world. When I saw security escort him off campus—some months after he disappeared into the light on the hatemyprofessor stage—our eyes locked and he saw my smile. Perhaps he thought I smiled out of cruelty. It wasn't that, at least not mostly. My only thought: *It's on.* I smiled not at his misfortune, but at all the dreams of our shadow university growing right here in the shell of Freedman's decaying husk. Everything was now coming to fruition, I thought. Maybe in that moment he realized it was I who sent his essay to the entire campus. Chambers is, after all, a smart guy

I like the river version best.* In the river Umar the Octopus surfaces his tentacles to snatch at all things that pass; Allen the Alligator sticks his snout out of the water to get a bite of every flying, swimming, or creeping thing; Danny the River Dolphin lets children ride his back; and most fearsome is Fearsome the Frog and his sticky tongue hunting to make a feast of all flies like Freddy. So Freddy and his little cousins sit in the soil at river's edge or they hover just above the ground, flying in pointless elliptical arcs, contemplating whether or not to buzz over the water to that other side.

What's on the other side, anyway, huh? Freddy asks. His cousins watch him, confused. Shangri-la, Freddy, one says. A party with the most beautiful flies from all over, says another one. They greet you with gold necklaces. Says one cousin: You meet yourself past, present, and future in the journey. In the party you become one with the universe, Freddy. If only you have the courage, Freddy.

And then the last cousin who spoke flies off greedily into the haze of the river. Freddy shudders with fear, calls his cousin's name, but he's gone. And soon flies another and another and another. They appear to Freddy, with the glow of the dusk moon making metallic light across their wings and their hard backs, like fireflies skimming the surface of the water.

Eventually all the cousins fly away and Freddy sits alone in the dirt watching the river. He can't see the other side in the dark. It seems so far. He makes to fly, but lands after a second. He thinks of the sea monsters of the deep, Fearsome the Frog, who always taunts with the thick of his tongue. Flies are not

---

* Of course Chambers would prefer this version, it is perhaps the blandest and most milque-toast. The version collected and published in the book *The Vexations: Fables*, by seminal Cross Riverian folklorists the River Brothers (a team consisting of three women, none of them siblings), features Freddy killing his cousins, becoming drunk off their blood, and serving their wings, torsos, legs, and bulging fly eyes to the forest creatures of Cross River in a nice stew. Later versions of this and other River Brothers fables were sanitized for the capitalist machine (cartoons, movies, comic strips, and books), thus manufacturing generation after generation of weak and feebleminded Cross Riverian children.

chickens. They don't need to cross roads or rivers to get to the other side. As with all creatures, it's their responsibility to die. Just give it a few weeks, is all. Flies don't last too long and Freddy is no different. Poor lonely fly. In some stories a bird with a long beak roots about the dirt and picks him off, and down the throat Freddy goes. I prefer the simpler version: Freddy, dead from the passage of time, his six legs up in the air, slowly becoming a dried husk. Pieces of him carried away by enterprising ants. Poor Freddy, never again seeing his cousins, never seeing that other side.

Careful what you call yourself, beloveds. I said I was as fly as Freddy, not knowing I had stranded myself at the river's side, afraid to use the wings on my back.

Chambers and I can agree on one thing, he did have wings and they were beautiful. Actually, our conceptions of the relative beauty of his wings is where we diverge. To me they were angel wings, silky with the span of a 747. To Chambers they were the thin disgusting silvery rainbow-tinged wings of a shit-eating housefly. No wonder it was so easy for the administration to take him down.

The administration—led by Mean Dean Jean Greene—took Chambers's porn essay as proof of his mental instability. Well, not just the essay—that was only the catalyst—the essay coupled with student complaints, and his behavior at Moments of Hate was enough to get him banished from campus. Suspended pending a firing.

And where did Chambers go to put himself back together again? Well, I'll let him tell it:

When all came crashing on me and Dean Greene ripped my heart from my chest, I went to my source of fresh water, my life-giver,* my love, my Christine. I found her sitting in the dim,

---

* This is similar to how I find refuge in Idra. I spend most of my nights with my head to her breast listening to her heartbeat. She says I am mentally ill and she will nurse me back to health, but I don't see where I'm more ill than anyone else. Idra wants to possess me physically, mentally,

the quiet of our living room. Not alone, but with our son, sick and shallow-sleeping on her lap.

Christine, I said. Christine.

She shushed me, pointed to our child.

Christine, baby, you know how I knew I loved you? She turned to look up at me. The expression on her face was intrigue mixed with disgust. I took that as a cue to continue. I knew because I wanted you to know everything about me, all my intimate thoughts. Before you, I never wanted a woman to know anything. They'd ask me about myself and I'd deflect with a joke or I'd ask them to tell me more about themselves and they'd comply. People like talking about themselves. I had their stories, Christine. I had so much of them. I was a vampire that way. But you, baby, you, I poured out all of me into you for a while. I never realized how difficult that was to maintain, though. Your eyes are like twin suns, Christine. You know that? You know what that heat on my skin is like? My skin is dark, but it's sensitive to the sun and to heat. You see the number the summer does to me? Turning my flesh raw. I couldn't stand naked in front of you anymore. I was afraid I'd get sunburnt and skin cancer and shit. So I put on sunblock and you put on sunblock. And then I put on a shirt and pants and then a layer over that and you put on a layer. And another layer and another. You and me sweating under the weight of all these fly clothes. I'm here now, Christine, though. I want to get naked with you. I mean, literally of course, but where it counts more, though. It's the only way I get through this midnight, this Rebecca Montana shit, this hatemyprofessor shit, this Freedman's kicking me to the curb shit. It's fucking with me, Christine.

---

spiritually, and temporally. If she could lock me in a room with her and keep me there until the sky cracks you'd never see or hear from me again. This, she says, would be for my own good, but I am skeptical, so I escape to the morgue. Idra's breast is a refuge from the morgue and the morgue is a refuge from Idra's breast.

I paused, let the silence of the moment hang. Christine shrugged. Moved the child from the pillow of one breast to the next.

She sighed. You know what . . . She paused. You don't think I've had crises too? Your dark semesters of the soul? Where were you, huh? In that dark abyss you said I can't possibly understand? I'm supposed to drop my drawers for you because you finally realize I exist? Why don't you go to the Adjunct, or to a swarm of fruit flies or something?

They don't have what you have, Christine. You know, that thing—and here I grabbed her hand, threaded her slender brown fingers with my own, brushed my fingertips along her red polished nails—where you close your eyes and touch my forehead and make my pain lift from me and you fly it away into the sky?

You think when I do that the pain just flies off to the sky? That's pretty cute, Reg.

Christine stood, carrying our youngest child to his room. After a while when she didn't return, I went searching for her. I found her in our bedroom changing into her nightclothes. She turned herself from me, covered her body as if I were a stranger to her.

Could you knock?

Knock?

Yes, knock. Damn.

I wandered from the room mourning our lost intimacy; I didn't even know when it had left us to rot beneath the earth. I slumped onto the couch in the warm divot her body had made. Submerge me in water and envelope me in darkness and this must be exactly how a womb feels. I touched my forehead, hoping somehow to do that thing that Christine can do. I felt no lighter.

She returned and sat on the opposite end of the couch from me, her body stiffened, an elbow on the couch's arm propping up her cheek. Christine stared for a while into our darkened TV, and when she turned her eyes to me she watched me as if I were an indelible stain on her heart.

Her face, the disdain of her cute-even-when-disdainful face, reminded me of the first time Christine put her hand to my forehead and removed my pain.

This was late in college, and loneliness felt to me like wading into the deepest and longest tunnel. Loneliness had been my oldest companion, but this strain of loneliness felt new, for some reason. I was twenty-one then. An adult. My loneliness had reached maturity alongside me. My old friend could drink now, and entertaining him felt like entertaining an abusive drunk. This crime of slowly killing me was an adult felony now.

Christine was new and I liked having her newness by my side. I sat in her dorm room with my head in my hands. She remained quiet as I tried to explain to her this emptiness inside me. Close your eyes, she whispered. And I did, preparing to receive her body, but instead she placed her hand at the spot right between my eyes.

I jerked my head from side to side. Why you touching my face? I chuckled a bit. There was a laugh in my voice, but my fight-or-flight reactions had been triggered. Relax, Reg. She spoke softly. Calm your ass down. Stop. I stopped. Looked up at her. She said: You trust me, right? You trust me? I wanted to nod, but I didn't. I just watched the brown pools of her eyes. Trust me, Reg.* She eased her hand onto my forehead. Close your eyes. I did, and the black at my eyes became tinged in blue. I felt a heaviness lift from my limbs, my muscles. I opened my eyes and it looked like soot rising from me and swirling away in a cyclone.

How do you feel? she asked, taking wobbly steps to slump

---

* The playfulness! The tenderness! So endearing, the way Chambers would like us to see him as nothing if not fully human.

herself into the chair at her desk. I noticed she limped a bit and I wondered whether she had limped that way before. I couldn't remember.

What's wrong? I asked.

I'm good, she said. How do you feel?

I'm good, now. 'Cause of you, I'm good.

I didn't feel happy, not exactly, but I felt fine. I felt that me and Christine were one and me and the desk were one and everyone else, even the stray cats who wandered campus, they and I were one. I felt this matter-of-factly. Everything's beautiful, Christine, I said.

And everything was. Objectively beautiful, and that was all fine.

How did you learn to do that? I asked.

Remember that house I showed you over on the Northside, the one over in Hilltop?

Beautiful House?

Yep, that's what I used to call it when I was a little girl. Beautiful House. Twenty-one September Lane. Loved living there. Beautiful House. My parents even had a sign out front made after I named it Beautiful House. Man, Reg, that made me feel special. Beautiful. I never ever felt lonely until when my father told me he was leaving. His apartment wasn't beautiful. Not in the least. And when I was at Beautiful House it was just me and my mother, her sad eyes and her mouth that opened only to tell me, Go out back and play, Christie. Go play. Enjoy this place. This not gonna be our place much longer.

So I went out to play all by myself all day long sometimes. Only so much you can play alone before you go inward. I don't know how to explain this, Reg, but there is this blue river in there, and— You know what? I sound crazy, never mind.

No, Christine. You're fine. I'm the crazy one.* Go ahead.

---

* Indeed.

Somehow I knew I could touch my mother's forehead and free her a little bit. It wouldn't last, but I could do it, and I did. Took three years before the sheriffs came to drag us out of Beautiful House. I hate that day, Reg. I don't need Beautiful House anymore, though.

No?

She rested her head on my chest. You're my Beautiful House now. My mansion with many rooms. I'm never leaving my Beautiful House.

I blinked back into the present, still feeling the weight of college Christine on my breastplate, but when I looked over at her face—she appeared forlorn and old, nearly distraught, a haze beneath a blankness—the feeling began to fade.

In this dark, a blue wall and many oceans lay between us; I rubbed my forehead by reflex, thinking of Christine's hand there.

Stop touching your forehead, she said. It's like you're playing with yourself.

This elicited a chuckle from both of us.

Lean back, she said. Close your eyes.

Lines and fields of blue. Pure blue. Electric. It came at me fast in beams and balls of bluelight. I shorted out in all that blue, and when I opened my eyes, Christine limped from me, hunched nearly into a ball.

Good night, she rasped.

It's too early, I said. Don't go.

I have to work in the morning, she said. One of us has to work.

I nodded, watching my wife limp away and dissolve into the darkness of our home.[*]

---

[*] Choosing the proper email sign-off is an art, and for this message Chambers selected an excerpt from an unpublished and unfinished Roland Hudson poem I had never heard of titled "Hail Marys on the Bridge." (Some sources list the title as "I'm Going to Tell You What My Water-Woman Told Me" Others list it as "The Negro Speaks of the Cross River," but that's just a refrain in the poem. The story of how Langston Hughes came to lift the line for the title of his famous poem, thus angering the people of Cross River and earning a lifetime ban from

. . .

I'm not sure how to explain the feeling I got reading the final lines of Chambers's email. Perhaps it was just a shudder I felt throughout my body, but it sure did feel like some sort of living spirit passing through me. Perhaps it was simply a moment of recognition, of seeing myself in Chambers's words. His words on the screen swirled again, this time forming, briefly, my own face.

I remembered coming back one night from an evening class. As the bell tolled I could've sworn I felt eyes burrowing into me from above, and I looked up at the library tower and saw a twinkling blue light. I looked away, and when I peered again, I wasn't sure, but I think I saw a hint of Chambers's face, skeletal, looking down upon me. At first I stood paralyzed, unable to even conceive of moving. But the blue light! That skeletal outline. I dashed back toward the tower and snatched open the library door. I ran past the late-night scholars, past the lovers attempting discretion in a shadowy corner. I ran up the stairs. Up. Up. Up. Up until I reached the top. When I arrived, winded and pained in the chest, light-headed, I looked around at the nesting birds cooing gently. The scattered tobacco guts dumped from split cigars. A faint hint of reefer smoke. Other than that, there was nothing but darkness as if I entered a dimension made of just blueblackness. I looked out on the campus and saw the blue expanse of it as I had never seen it before. I became dislocated standing there, and for several moments I felt myself hover, spectral and blue.

Reading Chambers's email now, I wondered, could this be the same

---

the town [enforced by Cross River's three major crime families] is an interesting one, but perhaps one for a different time.)

The river has faces
The river has arms

The river knows laughter
The river knows harm

Is this what you want?
For me to jump?

night, the same time? He closed his final message to Freedman's University with this:

> After Christine left, I felt light, but tired. I closed my eyes for a second, and without warning I became disassociated from myself. I floated above my body, a blue ghost, a puppet dangling from the rafters. I watched myself as one observes another person.
>
> He put earbuds into his ears and milled about as if unsure what to do next. I wondered what he was listening to, but I could only hear a tinny tinkling. Soon he walked through the front door and into the night's darkness. And before long he became enveloped in the evening and I could no longer see any trace of him.

Acknowledgments

The world certainly doesn't require me, but my world has required so many who have offered a love and kindness that has been unimaginable. Far too many to name here.

First, I would like to thank the people of Cross River, Maryland, for tolerating my presence in their lives.

Thank you to Katie Adams, Gina Iaquinta, and Robert Weil, and everyone at W. W. Norton/Liveright for believing in my stories and for taking such great care with the work.

My gratitude to the editors who published previous versions of many of these stories in their literary journals and anthologies. Special thank you to Lauren O'Neal for reanimating David Sherman with your brilliant editing. Thanks to PEN America, the Fellowship of Southern Writers, Kimbilio, Bowie State University, and the Bread Loaf Writers' Conference for providing support.

Much love and respect to Kima Jones, Allison Conner, and Jack Jones Literary Arts. Words are too weak to express my gratitude.

To my agent, Monika Woods, thank you for getting me.

Thank you to friends and colleagues who have shared their time, jokes, and hearts with me over the years. Thank you to Eugenia Tsutsumi for the sentence. You know which one. Ricki, thank you for reading my drafts and for your encouragement. Special thanks to Andrea Cauthen for designing the Freedman's University logo, but also for the years of friendship.

Rest in peace to my cat friend Isis, who passed while I was completing this book.

Thanks to Leroy for constantly showing me the true meaning of friendship.

The Yasiin Bey quote that opens Dr. Chambers's essay in *Special Topics in Loneliness Studies* (p. 192) was said during a concert at the Kennedy Center for the Performing Arts in Washington, D.C., on December 31, 2016.

Most of all, my world requires my family, the one that made me (Mom, Pop, Duane, Omar, RIP Granny) and the one that I made. My mother, Monica Scott, passed away while production of this book was in its final stages. I'll never forget that her encouragement started this writing thing for me and sustained me along the way. Rest in love, Ma. Samaadi and Madiba, Daddy loves you. Love you, Sufiya, my everything.

The Cross River Saga continues . . .